Praise for Lynn Michaels and
MOTHER OF THE BRIDE

"Throw the rice and cut the cake! *Mother of the Bride* is a winner!"
—JULIE GARWOOD

"This humorous romantic comedy warms the heart with its zany yet believable characters and snappy dialog. . . . Michaels' keen sense of comic timing and oddball characters never fail to entertain."
—*Publishers Weekly*

"*Mother of the Bride* is filled to the brim with wonderfully eccentric characters, layered emotions and downright hilarious antics."
—*Romantic Times* (Gold Medal, Top Pick)

Praise for
HONEYMOON SUITE

"Marvelously quirky supporting characters and wickedly pointed dialogue and description add up to a wildly improbable yet hilarious scenario . . . in a well-told romp that will delight fans of Jenny Crusie's *Bet Me*."

—*Booklist*

"Michaels has a gift for humor."
—*Publishers Weekly*

"Lynn Michaels has a way with characters that is unbelievable. . . . The most interesting and entertaining book I've read in months!"
—Once Upon a Romance

"Michaels uses her special combination of warmth and outrageous humor to great effect in this offbeat tale."
—*Romantic Times*

"On the surface, *Honeymoon Suite* is reminiscent of that classic, twice-made movie, *Sabrina*. . . . A lovely, beautifully written story of good people overcoming adversity with grace and affection."
—Romance Reviews Today

Also by Lynn Michaels
(*published by Ballantine Books*)

MOTHER OF THE BRIDE
RETURN ENGAGEMENT
HONEYMOON SUITE

Marriage by Design

A Novel

Lynn Michaels

BALLANTINE BOOKS • NEW YORK

An Ivy Books Mass Market Original

Copyright © 2006 by Lynne Smith

Published in the United States by Ivy Books, an imprint of The Random House Publishing Group, a division of Random House, Inc., New York.

Ivy Books and colophon are trademarks of Random House, Inc.

ISBN 0-345-47601-8

Cover art and design by Anne Higgins

Printed in the United States of America

www.ballantinebooks.com

OPM   9 8 7 6 5 4 3 2 1

For

Marguerite,
Queen of All Things Artsy-Fartsy.
Thanks for letting me steal both your names!

And

Nancy Haddock,
world's best friend and critique partner.

MIA SAVARD LOVED FASHION. Anyone who looked in her closet could tell you that, once they picked their jaw up from the floor.

In design school Mia excelled at classes in textiles and pattern-making. Blindfolded she could sew a seam straight as a laser. She dreamed designs. Her illustrations won awards that hung on her father Lucien's office wall.

Mia simply hated brides.

It was nothing personal. Some of her best friends were brides, had been brides or were about to become brides. Which had absolutely nothing to do, Mia swore to her father, with her loathing for brides.

"I'm simply up to here with bridal gowns." Mia held her index finger against her eyebrows, in her father's office one snowy Thursday morning in November. "If I have to design another one, I'll scream."

"Pish." Lucien didn't even bother to look up from the stack of sketches on his desk. "You're having a snit because all your friends are getting married and that bum What's-His-Name dumped you."

"The bum's name is Terence and this is not a snit," Mia insisted. She couldn't argue about being dumped; it was true and the hurt still throbbed like a stubbed toe.

"I'm bored as stiff as a bolt of tulle with bridal gowns. Move me to the trousseau line."

Lucien plucked a sketch off the stack, crumpled it and threw it over his right shoulder. "No."

"Move me," Mia said. "Or I'll quit."

"Absolutely not," her father replied.

"All right. If that's the way you want it."

Lucien's Paul Newman–blue eyes lifted and narrowed at her over the silver-framed half-lenses perched on his fine patrician nose. Mia had her mother's snipped-off pixie nose. She hated it. These days she hated almost everything. Especially Terence the Bum, the *GQ* hunk formerly known as Terence the Love of Her Life.

"I battled your brother, Mia, and I battled your sister." While Mia was still in design school, but she'd heard about the Sibling Wars from nonfamily Savard employees. "Do not threaten me. You will *not* win."

"You're stifling my creativity."

"I'm trying to run a business."

"You're trying to run my life."

"You're a Savard. This business is your life."

"That's what I just said. You're running my life."

"Mi-*ah*." Lucien threw an "h" on the end of her name to let her know that he was losing patience. "Go find yourself a new boyfriend. You'll start dreaming about weddings again and everything will be fine."

"Not this time," she retorted. "I'm finished with men. I don't want to be a bride—not *ever*—and I do not want to design brides' dresses anymore. I need a change. I'm bored. Stale—"

"You're depressed," Lucien cut her off. "You're an artist. You're prone to depression. Go shopping. It'll cheer you up."

"Move me," Mia said between her teeth, "to the trous-seau line."

"We design one-of-a-kind bridal gowns, Mia. It's what we do, how I built Savard Creations. I'd need my head examined if I moved one of my best designers from our custom line into ready-to-wear."

"Move me or I'll quit."

Lucien bent his head over the sketches. "No."

Mia drew a deep breath. "Then I quit."

Her father crumpled another sketch and tossed it with-out so much as a glance at her. "Are you coming to dinner tonight?"

"No." Mia wheeled away from his pool table–size desk, thought about slamming the door on her way out of the office but didn't.

She was too old to slam doors. Thirty and unmarried, unattached and unappreciated—*Waa-waa,* she thought, *have a little cheese with your whine, Mia*—plus she'd rather stick her right hand, her drawing hand, into a gar-bage disposal than give her father the satisfaction.

Mia stalked to the elevator, rode the car to the fourth floor and stomped down the hallway—her body so stiff with fury that her knees refused to bend—and turned into her office.

Her cousin Robin leaned his folded elbows against the edge of her drawing table, his Lucille Ball–red hair dull and dark against the gray sky framed by the wall full of windows behind him. His father, Rudy, Lucien's younger brother, was CFO of Savard Creations; Robin, his second in command. He glanced up at Mia from the sketch on her board.

"What are you doing?" she asked.

"Snooping." Robin cocked an eyebrow at Mia as she

yanked the chair away from her desk and sat down. "What are you doing?"

"Typing my letter of resignation." Mia pulled out the keyboard tray, shook the wireless mouse to clear the Colin Farrell screen saver from the flat screen monitor of her PC and glanced at her cousin. "I'll drop it off on our way to lunch. Are we eating in or going out?"

"Neither." Robin pushed off her board. "I just remembered I made an appointment to have bamboo shoots shoved under my fingernails."

"Coward." Mia snorted and started typing. "Some friend you are."

"This isn't about friendship, mighty mite," Robin replied. "This is about business and blood, which happen to be the same thing if your name is Savard. Love you, cuz, but I want to keep my job."

"What makes you think Lucien will fire you if I quit?"

"He fired my dad, his own brother, last year. He fired the whole accounting department twice." Robin perched on the corner of her desk and eyed her soberly. "One of these days, Mia, he could mean it."

"He never means it. He's fired the design staff a dozen times."

"He's never fired you."

"He doesn't dare. I'm the baby. Mother would kill him."

"If you're still alive later, call me." Robin stood up and kissed the top of her head. "Give me ten minutes to get out of the building."

"Hurry, Chicken Little. The sky is falling."

"Cluck, cluck." Robin grinned and strolled out of her office.

Mia shut and locked the door. The front wall of her office was glass. So was the front wall of the design department across the hall. Anyone could see her—Jordan, for instance, her best friend in the design department, the biggest nosey-pocus in the entire Savard Building, who occupied the second cubicle on the left—but Mia didn't care who saw her, so long as no one could hear her.

She reached for the phone and placed a conference call to her sister, Jenna, in LA and her brother, Luke, in New York. Jenna, the overachieving middle child, ran the Savard's boutique on Rodeo Drive, Luke the Fifth Avenue showroom. They'd both fled as far away from Lucien as they could without jumping into an ocean.

"Well?" Jenna demanded, her voice hollow on the speakerphone. "Did he agree to move you to the trousseau line?"

"No. He said absolutely not, so I quit. I spoke the words. I said, 'I quit.' He asked me if I was coming to dinner tonight."

"It was worth a shot," Jenna said. "Tell us what he said."

"Exactly," Luke said. "Word for word."

Mia told them. Exactly, word for word. When she finished, Jenna said, "You should've slammed the door on your way out."

"I thought about it," Mia said. "But I'm not you."

Jenna was the Queen of Slamming, Banging and Breaking Things, a talent she'd inherited from their father. Jenna once threw a lunch tray at Lucien in the employee cafeteria. It missed his head but drenched him in chili mac and peach cobbler. The Chili Mac Skirmish was considered one of the turning-point battles of the Sibling Wars.

"Have you written your resignation letter?" Luke asked.

"Yes." Mia read from the screen: "Dear Dad, I quit. Love, Mia."

"Short, sweet and to the point," Luke said. "Sign it and deliver it."

"I'm going to, on my way to lunch," Mia said, and hit Print.

She folded her resignation into a pale mauve envelope with Savard Creations, 4700 Ward Parkway, Kansas City, Missouri, 64111, scripted in dark burgundy ink in the upper-left corner, licked the flap shut and headed for the elevator. Lucien's secretary Selma, whose desk sat in the reception area outside the closed double doors of his office on the seventh floor, eyed the envelope warily when Mia handed it to her.

"Is this," she asked, "what I think it is?"

"My resignation," Mia said.

"Oh, boy." Selma sighed. "Here we go again."

Mia went back to her office, hoping she could grab Jordan for lunch. Her friend's cubicle was empty, so Mia put on her boots and her coat, picked up her purse and left the Savard Building. Under the canopy over the revolving front doors, she flipped up the hood on her purple merino wool stadium coat.

The bleak sky was spitting snow, tiny, dry flakes the wind swirled into curlicues along the sidewalk. Mia dug her cell phone out of her purse, dialed Savard Creations, then Jordan's extension. She meant to leave a message on her voice mail, but Jordan answered.

"I did it," Mia told her. "I quit."

"You *go!*" Jordan cheered. "Where are you?"

"Standing on the sidewalk wondering if I should throw myself under a bus and be done with it."

"He's a tyrant. A genius, but a tyrant," said Jordan,

whose whimsical, Laura Ashley–esque designs were frequently and roundly praised by Lucien. "Want me to come down and we'll go to lunch?"

Mia thought about it. If Robin the Wuss hadn't bailed on her she might've been able to choke down half a sandwich. Now she felt too nervous to eat, her stomach jumping with dread.

"No. I think I'll take a walk. I just wanted you to know."

"He won't let you quit," Jordan said. "You watch."

Mia disconnected and crossed Ward Parkway, waded through three inches of snow, swept a bench with her gloved hand and sat on the banks of Brush Creek watching a pair of mallard ducks asleep in their nest with their heads tucked under their wings. She gave her father half an hour to think about her resignation, then sighed and stood up.

"This will work or it won't," she said to the sleeping ducks. "Lucien will give in, or he won't. Nice chatting with you."

Mia half expected to be nabbed on her way into the Savard Building, turned around and pushed back through the revolving doors, persona non grata. But Pete Onslow, head of Savard Security, a burly, retired KCMO cop with a bald, round head, looked up at her and smiled from his half-moon kiosk in the three-story atrium lobby.

"Too bad you went out, Mia," he said. "You missed the chili mac."

Her office wasn't locked; no alarms or sirens went off when she crossed the threshold. Mia took off her boots and put on her shoes, hung her coat in the closet, tucked her gloves in the pockets, rubbed her cold, stiff cheeks with her numb fingers to warm them and poked herself in the eye when the intercom on her desk phone buzzed and she jumped.

"What does this mean?" Lucien demanded when she lifted the receiver. "'Dear Dad, I quit. Love, Mia.'"

"It means," Mia said, rubbing her watering eye, "I quit."

"I don't give in to blackmail. Ask your brother, Luke. He tried it."

"Move me to the trousseau line."

"No!" Lucien barked, and the line went dead.

Mia dialed her mother. "I'm not coming to dinner tonight," she told her. "Dad won't move me so I quit."

"Oh, boy. Here we go again." Petra Savard sighed and hung up.

Mia placed another conference call to Jenna and Luke.

"Dad said he doesn't give in to blackmail," she told them. "He told me I should ask my brother, Luke."

"Hot damn." Luke laughed. "We're on the right track."

"Don't waver," Jenna said sternly. "Don't weaken."

"I won't," Mia promised, though she felt tears in her eyes.

"Pack your stuff and clear out," Luke said. "It's the only way."

"I know." Mia sighed and hung up the phone.

She opened the closet and stared at the banker's boxes she'd bought on sale at Office Max. If she had them, Mia figured she wouldn't need them. She'd been so sure Lucien would relent, so positive that he'd give in. He'd fought Luke and Jenna tooth and claw. Surely he wouldn't fight her, surely he'd learned his lesson.

Mia wanted to cry but tears didn't work on Lucien. They hadn't worked on Terence the Bum, either. She pulled the boxes out of the closet and peeled off the cellophane, put them together and carried them to the wide Formica sill under the windows by her drawing board. Her spider plants, philodendrons and pots full of ivy had given her something cheery to look at instead of the roof of the parking garage.

She had no idea what she was looking at now.

"Need some help?" Robin's sister, Becca, asked from the doorway.

Mia turned and saw her younger cousin leaning into her office from the hallway, a tentative smile on her face, her dark, straight hair tucked behind her thrice-pierced ears. She worked for her father, too. Uncle Rudy wisely kept his chicks close.

"Maybe you shouldn't be here," Mia said. "Just in case."

"I'm not Robin." Becca stepped through the doorway. "I don't bail on my friends or my family."

"That's why Robin called you," Mia said. "Where was he?"

"Who cares?" Becca shrugged. "What can I do?"

It took them most of the afternoon to pack up Mia's belongings—the plants, the knickknacks, the framed posters and prints on the wall. Half a dozen times Mia almost said, *Stop. I don't want to quit. I don't know how I let myself get talked into this.*

Which wasn't true, she knew exactly how. She'd cried on Luke's shoulder about Terence and she'd bitched to Jenna about Lucien.

"How long have you known Dad?" Jenna had said to her. "You're going about this all wrong."

"Then help me," Mia had pleaded. "Tell me what to do."

It was the worst thing she could've said. Jenna was a

Scorpio and Scorpios *love* to plot and scheme. Jenna called Luke and the next thing Mia knew, her brother and sister had launched a campaign to liberate her, like she was a Third World country. She'd never meant it to go this far, but she'd felt so lost at the time—barely a week after Terence dumped her—so sad and so vulnerable. Being the baby again, just for a little while, letting Jenna and Luke take charge of her life and lead her by the hand, had made her feel loved and given her comfort.

Now it was giving her a migraine and a really, *really* bad feeling.

By three o'clock, a pile of banker's boxes the size of the Great Pyramid at Giza occupied the center of Mia's office and she and Becca hadn't even touched the bookshelves. Five tall oak stacks crammed with books on fabrics and techniques, classic designs and pattern-making.

"I had no idea," Mia said, "that I'd dragged so much crap in here."

"We need a cart," Becca said. "I'll call maintenance."

She was halfway to the phone when Lucien burst into the office. Becca froze like a rabbit at the thunderous expression on his face. Mia's heart leaped up her throat.

"The employee cafeteria!" Lucien bellowed. "Both of you!"

" 'Scuse me. Remember me?" Mia held up one finger. "I quit."

"Did you resign as my daughter?" Lucien snapped.

"No," Mia said. "Of course not."

"Then get yourself to the cafeteria," Lucien growled. "*Now!*"

He whirled and stalked across the hall into the design department.

"The employee cafeteria!" He shouted at the four designers perched at their drawing boards. "All of you! Every last one of you! *Now!*"

Jordan's spiked red and blond head popped over the wall of her cubicle to watch Typhoon Lucien storm past; the other three designers dove for the floor. Mia dashed to her desk with Becca for a better view through the glass wall—of her father making a beeline toward the office of Damien DeMello, Savard's head designer, Lucien's most trusted and valued employee. He'd been fired only three times in his twenty-plus years at Savard's.

Damien's office door was closed. Mia expected Lucien to blow it down like the Big Bad Wolf, but he flew past it like it wasn't even there and slammed out the Exit Only door at the far end of the department.

"Uh-oh," Becca said. "Do you think Damien's already dead?"

"If he isn't in the cafeteria," Mia said, "we'll call 911."

Jordan met them in the hallway, her eyes wide. "Who do you think did it?" she said. "Which one of us screwed the pooch?"

"Whatever has happened, it isn't confined to the design department," Mia said. "Lucien ordered Becca to the cafeteria, too."

They hurried down the hallway, turned the corner toward the elevator and stopped. The lobby was packed with Savard personnel milling and muttering while they waited for a car.

"Well," Becca said. "Looks like he ordered everyone on the fourth floor to the cafeteria."

"C'mon," Mia said. "We'll take the stairs."

She opened the stairwell door and stopped short at

the stream of employees from the first three floors climbing toward the sixth.

"Correction," Becca said. "Make that everybody in the building."

The employee cafeteria took up half of the sixth floor, which made it plenty big enough to hold all of Savard's two hundred forty-three employees. At least half of them were already there when Mia and Becca and Jordan wormed their way into the room. The lunch tables were gone, the mauve and green padded chairs that went with them lined up in theater rows facing the portable stage that came out of storage at Christmas to seat the band Lucien hired every year to entertain the troops.

In the center of the stage sat three chairs. Uncle Rudy sat in the middle chair. With his shock of black-streaked silver hair he could pass for Lucien's twin or Jay Leno. A relieved smile lifted his mouth when he caught sight of Becca with Mia.

Next to Uncle Rudy sat dark-as-the-devil Damien, dressed in his signature black with his legs crossed at the knee and his elegant, clever hands folded in his lap.

"Your boss is alive," Becca said, and waved to her father.

"What is this, Mia?" Jordan whispered in her ear. Like she was clairvoyant or she had a clue. "Has Lucien ever done this before? Pulled everybody into one big meeting?"

"Not that I've ever heard," Mia whispered back, and she'd heard it all from Luke and Jenna, Selma and Damien. Every clash, every skirmish of the Sibling Wars, every temper tantrum Lucien had ever thrown. "Whatever it is, Damien and Uncle Rudy obviously know."

"Right. 'Cause they're sitting up front." Jordan nodded, frowning around the room at the rapidly filling chairs. "Where should we sit?"

"As close to the door as possible," Mia said, and led the way.

In case we need to make a quick getaway, she thought, but didn't say it. She slid into a chair on the end of the last row, with Jordan between her and Becca. A moment later both sides of the big double doors that led into the cafeteria boomed open and Lucien appeared, towing up the center aisle a dress form on wheels that was covered with a shroud.

Damien rose to help him lift it onto the stage, then sat down. Lucien wheeled the dress form to the center of the stage, gripped the shroud in one hand and faced his employees.

"This is a black, black day for Savard Creations," he said. "One of you has stabbed me in the heart."

He nodded at the back of the room. At Pete Onslow, Mia saw when she glanced over her shoulder, standing near the long wall of windows on the north side of the building. Pete worked the blind strings to close the slats, then stepped behind an overhead projector squared on a table.

"I'm about to show you," Lucien said, "an advertisement placed by our fiercest competitor, Heavenly Bridals, in this month's issue of *Today's Bride,* which hit newsstands today."

The lights went out, the switches flipped by one of Pete's men. The projector shot an image on the wall behind Lucien. An image twice his height, of a pink chintz bridal gown with puff sleeves and a tiered skirt tied in bows, like Cinderella's ball gown, where it draped above the hem.

"Oh my God, Mia!" Jordan gasped in a hush. "That's your design!"

Stabbed in the heart. That's exactly how Mia felt. Stabbed and bleeding, so shocked and horrified she could barely breathe.

The lights came on, fading the image into the wall. Lucien ripped the shroud off the dress form, revealing the gown Mia had designed. Every one of Savard Creations' employees gasped. Mia moaned and Jordan gripped her hand.

"This is the one-of-a-kind, no-other-like-it-on-the-planet gown we designed for Alicia Whitcomb, daughter of Governor and Mrs. Alexander Whitcomb, fiancée of Timothy Bowen, son of State Senator and Mrs. William Bowen. Alicia and Timothy are to be married on Christmas Eve in the Governor's Mansion. And this—*this!*" Lucien bellowed, his face nearly vermilion, "was to be her wedding gown!"

Gasps and shocked little outcries filled the employee cafeteria. Mia held her breath, waiting for Lucien to fling a pointed finger at her—and maybe a lightning bolt that would fry her in her chair.

"You are all fired!" Lucien roared. "All of you!"

Uncle Rudy and Damien sprang out of their chairs and closed in on Lucien. He threw them off and whirled on them.

"You're fired! Both of you!" He shouted at Damien and Uncle Rudy, then wheeled on the rest of his employees, his right arm flung out, his index finger, but no lighting bolts, flashing this way and that around the room. "Get out! All of you! GET OUT!"

Her father's temper was legendary, but this wasn't temper. This was a major blood vessel exploding in his brain right before her eyes. Mia leaped to her feet, her heart banging with alarm.

"I've got to call my mother," she said to Jordan and Becca, and ran toward the surge of Savard employees rushing the back of the room.

It wasn't a stampede but it was close. Pete and the second security guard pushed the doors open and got out of the way. The crush carried Mia into the lounge outside the cafeteria, where it peeled away from Petra Savard like water curling from the prow of a ship. Helen of Troy had nothing on her mother, a face that could launch a fleet, a shoulder-length mane of hair the same dyed blush blond as her silver fox jacket. Petra was the rudder that kept Lucien on course. Most of the time.

"Mother!" Mia cried, and jumped at her. "Someone stole one of our designs! One of *my* designs and—"

"I know. Rudy called me." Petra caught Mia by the arms, winced and cocked her head as Lucien bellowed again. "Not taking it well, is he?"

"He's going to rupture a vital organ. We've got to get in there."

Mia caught her mother's hand and tugged her forward. It was slow going, weaving their way through the crowd pouring through the doors.

"Where in hell," Petra snapped, "is everyone going?"

"I'd guess the unemployment office," Mia said over her shoulder. "Dad fired everyone in the building."

"He *what*?" Petra jerked her to a halt and pulled her around. "Oh, for God's sake! Go back to your office, Mia. Be calm. Set an example."

"I'd love to, Mother, but I—"

Someone bumped her and shoved her against Petra. Her mother's arms closed around her and a big hand settled on her shoulder.

"Sorry, Mia. Sorry, Mrs. Savard. Step over here." It was Pete Onslow, steering them out of the crush to one side of the doors.

Lucien roared and something smashed into a wall.

"Good Lord," her mother said. "What's going on in there, Pete?"

"He's throwing chairs, ma'am," Pete said calmly. "I'm to clear the building and lock all the offices, leave my keys and my employee badge on the security kiosk downstairs and get the hell out of his sight."

"Whoa," Mia said. Except for Damien, no one had been with Savard's longer than Pete.

"You keep your keys and your badge," Petra said firmly. "Get me in there, then you'd better do what he says. At least for today."

"Yes, ma'am." Pete said, and reached for the hand she offered.

"You, too, Mia," her mother said. "Get your things and leave."

"I'm on my way." She waited till Pete had wormed a path into the cafeteria for her mother, then turned into the stream of Savard employees rushing toward the elevators.

"Does he mean it?" Cindy Somebody asked. Mia was too rattled to remember her last name. "Are we all fired this time?"

"I don't know," Mia said honestly. "My mother is talking to him."

"Oh, good." Cindy Somebody sighed with relief.

At the stairwell Mia ducked out of the crowd and flew down the steps to the fourth floor. The design department was deserted; Jordan wasn't even there, but she'd left a note on Mia's desk: *Becca and I are out of here. Meet us at Blanko's. We'll get a table. J.*

Mia grabbed her purse, stuffed her boots in their tote and yanked her coat out of the closet. She was just about to put it on, when her phone buzzed. The caller ID said it was Jenna.

"This is too funny." Her sister was laughing. "Listen to this e-mail from Dad. 'Dear Jenna, you're fired. Love, Dad.' It came with a red flag and a 'sender requests confirmation of receipt.' Is this a scream? I'd say he's figured out who's been coaching you."

"No, Jen. That's not why Dad fired you. The most awful thing has happened—" The call waiting caller ID interrupted her. It was Luke. "Hang on," Mia said to Jenna. "It's Luke. I'll get him on the line."

Well, she tried, but her fingers were all thumbs with shock and she ended up disconnecting her brother and sister. Mia fumbled with the buttons some more and got them both back on the line.

"Christmas came early. Dad fired me." Luke laughed on the speakerphone. "Let's see, how many times is this? Ten? Twelve?"

"Hush," Jenna said. "Something's happened. What is it, Mia?"

"The gown we made for Governor Whitcomb's daugher? Somebody stole the design and gave it to Heavenly Bridals. There's a full-page ad for Alicia Whitcomb's wedding gown in this month's *Today's Bride,* with Heavenly Bridals' name all over it."

"*What?*" Jenna shrieked. Luke roared it, sounding so much like Lucien that tears sprang into Mia's eyes.

"Dad fired everyone. Damien, Uncle Rudy, Pete. He's

smashing chairs in the cafeteria. Mother is talking to him."

"I'll get the first flight I can," Jenna said, and hung up.

"Me, too," Luke said. "That was your design, Mia. Are you okay?"

"I don't know. If Dad had just looked at me." Mia sucked back her tears. "If he'd yelled at me I'd feel better, but he just raged at everyone. He can't think I gave the design to Heavenly Bridals, can he?"

"Don't be goofy. Of course he doesn't. I'll see you soon."

Luke hung up. So did Mia, spinning out of her chair with her purse and her tote, shrugging into her coat as she hurried down the silent hallway to the elevator. It was weird, eerie to hear not a sound in the building. All two hundred forty-three Savard employees must've already bailed and fled from Lucien's wrath. Just like Robin.

Her car was in the parking garage, but Blanko's was only a block away. She'd come back for it later, Mia decided, and got off the elevator in the half-dark lobby. She glanced at her watch: five-fifteen. The lights were set on a timer to dim at five P.M. Only the spots in the ceiling above the waterfall in the atrium were lit. The splash of the water tumbling down the limestone wall set her teeth on edge, made every nerve in her body twitch. She wasn't a traitor. Lucien couldn't think so. He wouldn't. She was his daughter. She'd rather die than hurt him like this.

The revolving doors were turning, slowly. Mia stepped into a wedge coming around to meet her, leaned the heel of her right hand against the bar and pushed. She was halfway through when a tall man in a dark overcoat swung off the sidewalk, under the canopy of the Savard Building, and stepped into the door.

He was hurrying, almost running. It was nearly dark outside and as dim as the bottom of a closet in the lobby. He couldn't see her. He didn't see her, just gave the door a mighty shove that pushed her through, stumbling and falling. Maybe he never saw her. Maybe he only heard the yelp she made as she tumbled out of the door and fell on her hands and knees on the thick rubber mat under the canopy. She lost her grip on her tote and her boots spilled out. The strap of her purse caught on her wrist and swung her bag in an arc that landed it with a *thump* on the mat. The doors whooshed behind her.

"Oh, hell. I'm sorry, miss. I didn't see you." Mia felt him behind her, bending over her, spreading his legs on either side of her, his hands closing on her arms. "Are you okay?"

"Yes, I . . ." She sucked a breath, winded. "I think so."

"Can I lift you up?"

Mia nodded. "Sure."

He tightened his grip on her arms, picked her up like a sack of spilled groceries, set her on her feet and turned her around to face him. Mia gripped his sleeves to steady herself and felt fine, tightly woven wool beneath her fingertips. Soft, probably merino. Definitely not off the rack.

She drew another breath to fill her lungs and lost it in a whoosh when she looked up at his face. He wasn't off the rack, either. Dark hair, a lock of it fallen over his forehead, probably when he'd bent over her. Well-shaped eyebrows and deep blue eyes lit by one of the spots on the underside of the canopy. *GQ* hunk material. Mia felt her heart twist. Oh God, not another Terence. She let go of his sleeves. He held on to her upper arms.

"Thank you." Mia stepped back, out of reach, to break his hold.

He cocked his head to one side. "Are you all right?"

"I'm fine. Thanks again." She tugged her purse strap over her shoulder and turned away to pick up her boots.

He stepped around her and scooped them up, one at a time from the mat, and gave them to her. "You look a little shaken."

"Knocked the breath out of me, that's all." Mia pressed a hand to her chest. Through the heavy wool of her stadium coat she could feel her sucker-for-a-pretty-face heart thumping against her palm. "I've got iron knees. I used to play field hockey."

"If your iron knees feel like mush in the morning, call me." He drew a leather case from the breast pocket of his overcoat, thumbed out a card and slipped it between her fingers. "I'd like to make sure you're all right."

He gave her arm a squeeze, a smile that made her heart flip, and pushed through the door. He didn't look back. Mia watched him stride across the darkened lobby toward the elevator banks and turned away.

"Close one." She sighed and stepped under a spotlight, held his card up and read:

Joseph Kerr, Inc.
Private Investigations

There was more, an address, office number, cell phone, e-mail, but that's all Mia saw. Her heart stopped thumping and shot up her throat. She spun around on one foot but the lobby was empty. He was gone.

2

"It's one of us, isn't it?" Jordan asked. "It has to be."

"One of us personally? No," Mia replied. "A Savard employee? Yes. I don't see how it couldn't be."

Neither could Jordan or Becca. Mia could tell by their worried who-is-it, who-could-it-be expressions. They made a glum threesome, elbows on their favorite back-corner table at Blanko's. In front of a diamond-paned window that gave Mia a view of wind-driven snow slanting earthward in the foggy glow of the streetlamps.

A margarita sat in front of Jordan, a light beer before Becca. Mia fiddled with the celery stalk in her virgin Bloody Mary. She took after Lucien when it came to alcohol; one highball and she was dancing the boogaloo with a lamp shade on her head.

"Firing everybody made sure Uncle Lucien got rid of the traitor," Becca said. "But it doesn't catch him."

"Or her," Jordan added. "Or them."

Becca turned her head toward Jordan, the largest of the three silver hoops pierced through her left earlobe swinging against the curve of her neck. "Do you think it's more than one person?"

"For all I know"—Jordan licked salt off the rim of her margarita—"it could be the mailman."

"It's not the mailman. It's a mole," Mia said, bumping an ice cube with her celery stalk. "Someone on Heavenly Bridals' payroll who infiltrated Savard's. Someone with access to the design department."

"That's everybody in the building," Jordan said. "People flit in and out of design all day, every day."

"That's one of the things that made Luke crazy," Mia said. "But Lucien flatly refused to run Savard's like a gulag."

"I'll bet that changes," Becca said. "I wonder if any of us will be around to see it?"

"Of course we'll be around," Mia said. She'd already decided to unresign first thing in the morning. "Everyone will. As soon as Mother gets Lucien calmed down he'll rehire everyone. He always does."

"He's never fired the entire company," Jordan said. "The design department, yes. In the five years I've been at Savard's, he's fired us twice. One of these days he could actually mean it. All of us think so."

"All of us? You mean you and Evan and Arlene and Kylie?"

Mia named the other three designers who worked under the direction of Damien DeMello—Evan Larsen, Arlene Bitterman and Kylie Northcote—and Jordan nodded.

"I don't see how Uncle Lucien can rehire anyone," Becca said, "until he catches the rat who gave your design to Heavenly Bridals."

The card the *GQ* model had given her burned in Mia's pocket. *Lucien is on it,* she wanted to say, but didn't. She had absolute faith in Becca and Jordan's innocence, but Jordan would blab—she loved gossip and being in the know—and she might blab to the wrong person. Like the fink who slipped her design for Alicia Whitcomb's wedding dress—the governor's daughter; oh, wasn't that swell?—to Heavenly Bridals.

"*Gave* Mia's design to Heavenly Bridals?" Jordan snorted. "Sold, Becca. Sold for a boatload of money, or whoever did this is a fool."

"There are other motives besides money," Becca said.

"Oh really?" Jordan laughed. "Like what?"

"Sticking it to Lucien Savard." Robin appeared behind Becca, his red hair dark and sparkling with melting snow. He slid into the chair beside his sister and looked at Mia. "No offense, mighty mite, but how many people do you think Uncle Lucien has driven to Prozac? Besides our father, who art in therapy?"

Becca made a face at him and Robin grinned.

Uncle Rudy was on Prozac? This was news to Mia. He'd always seemed as calm and steady to her as Lucien was explosive. He'd called Petra and told her about the theft, which made Mia wonder who had discovered the Heavenly Bridals ad in *Today's Bride* magazine. And who had called Joseph Kerr of Joseph Kerr, Inc., Private Investigations.

"Who called and told you what happened?" she asked Robin.

"Dad," he said, filching a sip of Becca's beer. "I figured the three of you would be here."

"Actually, dear brother," Becca said, "we were surprised not to find *you* here, in the back room shooting pool when you should be working."

"On Thursday afternoon?" Robin shrugged. "Nobody to hustle."

Mia and Jordan laughed. Becca glared at her brother and asked, "So where were you all afternoon?"

"As far away from the Savard Building as I could get without leaving the state." Robin swiveled in his chair, signaled the waitress and ordered coffee. When it came, steaming in a heavy white mug, he took a sip and asked, "So who's going back in the morning?"

"I am," Mia said, and Robin blinked at her. "I thought you'd quit."

"I can't quit now," Mia said. Maybe later, but not now. "Jenna and Luke are both on their way home."

"Circling the wagons. That's good." Robin nodded. "Savard's is under attack by those heathens at Heavenly Bridals."

"This is nothing to joke about, Robin," Becca snapped.

"I'm not joking, Beck, but I'm not joining the Grim and Morose Club." Robin waved a hand over the table and shook his head. "The three of you look like somebody ran over your dog. When I came through the door I could see the black cloud hanging over your heads. Swilling booze doesn't change what happened and it doesn't help Savard's."

"This," Mia said sourly, "from the king of cutting and running when the going gets tough."

"Self-preservation." Robin turned his head toward Mia, a steely glint in his eyes that she'd never seen before. "Uncle Lucien blows up a dozen times a day. The only thing that standing in the blast pattern gets you is an uncontrollable twitch or a stretch on the couch. I haven't seen anything worth standing at ground zero for until today, till somebody sold us out to Heavenly Bridals. Now it's time to fight."

"Whoa," Becca said, her eyes round. "You do have a backbone."

"Okay, Rob." Jordan pushed her margarita away and folded her arms on the table. "Where do we start?"

"Beats me." Robin shrugged again. "I'm not a detective."

Mia wanted to say, *But Joseph Kerr of Joseph Kerr, Inc., Private Investigations* is *a detective and he's on the job.* Instead, she shoved the celery stalk in her mouth. This was not the time to come down with blabbermouthitis, otherwise known in the design department as Jordan's Disease.

She could barely chew, let alone talk, so of course her cell phone rang. Mia rose and turned from the table, spit the celery into a napkin and dug her phone out of her purse. The caller ID said it was Jenna.

"I'm on United flight 1218. Luke is on flight 1307. My plane lands at 10:12. Luke's at 10:35. Terminal A, gates 11 and 12," said Jenna, the queen of details. "Can you pick us up?"

"What? No limo?" Mia asked.

"Not tonight. We need to talk," Jenna answered. "Where's Dad?"

"I don't know." Mia moved to the window. "I'm at Blanko's with Robin and Becca and Jordan."

"So you can't talk. Never mind, then. See you later."

Jenna disconnected. Mia flipped her phone shut and slipped it in her pocket, leaned the heels of her hands on the narrow windowsill and eyed the street. The snow had nearly stopped; only a few flakes fluttered around the foggy streetlamps. The pavement glittered with tire-tracked slush that would freeze later as the temperature dropped, but Mia drove a Subaru, a sure-footed all-wheel drive. She'd have no problem getting to KCI and back.

As she turned toward the table her gaze raked over the piles of dirty snow pushed against the curb by the plows. Enough light spilled outside to etch the diamond-paned pattern of the window on the swept-bare-by-the-wind sidewalk—and glisten on the footprints stamped into the snow drifted near the building. Someone had been standing there, close enough to the window to see inside.

If he—or she, Mia supposed—was tall enough, which Mia wasn't. She had to rock up on her toes and press her forehead to the glass to make sure she was seeing footprints and not a shadow.

"Mia's on point," Robin said behind her. "Must be a Hunk Alert."

"Hardly." She turned and wrinkled her nose at him. "I'm eyeballing the roads. I have to pick up Jenna and Luke at KCI."

"I'd go with you," Becca said, "but I have yoga tonight."

"My sister invited me to dinner," Jordan said.

"I'd sooner walk to KCI and back barefoot," Robin said, "than be stuck in a car with Lucien Junior on the warpath."

"Do you mean Luke?" Mia put her hands on her hips. "Or Jenna?"

"I mean both of them."

Mia stuck out her tongue. Robin laughed. Mia grinned and picked up her purse and the tote with her boots inside. "See you tomorrow."

It took her ten seconds in Blanko's wood-floored foyer to trade her shoes for her boots, yank her stadium coat off a peg above an oak bench, shrug into it and flip up the hood, pull on her gloves and push through the heavy glass-paned door.

Blanko's occupied the first floor of a brick building on the southeast corner of 47th Street and Broadway. The Country Club Plaza climbed the hills above Brush Creek like a flight of stairs, so most of the northbound streets soared like ski slopes. Mia knew to duck her head to keep the wind from snatching her breath as she rounded the corner onto Broadway and trudged uphill to the diamond-paned window.

She found the footprints in the snow drifted against the cement foundation of Blanko's, where the light from the window pooled on the dark sidewalk, and dropped to her heels for a better look.

The soles of the shoes that had made the prints were flat, like men's dress shoes. No boot cleats or athletic shoe treads. Whoever had stood here hadn't jiggled from the cold or shifted from foot to foot—there were only two clear prints and a heel impression where the Peeping Tom had stepped out of the snow and onto the cleared walk.

Mia rose, looped her purse and tote over her left shoulder, braced her right palm against the brick wall of the building and lifted her right foot over the right print in the snow. The shoe that had left its mark was at least four sizes larger than her six and a half. She backed up a couple feet, but could only see the brass fixture hung over the table. She had to back up a good bit more, maybe another five feet, before she could see the top of Jordan's red and blond spiked head through the window.

Someone a lot taller than her five feet three inches had stood here. Why? Mia turned her head and looked up and down the street. No apartment buildings on this block, only small boutiques that closed at five, their dimly lit windows and locked doorways hung with shadows thrown by the mist-shrouded streetlights.

She'd arrived at Blanko's around five-thirty, just as the snow was beginning. A couple stray flakes caught in Mia's lashes as she fished her phone out of her pocket— the clock on the color screen read 6:42 P.M. She bit off her glove, pressed Menu and checked the time of Jenna's call: 6:35.

Sometime between five-thirty and six-thirty someone had stood here looking in Blanko's window—there was no place else to look, nothing else to see—straight at the table where she'd been sitting, where Jordan and Becca and Robin still sat. Who? A homeless person, gazing inside at the light and warmth like a character in a Dickens novel?

In dress shoes? In the swankiest neighborhood in Kansas City? Doubtful. The cops kept homeless people hustled off the Plaza. God forbid the rich should be offended by a brush with poverty. So if not a homeless person, who had been looking in Blanko's window? And why?

On any other day Mia wouldn't have blinked at footprints in the snow outside a window. But on this day, after the theft of Alicia Whitcomb's wedding dress . . . was someone following her?

It was her design that Heavenly Bridals stole. If someone, say Joseph Kerr, the *GQ* detective, was compiling a list of suspects, wouldn't that put her at the top?

His cover model face flashed in her head. Dark hair, a lock of it fallen over his forehead, well-shaped eyebrows and deep blue eyes. The barely there brush of his fingers as he'd slipped her his card and said, "Call me." With any luck it would put her at the top of his list.

"Oh for God's sake, Mia," she said disgustedly. "Get a date."

What was she doing out here, sniffing around like a bloodhound? She wasn't a detective—she was a nitwit. Her nose felt drippy and numb with cold. Her stomach like a rock, remembering the stricken look on her father's face when he'd whipped the shroud off the dress form and Alicia Whitcomb's wedding dress.

If only Lucien had looked at her, glanced at her or something, anything to let her know he didn't suspect her. But he'd fired her along with everyone else. He'd fired Jenna and Luke, too. His own children.

"Where's Dad?" Jenna had asked her. Mia hoped he was still in the cafeteria busting up chairs. A flash of Lucien strapped to a gurney with a heart monitor stuck to his chest leaped into her head, but she pushed it away and speed dialed her mother. Petra's voice mail answered.

"Luke and Jenna are on their way home. I'm picking them up at ten-thirty," Mia said, and disconnected.

She dialed Uncle Rudy, got his voice mail, too, and hung up.

Petra had told her to clear out of the Savard Building with everyone else and she'd done it. What a stupid thing to do, the worst thing she could've done. Hindsight being 20/20, Mia could see that now.

She should've stayed. Broken a chair if she'd had to to get Lucien's attention and told him she'd had nothing to do with the theft, that if he'd thought so—even for a nanosecond—he was wrong and she was resigning as his daughter. And she should've done it right there and then in the cafeteria, in front of her mother and Uncle Rudy and Damien.

Mia looked at her phone—6:46. Plenty of time to do it now before she headed for KCI to pick up Jenna and Luke.

She put her phone away, her right glove on, closed her hand around the straps on her shoulder and struck off downhill. The sidewalk wasn't as clear as it looked. She took a slip on black ice at the corner, twisting her left knee and making it throb all the way to the Savard Building. Like her heart had throbbed when she'd looked into Joseph Kerr's blue eyes.

The revolving door and the glass side doors were locked, the chain-mail security gate glittering in the half-light between the vestibule and the lobby. Mia used her key to let herself in and relock the door, raised and lowered the gate by the wall buttons and made for the elevator.

She was looking at her feet, wiggling her cold toes inside her boots, when the doors opened on six. She started out of the elevator, lifted her chin and stopped. Joseph Kerr stood in front of her.

Mia didn't stumble or miss a step—though her heart skipped—she simply stopped before she walked nose-first into the third button of his sage green linen shirt. A Perry Ellis, she thought. And if the tie he'd loosened at his throat wasn't a Ralph Lauren, she'd eat it.

"You again." He caught her by the arms and smiled. "Hi there."

"Hello, Joseph Kerr, Inc.," Mia said, and his smile widened.

Oh no. Dimples. One, anyway, at the left corner of his mouth.

"And you are . . . ?" he asked.

"Mia Savard. Is my father here?"

"No. He left with your mother."

"Not in an ambulance, I hope?"

"No," he replied, his dimple flashing. "On his own two feet."

The elevator started to close. Joseph Kerr stepped back, drawing Mia with him. The doors slipped together behind her and still he held her. Not exactly like he never wanted to let her go. More like she was a specimen under a microscope. Or a suspect.

"And you're here because . . . ?" Mia asked.

"Your father hired me to find out who stole the design for Alicia Whitcomb's wedding dress and how it ended up with Heavenly Bridals."

"I figured that. I mean why are you in the building?"

The dimple and the smile faded. He let her go and stepped back.

"I'm detecting. Why are you here?"

"I came to talk to my father. Since he isn't here, I'll be going."

Before I start drooling, Mia thought, and turned away to push the call button. *What have you detected? What have you found?* she wanted to ask. She wished she hadn't come. She wished this wasn't happening, that Joseph Kerr wasn't here, that she could've met him on a slow night at Blanko's. She wished the elevator would hurry, but the car had returned to the lobby. After hours, the elevators did that automatically.

"Out all by yourself tonight?" Joseph Kerr asked.

"Yes." Mia glanced at him. "How'd you know I was in the building?"

"I heard the elevator." The doors slid open. He took her elbow, steered her into the car and stepped back. "Good night, Miss Savard."

"G'night, Joseph Kerr, Inc." The smile and the dimple flirted with the left side of his mouth again, then the doors closed between them.

In the nick of time, Joe thought. One more second and he would've laughed out loud and blown his tough-guy-detective image.

If he hadn't blown it already in these clothes. He was still reeling from the twelve-hundred-dollar hit to his American Express Card, but Moira had insisted. "You can't meet Lucien Savard looking like *that*," she'd said, and dragged him to Jack Henry's.

An hour later he'd emerged from Kansas City's most exclusive men's store with, among other things, a two-hundred-dollar pair of trousers and a shirt and tie that cost him another hundred and fifty. Lucien Savard hadn't seemed to notice, but his daughter had. She'd given his tie a particular once-over.

Joe plucked it off his shirtfront, turned it over and read the label. Ralph Lauren. Whoever the hell he was.

"That was Mia," Pete Onslow, chief of Savard Security, said behind him. "Cute as a bug's ear, isn't she?"

"Yeah, she is." Dark hair, dark eyes, smart, quick-witted and funny. "Be a shame if she's the one who sold out her family."

"She didn't. Neither did Luke or Jenna. Fight like cats and dogs, the Savards, but just let somebody who isn't family come after 'em."

"Don't tell me things like that. Let me make my own judgments." Joe turned toward Pete. "That's how Savard wants it. Everybody is a suspect. No favoritism, no special treatment. He was adamant."

"Guess that includes me, too."

"I'd say that especially includes you, Uncle Pete," Joe said, and they both grinned. Then Pete shook his head. "That's the thanks I get for hooking Savard up with the best damn detective in the Midwest."

Naturally his mother's only brother thought he was the best. What surprised Joe was Lucien Savard hiring him on the spot.

"I want this SOB caught and prosecuted ASAP," the CEO of Savard Creations had told him, standing next to a pile of broken chairs in the cafeteria. "I don't have time to sift through bids. You're Pete's nephew. That's all the recommendation I need. Oh—and tell Pete he's not fired."

Savard's wife, Petra, sitting in one of the few chairs that still had legs, cleared her throat. When Savard glanced at her, she raised a brow.

"Never mind. I'll tell him myself." Savard sighed and strode out of the cafeteria, bellowing, "Pete? Pete! Where are you?"

Petra Savard smiled at Joe. "Lucien considers himself an artist. He thinks he has to behave like this. His bark is worse than his bite."

"Here's hoping," he'd said, and Petra Savard had laughed.

"That's me. The best," Joe said to Pete now, and gave his uncle a clap on the shoulder. "Says so on my business card."

"You *are* the best," Pete insisted. "Your dad raised you to be."

And when Sam Kerr, a twenty-year veteran of the Kansas City Missouri Police Force, was killed on the job—shot by a punk running out of a liquor store with a hundred twenty-five bucks and the .38 he'd taken from the owner—Pete Onslow, Sam's former partner, stepped in and helped his baby sister, Evelyn, finish raising Sam's youngest son.

"The job," Evie Kerr complained bitterly when Joe graduated from the University of Missouri at Kansas City with a degree in criminal justice and joined the KCMOPD. "It's all about the damn job."

It was bad enough that Sam Junior, Joe's older brother, already had six years on the force. That her baby boy was following in his footsteps, and their father's, was too much for Evie.

For ten years Joe turned his head. Pretended not to notice his mother's hair growing whiter, the stoop she developed from the weight of all the religious medals draped around her neck. Then one night he'd turned his head the wrong way, as he came out of a Quik Trip on Linwood Boulevard. His service revolver snapped into his holster, a cup of coffee in one hand, his cell phone in the other—talking to Moira, teasing her about her birthday—and found himself staring at a chrome-plated 9mm Glock.

He froze. Just for a second, no longer than it took his heart rate to shoot to the moon. But any cop who freezes, who hesitates for even a pulse beat at the sight of a gun swinging toward him, usually ends up a dead cop.

If it hadn't been for his partner, Brian Hicks, he would've been dead, and Moira would've been an orphan for the second time in her young life.

The next day Joe quit the force.

"If you do this, Ma wins," Sam told him. "This is what she wants."

"Maybe it's what I want, too," Joe replied. "Ever think of that?"

"Bullshit," Sam snorted. "You were born to be a cop."

"No, Sam. You were born to be a cop."

"What will you do? How will you take care of Moira?"

"Don't, Sam," Joe warned. "Ma throws that at me all the time. If something happens to me, what happens to Moira? We'll be fine."

Moira had been three days shy of fifteen that night; now she was twenty-two and the brains that ran Joseph Kerr, Inc. Joe and Brian were the brawn. When Joe's cell phone rang on his belt clip, it was Brian.

"I'm in Pete's office," Brian said. "Got the disks from the security cameras in the lobby and the parking garage all loaded. Ready when you are for Thursday Night at the Movies. Did you call in the pizza?"

"Moira's bringing it." Joe looked at his watch. "She should be here anytime. When did you change the lobby security disk?"

" 'Bout twenty minutes ago."

"Change it again. We had a visitor up here. Mia Savard."

"Will do. Tell Pete the popcorn is in the microwave."

Brian hung up. So did Joe. "Popcorn?" he said to Pete. "A microwave in your office?"

"It's not for me," Pete claimed, pushing the call button for the elevator. "It's for the night and the weekend guys."

"Right, Orville Redenbacher. Whatever you say." Joe laughed and followed his uncle into the right-hand car.

Pete got off on the first floor to join Brian in the security office. Joe rode down to the parking garage to open

the gate—a metal mesh curtain like the one in the lobby—
for Moira.

The garage was cold enough to show him his breath
as he stepped out of the elevator, rounded a concrete pil-
lar and inhaled fresh exhaust. A car sat at the gate, engine
idling, snowflakes dancing in the headlights that flashed
at him twice. Joe waved at Moira and moved toward the
wall-mounted controls to let her in.

The gold Subaru Forester he'd seen earlier when he'd
walked this level of the garage was still parked in the
shadow of one of the farthest pillars. The car belonged
to Mia Savard. Joe knew because he'd run the plate
through his contact at the DMV. Odd that she hadn't
taken her car.

He hit the switch and the gate lifted. Moira's silver
BMW Roadster scooted past him, and he hit the switch
again to lower the gate. Then he walked up to the Subaru and laid his hand on the hood.

Cold as the look Mia Savard had given him when he'd
asked her if she was out alone tonight. Cute as a bug's
ear didn't mean she wasn't a liar, but the twenty-minute-
old security disk might tell him.

"In the market for an SUV, Jo-Jo?"

"Since you have pizza"—Joe could smell it, hot cardboard and tomato-soaked pepperoni—"I'll forgive you
for calling me that."

He turned away from the Subaru and caught Moira's
grin over the crust of half-melted snow sliding off the roof
of her car. Every day she looked more like her mother.
The resemblance didn't rip his heart out of his chest anymore, just gave him a pang and made him smile.

"Did you get one of those lousy Hawaiian pizzas for
Brian?"

"I did." Moira lifted two Pizza Hut boxes out of the BMW, pushed the door shut with her hip and came around the car to meet Joe. "There's just something wrong about pineapple on pizza, y'know?"

"Don't tell me. Tell Brian." He took the boxes from her, swung them out of the way and bent to give her a kiss. "We've got a long night ahead of us, Smoochy Lips."

Moira made a face. "If I promise not to call you Jo-Jo anymore, will you stop calling me Smoochy Lips? I'm not twelve anymore."

"If there's extra pepperoni on my pizza, I'll think about it."

"Start thinking. Any suspects yet?"

"Would you believe two hundred forty-three?"

"That's everyone who works for the company," Moira said, which proved she'd done her homework. "This could take a while."

"I don't think so." Joe looped his free arm around Moira and drew her toward the elevator. "I imagine we'll be able to eliminate two hundred thirty-one of them right off the top."

"Which leaves, let me guess . . ." Moira slid her arm around his waist, hooked her thumb through his belt loop like she used to when she was twelve so she could keep up with him. "The entire Savard family—Lucien and his wife, Petra. Their children, Luke, Jenna and Mia. Lucien's brother, Rudy, and his two kids, Robin and Rebecca. The head designer, Damien DeMello, and the four designers who work under him."

"Took your smart pill today." Joe gave Moira an affectionate jostle. "We'll give every Savard employee a good long look, but I'm pretty sure we can focus on upper management. That's usually where you find an industrial spy. Somebody with access and opportunity."

"And motive." Moira stopped in front of the elevator and slipped out from under Joe's arm. "Any disgruntled employees?"

"My guess is two hundred forty-three. Savard fired everyone in the company this afternoon." Joe pushed the call button. "When I got here, he was in the cafeteria smashing chairs against the wall."

"Sounds like the boss from hell." Moira grinned as the elevator opened. "I bet we'll find a few Lucien Savard voodoo dolls, too."

When the doors closed behind Joseph Kerr and the gorgeous brunette, Mia gave up peeking over the dashboard and straightened in her seat behind the wheel of her gold Subaru Forester.

Her cell phone was still in her hand. She opened it and redialed her mother. "I'm back. Found my keys," Mia lied. She'd told her mother she'd dropped them under the seat. "So has Dad calmed down?"

"He's as calm as he ever gets. He and Rudy and Damien have shut themselves in the library. I've only heard a couple books hit the wall."

"I don't know if I'm bringing Luke and Jenna there or what," Mia said. "Guess I'll find out when they get here. I'll call you when I know."

"I'd appreciate it, honey. Drive safely." Petra disconnected.

So did Mia, tossing her cell phone onto the passenger seat. She'd been sitting here minding her own business, talking to her mother, when the BMW Roadster pulled up to the gate. "Hang on," she'd said to Petra, then yelped the lie about dropping her keys and ducked out of sight when the elevator opened and Joseph Kerr stepped out of it. She'd heard the brunette call him Jo-Jo, seen him kiss her, put his arm around her.

"Thank God." Mia sighed. "Thank God he's married."

3

"IF THERE'S WALL BANGING going on," Jenna said, as she settled herself in the front seat of Mia's Forester. "I want no part of it."

Neither did Luke, so instead of taking her brother and sister home to Mumsy and Dadums, Mia dropped them at the Fairmont Hotel on the Plaza, a two-block walk from the Savard Building.

"We'll see you in the morning," Jenna said as she slid out of the SUV into the frosty night air. "In your office. Seven-thirty. Have the coffee ready."

"Yes, *ma'am*," Mia said, and snapped a salute Jenna didn't see.

Her sister had already slammed the door and wheeled toward the front entrance of the Fairmont. Luke saw it and slid Mia a grin as he swung their bags out of the backseat.

"Lucien Junior," he said, and winked.

"Ai-yi-yi." Mia let her head thud against the steering wheel.

In the last twelve hours she'd resigned, she'd been fired and now Jenna was mounting a hostile takeover of her life. On their way out of the United terminal, with

Luke trailing behind with the bags, Jenna had said Mia was absolutely, positively *not* going back to Savard's.

"But it's my design that was stolen," Mia argued. "If I don't go back I'll look guilty, like I had something to do with it."

"Pish," Jenna had snorted. "If you go back, our campaign to get you out of bridal and into trousseau will have been for naught."

"I think this theft is just a tad more important, Jenna."

"Mia's right," Luke said. "She needs to be at Savard's tomorrow. We *all* need to be there."

Because Luke agreed with Mia, Jenna backed off. She wasn't happy about it—that's what slamming the door meant—but she'd get over it.

Mia was already over her two-hour infatuation with Joeseph Kerr, Inc., but the headache that had started in her office, the I-don't-want-to-quit-how-did-I-end-up-here throb still pulsed between her eyes.

When the cabby behind her honked, she lifted her head and pulled away from the entrance, turned left out of the Fairmont drive and stopped at the red light. When the turn arrow flashed, Mia made a left and followed Ward Parkway to the three-story brick Tudor house where she'd grown up. It was pushing eleven-thirty, but she had a feeling her parents would be awake.

Sure enough, the lights were on, and her mother was in the kitchen. When Mia used her key to let herself in the back door, Petra turned away from the sink with the electric teakettle in her hands.

"Mia," she said hopefully. "Are Jenna and Luke with you?"

"No." Mia swung her purse onto a chair at the round oak kitchen table. "I dropped them at the Fairmont."

Petra sighed and placed the kettle on its element. "I shouldn't have told you your father was throwing books."

Mia took off her coat. "He isn't still throwing them, is he?"

"No. He's on the phone."

"He doesn't think I'm involved in this, does he?"

"Good heavens, no!" Petra swung toward her with a startled blink. "Why would you think such a thing?"

"I did quit this morning, Mother." Mia hung her coat over the chair. "Which could look like I was getting out of Dodge ahead of the sheriff."

"It doesn't look that way to your father." Petra held her arms out with a come-here-baby smile. "Or to me."

Why the heck not? She was the baby. Mia went to her mother and laid her head on her shoulder. "Who found the Heavenly Bridals ad?"

"Celeste," Petra said—Savard's director of advertising—as she stroked Mia's hair. "She took the ad to Rudy and he called me. I told him to tell Damien before he told your father."

"Who's Dad talking to on the phone this late at night?"

"Walter Vance," Petra named Savard's attorney. "We're suing, of course. Your father's been on the phone most of the evening, calling everyone who works for Savard's to tell them they aren't fired."

Mia sighed with relief. *See, Cindy Somebody? Told you so.*

The automatic kettle shut itself off with a *click*. Petra put a kiss on Mia's forehead, turned away and poured hot water over the chamomile tea bags in the china teapot. Mia slid onto a stool at the crescent-shaped island

and opened the Pillsbury Dough Boy cookie jar she'd given Petra for Mother's Day when she was twelve.

"I went back to Savard's around seven," Mia said, biting into an oatmeal cookie. Suddenly she was starving. All she'd eaten today was yogurt for breakfast, half a Virgin Mary and a mouthful of celery. "You were gone, but I met the detective Dad hired."

"He came highly recommended." Petra put the lid on the teapot and came to sit on the stool beside Mia. "He's Pete Onslow's nephew."

"Really?" Mia said. "Zero family resemblance."

"Thirty years ago there was. I've seen pictures of Pete in uniform." Petra took a cookie out of the jar. When Mia finished hers, Petra handed it to her. "You've been worrying all day, haven't you?"

"I wouldn't say worrying." Mia broke the cookie in two and gave half to her mother. "I'd say scared to death that Dad thinks I'm a thief."

"Your father and I know better." Petra laid her hand over Mia's. "But Pete's nephew may not. Your father put Joseph Kerr in complete charge of the investigation. He told him specifically not to play favorites."

"Nor should he," Mia agreed. "The Savards shouldn't be above suspicion just because our name is Savard."

Petra smiled. "Your father gets to tell Jenna."

"Oh, boy," Mia said. "Hide the chili mac."

Her mother laughed and got up to pour the tea. Mia ate her half a cookie and thought about the footsteps in the snow outside Blanko's window. Joseph Kerr, Inc., had asked who she was when she stepped out of the elevator—*and* he'd been wearing dress shoes. Top-end Florsheims.

Mia Savard wasn't a household name. Lucien Savard

was, so she supposed Joseph Kerr genuinely might not have known her from Adam, but her face—Jenna's and Luke's, too—were all over the Savard Creations website. A couple mouse clicks before he'd pushed her through the revolving door and he would've known who she was. Had he pretended not to, just to see if she'd tell the truth? If he'd known who she was when he pushed her, had he followed her and left the footprints outside Blanko's window?

Petra slid a cup of steaming chamomile tea in front of her. "You look like you're worrying again, Mia."

"No. I'm wondering why Heavenly Bridals bought a full-page ad for a stolen design. If they'd slipped Alicia's dress into their spring collection, they could've claimed coincidence and maybe gotten away with it. But pasting it all over *Today's Bride*? They had to know we'd see it."

"That's the first thing I thought." Petra lifted her cup and blew on her tea. "Say what you will about Oren Angel, he built Heavenly Bridals from the ground up like your father built Savard's. He's too smart to do something so stupid."

Her mother, Mia knew, could say plenty about Oren Angel. He'd started his career at Savard's. Forty years ago he was Lucien's best designer, his pet protégé, till he'd stabbed Lucien in the back—the way her father told it—by leaving and setting up Heavenly Bridals in direct competition to Savard's.

"Then why did he run the ad?" Mia asked.

"Your father disagrees with me," Petra said, and sipped her tea, "but I don't think Oren has any idea the design is stolen."

"Blasphemy!" Lucien exploded into the kitchen from

the arched hallway that led to his library. "In my own home!"

Mia nearly jumped off her stool at her father's roar. The delicate Spode teacup in her mother's hand never wavered.

"Be quiet, Lucien," Petra said. "That's enough shouting."

"How can you defend that ingrate? That backstabber!" Lucien paced in front of the island, his tie askew, his mostly silver hair in disarray, like he'd been raking it with his fingers. "I taught him everything he knows! I *made* him! I offered him a partnership—but no, not good enough for the great Oren Angel! He turned up his nose and—" In mid-tirade Lucien swung around toward Mia. "Where are Luke and Jenna?"

"At the Fairmont," Mia said. "You were throwing books."

"Well, I would have stopped," Lucien said indignantly, then kicked a stool away from the other side of the island and plunked down on it. "We're suing Angel for fifty million dollars."

"That's a nice round figure." Petra rose, poured him a cup of tea and put it in front of him. Lucien wrinkled his nose. "I hate tea."

"It's chamomile. Drink it or you won't sleep." Her mother sat down and calmly stared at her father until he took a swallow. "I think you should talk to Oren before you start accusing him and filing lawsuits."

"My tongue will rot in my mouth before I speak to that Benedict Arnold." Lucien drank more tea and shuddered. "Pete's nephew is going to see him in the morning."

"I'm not sure that's wise," Petra said. "If Oren doesn't know the design is stolen, he could take a visit from a private investigator hired by you as an accusation. He could turn around and sue Savard Creations."

Her father's eyes flared. "Let him try."

"Lucien, please," her mother said. "Just call him."

"When hell freezes," Lucien snarled. "That's when I'll talk to him."

"All right. Then talk to your daughter." Petra lifted a hand toward Mia. "She's been worried all day, afraid that you thought she had something to do with the theft."

"Mia!" Lucien gaped at her, shocked. "How could you?"

"Well, Dad," she said, "you did fire me."

"Oh, for God's sake," Lucien said disgustedly. "I fired everyone."

"Did you rehire everyone?" Petra asked.

"You mean did I talk to everyone? No. I left messages. No one wants to talk to me, apparently." Lucien glanced at Mia again. He looked tired; his eyes red, his face drawn. "I'm surprised you want to talk to me."

"I didn't resign as your daughter. And I'm not quitting."

"Of course you're not. I knew that." Lucien bent his elbows and dragged his hands through his hair. "I wish Luke and Jenna were here."

"They'll be at Savard's in the morning," Mia said around the lump swelling in her throat at the sight of her father the dynamo sagging on the stool across from her. "At seven-thirty. In my office."

"I'll talk to them then." Lucien straightened, closed his hands on Mia's wrists and tugged her toward him, leaned across the island and kissed her. "Good night, little mite." He leaned on one elbow and kissed her mother as Petra stretched to meet his lips. "Good night, my love."

Mia watched Lucien drag himself out of the kitchen, then turned to look at her mother. Petra's lips were pursed, her head tilted to one side.

"I like Dad a lot better when he's yelling," Mia said.

"Not to worry." Petra collected the teacups and carried them to the sink. "If your father won't talk to Oren, then I will." She turned and smiled at Mia. "That should bring the roof down on all our heads."

Joe had been tossed out of better places than Heavenly Bridals.

He was literally thrown, kicked to the curb like the garbage by Oren Angel. After spending half the night staring at flat-line boring security tapes, and listening to Savard bellow on the phone for half an hour about his former protégé, it felt kind of good to just lie on the sidewalk for a minute.

He hadn't resisted when Angel grabbed him. It was much better for business to be the assault*ee* rather than the assault*er*. The snow that had fallen overnight, already shoveled off the sidewalk into piles, cushioned his landing. Thanks to the KCMO Police Academy, he knew how to fall on concrete so he didn't bash in his head or break a bone.

He was due at Savard Creations at nine-thirty to meet with Savard, his family, his attorney and Damien DeMello, head of the design department. He had plenty of time to swing by the office, where he kept a couple changes of clothes, but Joe smiled and brushed off, swung into his decade-old Ford Explorer and dialed Moira on his cell. Clients, he'd discovered, responded better to seeing what he did for them rather than hearing about it.

"Grab something out of the closet in my office and

meet me at Savard's at eleven-thirty," he said. "I'll take you to lunch."

"Slop Cocoa Puffs on your shirt again?"

"Smoochy Lips, Smoochy Lips, Smoochy—"

"Okay, okay," Moira laughed. "What happened?"

"Oren Angel gave me the boot."

"I'll bring something snazzy so you can take me somewhere nice."

"I don't own anything snazzy."

"You will by eleven-thirty," Moira said merrily, and hung up.

Lucien Savard's secretary, Selma Daniels, didn't bat an eye when he turned up in front of her desk dripping slush and Ice Melt. She was sixty-something, wore a plum-colored suit and an expression that said she'd seen it all during her twenty-five years as Savard's Girl Friday. She nodded at his name, led him into the conference room adjacent to Lucien Savard's office and sat down in a corner chair with a steno pad.

Neither the room nor the polished cherry table where Savard sat, at the head of course, was especially large. The walls were pale mustard hung with silver-framed modern art, the carpet paprika red. Ugliest rug Joe had ever seen, but the view through the window behind Savard—pale winter blue sky streaked with thin white clouds above the downtown skyline—would make a great postcard.

Savard's wife, Petra, sat on his right, with Luke, Jenna and Mia Savard and Damien DeMello. On the left side of the table sat Rudy Savard, who looked enough like Lucien to be Lucien, the attorney Walter Vance, Rudy's son, Robin—short for Robert—and his daughter, Rebecca, called Becca. When he'd finished the security tapes,

Joe had spent two hours reviewing the Savard management files before he fell on his face.

The CEO looked like he'd had a rough start to his day, too. Joe didn't know diddly about clothes, but he knew stains. The splash pattern on Lucien's peach-colored shirt suggested a cup of coffee. Last night over pizza and the security tapes, Pete told him about the Sibling Wars. Joe glanced around the table, zeroed in on the fire in Jenna Savard's eyes and decided the battle had been rejoined.

"Everyone," Lucien said, "this is Joseph Kerr, the private investigator I've retained to discover who stole Alicia Whitcomb's dress. I expect you all to make yourselves available to him for interviews."

Savard introduced the men first. Sexist, but it didn't surprise Joe. Savard's brother, his son, his nephew and Walter Vance all came around the table to shake hands. Damien DeMello did not. He pushed his chair away from the table and sat sketching on the pad of paper in his lap. Mia Savard leaned on the elbow of her chair watching him.

"You met my wife, Petra, last night," Lucien said, and Mrs. Savard nodded. "My niece, Rebecca." A brunette with big dark eyes peeked at him shyly. "My older daughter, Jenna." The fiery-eyed blonde looked like Michelle Pfeiffer with lockjaw. "And Mia, my youngest."

Miss Cute as a Bug's Ear glanced at him with a smile, then leaned closer to DeMello. Huh. Last night, Joe would've sworn she'd thought he was pretty cute, too. A good reason why he never trusted first impressions.

"You look a little damp around the edges, Mr. Kerr," Lucien Savard said. "Problem this morning?"

"I gave Oren Angel my card, told him I'd been retained by Savard Creations and he showed me the door by the seat of my pants."

"*You* should have called Oren, Lucien," Petra said to her husband, then to Joe, "I'm so sorry, Joseph. Are you all right?"

"I'm fine, Mrs. Savard. No apology needed."

"Selma. Coffee, please," Savard said. "Sit, Mr. Kerr." Selma appeared at his elbow, put a silver tray that held a cup and saucer, a mini sugar bowl and cream pitcher and a small carafe in front of him. Joe thanked her and sat down.

"I was airborne at the time so I may have misunderstood," he said to Savard. "But I think Angel said you'd be hearing from his attorney."

A glint of relish lit Lucien Savard's eyes. His brother Rudy's bland smile didn't flicker. Savard's attorney, Walter Vance, opened a leather portfolio on the table in front of him and clicked a gold ballpoint pen.

"Howard Edwards represents Heavenly Bridals," Vance said as he wrote. "When I hear from him, I'll let you know."

"Apprise Mr. Kerr as well, Walter," Savard said. "Selma has his contact information."

Vance nodded and glanced at Joe. "Were you able to ask Angel anything about the design in *Today's Bride*?"

"No. He heard the name Lucien Savard and I was on the sidewalk."

"Exactly as I expected." Savard smacked his hands gleefully on the padded arms of his chair. "I think that's all the proof we need."

"All it proves," Joe said, "is that Oren Angel dislikes you."

"He hates my guts, Mr. Kerr, and I hate his."

"Yes, Lucien, so you've told us." Walter Vance didn't say *a million times* but Joe heard it in his voice. Vance had been Savard Creations' counsel since its founding. "Mr. Kerr is right. Angel tossing him into the street tells us nothing about how the design came into his hands."

"I still say," Petra Savard stated firmly, "that it's entirely possible Oren has no idea the design was stolen from Savard's."

"Oh, Mother," Jenna snapped. "Heavenly Bridals is our fiercest competitor. Oren Angel's been holding his breath for twenty years *waiting* for a chance to stick it to Dad. What better way than to steal Alicia Whitcomb's dress? Hoping, of course, that Governor Whitcomb will hit the roof, vent to the press and Savard's will be humiliated all over the papers and the evening news."

"That hasn't happened yet," Luke Savard said. "Governor and Mrs. Whitcomb and Alicia will be here at two o'clock this afternoon. Heavenly Bridals must be dealt with, but at the moment we need to focus on damage control and making Alicia Whitcomb happy." Savard's son slid Joe an amiable glance. "No offense, Mr. Kerr."

"None taken," Joe said easily, and poured a cup of coffee.

"Fine, Luke," Jenna Savard said. "You focus on damage control. I'll focus on breaking Oren Angel's kneecaps."

"Jen*na*, really," Petra Savard said. *Not in front of company* said the look she gave her daughter.

"Oren Angel is despicable, Mother," Jenna replied. "He's been accused of lifting designs from other houses."

"Accused," Walter Vance said pointedly. "The charges were never proved, and to my knowledge no settlements were ever paid."

"He doesn't need to steal," Damien DeMello said without looking up from his sketch. "Oren Angel is a genius."

"Perhaps, Damien," Lucien Savard said with a scowl that could scorch paper, "you'd be happier at Heavenly Bridals."

"Oren has made overtures, Lucien, which you know, since I've reported every single one of them to you." DeMello glanced up from his sketch at Savard, then at Joe. "You'll want to make a note of that. Perhaps work me over later with a rubber hose."

Terrific, Joe thought. *A smart-ass who wants to play Columbo.*

"I'll jot that down," he said, but didn't. "Mrs. Savard? What makes you think Angel may not know the design was stolen?"

"As Mia pointed out last night," Petra said, and Miss Cute as a Bug's Ear glanced up at her, "it defies logic that Heavenly Bridals would advertise a design they know was stolen from Savard's in a publication we're guaranteed to see."

"He did it to provoke me," Lucien snarled. "To incite a war."

"A war isn't good for business," Petra said. "Ours or theirs."

"Scandal grabs headlines, Mother," Jenna said. "What a coup for Angel if he can snatch Alicia Whitcomb away from us. Savard Creations gets a black eye and Heavenly Bridals reaps millions in business and referrals from Governor Whitcomb's high-roller friends."

"Thank you, Jenna, for bringing us back on point." Luke Savard bent his left wrist and tapped his watch. "It's after ten. The Whitcombs will be here at two. Do we have a plan? New designs to show Alicia?"

"I'm on it, Junior," DeMello said.

Luke Savard shot him a scowl. DeMello tore two sheets of thin paper off his pad and slid them across the table. Luke snatched them up.

"Why are you sketching for Alicia? She chose one of Mia's designs."

"Mia is taking a break from bridal," Lucien announced. "She's going to try her hand at trousseau."

"I am?" Cute as a Bug's Ear swung her chair toward her father.

"Merry Christmas, Mia." Savard smiled at her, then spread his hands on the polished surface in front of him and looked around the table. "Damien, keep drawing. I'll see you in the workroom at eleven-thirty. Jenna, I want you there to go over fabrics. Walter, I want our suit against Heavenly Bridals filed before lunch."

"I wouldn't, Mr. Savard," Joe said. "Give Angel a chance to make good his threat to sue. He'll have to site grounds. Let's see what he says."

Savard glanced at Vance, who nodded. "A good point, Mr. Kerr. All right, Walter. Draft the suit but sit on it. Luke, press releases. We confirm, we deny, we're shocked, blah blah. I'll see you all back here at one. Wear your charming faces. Mr. Kerr? May I have a moment?"

"What about me?" Mia asked. "What am I supposed to do?"

"Take your mother to lunch," Savard said.

Petra and Mia Savard rolled their eyes at each other and followed everyone else out of the room. Joe was kinda disappointed that Cute as a Bug's Ear didn't even glance at him. When Selma Daniels closed the conference room door, Savard leaned back in his chair.

"Five resignations so far this morning. The one in security, which you've already filled for us. One in human resources, one in the mailroom, one in IT. Plus the design department needs a new administrative assistant. Can the rest of your people fill those positions?"

"Absolutely," said Joe. "The assistant in design is most critical. Your problem may not have started there, but that's where it ended. I assume any candidate will have to be vetted by DeMello?"

"Make it a she with a pretty face. Make it today and Damien will adore her. He loathes paperwork. Our head of human resources is—"

"George Burkholtz," Joe put in, just to show off. "His office is on the first floor, his extension number is one-four-two."

"We call him Ziploc," Savard said. "Zippy for short, because George never leaks. He'll keep an eye on your people and whoever you put in HR will have George's full cooperation."

"How quickly can we fill these positions without raising eyebrows among the rest of your employees?"

"Instantly if not sooner. Anyone interested in working in bridal fashion in a big way in Kansas City has two choices—Savard Creations or Heavenly Bridals. Zippy is always up to his armpits in applications."

"So if the new kids are in place bright and early Monday morning, no one will think, whoa, that was fast?"

"Fashion is a very stressful field. We have a high turnover."

An astronomical turnover after one of Savard's tantrums, according to Pete, who kept telling Joe things even after he'd begged him to stop.

"Nerves of steel," Pete had said. "That's what you need to work here."

So long as Lucien didn't pull a gun on him, Joe figured he had all the nerve he needed to find the viper in Savard's bosom.

"Your professional opinion, Mr. Kerr. Is it possible that Angel has no idea the design was stolen from us?"

"Anything is possible." Joe shrugged. "I try not to form opinions this early in an investigation. I'll take another shot at Angel."

Savard sighed, irritated. "If you think it's necessary."

"I won't waste my time or your money, Mr. Savard. Your wife raised the question. I'd like to hear Angel's answer."

"All right, Mr. Kerr." Savard spread his hands on the table. "I gave you complete control of the investigation."

And it was killing him. Joe knew the signs. He'd been well on his way to becoming Lucien Savard. A royal, Type A pain in the ass. A fire-breathing, hair-triggered heart attack hurtling toward an intensive care unit. Until that night outside the Quik Trip on Linwood Boulevard.

"Sounds like you and your staff will have your hands full with Governor Whitcomb and his wife and daughter," Joe said. "The new assistant will be in place Monday morning. I'll wander around the design department this afternoon. Scope it out, get the lay of the land."

Talk to the other designers, see what he could coax out of them. Complaints, grudges, gossip. They were far more likely to dish the dirt with DeMello and Cute as a Bug's Ear up here in the conference room.

"This weekend you'll install the new security devices?"

"That's the plan." Joe stood up. "Should be up and running by two o'clock Sunday if you'd like a walk-through."

"I suppose I do." Savard sighed and pushed to his feet. "My son, Luke, will. He's been hounding me for years to upgrade our security system. I suppose I should have listened to him."

"The idea of security, Mr. Savard, especially cameras, is to deter amateurs, make them think twice. A determined thief can find a way around almost anything."

"How determined a thief do you think we have, Mr. Kerr?"

"I'd say very determined. Someone with access to the design, the opportunity to lift it and a reason to hand it over to Heavenly Bridals. Does anyone besides Oren Angel hate your guts?"

"At one time or another, probably everyone who's ever worked for me." Savard smiled wryly. "My wife tells me I'm not an easy man."

Typical egomaniac response. "Anyone with an ax to grind? Fired anyone recently from a key position?"

"No." Savard shook his head. "But you might check with Zippy."

"I'll call you on Sunday when the installations are complete."

"Do, please. Luke and I will come down."

Jenna, too, Joe bet. Maybe Mrs. Savard. Mia, he wasn't sure.

Cute as she was, she was in the thick of this. She'd created the stolen design, she'd quit yesterday morning—another thing he'd begged Pete not to tell him—and she'd returned to the Savard Building looking for her father. Alone, she'd claimed, which the lobby security camera confirmed. The garage camera was old, beat to hell and set at a piss-poor angle. He'd only seen Mia Savard exit the elevator and walk toward her Subaru

Forester. Had she deliberately parked out of range? Made a wide loop around the garage to avoid the camera as she left?

"Your daughter Mia came back here last night looking for you."

"Yes, I know. She came by the house."

Savard smiled, a pleasant, that's-all-I'm-going-to-say smile.

"Good luck with the governor. I'll keep in touch."

He and Savard shook hands and Joe left, nodding at Selma on his way to the elevator. He rode down to the first-floor atrium lobby, where the new security guard—his former partner, Brian Hicks, the man he owed his life to—sat in a Savard security uniform at the half-moon kiosk.

Sun glinted on the tinted glass walls and on Brian's long blond hair, which he tied back in a queue. The tropical plants rising in mossy tiers from the rock terraces flanking the waterfall seemed unnaturally green against the outside snowscape. There was no one in the lobby but Brian and a frog croaking somewhere in the pool at the foot of the waterfall.

"Lookin' good back in blue, Bri," Joe said with a grin.

"I'm breaking out in hives." Brian handed Joe a clipboard. "Here's the tally so far. Of the two hundred forty-three people Savard fired yesterday, two hundred thirty-two of them showed up for work this morning. Including the five resignations, that's only six no-shows. Amazing. How much does Savard pay? I may apply."

"The boss just explained to me that Savard Creations and Heavenly Bridals are the two biggest bridal fashion employers in this town." Joe scanned the check-in sheet and gave the clipboard back to Brian. "You got the troops rounded up to fill the other vacancies?"

"Yep. Told 'em to report to HR after lunch. Moira's here." Brian grinned. "She came in with two giant shopping bags from Jack Henry's."

"Swell." Joe groaned. "Poorhouse, here I come."

4

HER MOTHER HATED to drive on the Plaza. Traffic lights were few, stop signs far between and crosswalks nonexistent, which turned intersections into games of chicken with pedestrians. When Petra offered to drive to PF Chang's for lunch Mia should have been suspicious, but she wasn't until Petra made a right instead of a left leaving the restaurant.

"Mother," she said, sliding her sunglasses over her nose against the glare of sun on snow. "The Savard Building is the other way."

"We aren't going to Savard's. We're going to Heavenly Bridals."

"You said you were going to *talk* to Oren Angel," Mia reminded her. "You didn't say you were going to drive over to Heavenly Bridals to do it."

Petra's fingers flexed on the steering wheel of her champagne beige Cadillac Escalade. "I don't want to go alone, Mia."

"I don't want you to go, period. Pete's nephew is named Kerr, and he got tossed in the snow. Our name is *Savard.*"

"Oren won't throw us in the snow." Petra gave her a quick at-least-I-don't-think-so glance. "Someone needs to talk to him. We have to know how the design ended up at Heavenly Bridals. If Oren was duped, then we can stop this before your father blows it all out of proportion."

And maybe blow a heart valve in the process. Her mother didn't say so, but Mia heard the worry in her voice. She still didn't like this foolhardy quest, but now she understood why they were charging off to Prairie Village, Kansas, like Don Quixote and Sancho Panza.

"Angel can claim he was duped and still be a thief," Mia said. "How do you know you can believe him?"

"I've known Oren for forty years. We were students together, all three of us—your father and Oren and me—at the Kansas City Art Institute. I met your father there. You know that." Petra glanced at Mia. "Well, I met Oren there, too. He was in my sculpting class."

Something about the way her mother said it—maybe the "Well" that quavered a bit—made Mia turn sideways in the Escalade's deep leather seat and lift her sunglasses.

"Did you go out with him, Mother?"

"Yes. I did." Petra glanced at her. "Oren and I dated for almost a year before your father swept me off my feet."

Her parents were art students in the sixties. Her mother dated Oren Angel in the sixties. The freewheeling, freeloving sixties. Peace signs, sit-ins and hash. Not the kind you ate with eggs sunny-side up, either.

"Why are you telling me this, Mother?"

"You asked how I could believe him. That's your answer. That's how I'll know." Petra clenched her jaw and the steering wheel. "If Oren lies to me, believe me, I'll *know*."

He'd lied to her before, Mia guessed, more than once. Which cast the Sir-Lucien-on-his-white-charger story she'd heard all her life in serious doubt. It sounded like Petra caught Angel in a big one and Lucien, who was in her mother's drawing class, was waiting to snatch her up.

This was way more than Mia wanted to know about her mother's love life. Especially on top of Szechuan pork. She shut her mouth and rubbed her stomach. If Angel called the cops, she'd call Luke for bail money. He'd go off like Lucien, but he wouldn't break kneecaps like Jenna.

Heavenly Bridals' corporate offices occupied a two-story redbrick building in Prairie Village, Kansas, one of the oldest and most charming of Kansas City's suburbs. Mia had never been to Heavenly Bridals, but she'd seen photos in trade journals of the building and the long stucco wing on the back that housed the production facility.

Eighty-Second Street wasn't as posh an address as 4700 Ward Parkway, but it was classy. Driving through Prairie Village was like driving through small-town New England. Streets lined with stately trees, brick and shingle bungalows with deep eaves and painted shutters, clipped hedges of yew and holly. (Didn't these people *know* they were in Kansas?) There were even a few Christmas lights and decorations up here and there, two weeks before Thanksgiving.

Her mother drove straight to Heavenly Bridals, like she'd been there before. That rattled Mia. So did the empty parking lot. The dash clock said it was twelve-ten, but there wasn't a single car in sight. Petra crawled the Escalade around the curved drive in front of the building. Mia stretched in her seat to peer at the double glass doors.

"Do you think Angel closes the whole place for lunch?"

"I wouldn't, but maybe Oren does." Petra turned the Cadillac into the lot and parked. "Heavenly Bridals is half the size of Savard's. Only one hundred twenty-five employees."

"Do you suppose they all took the bus to work today?"

"I think they're closed." Petra shut off the engine and tucked her keys in the pocket of her blush-dyed silver fox jacket. "Let's find out."

Mia slipped off her seat belt and her shades. The sun had vanished behind a bank of gray clouds. She followed Petra up the walk, shivering in a skiff of snow lifted off a close-by snowbank by the wind.

The double glass doors were locked. No note that said "Gone to Lunch" or "Gone Fishing." No hours posted. No nothing. Petra cupped her gloved hands around her eyes and peered inside. So did Mia.

"No lights on," her mother said.

The lobby was dim but Mia could make out the reception desk. On the wall above it an angel with feathered wings and a harp in her hands floated in a wedding gown and veil spun out of cloud.

"That is the dopiest logo," she said. "Do you think Angel tossed Pete's nephew on his ear and hopped a plane for Brazil?"

"Don't talk like your father, Mia." Petra wheeled away from the door, stepped over the pile of snow shoveled off the walk and waded out of sight around a giant yew that grew at the corner of the building.

"Mother?" Mia hopped the snowbank, slogged through ankle-deep snow around the bush and the building and saw Petra peering in a window. "Mother! What are you doing?"

Petra frowned at her. "What does it look like I'm doing?"

She pushed off the brick sill, picked her way through the snow to the next window and pressed her gloved hands and her face to the glass. Mia threw a panicked look around.

About twenty yards of snowy slope separated Heavenly Bridals from its nearest neighbor, a small brick office park. There were cars in the lot, snow piled along the edge and a line of trees. Pin oaks that held their leaves most of the year, drooping under the weight of iced-over snow. Mia couldn't see much through their sagging branches; icicles stuck to a couple of car bumpers, a dirty windshield, the corner of a FedEx drop box. Hopefully no one could see them, either.

Still, it was daylight. Gloomy and spitting snow again, but daylight. She had to get her mother out of here before someone saw them or Oren Angel and his employees came back from lunch. Or Timbuktu.

Petra had given up on the windows. Now she was striding around the back of the building. Out of sight of the street, thank God, the lion's mane collar of her jacket fluttering around her ears. Mia flipped up the hood of her purple stadium coat and crunched after her, rounded the corner and found herself in a blacktop lot plowed clean of snow, the fence at the back stacked with slated wooden skids.

She didn't see her mother till she heard leather-soled boots scrape on concrete, glanced up at the loading dock ten feet above her head and saw Petra peering in a dirty, wire-meshed window.

Mia groaned, then cut around the front side of the dock where eighteen-wheelers backed up to the tall overhead doors to unload. Near the corner she found a flight of steel steps and rushed up them, smelling creosote on the railroad ties stuck to the edge of the dock to cushion the impact of concrete against trailer bumpers.

She sidled up to her mother, leaned her face close to the window and looked inside Heavenly Bridals' warehouse. Mia saw rows of racks down the center that held boxes and crates, long, long rows of locked steel cabinets bolted to the walls. Certainly the space was climate controlled, as Savard's warehouse was, to protect the delicate fabrics they worked with, but it was about a tenth of the size.

"What are we looking for?" Mia asked.

"I don't know. We're here. I thought we might as well look."

"You mean snoop."

"Whatever." Petra shrugged her fur-covered shoulders.

"Ladies," said a quiet male voice. "This way, please."

Mia backed, startled, and spun one-footed away from the window. Standing halfway up the snowy slope between Heavenly Bridals and the office park, a man in tan cords and a green suede jacket lifted a camera mounted with a digital flash. *Piiiiing.* The photocell blinked and so did Mia, blinded by green rings.

It took a second for the afterimage to clear from her eyes. She blinked again, saw the grin on the man's face but not his features—not clearly, her vision was still blurred—then he cocked a salute.

"Thank you, Mrs. Savard. And you—which kid are you?"

"Mia!" She blurted and bolted down the steel steps.

The man gave a whoop of laughter, wheeled and plowed at a run through the snow, up the slope toward the office park. He was taller and stronger and he had a ten-yard jump on her. Mia chased him anyway, her eyes stinging from the snow kicked up in his wake.

"Mia!" Her mother's voice rang behind her. "Let him go!"

He'd already reached the parking lot. Mia thrashed up the slope, saw him racing toward a dirty gray Kia Sportage. She heard the engine gun as she stumbled over a pile of plowed snow, swooped and grabbed a handful. The mini SUV shot backward out of a parking space. Mia hurled her snowball, watched it sail then smack the rear window with a *splat*. The man with the camera gave two cheery toots of the horn and the Kia scooted out of the parking lot.

"Dammit!" Mia spat between cold-chapped lips, her nose dripping and her breath coming in stinging gasps.

"Mia!" Petra came up behind her, almost as out of breath as Mia was, turned her by the shoulders and engulfed her in a soft, silver fox hug. Mia clung to her, inhaling Shalimar, her mother's perfume. "Who was that, Mother? He knew you."

"He doesn't know me. He recognized me."

"Where do you suppose that photograph is going to turn up?"

"I don't know. I shudder to think."

So did Mia. "Cee-em-kay-zero-three-nine," she said.

"What?" Her mother held her at arm's length.

"That's his license number. Cee-em-kay-zero-three-nine."

"That's my girl." Petra hugged her again, tightly, fiercely. "When that photograph surfaces, your father is going to kill us."

Mia noted that Petra didn't say *if*. She sighed and laid her cheek on her mother's blush-dyed shoulder. "Not if we hop a plane to Brazil."

Alicia Whitcomb took the news that her wedding dress had been pirated by Heavenly Bridals like a brick. Only for a second or so did she look like she wanted to bash Lucien over the head with said brick.

It was a long second that had Mia's heart banging in her throat; Petra, Jenna and Luke holding their breath; the governor and his wife looking grave but clearly leaving the ball in their daughter's hands.

"We are as pierced through the heart as you are," Lucien told Alicia. "We will craft you another gown. We have prepared new designs. It is our dearest wish that you accept this gown as our wedding gift to you."

He went down on one knee and presented her with a check.

"My wedding is six weeks from Sunday," Alicia said. "Can you make me another gown by then?"

"Absolutely," Lucien vowed. "We will sew night and day."

Alicia eyed the check, a full seventy-five-thousand-dollar refund for the dress Mia had designed, and glanced at her father. They exchanged a look, one politician to another, and Alicia smiled.

"All right, Mr. Savard. Show me the designs."

Lucien kissed her hand and waved Damien forward.

He came with a bow, the sketches he'd made that morning, his pad and pencil, and sat down at the conference table with Alicia.

Lucien got to his feet, looking relieved enough to weep. Guilt stabbed Mia. He'd set her free, released her from bridal, and she'd paid him back by getting caught in a photograph with her mother that would, when it surfaced, look like they were breaking into Heavenly Bridals.

Mia wanted a drink. A real Bloody Mary. Maybe a double. She'd throw caution to the wind later at Blanko's and risk one.

When she'd rushed into her office after lunch, she'd found a note on her desk from Jordan: *OMG! He's gorgeous! Why didn't you tell me? B's at 5:30—J.*

The only gorgeous "he" that Mia hadn't told Jordan about was Joseph Kerr, Inc.

"Down girl," she'd said as she crumpled the note. "He's married."

When Mia had bailed out of her mother's Escalade, cold and wet and filthy, she'd pushed through the revolving door and for the second time in less than twenty-four hours nearly collided with his chest.

He'd caught her by the shoulders, as he had the night before when she stepped out of the elevator—awful damn friendly for a married guy—and gave her a dimpled smile.

"What did you do on your lunch hour? Play ice hockey?"

"How'd you guess?" Mia laughed, certain that it sounded as fake and forced to him as it did to her.

His dimple vanished and he let go of her shoulders. "I'd like to ask you a couple of questions. I'll swing by your office later if that's okay."

"That's fine," she'd said, and fled to the elevator.

She'd gotten into the habit of keeping an assortment of clothes at work. Terence was notorious for calling her at two in the afternoon to invite her to a black-tie soiree, a Royals baseball game or anything in between. She'd been so besotted she'd let him get away with it.

Most of her office was still piled in the middle of the floor. This morning she'd had time only to put the plants back on the windowsill and hang the clothes in the closet.

She tugged a pair of quilted silk patchwork pants she'd designed and sewn herself off a hanger along with a mulberry sweater knitted by Petra from yarn she'd spun on her own wheel. She dug tights that matched the sweater out of plastic drawers in the corner, lifted a pair of black suede ballerina slippers off the shelf and ducked into her private bathroom.

She locked the door and turned toward the sink, saw the dirt on her chin, the snarled wreck of her hair and teeth marks where she'd bit her lower lip and the chapped skin had cracked and bled.

"Oh," she said. "That's what he meant about ice hockey."

Her lip didn't hurt till she cleaned it. Then it bled a little more while she'd washed and changed, redid her makeup and her hair. She dabbed Neosporin on the cut and covered it with lip balm and lipstick.

Now it throbbed along with her conscience as she watched her father and Governor Whitcomb give each other a companionable slap.

Alexander Whitcomb was in his second term as governor. How long he'd been a friend/acquaintance/associate of her father's Mia had no idea. Following Petra's revelation on the way to Heavenly Bridals, she'd made her first resolution for the coming new year: pay *waaay* more attention to the people her parents hung out with.

Her mother looked serene as a Buddha, standing at the conference room window with the governor's wife. Felicia Whitcomb was enchanted with the delicate, multi-colored shawl, another of her mother's creations, that Petra had tossed over a winter white suit. She'd dashed home to change after she'd dropped off Mia, which gave them only a moment together on their way into the conference room.

"Mother," Mia said under her breath, "there's no way that guy just happened to be there with a camera. He must've followed us."

"I know," Petra murmured. "I'm going to tell your father."

Soon, Mia hoped. The dread and the worry—Who *was* that guy? Why had she told him her name?—had her nerves jumping.

On the credenza beneath the windows stood a silver urn of coffee, another of hot water and a treasure chest of teas. The best corporate china, delicate, cream-colored, hand-painted with a 24-carat "S." Two silver, three-tiered servers, artfully arranged with delicate cookies and divinely filled phyllo puffs.

Jenna was charming the governor's chief of staff. Luke had Whitcomb's plainclothes state trooper bodyguards laughing.

No one else paid the least bit of attention to the pastries, but they were calling to Mia. She headed toward them, smiling at Alicia—charming face, charming face—as she passed the conference table.

"Excuse me," Alicia said to her. "You're Mia, aren't you?"

"Yes," Mia said.

"You designed my dress, didn't you? The first one, I mean?"

"Um," Mia said. *Uh-oh,* she thought. "Yes, I did."

"I thought so." Alicia beamed. "Then I want you to design this one."

"Oh." Mia blinked. *Oh, no!* "I'd be glad to, but—"

"Here, Mia. Come." Damien vacated the chair beside Alicia. "Sit."

This is the governor's daughter, said the partly amused but mostly pissed-off glint in his dark eyes. *Get over here and make her happy.*

Mia's heart sank. The last thing she wanted to do was design another wedding dress, but what could she do? She was a Savard and this was war. Someone had stolen the design for Alicia's dress, *her* design for Alicia's dress.

And there was this: Lucien wouldn't kill her for the photograph if she had to design another gown for the governor's daughter.

So Mia smiled and said to Alicia Whitcomb, "I'd be delighted to design your wedding gown."

Lucien appeared beside her, put his arm around her, a kiss on her temple and murmured in her ear, "One more, Mia. Just one more."

5

JOE SPENT THE AFTERNOON in the design department.

Mia Savard and four other designers worked under Damien "Let's Play Columbo" DeMello:

Arlene Bitterman, Jewish mother. Third in seniority to DeMello, for almost twelve years. Good jewelry, perfectly coifed auburn hair. Sixty-two next June. Retired husband, two grown sons, four grandkids—three boys and a girl—who shared photo space on the padded, pale burgundy walls of her spacious cubicle along with snaps of her two Yorkies, Posh and Beck.

"The kids around here keep me hip," she said, and Joe grinned.

"Is fashion mostly a young person's field?" he asked.

"It's not a job for the faint of heart of any age. Nerves of titanium. That's what you need to work in fashion."

"To work in fashion or to work for Lucien Savard?"

"Did your homework." Arlene nodded. "He can be a terror and a tyrant, but he's a softy underneath. He blows up a lot to hide that."

"How long has your department been without an assistant?"

"Since Cherie went out on maternity leave? Two months." Arlene shook her head, and not one strand of her hair moved. "We're knee-deep in stuff that needs to be filed. Damien is beyond picky."

"I'm trying to establish a time line for the theft. Do you know when Alicia approved the design for her wedding gown?"

"She was awfully hard to please. Mia was pulling her hair. It took Alicia about a month to settle on what she wanted. I don't know the exact date, but I'd say end of August, first part of September."

"Was the gown made? Is it finished?"

"For the governor's daughter? Are you kidding? Her gown was top priority. It's ironic, really. Alicia was supposed to pick it up today."

Kylie Northcote was two years out of design school, strawberry blond and thin as David Bowie. Engaged to a loan officer at Lambert Bank and Trust named Phillip. Shy, starry-eyed, the walls of her cubicle decorated with photos of her fiancé, her two cats—Puffy and Snowball— and drawings she'd done herself of fairies and unicorns.

"Mr. Savard scares me sometimes," she said. "Like yesterday. He fired us all, I mean everybody who works for Savard's. I went home and threw up. I threw up again when he called and said I wasn't fired after all and then I cried myself to sleep."

Anorexic, bulimic or nerves of limp linguini, Joe figured.

"Ever thought of working for Heavenly Bridals?"

"No. I worked summers there when I was at KU." The University of Kansas in Lawrence. "Never again."

Joe already knew this; he'd read all of the designers' files in Zippy Burkholtz's office before Moira dragged him to Peppercorn Duck Club. He gave Kylie points for volunteering the connection.

"What was the problem? Lousy pay? Bad food in the cafeteria?"

"Oren Angel." Kylie's nose wrinkled again. "His designers have to sign a paper that says he gets the credit for their work. Their designs appear in Heavenly Bridals' catalog under his name."

"That's not how it works here?"

"No. Savard Creations owns our designs, of course, but we get the credit. Our names are listed with our work in the catalog. It's how designers build their name and reputation."

"I'm trying to establish a time line for the theft. Do you know when Alicia approved the design for her wedding gown?"

"Oh, no. I don't have any idea." Kiley's eyes grew huge. "I keep my head down and do my work."

The live wire in DeMello's merry band was Jordan Branch. Clean but cluttered cubicle plastered with faces: Jude Law, Colin Farrell, Brad Pitt with a black "X" drawn over his pretty-boy mug and Clint Eastwood in his Dirty Harry days. She gave Joe several c'mon-big-boy-make-my-day smiles. Funky dresser, red and blond spiked hair, fake nails tipped with tiny jewels. Flash and trash and a lot of fun at parties, Joe bet.

"Me and Mia. We're like this." Jordon crossed her fingers and gave Joe a look that said she wouldn't mind being that way with him. "Total buds. Through thick and thin."

"Do you hang with her after work?"

"Almost every day at Blanko's. On Broadway. You know it?"

Joe nodded. He knew every bar and hangout in Kansas City. Most professionally, a few socially.

"We hook up with Mia's cuz Becca, sometimes Becca's brother, Robin. Except on Tuesdays, every other Thursday and the first and third Friday of the month."

"Where are you on those days? AA meetings?"

Jordan laughed. "Mia doesn't drink. The Tuesday, Thursday, Friday thing is since she and Terence split. They met at Blanko's, so it was like their place till the breakup. Now it's like a time-share."

"Do you know when Alicia approved the design for her gown?"

"Not off the top of my head. Do you need the exact date?"

"It would help me establish a time line for the theft."

"Okay." Jordan hopped off her stool. "Let's go find out."

She led Joe out of her cubicle into the design department storage room, a fair-sized space with two large steel utility cabinets on one wall, a bank of lateral file cabinets on another, a Xerox machine the size of a Volkswagen and a laminated rectangular table.

Jordan dropped to her heels in front of the end lateral file and opened the bottom drawer, flipped past "U" and "V" to "W," and pulled out a large manila envelope. She took it to the table and opened it, looked through it, pulled out a folded spreadsheet and handed it to Joe.

"The production schedule for Alicia's gown," she said.

"Design approved September sixth," Joe read. He scanned a couple other lines: Pattern Completed/Fitted; Muslin Completed/Fitted—whatever the heck a muslin was. "Gown completed October twenty-eighth. This is great. Just what I need. Could you make me a copy?"

Jordan buzzed one off for him on the giant Xerox. Joe

watched, wondering if the thief had used the whiz-bang machine to copy the design. He said thanks, tucked the folded copy of the production schedule into the inside pocket of his sport jacket and moved on to Evan Larson, the only man in design besides DeMello. Second in seniority, with fifteen years.

Evan gave Joe a cup of coffee and admired Moira's taste in clothes.

"You should wear blue, always," he said. "At least a small touch here or there. It really enhances the blue of your eyes."

Evan and his partner held Chiefs season tickets, primo seats on the 50-yard line. A framed photo of Evan and his SO, Felix, sat on the modular desk. Faces painted Chiefs red and yellow, Larson in a bright red clown wig, Felix in a yellow one. Both bare-chested and howling their lungs out at Arrowhead Stadium in a January blizzard.

These days Evan designed mostly for the Lucien signature line of men's bridal wear. The collection was Luke Savard's idea, in its second year and selling like hotcakes at a Cub Scout pancake breakfast.

"Luke's brainchild but it carries Lucien's name?"

"Well, hell yes," Evan said. "Lucifer is the boss."

Joe managed not to spew coffee.

"Sorry." Evan grinned. "That's our nickname for Lucien."

"Ever screw up and call him Lucifer to his face?"

"Not so far." Evan kissed his fingertips and touched them to a photo of Sir Elton John with his gap-tooth grin and a pink boa.

"Were you ever in the running to design Alicia's gown?"

"No. But Damien was convinced she'd choose one of

his designs. He swanned around here like Valentino. What the man lacks in talent, he makes up for in ego, but I never said that."

"How did he react when Alicia chose Mia's design?"

"He was apoplectic. He's all smiles today. He's positive Lucifer will talk Alicia into allowing us to make her another gown and he's convinced that this time she'll choose one of his designs." Larson winked. "I have twenty bucks in the pool that says she chooses Mia again."

"The average lead time for magazines is four to six months. The December issue of *Today's Bride* came out yesterday. Any idea how Heavenly Bridals got their ad into that issue in such a short time?"

"Advertising *space* is reserved four to six months in advance. Content is dropped in pretty close to deadline. I'd say Heavenly Bridals already had that full page reserved and simply changed the copy."

Joe smiled. "So would I."

On his way out of the department, he thanked each designer for their time. When he asked could he come back if he had more questions, they all said "Yeah" or "Sure" without ducking his gaze. Jordan Branch said, "Anytime," with a hint of *Anyplace, any way you want it* in her voice.

Miss Cute as a Bug's Ear Savard wasn't in her office. Her doe-eyed cousin Becca was, loading a bookcase with tall, artsy-looking books.

The door was pushed open against the wall. Joe stopped beside it and knocked lightly. "Miss Savard?"

She glanced over her shoulder. "Mr. Kerr." She shoved the books in her hands on a shelf and turned around. "Mia is still upstairs with the governor and Alicia."

"Why aren't you? I thought it was supposed to be a family affair."

"Dad and Robin and I got a reprieve." She smiled wryly. "We're only bean counters."

Rebecca Savard was modest. She was head of payroll for Savard Creations, held an accounting degree from Penn State and a CPA license.

"Seems to be going on awhile. Is that a good sign or a bad sign?"

She shrugged. "It's neither. It is what it is."

A philosophical bean counter. Didn't meet one of those every day.

Joe nodded at the boxes piled in the middle of the floor. "I heard your cousin Mia quit yesterday."

"She resigned to make a point, but she's staying. I know where most of these things go, so I thought I'd give her a hand."

"No beans to count?" Joe smiled. Becca Savard did not. "I've counted my allotment for today."

"When Celeste Taylor"—Joe named the director of advertising—"found Alicia Whitcomb's dress in *Today's Bridal,* she called your father, not your uncle. Why didn't she go straight to the boss?"

"You should ask Celeste."

"I did. I'd like to know why you think she handled it that way."

"Uncle Lucien tends to explode a lot, so no one on staff likes to give him bad news. If something has to be broken to Uncle Lucien, my father, because he's his brother, gets to break it."

He'd heard the same thing from Celeste Taylor, but without the edge of resentment in Becca Savard's voice.

"Are they close, your father and your uncle Lucien?"

"I've already answered that question." She turned away, picked up more books and pushed them onto a shelf.

"I'm looking for a thief, Miss Savard. It's not in your best interests or your father's if you leave me to assume things."

She turned and faced him again. "If they weren't close, my father wouldn't be the designated bearer of bad tidings."

"See?" Joe smiled. "That wasn't hard, was it?"

"I'm sorry." She puffed out a breath that fluttered her dark bangs. "It's been a rough two days. I've worked with everyone here for the last six years. Now I'm not sure who I can trust and who I can't."

"The sooner we catch this person, the better. The quicker things get back to normal. I'd appreciate your help."

"I'll be glad to do whatever I can." She smiled. "And I am sorry."

"No problem." Joe nodded. "We'll talk again."

He turned out of the doorway and headed for the elevator. A car coming down opened on four and Damien DeMello burst out of it, the expression on his face as dark as his black suit and shirt.

"Mr. DeMello," Joe said. "Could I have a few minutes?"

"No," he snapped, and stalked down the hallway.

Joe followed him to design, hanging back till he heard a door slam like a sonic boom. Then he stepped into DeMello's department.

Three of the designers were on their feet. Evan Larson shaking his head at DeMello's closed office door, Jordan and Kylie murmuring over the shoulder-high wall between them. Arlene Bitterman hadn't budged off the stool at her drawing board in the cubicle closest to the open doorway. She glanced up at Joe.

"What was that about?" Joe asked. "Did he say?"

"No," Arlene replied. "And I didn't ask."

"Want to take a guess?"

"Well." Arlene crooked a finger. Joe stepped into her cubicle and she lowered her voice. "I'd say the governor's daughter didn't like any of his designs for her new wedding dress."

Joe's cell phone vibrated on his belt. He unclipped it, read the text message from Brian—LOBBY ASAP—thanked Arlene and turned out of the design department. He smiled at Becca Savard, craning her neck at the glass wall of Mia's office across the hall. She smiled back.

When the elevator opened on one, Joe looked across the lobby and saw his brother, Sam, talking to Brian. He was in uniform, leaning his elbows on the security kiosk, his badge and his sergeant's stripes gleaming on the shoulders of his padded black nylon KCMOPD jacket.

Sam saw Joe and straightened. He was an inch taller and twenty pounds heavier, but had the same dark hair and blue eyes. Evie Kerr said that both her boys looked like Sam Senior had spit them.

"Sorry, Joe," Sam said. "The captain asked me to make this courtesy call for Prairie Village PD."

"No kidding." Joe was surprised. He hadn't expected his visit to Heavenly Bridals to pay off so quickly. "What did I do? Allegedly?"

"According to a Mr. Oren Angel, owner of Heavenly Bridals, you assaulted him this morning at his place of business."

"Since when is offering your business card considered assault?"

"I know." Sam held up a hand. "This Angel guy is a pain in the ass, but he's also a big cheese out there. The Prairie Village chief called the captain, they commiserated, the captain called me 'cause you're my brother, and here I am."

"Okay. What do I need to do to square the chief with Angel?"

"Pay him a visit before the end of the day. Chief said he'd be in his office till five-thirty. Tell him your side. It'll be he said, he said, but the chief seems to think your statement will shut Angel up."

"I'll head that way now." Joe grinned at Brian. "You have the bridge, Number One."

"May the Force be with you, Obi-Wan," Brian deadpanned.

"Mixing your movies again, Brian. I'll report in to Moira on my cell. You've got the overnight worked out with Uncle Pete?"

"Handled," Brian said. "I'm here till seven, then Pete takes over with two of his Savard guys. Squeaky clean. Moira did their background checks. Carlos and Stink have the overnight roam on the building."

"Make it so." Joe rapped his knuckles on the kiosk as he swung away from it with his brother.

"Ma's pissed 'cause you and Moira can't make dinner and the Chiefs game on Sunday," Sam said. "Just thought I'd warn you."

"Thanks for the heads-up," Joe said, falling out of step with his brother as Sam pushed through the door to go to his squad car idling at the curb and Joe headed for his Explorer in the parking garage.

The day planner Moira insisted he carry lay open on the passenger seat.

"Whattaya know," Joe murmured. "It's the second Friday."

He'd make a quick trip to Prairie Village, then a swing by Blanko's on Broadway to talk to Miss Cute as a Bug's Ear Savard.

6

Mɪᴀ ᴀʟᴍᴏsᴛ ᴅɪᴅɴ'ᴛ ɢᴏ to Blanko's. She almost went home to wrap her head in aluminum foil and stick it in the microwave.

What a depressing day. No chance to celebrate her liberation from bridal. Only a high-five from Jordan after this morning's conference, a green tea toast and a smiling "See? Your father *can* learn" from her mother before Alicia Whitcomb decided she liked Mia's designs best.

She'd never seen Damien so pissed. And he was, royally, enough to bow out early on Governor Whitcomb. So pissed that Mia was sure he'd killed himself to beat her back to the design department to announce that she wouldn't be joining Arlene and Kylie on the trousseau line after all. She'd wanted to tell them herself, but it was after five when the Whitcombs left, and everyone in design was gone.

Then there was Joseph Kerr, Inc. The best-looking and, from what she'd seen so far, nicest man she'd met since Terence broke up with her the night of Becca and Robin's Halloween party. How utterly pass-the-singles-ads dismal that he was married.

Personally, Mia thought the gorgeous brunette looked

just a teensy bit too young for him—say a decade—but who was she? The dope who fell for Terence the Bum.

After he dumped her, everyone from Jenna to Jordan informed her that (a) Terence was a jerk, (b) he was completely wrong for her and (c) he'd been seen several times at Blanko's, which was supposed to be *their* place, with someone else.

But it was Friday, *her* Friday for Blanko's, and she really wanted that Bloody Mary. If her father was going to kill her, she wanted to taste vodka before she died. While she cruised around Blanko's block looking for a parking spot on the street, Mia speed dialed her mother.

"You haven't told Dad yet, have you."

"What makes you think that?"

"You're still alive to answer the phone."

"Yesterday he was down, today he's up. I'll tell him tomorrow."

"You need to tell him before the king of damage control goes back to New York."

"Luke is staying till Sunday. I'll tell your father tomorrow," Petra said firmly, and hung up.

Mia gave up finding a spot on the street and turned into a parking garage a block from Blanko's. She didn't blame her mother for not wanting to tell Lucien about their foray to Heavenly Bridals. Till Alicia Whitcomb opened her big mouth, Mia was thinking how nice it would be to spend Thanksgiving in the Bahamas.

Blanko's was crawling with people and jumping with noise. Music and laughter, shouted snatches of conversation. It was always packed on Fridays, one of the best get-lucky spots in Kansas City. She'd met Terence here on a Friday night.

"The cheery thoughts just keep coming," Mia muttered as she wove her way around crowded tables toward the round one in the back corner by the diamond-paned window.

She saw Jordan and Becca before they saw her, the cardboard CONGRATS cutout turning by a string from the light fixture over their heads and the white paper cloth on the table scattered with foil confetti.

"Oh, no," Mia murmured, her spirits sinking.

That's when Becca saw her and jumped up to light the silver candle on a coconut cake. Jordan sprang up beside her, raised a spangled noisemaker to her lips and blew— *wauughaa-wauughaa.*

A few heads turned in their direction with good-natured grins and Mia started to smile. *Oh, what the hell,* she decided. *It's Friday.*

She struck a runway pose, pranced up to the table and blew out the candle on the cake. Jordan and Becca applauded.

"What's your pleasure, Mia?" asked Bev, the redheaded waitress who usually waited on them. "This one's on the house."

"Bloody Mary. A real one," she said.

Becca oohed and Jordan ahhed.

"I'm throwing caution to the wind." She threw off her coat, dropped into a chair across from Jordan and Becca and swiped a fingertip of icing off the cake plate.

"Coconut, my favorite. This is great. Premature, but great."

"We know." Jordan smirked. "Damien couldn't wait to tell us that Alicia Whitcomb gave him the boot in favor of you."

"Not *me.*" Mia licked icing off her finger. "My design."

"Tell that to a conceited ass," Jordan said as Bev delivered Mia's Bloody Mary. "We'd already ordered the cake, so . . ." Jordan lifted her margarita. "Here's to Mia for saving Savard's butt."

"We all saved Savard's," Mia said. "Everyone who showed up for work today after yesterday's fiasco. I say we drink to us all."

"Here, here," Becca said, and raised her light beer draw.

"Right on," said Jordan.

Mia raised her Bloody Mary, they clinked glasses and drank. The vodka burned Mia's throat but her head didn't spin.

"So," Jordan said. "Did you come up with a new design for Alicia?"

"I can't talk about it," Mia said. "Lucien's orders."

"Oh—right. Of course you can't. What's wrong with me?" Jordan gave herself a head slap. "How could I forget the spy in our midst?"

"You didn't forget," Becca said. "You put it out of your mind for a while. You have to so you can function, so you can cope. Otherwise it's too overwhelming."

"I'll tell you what's overwhelming. That detective, Joseph Kerr. Somebody beat that man senseless with the handsome stick."

Jordan feigned a swoon against Becca's shoulder. Becca laughed, shrugged her off and took a sip of her beer.

"Brace yourself," Mia said. "He's married."

"He's *what*?" Jordan clutched her heart and a handful of her pink velour turtleneck. "No!"

"Yes," Mia said. "He has a wife. I've seen her. She's gorgeous."

Jordan keened and fell against Becca again. Becca leaned her cheek sympathetically, and carefully, against the top of Jordan's spiked head.

"Wait." Jordan sprang up in her chair. "He doesn't wear a ring."

"Some married men don't," Mia said. "It should be the law. If you're a man and you're married, you must wear a wedding band right here." She made a circle of her thumb and index finger and pinched the tip of her nose. "So us poor single girls don't get our hopes up."

"Well, mine are dashed." Jordan sighed and lifted her margarita. "Ladies, here's to my broken heart."

They clinked glasses again, drank again. The vodka didn't burn this time, only warmed Mia's throat.

"Wait a minute." Jordan frowned at Becca. "I saw you talking to him in Mia's office. Why didn't you tell me he's married?"

Becca shrugged. "I didn't get any married vibes off him at all."

"Phooey." Jordan snorted. "Your antenna needs a tune-up."

"Does not," Becca said indignantly. "My radar is just fine."

And astonishing. Becca could pick married men out in a crowd almost without fail. Mia had no idea how, but Becca rarely missed.

Bev appeared with three small plates, three forks, a knife and a wink. "Here you are, girls. Life is short. Eat dessert first."

Mia cut the coconut cake and gave a slice to Bev on a napkin.

"Thanks for reshelving my books, Beck," Mia said. "I only had time to put the plants back this morning."

"The handsome detective," Becca said, "knew you'd quit."

"Really?" Mia blinked. "I wonder who told him?"

"He just said he'd heard, but he asked me about it. I didn't like it."

"What else did he ask you?" Mia held up her hand. "No. Sorry. We probably shouldn't compare notes about Mr. Kerr's investigation."

"Why not? Did Uncle Lucien put a gag on that, too?"

"Well—no. But we might say something to the wrong person."

Becca and Jordan stiffened, both startled and insulted.

"Knock it off." Mia waved her fork at them. "I don't mean you two."

"Then I think we should discuss it," Becca declared. "It will help us handle the stress of having Mr. Kerr wandering around grilling people."

"Cute as he is," Jordan said around a mouthful of cake, "playing twenty questions with him every day will get real old, real quick."

"Plus, he's an outsider," Becca said. "He doesn't know Savard's like we do. We could pick up on things that he misses. Wouldn't it be cool if we could beat him to the punch and catch the spy ourselves?"

"The three of us?" Mia took a sip of her Bloody Mary. It tasted only mildly disgusting with coconut cake. "You think we could?"

"Three heads are better than one," Jordan said.

"He's probably got other people working on this with him," Mia said, thinking of the gorgeous Mrs. Kerr bringing pizza the night before.

"So what?" Becca shrugged. "They're outsiders, too."

"Yes, but they're probably detectives and we aren't,"

Mia said. "I'm a designer, Jordan's a designer and you're a CPA."

"Which means," Becca said, "that I can add two and two and get four a lot quicker than most people."

"Yeah." Jordan pointed a forkful of cake at Mia. "And you and I can connect dots at the speed of light."

"We'd be doing something, wouldn't we?" Mia thought out loud. "At first I felt shocked, then I felt scared and violated. Now I'm angry. I don't want to just sit around wondering who did this. I want to *know*."

"Me, too," Becca said. "I hate being suspicious of everyone. I want to narrow the field."

"Then let's do it." Mia raised her Bloody Mary. "Let's catch a thief."

They drank a third toast, which left Mia with little more than ice cubes. She plucked the swizzle stick out of her glass, bit one of the olives off the end and munched. Mmm. Yummy soaked in vodka.

Jordan signaled for another round. When Bev brought it to the table she gave Mia the peace sign. "How many fingers?"

"Ha-ha," she said with a grin. "You know, vodka really improves the taste of green olives."

Bev raised an eyebrow. "You two keep an eye on her," she said to Becca and Jordan, and turned away.

"Mr. Kerr asked me about Dad and Uncle Lucien." Becca hunched on her elbows over the table. "Their relationship, are they close. He wanted to know why I thought Celeste took the ad in *Today's Bride* to Dad first. I told him Dad is the designated bearer of bad news."

"He didn't ask me much about Savard's," Jordan said. "A couple questions about Damien, was he a good boss, fair, stuff like that. He asked Arlene and Kylie and Evan the same questions."

"Sounds like he's trying to get a feel for us and how things work at Savard's." Mia leaned close to the table. "He went to Heavenly Bridals this morning. Oren Angel threw him out. Wouldn't even talk to him."

"Whoa." Becca sat back in her chair. "That sounds guilty as hell."

Jordan's gaze lifted over Mia's head. "Whoa—*ho.* Okay, Radar." She poked Becca. "At the bar, by the corner. Third guy from the left in the lawyer suit"—shorthand for pinstripes—"single or married?"

Becca leaned on her elbow toward Jordan, her lips pursed.

"Married," she pronounced. "Definitely married."

"Oh, *man.* Are you *sure?*"

"He has 'wife and two kids' rolling off him like too much cologne." Becca looked down her nose at Jordan. "Do you doubt me?"

"No. But that man is *fine* and I'm gonna go make sure." Jordan pushed to her feet and froze, her eyes wide. "Oh, my God—Terence."

Mia's breath seized. She supposed it was inevitable that one of them would get their days screwed up, but why did it have to be today?

"Oh, great." She sighed, disgusted. "What's he doing here?"

"He's coming this way," Becca said. "He's looking for someone."

"Not me," Mia said, relieved. "That's all I care about."

Jordan blinked and sat down. "Uh, Mia?"

"What?" she said as Terence came around the table

on her left, looking like he'd stepped out of *GQ*, in sharp dark trousers and a lime green shirt under a multi-colored pullover.

"Hello, Mia," he said. "I thought I'd find you here."

"Of course you did." She glared up at Terence's Greek god face and gilt hair. "It's my night to be here. Not yours. Good-bye."

"I tried to call you, but you've got my number blocked," Terence said. "At home, on your cell and at Savard's."

He looked surprised, like the thought that a woman would block his phone number had never entered his beautiful head.

Blocking his calls was petty, but it was the only thing Mia could think of to do that took control away from Terence. He'd given her the standard "We have nothing in common and our lives are going in separate directions" breakup speech. "What are you talking about?" she'd wanted to shout at him. "I'm a fashion designer and you're a model!" But she'd been too stricken to open her mouth.

"I blocked your number because I don't want to talk to you."

"Could I have five minutes? That's all. I swear."

He held up his hand, fingers spread, and gave Mia the smile that stopped her heart the night she'd met him. Now it just made her seethe.

Mia glanced at Becca and Jordan. "Would you mind?"

"We'll check out the pool room." Jordan pulled Becca, frowning and clearly not happy about this, to her feet. "We'll be back in five minutes."

"That's better," Terence said as Jordan yanked Becca

out of earshot. "Now you don't have to put on a show for your girlfriends."

"This isn't a show. I'm willing to give you five minutes if you promise to go away and never talk to me again."

"I'm sorry you're still taking this so hard." Terence sat down. "I thought you would've realized by now that I was right about us."

"What I've *realized*, Terence, is that you're a liar and a cheat. Jordan saw you here, right here at Blanko's, with someone else."

"A true friend wouldn't tell you something like that." An expression of such dripping pity came over Terence's face that Mia wanted to throw what was left of her cake at him. "I tried not to hurt you, Mia."

"Did you have something important to say? If so, get to it."

"All right. Here it is." Terence bent his elbow on the table, leaned toward her and lowered his voice. "I saw Terri Baxter at the gym this afternoon. She does catalog work for Heavenly Bridals. She was on the recumbent bike next to me and she was pissed. She was supposed to do a shoot this afternoon for Oren Angel but it was canceled at the last minute. No explanation. She said, 'If there's a spool of thread left when Savard gets through with him, I'll be amazed.' When I asked what she meant, she told me to buy a copy of *Today's Bride* and see for myself."

Uh-oh, Mia thought. *Somebody blabbed.*

Like most industries, fashion was incestuous. Designers hung with designers, seamstresses with seamstresses, models with models. Any one of Savard's employees could have said something indiscreet to one of their counterparts at another company. Not just Heavenly Bridals.

There were smaller fashion houses in Kansas City. Lucien hadn't screamed at them to keep their mouths shut. He'd screamed, "You're fired!"

Since all was forgiven with Governor Whitcomb and Alicia, Mia wasn't sure Terri Baxter's comment mattered, but gossip was a forerunner of scandal. She agreed with her mother that scandal wasn't good for business. Or for pending lawsuits.

"So did you?" she asked Terence, pausing to take a swig of her Bloody Mary. "Did you buy a copy and see for yourself?"

"I did, yes, but I didn't see anything about Savard's. I saw a full-page ad placed by Heavenly Bridals for—" Terence broke off and leaned closer to Mia. "That's it. The Heavenly Bridals ad. That's why Governor Whitcomb was at Savard's today."

No empty-headed boy toy, Terence. His intellect was every bit as stunning as his looks. Dammit. Mia took another slug of her drink. Where was Luke, the king of damage control, when she needed him?

"I don't recall seeing Governor Whitcomb today," Mia lied, certain that the fewer people who knew about the theft of Alicia's dress, the better. "I'm sure I'd remember. Kind of hard to miss the governor."

"Kind of hard to miss his limo, too." Terence smiled. "My gym is only a block from Savard's. The motorcade went past while Terri and I were on the bikes, right in front of the window. I just put it together."

"All right, Terence." Mia scooted forward in her chair and dropped her voice. "You can't tell anyone. Alicia has a thing for Twinkies, okay? She's been overindulging— nerves, I guess. We have to alter her dress."

"All the trappings of the governor's office for ten

pounds of Twinkie fat? I don't think so. On top of Terri's crack about Savard's? On top of the ad in *Today's Bride*? Did you design that dress, Mia?"

"As a matter of fact," Joseph Kerr, Inc., said behind her, "she did."

7

JOE ENJOYED THE HELL out of surprising people. Especially suspects.

He didn't get to do it much, but Blanko's was the perfect place for it. Dim lighting, loud music. He really got a kick out of Tall, Blond and Beautiful jumping to his feet like he'd sat on a whoopee cushion.

Miss Cute as a Bug's Ear Savard swung a wide-eyed look at Joe over her shoulder. A look that followed him as he stepped around her chair and offered his hand to TB&B.

"Joe Kerr. I'm a private investigator. Lucien Savard hired me to find out who stole the design for Alicia Whitcomb's wedding dress. The dress in the Heavenly Bridals ad in this month's issue of *Today's Bride*."

"Terence Parker." TB&B shook his hand.

Ah, Joe thought, the ex. Parker's grip was dry, cool and steady; the glance he dropped on Mia was amused. "Twinkies?"

"I was making it up as I went along," she said sheepishly.

"Here's my card." Joe offered TB&B one from the breast pocket of his brand-new tweed jacket. Moira had wisely cut off the price tag before she'd forced him to put it on. "If you pick up any more interesting comments at the gym, I'd like to hear them."

"I'll pass them along." TB&B slipped the card in his back pocket and smiled at Cute as a Bug's Ear. "I do miss your sense of humor, Mia."

He nodded to Joe and turned toward the bar. Mia Savard watched him, her expression part there-goes-my-everything, part good-riddance.

Joe sat down in TB&B's chair. "I can't see you with him."

"Terence couldn't see me with him, either," she replied without missing a beat. "Are you a psychic detective, Mr. Kerr?"

"Joe. And no. Jordan Branch told me about Terence the Bum."

Cute as a Bug's Ear laughed. "We call her Blabbermouth."

"Looks like a party." Joe flicked at the foil confetti littering the white paper tablecloth. "Am I crashing?"

"No. We do this every Friday to celebrate that we still have jobs." Mia Savard grinned at him. "Would you like a piece of cake?"

"No, thanks. You shouldn't lie, Miss Savard. You're not good at it."

"I know." She made a wrinkle-nosed face. "I suck."

"Why didn't you tell him the truth?"

"I thought the fewer people who know about this, the better."

"Anyone who works in fashion in Kansas City either knows by now or has heard enough to figure it out. People like your friend Terence don't bother me. I'm more concerned about this ending up in the newspapers or on the six o'clock news."

"Really?" She reached for her drink—a glass of melted ice and diluted tomato juice. A Virgin Mary, Joe figured, since Jordan Branch said that Mia Savard didn't drink. She downed the whole thing.

"If you hear from any reporters, don't talk to them," Joe said. "If they call you on the phone, hang up. If they approach you on the street, simply say 'No comment' and walk away."

"Should I put a book over my face like they do on *Law & Order*?"

"If you feel the need and you have one handy, go for it." Joe nodded at her empty glass. "Would you like a refill?" He gave her an I-won't-tell-if-you-won't smile. "I can pad my expense account."

"Well, if Lucien's paying, absolutely," she said merrily. "You should try the buffalo wings. They're great here."

Joe signaled the waitress, ordered the wings, a Bud on tap and "Another one for the lady."

"Yes, sir." The chunky, middle-aged redhead glanced at Mia, raised her hand and made the Vulcan sign of peace.

"Live long and prosper, Bev." Mia Savard laughed. "All five fingers."

"Okeydokey," the waitress said, and turned away from the table.

"Bev waits on us all the time," Mia explained. "She's a big kidder."

There were two other plates, a margarita and a beer on the table.

"Your friend Jordan said the two of you and your cousin Becca come here after work. Have they left already?"

"No. They're checking out the action in the pool room." Mia bit an olive off her swizzle stick. "Did you follow me here from Savard's?"

"No way." Joe held up both hands. Moira had followed her, then passed Mia off to him. "You can get in a lot of trouble following women."

"I'll bet you can," she said, with enough emphasis on *you* to give Joe the idea that she meant he personally could get in a lot of trouble.

"I know why I'd prefer to keep this out of the media," Mia said. "Politicians don't like negative press. Lucien sweet-talked Alicia into letting us make her another gown. But if he and Oren Angel get into it, especially in public, her father might convince her it would be less hassle to buy her wedding dress off the rack at JCPenney."

"Me?" Joe shrugged. "I'd just like to keep the lawyers out of it."

The waitress delivered their drinks, the wings and two plates. Joe gave Mia first pick of the wings, then loaded his plate from the wax paper-lined basket and dug in. He polished off a dozen.

"You're right." He wiped his mouth with a paper napkin. "Best wings I've had in a while."

"I love the sauce. It's spicy but not too—ouch." Mia winced, dipped the corner of her napkin in her glass of water and pressed it to the split that had opened in her bottom lip. "Sorry. My ice hockey injury." She took the napkin away from her lip. "Did I get it?"

"Nope. Still bleeding." Joe drew a handkerchief out of his breast pocket and gave it to her. "Try this."

"Thanks." She dipped and pressed and smiled at him. Joe was ninety percent sure that the thief—or if not the thief, his or her accomplice—was in the design department, but he hoped to hell it wasn't Mia Savard. He'd had some fine-looking clients in his day, but he'd never felt this strong an attraction to one. Technically, Mia wasn't his client, her father was; still, it was too close for comfort or objectivity.

"You weren't playing ice hockey on your lunch hour, were you?"

"No." She took his handkerchief away from her lip. "Better?"

"Looks like it's stopped. Where were you at lunch?"

She hesitated, touching her tongue to the split in her lip. "If I ask you a question about the investigation, will you tell me the truth?"

"Yes. Cooperate with me and I'll cooperate with you."

"Did you have someone following my mother and me today?"

"No." Joe hadn't decided to put a tail on each of the designers till he'd interviewed them and realized that whichever one of them it was who stole the design was damn smart and cool as an iced-over pond.

"Oh." Mia gulped half her drink and made a face like there was way too much Tabasco sauce.

"Did someone follow you today? Is that why you thought I'd tailed you here from the Savard Building?"

"I wondered, but now I think I'm just paranoid." Mia turned her head and nodded at the window, the light fixture over the table giving Joe a breath-hitching glimpse of her long, dark and very thick eyelashes. "Last night, I saw footprints in the snow, out there on the sidewalk, and thought the same thing, that someone had followed me here."

She probably was paranoid, but if someone was following her, Moira or whoever he assigned to tail her would find out.

"Still." She turned her head toward him, the light streaking red highlights in her hair. "It's not coincidence that you're here, is it?"

"No. I have a few questions I'd like to ask you."

"Jordan said you'd talked to her today." She took another slug of her Virgin Mary—a big one—and made an oh-man-that's-awful face. "She said you talked to Arlene and Evan and Kylie, too."

"Did Alicia approve the design for her dress in person?"

"No. I scanned the drawing and e-mailed it to her at the Governor's Mansion in Jefferson City. She and I came up with a new design today, so we won't have to e-mail back and forth on this gown."

"I thought DeMello was designing the replacement dress."

"So did I, but Alicia didn't like his ideas. She asked for me."

"How did that go over with DeMello?"

She smiled wryly. "Like a lead balloon."

"Have you seen the ad in *Today's Bride*?"

"I saw it yesterday, blown up on the wall, but not up close."

Joe took a tear sheet from the magazine out of his pocket and unfolded it on the table. Mia moved the coconut cake out of the way and leaned over the ad on her elbows. Joe pulled the candle flickering inside a glass holder closer to give her more light and wished he hadn't. The flame lit her dark eyes with a soft amber glow.

"This is the dress I designed, but it's not my drawing.

This isn't my style, and it's a different view from the final one I e-mailed to Alicia."

"So it's your design rendered by someone else?"

"Yes." Mia gave the tear sheet a one-fingered push toward him.

Joe moved to pick it up but Jordan Branch snatched it off the table and gave it an eyeball. He'd seen her coming through the doorway in the far back wall with Becca Savard trailing behind her. They'd drawn together, whispered something and then approached the table.

"Absolutely Mia didn't draw this." Jordan dropped the tear sheet on the table with a grin. "Just my professional opinion."

"This isn't your style," Joe said to Mia. "Is it a style you recognize?"

"Do I know anyone who draws like that?" she asked. Joe nodded and Mia shook her head. "It's not anyone who works for Savard's. Drawing styles are as distinctive as handwriting. I could pick Jordan's stack out of a stuff—I mean, Jordan's stuff out of a stack of sketches. Evan's, Arlene's, Kylie's and Damien's, too."

"Could someone forge one of your drawings?"

Joe asked the question of Mia but Jordan answered it with a cheery "Oh, sure" as she dropped into her chair across the table. He didn't miss the don't-help glare Mia shot Jordan. Neither did Becca Savard, who frowned as she, too, sat down.

"What I mean is," Jordan corrected herself, "I could mimic Mia's technique but not her style—the little nuances and touches she throws in. She could mimic mine, too, like fine artists who copy the *Mona Lisa* but never quite get it right. A sharp-enough eye can spot a forgery."

"Who has an eye that sharp?" Joe asked, and Mia, Jordan and Becca all said, "Lucien."

"But this isn't a forgery," Mia snatched up the tear sheet, a don't-you-get-it? snap in her voice. "It's not even a good drawing. It's a, uh . . ." She blinked at Joe, the glow in her eyes now an overbright gleam. "What did you call it?"

"A rendering," he filled in, noticing the uh-oh glance Becca Savard exchanged with Jordan.

"That's it. It's a rendering of my design, not a forgery." Mia slapped the tear sheet on the table. "So why are you asking questions about it?"

"I'm trying to get a handle on how the theft was accomplished."

"Do you think the person who made that drawing for Heavenly Bridals is the thief?" Becca asked.

"I don't know." Joe shrugged. "Like I said, I'm just trying to figure out how the design made it from Savard's to Heavenly Bridals."

"Pssst." Mia leaned toward him, cupped a hand over her mouth and whispered, "Somebody took it."

Then she threw her head back and cackled, her arms wrapped around her waist, her heels drumming the floor like she'd just said the funniest thing anyone had ever said since the dawn of time.

"Oh, no," Becca Savard said. "She's gone."

Joe picked up Mia's drink and took a whiff. His eyes watered.

"There's enough vodka in this to pickle an elephant," he said to Jordan Branch. "You told me she doesn't drink."

"She doesn't. I don't know what got into her." Jordan shouldered her purse and her coat, rose and pulled on

Becca's elbow. "She told Bev she was throwing caution to the wind and ordered a Bloody Mary."

"A cup of coffee and she'll be fine." Becca wound a red scarf around her neck and stood up. "We'll be with Robin. He's finishing a game of nine-ball, then we're heading to a party. Tell Mia we'll wait for her."

She smiled and lifted her coat from the back of her chair. Jordan slipped into hers and dropped him a wink. Mia was still laughing and now she was smacking her palm on the table.

"As friends go," Joe said, "you two make great strangers."

Becca looked wounded. Jordan laughed, spread her hands on the gilt confetti and leaned toward him over the table.

"You're positively luscious, Joe, but you're off-limits," she said in a husky voice. "It's Friday night, fun night, and there are two very cute guys in the poolroom looking for a good time. So see ya, handsome."

"Black! Two sugars!" Becca called as Jordan dragged her off.

Mia was still laughing and slapping the table. At least she was a happy drunk. Joe pushed his chair around to signal Bev and saw that she was already on the way with a super-size white mug on a tray.

"Black coffee, two sugars." Bev put the mug down in front of Mia. "Is she laughing or crying?"

"Laughing. Smell this." Joe handed her the Bloody Mary.

"Woo." Bev turned her nose up. "I told Charlie to make 'em weak."

"Is Charlie the only one behind the bar tonight?"

"Yes. And he's gonna hear about this."

"The guy who was with Mia. Terence Parker. Is he still here?"

"No. He spoke to a couple folks at the bar and left." Bev looked at the two empty chairs across the table. "Where's Becca and Jordan?"

"Two cute guys in the pool room." Joe tore open the sugar packets.

"I told them to keep an eye on Mia. They'll hear about this, too." Bev turned a stern eye on Joe. "Can I trust you with Mia?"

"You can." Joe showed her his ID. "I'm working for Lucien Savard."

Bev didn't just glance at his state-issued investigator's license in its leather case; she took it out of his hand and read every word.

"Good enough." She shut the case and gave it back, picked up the lethal Bloody Mary and took it away with her.

Joe dumped the sugar and stirred it into Mia's coffee. Her cackle wound down to giggles, then she sighed and blinked at him.

"Hey, Joe. Whattaya know?" she said, and went off in another spasm of cackling, table-slapping laughter. When it passed, Mia grinned at him and said, "Knock knock."

"Who's there?"

"Private eyes."

"Private eyes, who?"

"Private eyes are watching you." She sang the old Hall and Oates song, way off-key and reeled off into another round of cackles.

Joe pushed the mug at her. "Drink this coffee."

"Joe." Mia giggled. "That's slang for coffee, y'know.

Hey, Bev!" she called to the waitress. "Joe wants me to drink my joe!"

She thought that was hilarious and started laughing again. Then she started singing again—rather, butchering an ancient Nescafé TV commercial: "Let's have another cup of coffee, then let's have another cup of joe!"

This wasn't how he'd planned to spend his evening. Spooning coffee into Mia Savard's pretty mouth when she paused to draw breath between choruses. He had employee files to read, the new security installations to discuss with Brian, but here he sat, dribbling coffee past Mia's lips and wondering if this was accident or design. Had Charlie tipped the Absolut bottle just a bit too far or had someone spiked her drink?

Why would Terence bother? Why would Becca and Jordan abandon Mia? Was the idea to get him out of the way by sticking him with a happy drunk who sang about as well as she lied? And if so, why?

Bev appeared at Joe's elbow. "Not going well, is it?"

"Not well at all. I think I should take her home."

"Mia, honey," Bev said, "can you stand up?"

"Me? Stand?" She blinked and grinned at Bev. "Suurre."

Mia spread her hands on the table and pushed to her feet. So did Joe, in time to catch her and keep her from nose-diving into the cake. She thought that was hilariously funny and started laughing, limp as a rag doll in Joe's hands.

"I'll take her," Bev said. "Go get your car. I'll meet you up front."

He folded the Heavenly Bridals ad into his pocket and headed for the door. On the off chance Bev had missed Terence Parker, Joe took a look around for him. He didn't see him and was almost disappointed.

It was spitting snow and nose-freezingly cold. While he gave the Explorer a minute to warm up, Joe checked his watch—eight-fifteen—and called his uncle Pete at the security kiosk in the Savard Building.

"Hey, Unk. It's Joe. Are Carlos and Stink there?"

"Yep. They're cruising the building and I'm riding the desk."

"I've been held up. Mia Savard had too much to drink so I'm taking her home. Couple odd things going on here."

Joe flipped on the heater—still blowing cold, so he turned the fan off—and told Pete about Terence, and Becca and Jordan dumping Mia.

"Probably nothing, but better to be safe," Pete said. "I'll send Carlos down to the garage. I won't let anybody in the front, not even Lucien."

"Check Mia's office," Joe said. "Make sure it's locked."

Joe disconnected, flipped the heater on—warm at last—and swung the Explorer out of its spot on the street. He doubled-parked in front of Blanko's, flipped on the emergency flashers and met Bev, lugging Mia stuffed into her coat with her purse hung around her neck like a canteen, just inside the door. Mia was still singing.

"I can handle her from here." Joe slipped Bev a fifty-dollar bill for service above and beyond. "Keep the cake."

The frigid slap of air in her face made Mia gasp as Joe tucked her under his arm and hustled her into the truck. He buckled her into the passenger seat, swung behind the wheel and kicked the heater on high.

Mia blinked at him. "Where are you taking me?"

"Home." Joe watched in the mirrors and pulled into traffic.

"Ohhh, thank you." Mia sighed, her head thunking against the passenger window. "I don't feel so good."

"After coconut cake and buffalo wings on top of Bloody Marys," Joe said as he switched on the wipers, "I'm not surprised."

"I ate buffalo wings with coconut cake? Oh, God." She moaned and curled in a ball against the armrest. "I will never drink again."

8

MIA SHARED A TRIPLEX with Becca and Robin Savard. A three-story pink stucco Mediterranean with a red tile roof, just off Ward Parkway, within spitting distance of her parents' house.

Robin had the first floor, Becca the second and Mia the top floor.

Courtesy of Moira, who gathered all the vital statistics on all the Savards from Petra, Joe knew the house had an elevator and a four-car garage around back, with an attached three-bay aluminum carport.

The driveway sloped uphill, but it was plowed. Snow skittered across the blacktop, clung to the snowpacked edges and glistened with the promise of ice in the headlights. The motion-activated security lights came on when Joe swung the Explorer into the carport, shut off the engine and went around the SUV to collect Mia. If he hadn't belted her in she would've fallen out when he opened the door.

"Hey, Joe." She smiled at him weakly, her purse swinging like a pendulum around her neck. "What do you know?"

"Where are your house keys?"

She had to think about it for a second. "In my purse."

"How about the design for Alicia's new dress?"

Another second, then she said, "In my purse. I didn't think it was smart to leave it on the drawing board in my office."

"A sober mind is an amazing thing, isn't it?"

Mia squinted in the bright glare of the security lights. "You're one of those obnoxious people who can actually hold their liquor, aren't you?"

Joe grinned at her. "Guilty. I'm Irish."

"My luck." She groped for her purse strap, got her hand caught in the seat belt, gave up and made a disgusted noise. "Get this thing off me, would you?"

Joe drew her purse over her head, unzipped it to fish out her keys, hung it over his shoulder and unhooked her seat belt. "Can you walk?"

"Of course I can," she said, and oozed out of the SUV.

If Joe hadn't caught her she would've ended up a bright purple Popsicle on the driveway come morning. He slid one arm under her shoulders, hooked the other under her knees, kicked the door shut and carried her toward the house.

"Am I walking?" She blinked at him with snowflakes in her lashes.

"No. I'm carrying you."

"Oh, boy. Smoochy Lips is gonna love this."

Joe's laugh fogged on the frigid night air. "Her name is Moira."

"Pretty name." Mia swallowed and closed her eyes. "Pretty girl."

"You were in your car last night in the parking garage."

"Yes. Hiding under the dash like a fool." She opened

her eyes as he climbed the steps to the cement back porch, and the motion light under the eaves came on over their heads. "How'd you know my car is my car?"

"I have a friend at the DMV. I ran the plate."

Joe leaned Mia against the shoulder-high railing, unlocked the storm door, the inside steel security door, took her by the shoulders and walked her inside.

Two round globes suspended from the ceiling by heavy black chains lit the white plaster walls and the black and white tile floor. Joe leaned Mia in a corner while he locked up. When he turned back to her, she'd slid halfway down the wall.

"Look," she said. "I'm standing."

"Not quite, but you're getting there." Joe pulled her up and steered her across the tile floor to the elevator in the wall opposite the doors.

A custom job with a black-grilled gate on the front. One on the back wall, too, that opened when the car reached three. Another glass globe on a black chain lit the foyer. There were two doors: one on Joe's left, the other on his right on the far side of the foyer.

The bright red runner covering the white carpet angled from the elevator to the left-hand door. Joe guided Mia toward it.

"What's behind door number two?" He hooked his thumb over his shoulder. "Storage?"

Mia peered across the foyer and blinked. "That's my sewing room."

Her apartment door had two locks: one in the knob, a brass dead bolt above. Joe held Mia against the wall with one hand, found the correct keys on her ring—a silver circle dangling a plastic fob that said in bright yellow letters on a hot pink background KISS MY TIARA—and opened the door.

He pried Mia off the wall and steered her inside ahead of him. The wall switch he flipped turned on two crystal table lamps with pleated white shades. Mia wove unsteadily away from him and collapsed face-first on a pink-flowered sofa. The cushions piled along the back exploded like shrapnel and tumbled off onto the white carpet.

Joe grinned and threw the dead bolt. Mia made a sound that was part moan, the rest groan. He put her purse on a cherry credenza with a glass top by the door, dropped her keys in a pewter bowl that held a pair of white knit gloves turned neatly inside out and a pair of sunglasses.

Turning lights on as he went, Joe checked the rest of the apartment. The place was monstrous, the rooms huge. Twelve-foot ceilings, crown molding, plastered walls. A half wall with black iron spindles separated the living room from the dining room. The kitchen was ultramodern with a freestanding snack bar and two tall stools.

The hallway past the kitchen had two rooms on the right—one a guest bedroom, the other a home office—at the end a sun porch glassed in for the winter. On the left, in Mia's bedroom, French doors opened onto a terrace. Her walk-in closet was the size of Montana.

The bathroom was a Hollywood. Joe turned on the lights, traipsed past a Jacuzzi tub, a corner shower, a makeup counter with a giant mirror lit around the edges by round bulbs. He opened the door at the far end and found himself in the other half of the bathroom, which led into the kitchen.

Mia was still facedown on the couch. Joe sat on the coffee table, took her by the shoulders and sat her up. Her big, dark, bloodshot eyes blinked at him. Her ice hockey injury looked like a red pencil line on her bottom lip. Her face was a color Joe couldn't find a name for, a shade between chalk white and strained-baby-food green.

"Thanks for bringing me home," she said hoarsely. "Now go away."

"Do you have any 7-Up in the house?"

"Huh? Uh—I don't know. Why?"

"Because you look like you're about to be sick."

The words were barely out of his mouth when her eyes bulged and she shot off the couch with one hand clapped over her mouth. She made it into the bathroom off the kitchen before she started retching.

"Been there, done that," Joe murmured sympathetically.

On the other side of the front door stood a pretty cherry desk with curved legs, a dainty chair that he didn't dare sit on, a white French phone and an address book.

He had all the Savards' numbers stored on his cell, but this was a too-good-to-pass-up opportunity. While Mia puked, he opened her address book and read through it while he dialed Petra and Lucien Savard. He didn't find Oren Angel under A or Mammy and Pappy at home.

Joe left a message and dialed Jenna Savard's cell, got her voice mail and left a message. Same result with Luke. He left Mia's brother a message, too, flipped through H, didn't find Heavenly Bridals, and lifted Mia's cell phone out of her purse.

Five missed calls and two voice mail messages:

From Jenna Savard: "Where are you? At that damn bar? Why? You don't drink. Luke and I are having dinner at the American Restaurant." A grand eatery atop Hall's department store in Crown Center. "It's seven o'clock. Get over here."

From Petra Savard: "I'll tell your father after lunch to-morrow. I'm making crepes. Luke will be here. Twelve-thirty if you want to join us. Please join us. I could use the moral support. Love you."

Joe saved the messages, checked the missed calls. Three total from Jenna, the call from Petra and one from an unknown number.

The toilet flushed. Joe put Mia's phone back in her purse and went into the bathroom.

She lay on the white ceramic tile floor, her face tucked in the curve of her left elbow, her arms wrapped around the base of the commode. Joe leaned over her with his hands cupped on his knees.

"How're you doing, sunshine?"

"I'm going to sleep now," she croaked. "Good night."

"You can't sleep on the floor. You'll freeze to death."

"No I won't. I still have my coat on." She paused. "Don't I?"

"Come on." Joe reached for her. "I'll help you."

"No!" She went stiff. "Don't touch me. I'll throw up again."

"Okay," Joe said. "I'll give you a couple of minutes."

He went to the kitchen and looked for 7-Up. He found two cans in the fridge, the rest of the six-pack in a bottom cabinet. He pulled one out of the plastic collar, set it on the pink granite counter and popped the top to let some of the gas out. In the cabinet under the sink he found a green plastic dishpan that looked like it had never been used.

He put it on the floor beside Mia's bed, on top of a towel to protect the white rug, turned on the crystal lamp on the nightstand and killed the overhead lights on the two ceiling fans. He stripped the bed of its quilted pink silk shams and matching coverlet, backtracked to a linen closet in the hall for a cotton quilt and tossed that over her king-size bed.

He found pink polka-dot flannel pajamas in a drawer in the cherry armoire—a twenty-three-inch color TV behind the top doors—slippers on the closet floor beneath a hook that held a white terry-cloth robe. He tossed the pajamas and the robe on the bed and went back to the bathroom.

Mia was still hugging the toilet.

"Your pj's and your robe are on your bed."

"I wish them well," she said faintly. "They'll be very happy there."

"I put a dishpan by the bed in case you have to puke again."

Mia moaned. "Stop with the sweet talk or I'll tell Smoochy Lips."

"Great idea," Joe said. "I'll be right back."

He went to the living.room and dialed Moira's cell. When she answered he heard something roaring in the background.

"What are you doing? Mixing concrete?"

"Gramma Evie and I are making mincemeat."

"I was close," Joe said.

In the bathroom, Mia started retching again. Violently.

"Good grief," Moira said. "Where are *you*?"

"Mia Savard's apartment. She had too many Bloody Marys, too many buffalo wings and too much coconut cake."

"Get in there and help her, Joe! One hand on her stomach, the other on her forehead like you used to do for me when I was little."

"She's not you, Moira, and she's not ten years old. I need a hand."

"You've got two. Use 'em. G'bye."

"Ungrateful brat." Joe hung up and headed back to Mia.

The toilet flushed again. He leaned around the bathroom doorjamb and saw Mia crawling slowly toward her bedroom.

"Atta girl," Joe cheered her on. "You can do it."

"Go home," Mia panted, her arms quivering. "Please."

"I can't leave you like this. You're too sick. I'll stay awhile."

"You can't stay." Mia crawled out of sight into the other half of the bathroom. "Smoochy Lips won't like it."

"Smoochy Lips won't—what?" Joe broke off, puzzled.

It took him a second to figure out what she meant. Then he laughed, trailed Mia through the adjoining door and saw that she'd made it past the makeup counter, the shower and the tub.

"Moira and I," he said to her back, "are not married."

"Then she really won't like it." Mia crawled into her bedroom, raised her right knee off the floor and kicked the door shut in Joe's face.

When she woke up Saturday morning, still alive and breathing, Mia was the most astonished person on the planet.

Joseph Kerr, Inc., might be the second. If he was still speaking to her, that is, after she'd thrown up on him twice.

The first time was her fault. On the verge of crossing over to the Big Sweatshop in the Sky, run by one of her Savard ancestors, she'd croaked at him that if he insisted on staying he might as well make himself at home. She'd had no idea the smell of microwave popcorn would induce more vomiting.

The second time was his fault. She'd warned him after the popcorn incident that she could *not* swallow any more 7-Up or eat any more crackers. He'd insisted that she could and forced two mouthfuls of saltines soaked in pee-warm 7-Up down her throat. A surefire cure of his mother's that ended up on the front of his shirt.

Mia's right foot was still on the floor, her left hand no longer pressed against the wall, but limp on her stomach. One foot on the floor, the opposite hand on the wall wouldn't keep the room from spinning, Joe said, but it would keep it from turning end over end. Which it had, and that's how she'd finally managed to fall asleep.

Mia cracked her left eye and slowly rolled her head toward the French doors. Thank God she'd closed the sheers behind the drapes yesterday morning. The heavy white chiffon kept out the worst of the sun dazzling off the snow that had fallen on the terrace overnight.

She lifted her right foot onto the bed, stretched out the kinks and eased herself up, mostly on her right elbow in case her stomach came up again. When it stayed put, she pushed all the way up and swung her legs over the side of the bed.

Her head spun, but just a little. She closed her eyes till it passed. She had a sick-pulse headache, but if she could stand, Mia thought she might live. How she was going to sustain life without eating ever again was a question for later. At the moment she'd settle for getting to the bathroom before she wet her pants.

On her third try she made it to her feet and to the toilet. What a relief. Once she'd washed her hands and her face,

Mia rinsed her mouth with water, let a tiny bit leak down her throat and dropped to her knees in front of the toilet. Her heart pounded but the thimbleful of water stayed down. Thank God. She could brush her teeth.

Crest Multi-Care and Scope Minty Fresh had never tasted so good.

Mia took a hairbrush out of the vanity drawer, looked in the mirror and almost screamed. Then she realized that her pajama top was on backward, that her head hadn't turned completely around on her neck like poor Linda Blair in *The Exorcist*.

Mia tugged the top over her head and turned it, stuck her arms through the sleeves and blinked at her reflection. Wait a minute. She'd gone to bed in pink polka-dot flannel pajamas. She still wore the bottoms—but the top was blue cotton pinstripe. How had this happened?

She went back to her bedroom. The green dishpan was clean and empty. The guest half of the Hollywood bath was spotless and smelled faintly of Lysol. Mia was pretty sure, even as sick as she'd been, that she'd remember puking all over herself and changing her pajama top.

Something clinked, like a spoon against a cup, and then something rustled, like paper. A page turning in a newspaper. Mia crept to the bathroom doorway and peered into the kitchen.

Joseph Kerr sat on a white iron chair with a pink flowered seat at her glass-topped dining room table reading the *Kansas City Star*, a pink mug on a coaster beside him. Mia smelled coffee; glanced at the machine on the kitchen counter, the carafe half-full of Vanilla Bean, the blend she drank at home. Her stomach growled but she ignored it.

Clearly, Joseph Kerr had stayed all night. Clearly, he'd found the beans and the coffee grinder. Well, he *was* a detective; but clearly, he knew nothing about changing a sick and puking person's clothes.

Mia went back to her bedroom, stuck her feet in her slippers, pulled on her robe and stepped into her bathroom. She took one small, tender-headed tug at her hair, thought her scalp was going to come off with the brush and said "To hell with it" to her flyaway reflection.

She'd thrown up on the guy. Who cared what her hair looked like? Besides, he belonged to Smoochy Lips, the beautiful Moira, and Mia did not poach. She put her brush down and headed for the kitchen.

Joe Kerr glanced up from the paper. He'd changed the shirt she'd ruined for a sweatshirt, once black, she thought, now nearly gray, with faded gold KCMOPD across his chest. "How d'you feel?"

"I have a headache." Mia stopped where the Pergo kitchen floor joined the white dining room carpet. "I also have on pink polka-dot pajama bottoms and a blue pinstripe top. Can you explain this?"

"I checked on you about four. You were sopping wet, sweating out the booze. I thought you'd be more comfortable if you were dry."

"Did I throw up again?"

"No. You just moaned a lot."

Probably because he'd had his hands on her. Mia turned up the shawl collar of her robe to hide the flush she could feel.

"You're welcome." He smiled. "I do my best work in the dark."

Oh, what a disappointment. He was a chaser, another Terence.

"I'm sure Smoochy Lips can testify to that."

"I'm not married, Mia," Joe said. "Moira is my daughter. I was engaged to her mother. She died when Moira was twelve. I adopted her."

"Oh," Mia said. *I'm an idiot,* she thought. "I'm sorry for your loss."

The flush she'd felt coming on gushed up her throat. She ducked into the kitchen, grateful for the overhead cabinets that hid her face.

"You aren't the first person to jump to that conclusion," Joe said. "We have the same last name, so people assume. Especially when we're both working the same case."

"Moira works for Joseph Kerr, Inc., Private Investigations?"

"Some days I swear I work for her. She's a born detective."

"Women are good at ferreting things out and discovering secrets."

The fact that Joe Kerr wasn't married was one secret Mia intended to keep to herself. Mean, maybe, but no meaner than Becca and Jordan abandoning her in Blanko's. She'd have to remember to thank them.

She filled the stainless steel teakettle with cold water, turned a back burner on high and ducked her head so she could look through the gap between the ceramic range top and the built-in microwave.

"I'm making toast. Would you like a couple slices?"

Joe smiled at her. "Can't handle 7-Up and crackers, huh?"

"Uh, no." Mia shuddered. "Sorry about your shirt."

"Don't be. I wasn't that attached to it. Toast would be nice."

He went back to the paper while Mia made the toast

and a weak cup of tea. When she brought napkins and a plate of lightly buttered wheat toast to the table, he folded the sports section in half and moved it out of the way, said, "Thanks" and kept reading while he ate.

Perfectly relaxed, perfectly at home, while Mia thought how weird it felt to have him here, how weird it was to have any man except Robin here since Terence. He'd never been much for staying over; he'd spent the entire night maybe four times in the eight months they were together. After the fact, she'd realized that should've told her something.

Mia took tiny bites, chewed well and swallowed with small sips of tea. She'd made six slices of toast and ate one. Joe ate three.

"Is that all you want?" he asked.

"For now," Mia said. "Help yourself."

While he polished off the toast, she went to the bathroom for two Tylenol and swallowed them at the kitchen sink with a glass of water.

"So why did you hide under the dash in your car?" Joe asked.

The question startled Mia. She could've sworn he was paying no attention to her. She glanced through the gap under the cabinets, saw him still hunched over the sports section but looking at her.

"I don't know. I was on the phone with Mother. Dad was in the library throwing books. He'd already thrown chairs and fired everybody, even me and Luke and Jenna. Somebody had stolen Alicia's dress. You're a detective. I'd bumped into you twice already. I saw Moira's car pull up to the security gate, then you stepped off the elevator and I just freaked."

Mia gave an I-know-it-sounds-lame-but-there-it-is shrug.

"Okay. I was curious." He folded the paper and laid it aside. "When I checked the tape from the security camera for Thursday night, I didn't see your gold Subaru leave the garage."

"There's a security camera in the parking garage?" Mia blinked, surprised. "Really? Where?"

"Never mind. There'll be a new one installed by Monday. Actually, there'll be half a dozen cameras in the garage. High tech, zoom lenses."

"Luke will be thrilled. He's bitched for years because Savard's has no security. People flit from this department with that thing to that department with this thing." Mia collected the toast remains from the table, tossed the napkins in the trash can under the sink and rinsed the plate. "It drives Luke crazy. He thinks there should be more controls."

"Come Monday morning your brother is going to be a happy man." Joe sipped his coffee. "You have two messages on your cell phone. One from your sister, one from your mother."

Mia swung away from the sink. "You checked my messages?"

"I was trying to find someone to stay with you. Your sister wanted you to have dinner with her and Luke. Your mother invited you for lunch. She's making crepes at twelve-thirty."

Mia glanced at the clock on the microwave. It wasn't quite nine.

"Who do you think stole the design?" Joe asked.

"If I knew, I'd be the detective, wouldn't I?" Mia heard the snap in her voice and sighed. "I'm sorry. I'm not used to having my messages checked and being interrogated first thing in the morning."

"Your privacy and the privacy of every Savard employee went out the window when one of you stole the design for Alicia's dress." He sipped his coffee again, unfazed by her sharp tone. "If you don't like the way I'm doing my job, tell your father. He hired me and gave me carte blanche to find the thief, ASAP."

"You make it sound like you've already found her." Mia shoved her right fist on her hip. "Do you think I did it?"

"I hope not. I like you." Joe's dimple flashed just long enough to make her pulse flutter, then it vanished. "But nobody gets a pass."

"No preferential treatment because my name is Savard. Mother told me. I can't explain why you didn't see my car on the security tape." The snap crept back into Mia's voice, but she couldn't keep it out. Maybe it was the sick headache pulsing between her eyes. "I backed out of the space and made a loop around to the gate. I could've gone straight. If I had, maybe the camera would have picked me up. I don't know. I don't know why I backed up instead of going straight, either. I just did."

"Invading your privacy is one thing." Joe rose, pushed in his chair and picked up his cup. "But I've invaded your space long enough."

"I don't want you to leave," Mia said. "I don't want you to stay, either. I don't know what I want, other than this whole mess to be over."

"Then don't get bent out of shape every time I ask a question. The more information I have and the quicker I gather it, the better. The quicker I find the thief and you get your life back."

"I'll try not to take this personally, but that's hard for me. It's my design that was stolen. I realize that points the finger straight at me." Mia drew a breath to brace herself for the reply. "Doesn't it?"

"Yes. Let me tell you why. One, it was your design." Joe raised his thumb. "That's access and opportunity. Two, you wanted out of bridal, but your father wouldn't let you out. That's motive." He raised his index finger. "Three, you quit the morning the theft was discovered, which looks like you were trying to stay one jump ahead of the posse."

Last he raised his pinkie and his ring finger and pressed them together to make the Vulcan sign of peace. Mia laughed, remembering Bev holding up the same fingers to her last night. It occurred to her that Joe could be trying to disarm an uncooperative suspect, but she didn't care.

He smiled. "I'm not all suspicion and questions, Mia."

"I'm not guilty and I intend to prove it."

"Terrific. That'll make my job easier."

"You could finish the coffee if you like. I think I'll stick with tea."

"One more cup," Joe said, "then I'll split."

He stepped into the kitchen, which suddenly seemed much smaller and a lot warmer filled with Joseph Kerr, Inc. He didn't seem as tall as he seemed large and wide, especially across the chest and shoulders.

"Maybe I'll try yogurt." Mia opened the fridge, stuck her head inside and drew a breath. *Ahhh. Much cooler in here.*

The front door buzzed. Mia shut the fridge, crossed her apartment and pressed Talk on the intercom. "Hello. This is Mia."

"How many times," Jenna said, "have I told you not to identify yourself until you know who's down here?"

"Here" was the vestibule on the first floor, separated from the foyer outside Robin's apartment by a glass door and side panels constructed of pale green tinted blocks as thick as Coke bottles.

"Let me think," Mia said. "About a million?"

"Are you decent? Luke is with me."

"I'm in my pj's. Joseph Kerr is here."

"Excellent. He's on my list for today."

Jenna the Firebrand versus the Unflappable Joe Kerr. *This should be fun,* Mia thought. Too bad she didn't have time to sell tickets.

9

"Copy that, Blue Leader," Mia said. "Over and out."

She took her finger off Talk, pressed and held Open to buzz Jenna and Luke through the vestibule. Then she unlocked the front door and turned around. Joe stood between the dining room and the kitchen. His left shoulder against the cabinets, his pink coffee mug in his right hand.

"Why do you call your sister Blue Leader?"

"Just to razz her. When we were kids, if Luke or I didn't do what Jenna wanted, we ended up black and blue."

Joe smiled. "Good thing I'm bigger than her, huh?"

Jenna was first through the door. Born second but first in everything else. First to walk, first to talk, first to sock Mia or Luke in a squabble. Long ago, they'd learned to let Jenna lead—there was less socking that way—so Luke came in behind her, closed the door and tucked Mia under his arm for a quick kiss on the cheek.

Jenna was brilliant, brash and every bit as gorgeous as Petra.

When clients commented on his children's looks, Lucien told them that homely offspring were not allowed in the family. With a broad wink he'd say that before the

Savards emigrated from France, ugly children were sold to the Gypsies.

When he really got wound up at lunch parties, Lucien told clients that the Savards were descendents of European royalty. In fact, they sprang from a long line of fur traders and rapscallions who hightailed it out of New Orleans and up the Mississippi one jump ahead of the parish constable. But the royalty story made colorful copy in the fashion mags.

Jenna laid her purple leather day planner on the desk. She'd misplaced it once in her office and broke out in hives. She wore black jeans with red suede boots, a white sweater and Petra's sheared beaver jacket, which she tossed on the couch as she turned toward Mia.

"You don't look sick," she said. "You look pale, and you look like you got ready for bed in the dark, but you don't look sick."

"You should've been here last night," Joe said.

"Mr. Kerr." Jenna swung her dark brown gaze on him. "I apologize for not returning your call. I didn't check my voice mail till this morning. I allotted time for you this afternoon, but since Luke and I are here, would you like to interview us now?"

"I would." Joe looked at Luke, who nodded; then he glanced at Mia and pointed his thumb down the hall. "Can I use your office back there?"

"Sure," Mia said. It would give her a chance to practice on Luke what she planned to say to Lucien about the photograph.

"Ladies first," Joe said to Jenna. She picked up her day planner from the desk and swept down the hall. Joe followed.

"Tell me you've got coffee." Luke peeled off his navy

bomber and hung it on a dining room chair. "Jen's off caffeine again."

"What's the 'in' drink in LA this week?"

"Guava juice, I don't know. Where's the coffee?"

"In the kitchen. It's Vanilla Bean."

"I don't care if it's Beef Liver, so long as it's coffee."

Once Luke had a pink mug of Vanilla Bean and Mia had one of weak tea, they sat on the sofa and he cocked his head at her.

"You look like hell. What possessed you to drink last night?"

"The side trip Mother and I took at lunch yesterday," Mia said, and told Luke about their jaunt to Heavenly Bridals.

He didn't yell; the veins in his forehead didn't even pop out. When Mia finished, he asked, "Did you tell the detective about this?"

"No," she said. "But I probably should."

"Yes, you should, but not till Mother tells Dad." Luke took a big swig of his coffee. "What was she thinking?"

Oh, if you only knew, Mia thought, but didn't answer.

"Well?" Luke demanded. "You were there. What *was* she thinking?"

"What she said at the meeting. She doesn't believe Angel knows the design is stolen. She wanted Dad to call him Thursday night, but he refused. She said if Lucien wouldn't talk to him, then she would."

"Mother has a point. Did Angel know or didn't he? But she's not the one to find out. She's too soft-hearted."

That's what you think, Mia wanted to say. *You didn't see the fire in her eyes when she said, "If Oren lies to me, believe me, I'll know."*

"The guy with the camera wasn't there by accident,

Luke. I asked Joe if he had someone follow Mother and me yesterday. He said no. So who was that guy and why did he tail us to Heavenly Bridals?"

"Maybe he was already there," Luke said. "Maybe he works for Heavenly Bridals. Just because Mother didn't see anyone when she looked in the windows doesn't mean no one was there."

"But he was parked next door and he drove away."

"Of course he did, Mia. You were chasing him."

"He wasn't in a car. It was a Kia Sportage. When he drove off I—"

"Luke!" Jenna called, an edge in her voice. "Your turn!"

"Don't tell Jen about this." Luke gave Mia a quick kiss, picked up his coffee and headed for the study.

Mia's head was starting to spin again. Tell this, don't tell that. She sipped her tea and closed her eyes. When she opened them, Jenna was settling onto the sofa beside her, with a pink mug dangling a tea bag.

"That's not decaf," Mia said.

"I'm aware." Jenna set her mug on a coaster and faced Mia, a white line around her mouth. "How did you survive a night with that man?"

"I was sick and passed out for most of it. What happened?"

"I'm a Savard and he treated me like a suspect."

"At least you're not the number-one suspect. I am."

"That's outrageous!" Jenna's nostrils flared. "How dare—"

"Think about it, Jen. It's my design." Mia laid out the rationale for Jenna the way Joe had laid it out for her. "That doesn't mean I did it, because I didn't. That's just why it puts me at the top of the list."

"Your name is Savard," Jenna argued. "That should take you off the list. That should take us all off the list."

"No it shouldn't. Dad can't play favorites on this. Someone at Savard's stole the design. We can't be exempt from scrutiny or suspicion just because our name is Savard."

"That sounds like detective speak to me." Jenna picked up her cup. "Are you sure you were sick and passed out most of the night?"

"Go look in the clothes hamper. Be sure you hold your nose."

Jenna sipped her tea. "Mr. Kerr is awfully good-looking."

"I had a huge crush on him for two hours, then I got over it."

"Mmmm," Jenna said, and put her cup down. "Do you think you should be entertaining him in your pajamas and robe?"

"I'm not entertaining. I'm barely coherent. Joe stayed because I was sick. I threw up on him, not to mention that I've sworn off men."

"I wish you'd swear off hanging out in that bar. It's not a good environment. You met Terence there."

"Guess who was at Blanko's last night?"

"No," Jenna said. "Did he have the nerve to talk to you?"

"Oh, yes," Mia said, and told Jenna about Terence and Terri Baxter seeing Governor Whitcomb's motorcade from the recumbent bikes, the canceled photo shoot at Heavenly Bridals and Terri telling Terence to buy a copy of *Today's Bride*. "So someone who knows that the design was stolen is telling the world."

"People can't keep their mouths shut," Jenna said disgustedly. "At this rate, it will be on billboards by Monday morning. Did you tell Dad?"

"No, just you. Joe knows," Mia said. "He was at Blanko's, too, and overheard what Terence said. The Bloody Marys hit me right after that."

"What was Mr. Kerr's response to Terence's revelations?"

"Mr. Kerr will be glad to tell his response," Joe said behind them.

Mia turned on her knees, looked over the back of the sofa and through the spindles at Joe and Luke coming through the dining room. She sat down with her right foot tucked underneath her; Joe and Luke sat on the window seat in the living room bay window.

"Lawyers ball things up," Joe said. "So in the interests of keeping the lawyers out of it, I'd like to keep this out of the papers and off TV. I told Mia last night, and I'm telling you now, both of you"—Joe glanced at Luke, then Jenna—"don't talk to the media."

"As if." Jenna snorted.

Luke asked, "Who's going to gag Lucien?"

"We could draw straws," Mia suggested.

"We can't ask Uncle Rudy," Jenna said. "He broke the theft to Dad. That's enough for one week."

"I'll talk to him." Joe rose to his feet. "Thanks for your time," he said to Luke and Jenna, then smiled at Mia without the dimple. "Take care."

He left and Jenna frowned at the door. "That was abrupt."

"I think he has things to do." Luke slapped his hands on his knees. "So do we." He looked at Mia. "Are you coming to lunch?"

"Yes." She rose off the sofa. "Can you take me to get my car?"

"Sure," Luke replied. "We'll pick it up on the way."

"Thanks. I'll take a shower and get dressed."

On her way out of the living room, she heard Jenna say to Luke: "Well, lunch should be an interesting meal."

Lunch, the meal, was divine. Petra had a way with seafood and sauces. The salad, tiny leaves of baby spinach and bits of some prickly species of lettuce, melted in Mia's mouth under raspberry vinaigrette. She steered clear of the wine her mother served, but dared a couple of the stuffed pastries left over from yesterday's reception.

Lunch, the aftermath, was a disaster.

Mia stuck with tea, everyone else poured coffee, and they retired to the living room to powwow while Tilde the maid, who had been with Lucien longer than Petra, cleared the dining room.

"I've written press releases to cover every contingency," Luke said. "Celeste has them with instructions on when and where to distribute them. So really, Dad, there's no reason for you to talk to the media. And I agree with Mr. Kerr. If this leaks to the papers or God forbid TV, the less we say in public, the better."

"Yes, yes." Lucien waived an impatient hand. "I know all that."

"Good," Jenna said. "Then we can count on you to put a sock in it."

Lucien shot his middle child a scowl that was part irritation and part I-adore-you-you're-just-like-me.

"While we're on the subject of the media, Lucien." Petra linked and twisted her fingers in her lap and Mia held her breath. "There's something I need to tell you. It may be nothing, but—"

That's when the doorbell rang the first time.

"I'll get it," Luke said. "I'll get it, Tilde!" He called down the hallway that cut her parents' three-story Tudor home in half.

"Good!" Tilde shouted back from the dining room. "I'm busy!"

"Yes, my love? You were saying?" Lucien prompted Petra. "What about the media?"

"I was saying that I'm sure this is nothing, but—"

Luke stepped into the living room with Uncle Rudy.

"I hope I'm not interrupting," he said with a tentative smile.

Mia stifled a moan of frustration. Her mother rose from her green plaid upholstered wing chair by the white brick fireplace. If she'd jumped up and shouted, *Whoopee!* she couldn't have looked more relieved.

"Never, Rudy." Petra took her brother-in-law's hands and pecked a kiss on his cheek. "Come and have coffee. Have you had lunch?"

"Yes. I stopped for a bite when I left the office." He shed his dove gray, down-filled storm coat, gave it to Luke and followed Petra to the fire. "I think it would've been easier for me to get into Fort Knox this morning than the Savard Building."

"Excellent!" Lucien said. "It will be even tougher come Monday."

He clapped his brother on the shoulder and ushered him toward the chair that matched Petra's on the other side of the fireplace. "Are you sure you won't have a bite? Petra made crepes."

Rudy's smile tightened. Jenna slid Mia a look that said *They're doing it again*. Fawning and fussing. Since sweet, adorable Aunt Rose died three years ago, Lucien and Petra had been in perpetual hover.

Mia remembered Robin saying in Blanko's on Thursday night that his father was on Prozac—the implication, because of Lucien. Becca, who usually told Mia everything, hadn't breathed a word about Prozac. It seemed more likely that Uncle Rudy would need an antidepressant to help him deal with Aunt Rose's loss way more than he'd need one to deal with Lucien, which he'd been doing for fifty-eight years. How, Mia wondered, could she bring up Prozac with Uncle Rudy and find out?

She and Becca and Jordan were supposed to be working together to find out who stole the design, but since they'd abandoned her in Blanko's last night, Mia was having second thoughts. And she was doing her darnedest not to think about Joe Kerr being single.

"I am sorry I missed the crepes," Rudy said. "I do love them."

"They're your favorite," Petra said in a singsong voice. "Shrimp and crab with lobster sauce. We have plenty."

"No, you do *not* have plenty!" Tilde barked from the doorway.

Everyone jumped, Luke the worst, nearly off the sofa beside Mia. He used to have nightmares about Tilde the Terror. Or Tilde the Tank. They'd called her that, too, as children, because she was built like one. Short and stout, Lucien and Rudy's once-upon-a-time nurse. Tough as an old boot and utterly devoted to the Savard brothers.

"There's two lousy crepes left!" Tilde shouted at Petra. She wore her gray uniform with a white collar and cuffs and a white apron. "Maybe a teaspoon of sauce! Which, by the way, is separating 'cause you used too much milk! Just like I told you! But did you listen? No!"

"Thank you, Tilde," Petra said between her teeth.

"And that," Luke whispered to Mia, "is why Mother is the wrong person to talk to Oren Angel."

"Yes, Tilde dear. Thank you." Lucien hurried across the living room, swept her under his arm and kissed the top of her gnarly-curled gray head. "How about some coffee? Could Rudy have a cup of coffee?"

"Suuure," Tilde purred like a cat. "I'll be right back with it."

"I'm so sorry," Rudy murmured to Petra.

"It's all right, dear." She smiled at him. "I'll outlive her."

Tilde came with Rudy's coffee and left. Jenna got up behind her and shut the pocket doors.

"I don't want to cause trouble or muddy the waters any further." Rudy put his cup and saucer on the small round table beside his chair. "But something is bothering me and I feel I have to say it."

"Please do, Rudy," Lucien said. "You know I value your input."

"What bothers me is the assumption that the person who stole the design is a Savard employee. I realize the evidence points that way, but I'd hate to see us rush to judgment and overlook other possibilities. I just can't believe that anyone who works for Savard's would do this."

"I don't believe Pete's nephew is ruling out any possibility," Lucien said. "He's working from the most likely scenario. Has he spoken to you?"

"No. I'm sure he'll get around to me. This is nothing against Pete's nephew. He seems a fine young man. I'm sure he's very competent."

"Security is one of his strengths," Luke said. "The electronic devices his team is installing this weekend will make it damned difficult for something like this to ever happen again."

Aha, Mia thought. *Joe has a team. I knew it.* She'd *told* Becca and Jordan that Joe had other detectives working with him.

"What other possibilities do you see, Uncle Rudy?" Jenna asked.

"I see a prime candidate for the title of suspect that none of you are going to like," he said. "Governor Whitcomb."

"Doesn't bother me." Luke shrugged. "I didn't vote for him."

Lucien sat on the arm of the sofa nearest Rudy's chair, his hands on his knees, gazing at his brother as if he'd just said that Elvis had stolen the design for Alicia's dress.

"Why do you suggest the governor?" Lucien asked. "I can't see any political gain for him in the theft of his daughter's wedding gown."

"How about sympathy? The state budget is a disaster," said Uncle Rudy, Savard's CFO, who knew numbers like Mia knew fabrics. "Most of the mess Whitcomb inherited, but he's taking the hit. His job approval rating is in single digits. Politically, he has designs on the U.S. Senate when his term as governor expires. Everyone loves brides and weddings. We should know. It's how we make our living. Seems a perfect way to garner a swell of sympathy with the voters if his daughter's fairy-tale wedding hits an iceberg six weeks before the ceremony."

"If Alicia had demanded my head on a pike yesterday and Alex," Lucien said, referring to the governor, "had raced out of the room to hold a press conference, I would give your theory credence, Rudy. But that didn't happen, and it doesn't explain how Angel obtained the design."

"Alicia could have given it to him," Rudy replied. "Becca tells me that Mia e-mailed the final design to Alicia. Actually, anyone in the Governor's Mansion could have copied it out of her in-box."

"Alicia could have printed it," Jenna said, "and passed it around both houses of the state legislature."

"A clever hacker in Poughkeepsie," Luke tossed in, "could have pulled it off the 'Net and sent it to Heavenly Bridals for a tidy finder's fee."

"Preposterous possibilities, but they *are* possible," Rudy said. "And that's my point. A number of people besides Savard employees could have gotten their hands on the design for Alicia's dress."

"Any one of those things is possible, but they're not likely," Mia said. "*Likelihood* means probable, not possible. The cops say that all the time on *Law & Order*. Probable cause, not possible."

"Here we go again," Jenna said with an oh-isn't-my-baby-sister-cute smile. "More detective speak."

That's when the doorbell rang the second time.

"I'll get it." Luke rose off the couch and opened the pocket doors, turned right into the hallway and called, "I'll get it, Tilde!"

"'Bout time!" She shouted from what sounded like the kitchen.

Luke came back and stopped in the doorway, his expression tight, a muscle twitching in his jaw. "Dad. You need to come to the door."

"Yes?" Lucien pushed off the arm of the sofa. "What is it?"

"Stay calm," Luke said. "Remember what Mr. Kerr told you at the meeting yesterday morning about Oren Angel's attorney."

Her father remembered instantly. It took Mia a second, maybe because of the headache still pulsing between her eyes, to recall Joe saying: "I was airborne at the time so I may have misunderstood, but I think Angel said you'd be hearing from his attorney."

Lucien's eyes narrowed and his nostrils flared. "Petra. Get Walter on the phone and get him over here."

Her father stalked across the living room like a bull on the charge.

"Jenna," Petra said, following on his heels. "Call Walter."

Jenna wheeled out of her chair for the phone in the library across the hallway. Mia jumped to her feet. So did Rudy.

"Where can we hide?" she asked, and her uncle gave her a thin, strained grin.

"How about in the kitchen with Tilde?"

"You can," Mia said. "I'm the spawn of my mother."

Lucien bellowed. The door slammed and Mia and Rudy winced.

"That backstabbing Judas!" Her father roared. "That ingrate!"

Mia and her uncle raced for the pocket doors in time to see Lucien rage past with a folded rectangle of papers crushed in his fist. He turned into the library with Petra hot behind him. Mia caught her sleeve.

"What is it, Mother? What does Dad have in his hand?"

"A subpoena," Petra said breathlessly. "Oren Angel is suing your father for slander and harassment."

10

THE NIGHT JOE TOOK the Glock in the face, the slap of reality that made him realize he wasn't born to be a cop like his father, he'd wanted to crawl in a hole and howl.

He'd crawled home instead and found his mother asleep on the couch. His watch commander had called Evie to stay with Moira, but hadn't told her why. Joe didn't wake her. He'd bumped through the dark house and sat down on the foot of Moira's canopy bed.

It was three-thirty A.M. Almost seven hours since the kid on his third day of a meth high nearly shoved the muzzle of the Glock up his right nostril. His nose had stopped bleeding but his hands were still shaking.

Moira had sat up and blinked at him, her eyes glowing like a cat's in the shimmer of her night-light. Three days shy of fifteen and she slept with a night-light. A pink plastic seashell that Janine bought her before she went into the hospital the last time.

"You okay, Jo-Jo?" That's what Moira called him instead of Dad.

"I will be, Smooch." Joe pressed his thumb and index finger to his eyes to keep back tears. "How 'bout you?"

Moira went up on her knees, wrapped her arms around

his neck and laid her cheek against his shoulder. "I thought you'd been shot."

"No. What you heard was Brian's shotgun." All Joe heard when the meth head screeched at him to kiss the concrete and kicked the cell phone out of his hand was Moira's scream in his ear.

She didn't ask him if the kid with the Glock was dead. In all the years since, she'd never asked him.

"I'm going back tomorrow." Joe swept his arms around her, held her fiercely. "Just long enough to quit."

He didn't say *You're all I have left of Janine and I thought I'd never see you again.* It stuck in his throat, ached there, but he didn't say it.

"Go to sleep, Jo-Jo. We'll talk in the morning." Moira hugged him as tight as she could. "Can I stay home from school?"

Joe laughed. Moira smiled and crawled under the covers. After she fell asleep, he stretched out on the foot of her bed, buried his face in an armful of pink gingham quilt and cried.

He woke up at nine-thirty. Moira was in the kitchen in her school uniform mixing pancake batter.

"Where's Gramma Evie?" he asked cautiously.

"She went home." Moira grinned. "I promised her I'd go to school, so you'd better call and excuse me."

Joe made the phone call to St. Pius High, his alma mater, while Moira made the pancakes. They were perfect, feather light, perfectly brown. On bad days, when Janine couldn't breathe without oxygen, Joe would come home and find her in the kitchen teaching Moira how to make some dish, like scalloped potatoes. He'd force her to bed, carry her if necessary, but she wouldn't stay.

"I have to show Moira how to make the white sauce,"

she'd say. "I have a lot to teach her and not much time to do it."

While they ate, Joe told her what had happened. When he finished, Moira folded her still-skinny little-girl arms on the table.

"You like being a cop," she said. "But you don't like guns."

"It's not that I don't like them, Smooch. It's that I never want to have another one shoved up my nose. Ever again."

"So what can you do that's like being a cop only you don't have to carry a gun?"

"Dunno," Joe said. He still wasn't thinking clearly. "Drive a cab?"

"Oh, please, Jo-Jo. It's soooo simple. You should be a detective."

Since Joseph Kerr, Inc., Private Investigations was Moira's idea it was only fitting that she should be the first person he hired. She was in high school, so she could work only half days, but in the beginning Joe was lucky to have a half day's work.

Moira ran the office from her bedroom. Answered the phone, did the invoicing (such as it was) talked to clients and scheduled jobs on the PC she used for her school-work. Joe sleuthed by day and worked nights in the lime-stone caves along the Missouri River unloading freight.

When Moira graduated from St. Pius and enrolled at UMCK on a full academic scholarship, Joe quit unload-ing trucks at night. A year later Brian destroyed his left knee chasing a felon over a fence. He retired from the force with a small medical pension and Joe hired him.

The third person he hired was Stink, Andrew Stinken-sky, the geek down the block in Evie's neighborhood.

Stink had it bad to be a cop and less than a snowball's chance in hell of passing the physical. He ran track in college, joined the wrestling team and lifted weights, but there's only so much you can do with a ninety-seven-pound weakling physique.

When he flunked the department physical for the third time, Sam and his wife and kids and Joe and Moira and Brian were at Evie's for a cookout. Stink wandered over to have a beer with them. As gently as he could, Sam told Stink he really needed to find something else to do with his life. Stink burst into tears. Joe hired him on the spot.

"What are you doing, Joseph?" Sam looked at him like he was nuts. "Stink can't lift a sack of flour with both hands."

Joe tapped his temple. "No brawn, Sam, but brains out the kazoo. Stink has degrees in physics and computer science. Did you know that?"

"You've already got the Gonzo King." Sam nodded at Brian, his long hair tied back, a beer in one hand, a spatula in the other at the grill. "Now you've got Stink. A freak and a geek."

"Careful, Sam," Joe warned. "That freak saved my life."

"Hicks was a good cop, but he's a flake."

"Brian is my friend and Stink is all right."

"What're you gonna do, Joe? Hire every misfit and goofball you meet? Should I send all the department rejects your way?"

"Yeah," Joe said. "Why don't you do that, Sam?"

Now in its seventh year, Joseph Kerr, Inc., Private Investigations had a nice suite of offices in Brookside, southwest of the Country Club Plaza. Three dozen corporations depended on JKI for employee background checks and security clearances—Moira's area of expertise, two dozen legal firms counted on JKI to do their legwork and at any given time there were another half dozen or so jobs like the one at Savard Creations.

The agency specialized in white-collar crime and industrial espionage, pulled in nearly four million a year, paid its twenty-seven full-time employees exceptionally well and provided them with a benefits package that would make a U.S. congressman drool.

Most of Joe's employees were misfits or head cases like he was—an ex-cop who broke out in a cold sweat at the sight of a gun.

Next to his brother Sam, Brian was the savviest cop he'd ever known. Eyes in the back of his head and a sixth sense for danger like Will Robinson's robot on *Lost in Space*. Street smarts and a naturally suspicious mind. He spent most of his time in a Galaxy Far Far Away.

Now and then Joe let Stink do something like night rounds in the Savard Building with Carlos to make him feel less geeky, but his value was his expertise with computers and electronics. He understood quantum physics and could explain it so it almost made sense to Joe.

Carlos Garcia was a referral from Sam. A cop who truly loved donuts and had lost his battle to meet the department weight limit. Working for Joe, he could stay pleasantly plump, but it was a mistake to write him off as a lard-ass. Carlos was strong as an ox, fleet as a deer. He'd agreed to join the ranks of the maintenance department at Savard Creations.

Moira discovered Imogene Tyler in her kickboxing class. An EMT on sabbatical due to serious burnout.

When Lucien Savard told him to make sure the new assistant in design was a she with a pretty face, Joe thought of Imogene. Her street smarts rivaled Brian's.

For the mail room position Joe selected Ricky LeHay, one of the new kids on the JKI roster, a recent law grad taking night courses in law enforcement. Ricky loved alternative rock and spent Friday and Saturday nights hanging out in Westport listening to the newest bands.

To work with Zippy in human resources, Joe tapped Brian's ex-mother-in-law, Betty Sanders, one of JKI's part-timers, a retired legal secretary. Betty had a paralegal degree, astonishing computer skills and a nose that could smell a lie a mile away.

For the vacancy in IT, Stink was a natural. It would also keep him on-site to monitor the new security installations. He came to the meeting Joe called at one P.M. Saturday in the small break room in the security office of Savard's, brushing bits of drywall and insulation off his clothes.

"How's it going?" Joe asked. Stink and his team, eight of his techie friends he recruited for jobs like this, had been at it since six A.M.

"Good." Stink dropped into a chair, a small, thin man dwarfed by dark, brawny and big-as-a-house Carlos. "We're on schedule for the grand unveiling tomorrow afternoon."

"Everybody ready?" Joe looked around the break room table at his team: Moira, Imogene, Ricky, Brian, Betty. And Uncle Pete to answer any questions about the building or Savard employees. "Anybody need anything? Coffee?" Joe grinned at Carlos. "Donuts?"

"Bite me," Carlos said, and grinned back at him.

"Okay, Stink." Joe leaned back in his folding chair. "You're the leadoff hitter. Get us started."

"This place had no safeguards," Stink said. "Two ancient cameras in the parking garage, Pete at the kiosk, with three daytime guys and two for overnight. All five guys rotate the weekend watch. Five guys spread over seven floors, eight major departments and a dozen smaller ones. Three exits. The front, the parking garage and a fire door on three to the garage roof. Nearly twenty miles of stairwell. The rankest amateur on the planet could walk out of here with just about anything, anytime they wanted. No offense, Pete."

"None taken," Joe's uncle replied. "I harped and Luke Savard harped, but Lucien wouldn't hear of anything tougher. Till now, that is."

"No system is foolproof," Stink said. "But the one we're putting in should stop the amateurs. The garage cameras will cover every inch of every parking space. The ones we're putting in the building will watch the departments with the highest traffic, the most ins and outs during the day, and the cafeteria. Ready with the bugs, boss, when you are."

"I need to wander around some more to find the hot spots," Joe told him. "Hallways, alcoves, any nook or cranny that Savard folk duck into for a few out-of-earshot words. Brian, what do you have from subbing for Pete at the kiosk yesterday?"

"A lot of phone numbers." Brian grinned. "The log is instituted. Visitors and employees sign in and out. Visitors with their destination, and they will be tailed. I'm working with Pete's guys later today to show them how to shadow somebody."

"We can't cover every inch of this building," Stink

said. "It's too big and there aren't enough of us. Just thought I'd mention it."

"I know," Joe said. "Still, we're operating on the MO that the thief is inside and all we gotta do is catch him or her doing something hinky."

"Speaking of hinky," Brian said. "Pete and I went over his security logs this morning and double-checked them with our brothers in blue. No break-ins in the last year and only four false alarms. Two since the first of September, the date you gave me on the phone last night."

"Tell us about them," Joe said.

"On September seventeenth, Rudy Savard forgot his key for the garage gate and couldn't remember the override code. The second was on Thursday the twenty-first at eleven thirty-eight P.M. on the third floor. The fire door to the garage roof. I talked to the Savard security guy who had the watch that night. When he checked it, the door was ajar. Either someone went out of it, or opened it to draw him up there while they exited the building another way. It's not a goosey door. I checked it myself."

"First thing for you, Imogene," Joe said to the new assistant in the design department. "Find out if any of the designers were in the building late on Thursday, September twenty-first. Let me know ASAP."

"Will do, Joe," she replied.

"Is your paperwork with Zippy all in order?"

"Yes. The five of us," Imogene said, nodding at Ricky, Betty, Carlos and Stink, "went through orientation with Mr. Burkholtz yesterday."

"Can you all handle the positions here?" Joe asked. "If you can't, tell me now. You want to look new, not inept. That will draw attention."

"I have the assignments and the schedule for tailing the

members of the Savard family," Moira said. "I e-mailed
it to all of you this morning so you'll know who else is
working on this case with you. Keep your cell phones
charged but on vibrate. Same for your JKI beeper. Check
your messages every hour if you can. Return calls outside the Savard Building only. Do you all know the panic
code for this assignment?"

"One-one-two," everyone said in unison.

"Your JKI beeper has a GPS chip," Joe said. "If you
end up in a tight spot and feel threatened, use the code.
If any one of you receives a one-one-two on your beeper
from anyone else assigned to this case, call 911. Don't
assume someone else called. You call."

The JKI beepers and the panic code was SOP on every
job. Joe didn't imagine for one second that any of them
would need it.

"Next meeting is my place tomorrow at six P.M.," he
said. "We'll do a final run-through and eat chili."

Everyone groaned. Joe scowled.

"I'm not making the chili," he said. "My mother is."

Everyone cheered. Joe laughed and his cell phone
buzzed. The caller ID screen showed Lucien and Petra
Savard's home number.

"Hello, Joe. It's Mia Savard. Lucien was just served a
subpoena. Oren Angel is suing him for slander and harassment. Mother thought—" A loud bang in the background interrupted Mia. "That was a book hitting the
wall. Walter Vance is on his way. Mother thought you
should come, too, if you can."

"I'll be right there," Joe said, and disconnected.

11

SEVERAL TIMES MIA TRIED to introduce Terence to Lucien and Petra. She arranged a traditional meet-the-parents dinner, a couple of casual lunches, a Sunday brunch and a get-together at Blanko's for drinks.

Eich time Terence said he was too busy, he had an out-of-town shoot or he simply canceled at the last minute with no explanation.

Three good reasons why Mia should've known he was a bum.

Joe Kerr showed up at her parents' front door within ten minutes.

An excellent sign. Now, if she could just figure out if, when he said he liked her, he meant he liked her or he *liked* her.

He smiled when she opened the door. It was snowing again, just spitting. A few flecks of white glistened in his dark hair. The afternoon sky hung low and gray behind him. He stood on the brick porch between potted rosemary bushes that smelled fragrant in the cold air. Any day now her mother would tie red velvet bows on them for the holidays.

"Thanks for coming." Mia opened the door wider so he could step inside. He'd changed clothes since he'd left her apartment. Navy pants, a blue shirt, a multicolored striped sweater and the dark wool overcoat.

"Not a problem." He stood on the indoor mat and shrugged out of his coat. "I don't hear anything hitting the wall."

"He's calmed down. Walter Vance is here. They're in the library with Uncle Rudy. My mother, Luke and Jenna, too."

"Almost the whole fam damily." He smiled again and Mia's pulse fluttered. She was a fool for spoonerisms.

As she held her hand out to take Joe's coat, Tilde appeared out of nowhere and snatched it away from her.

"What do you think you're doing? I'm the maid around here!" she shouted at Mia, and glared at Joe. "I suppose you want coffee, too."

Joe held his hands up and backed away. "No, ma'am."

"Wipe your feet!" Tilde flung a gnarled finger at the mat and stalked away with Joe's fine merino wool overcoat.

"Jesus and Mary," he said. "Who the hell is that?"

"Tilde the Terrible," Mia said. "Our maid."

The library pocket doors were opened a notch, just enough for Petra to peer between them.

"I thought I heard Tilde," she said.

"You did," Mia said. "But she's gone now."

Petra slid the doors apart, stepped into the hallway and closed them behind her. Her mother looked wonderful—she always did—in a dusty pink sweater and trousers and one of her soft-hued shawls.

"Joseph." Petra held her hand out to Joe. "Thank you for coming. We were just having coffee. Would you like some?"

"No, thank you, Mrs. Savard. I'd like to see the sub-poena."

"So would Walter," Petra said. "You can both read it once Lucien has Scotch-taped it back together."

"Oh. Well." The corners of Joe's mouth twitched, but just a little. "Then coffee sounds nice. Thank you."

"Lovely. I'll be just a moment." Petra turned away.

A crash echoed up the hallway and her mother froze.

"Oh dear," she said. "Tilde is still in the kitchen."

"Look at your clock, Mother." Mia nodded at the Hepplewhite grandfather clock Petra had inherited from her great-aunt.

It stood against the walnut-paneled flank of the stair-case that rose up the wall just past the library doors. The clock was even older than Tilde. Joe cocked a curious eyebrow at Mia.

"Wait for it," she said, and a second later the gilt second-hand notched straight up on three P.M.

Three deep melodious chimes reverberated through the hallway. Mia stood close enough to feel them quiver in the nape of her neck. Then a boom echoed from the kitchen, the slam of Tilde's bedroom door.

"Saved by the bell," Petra said. "I really will be just a moment now."

She smiled at Joe and headed for the kitchen.

"Nap time," Mia explained. "Tilde won't wake up till after dinner."

"There's a break." Joe grinned.

"There's the living room." Mia waved him toward the open pocket door across from the library. "I'll check on your coat. Sometimes Tilde forgets where she puts things."

Tilde never forgot a thing, but the ruse got Mia away

from Joe. His overcoat lay over the back of a tartan plaid sofa in the great room that spread across the back of the house and adjoined the kitchen. Petra stood at the marble-topped counter that separated the two rooms, filling the gold-banded Spode server from a sterling silver urn the size of a small potbellied stove. She'd hauled it out for lunch to make sure Luke would have plenty of strong French Roast.

"Mother." Mia leaned on the counter from the great room side. "You've *got* to tell Dad about the photo. You can't put it off any longer."

"On top of a subpoena for slander and harassment?" Petra looked at her like she'd lost her mind. "I can't do that to him."

"What if Dad got the subpoena because of the photograph?"

"It says harassment. Not peering in a dirty warehouse window."

"That could be construed as harassment."

Petra frowned. "I wish you'd stop watching *Law & Order*."

"Listen to me, Mother. Luke made a good point. What if the guy with the camera didn't follow us? What if—"

"You told Luke?" Petra interrupted. "Why on earth?"

"If we end up dead, someone should know why. As Luke pointed out, maybe the guy was already there. Maybe he works for Heavenly Bridals. That would explain how he recognized you."

"Hmm." Petra's eyes narrowed, her lips pursed. She was thinking about it. Good. Then she shook her head and gave Mia a subject-closed look. "I still can't tell your father. He's had enough for one day."

"But Mother," Mia argued. "What if the two things are related?"

"What two things?" Luke asked.

Mia turned away from the counter and saw him coming toward them across the great room with his coffee cup.

"The photograph I told you about and the subpoena."

"Remind me." Luke stopped next to Mia and handed Petra his cup and saucer. "What time were you at Heavenly Bridals yesterday?"

Mia looked at her mother. "Noonish, wasn't it?"

"More or less." Petra shrugged.

"Then the wheels of justice would've had to turn at the speed of light," Luke said. "Why did you go out there, Mother?"

"Your father wouldn't talk to Oren, so I decided I would." Petra refilled Luke's cup from the urn and gave it back to him. "Now Mia wants me to rush in there and tell your father about the photograph."

"Hmm." Luke sipped his coffee and looked at Mia over the rim of his cup. "Not a good time, mite. Not today."

"You guys!" Mia stamped her foot and felt like an idiot. "Sorry. I just really think that the sooner Dad finds out about this, the better."

"Normally I'd agree," Luke said. "But he's foaming at the mouth already. And you don't have to listen to him when we leave. Mother does."

"Oh." Mia glanced at Petra. "Sorry, Mom."

"It's all right, Mia." She smiled. "It's been a long week for us all."

"And it's not over." Luke picked up the sterling silver

tray Petra had arranged with the Spode server, two cups and saucers, the cream, the sugar, napkins and spoons and carried it into the living room.

Joe sat on the flowered chintz sofa with Walter Vance, their knees pressed against the coffee table as they hunched over a trifolded set of taped-together papers. Jenna sat with Rudy on the window seat. Mia and her mother paused in the doorway.

Lucien paced like a caged white tiger in front of the fire.

"Tell me, Walter," he growled at Savard's legal counsel. "How did Benedict Arnold get that suit filed so quickly?"

"Angel told Mr. Kerr yesterday morning that you'd be hearing from his attorney." Walter put his pen down and glanced at Mia's mother. "And forgive me, Petra, but if Oren knew the design came from Savard's he could've been ready with the suit, anticipating Lucien's response."

"The subpoena doesn't prove that, does it?" Petra asked.

"No," Walter said. "And so far as proof goes, I'm amazed the court accepted such flimsy grounds. It cites 'accusations of fraud and theft,' but it doesn't give specifics, like where, when or to whom. The harassment proof is even weaker. 'Defendant sent persons to plaintiff's place of business for sole purpose of harassment.' Well." Walter glanced at Joe. "Maybe the judge who issued this sees double, but you look like only one person to me."

The other two persons, Mia suspected, stood in the doorway.

Thank God, she thought, linking fingers with Petra.

Thank God Oren Angel didn't list our names. Luke set the tray on a round table near the window seat, turned and shot Mia a keep-your-mouth-shut glare.

Only she wasn't sure how much longer she could. Mia tugged her mother's fingers. When Petra inclined her head, Mia whispered, "I can't stand this. I'm leaving before I shoot off my mouth."

"I *will* tell him," Petra whispered back, and kissed her cheek.

Mia went to the great room for Joe's overcoat. When she laid it over the arm of the flowered chintz sofa beside him, he glanced up at her from the notes Walter Vance was making on a small pad of paper.

"Thanks. Are you leaving?"

"Duty calls." Mia smiled and turned toward her father, caught Lucien as he turned to pace in the other direction and slipped her arms around his waist. "I'm sorry this happened, Dad. I have to go."

"You're leaving?" Lucien caught her hands. "Why?"

"I have a wedding gown to make for Alicia Whitcomb."

"I'd almost forgotten." Lucien pulled her close. "What a good girl you are to think of the governor and his daughter at a time like this." He put a kiss on her cheek and said in her ear, "You always were the best behaved, but don't tell your brother or your sister."

"They won't hear it from me." She gave him a peck on the cheek.

Mia felt Joe's eyes on her as she left the living room, and stifled a whimper. She'd planned to hang around till he left and sort of drift to the door with him in hopes that he'd ask her for coffee or something.

She'd hung her coat, a red wool jacket to replace her

purple stadium coat, which needed to be cleaned, in the closet under the stairs; her purse over the hanger inside the jacket. Mia opened the zipper and made sure Alicia's design was still tucked in the pocket in the lining.

She'd forgotten she was still carrying the design, but it was just as well. During lunch it struck her that the neckline she and Alicia had settled on reminded her of a neckline she thought she'd seen on a gown in another designer's line. She couldn't think whose, but it was bothering her. She really should check it out before she went any further.

The design department's vast library of bridal magazines and catalogs from other designers would've been the quickest way to double-check the neckline, but the Savard Building was off-limits this weekend while the new security system was installed. Uncle Rudy had been there this morning, but that was typical Uncle Rudy.

Mia had some reference materials at home in her sewing room, but she didn't want to go home. She wanted to gaze into Joe Kerr's blue eyes over a double mocha latte and melt as fast as the whipped cream, but that probably wasn't going to happen.

At least till Joe found out who stole Alicia's wedding dress and she figured out if he liked her or he *liked* her.

Mia shivered out to her Subaru, still ice-cold from spending the night in a parking garage. She started the engine, and while she waited for the heated seats to warm, she dug her cell phone out of her purse, stuck the hands-free bud in her right ear and speed dialed Jordan.

She got her voice mail and left a message, wove the Subaru around the house, made a right onto the curved drive in front and cruised past Walter Vance's silver Lincoln Town Car. She'd never seen the dark blue older model Ford Explorer parked behind it. Must be Joe's ride.

Mia grinned at herself in the rearview and wiggled in her toasty-warm seat. She loved detective speak.

She made a left out of her parents' driveway onto Ward Parkway and headed for the Plaza, turned the wipers on intermittent and speed dialed Becca. She answered on the second ring. Out of breath, like she'd just run up the stairs.

"I'm going shopping," Mia said. "Want to meet me?"

"Oh, gosh, I would, but my hair is a mess."

"Oh, please. Your hair. I spent half the night on the bathroom floor. How do you think *I* look?"

"I can't, Mia. I—" Something went *thump* in the background. "Ow!" Becca sucked air between her teeth. "I'm in the middle of something. Call me later. I'll wash my hair and we'll catch a movie."

Becca hung up. Mia pulled the bud out of her ear, turned off her phone and clenched the wheel, suddenly so angry she had a lump in her throat. She'd been abandoned by Becca and Jordan and betrayed by the person who'd stolen her design. Who was it? How could she find out?

Mia left the Subaru in a parking garage and started her rounds of the bridal boutiques on the Plaza. The shops were blocks apart, but it felt good to walk. The Christmas displays in the windows made her smile.

Well, it felt good for a couple of hours. By then, she'd looked at so many wedding gowns her eyes were starting to cross and her head was pounding. It was nearly five-thirty and nearly dark when she pushed through the glass door of the sixth boutique she'd visited onto an icy, snow-blown sidewalk. The temperature had dropped like a rock and it was snowing like crazy.

Time to go home, Mia decided. No one else had used the neckline Alicia wanted, so she could finish the design.

The outside lights that came on under the eaves of the house she shared with Robin and Becca glared like signal beacons on the new snow drifting across the front yard. The uphill drive looked nasty, but her sure-footed Subaru climbed it in first gear as easy as a cat went up a tree.

There were no lights on in Robin's first-floor apartment, which was typical on weekends. If he didn't stay with a girl, he took off on an overnight someplace with his friends.

Only a single lamp in the bay window burned on the second floor. That surprised Mia. Becca's big night out was Friday. She usually stayed in on Saturday.

Her place was dark, too. Mia hadn't thought she'd be out till—she glanced at the dash clock—almost six, so she hadn't left a light on.

She was cold and tired and her head felt like it was about to split open. No way could she focus on Alicia's dress with this headache.

Mia soaked in the Jacuzzi, which helped her head, slathered on moisturizer and slid into green flannel pj's. She wasn't hungry, but ate two pieces of toast with a cup of tea so she could take two more Tylenol.

No messages on the answering machine. Her cell phone was still off and could stay that way. Screw the world.

Mia felt her mad coming back and went to bed. Turned on the TV in the cherry armoire, curled under the covers and konked out. She slept through a Matt Damon movie and woke up partway through the ten o'clock news, in time to catch the weather. No more snow for at least the next week, the forecaster said.

"Yeah, right." Mia pushed Off on the remote. "I live in Missouri. I'll believe it when I see it."

She threw back the covers, made herself another cup of tea and looked around her apartment for a safer place than her purse to keep Alicia's design once she was finished with it. There was a small wall safe behind a Maxfield Parrish print in her study. Not much in it: insurance policies, her car title, the deed to the house, a few pieces of good jewelry she'd inherited from Lucien's mother. Probably the best place for the design.

Her sewing room would likely be cold from being closed up, so Mia put on jeans, a white cotton turtleneck under a red Kansas City Chiefs sweatshirt, warm socks and clogs. With her keys and the design, she let herself out the front door, which she left ajar because she'd probably be back and forth, and crossed the foyer to her sewing room. The vinyl-clad steel security door was just like her apartment door, a lock in the knob and a brass dead bolt above.

Mia undid both locks and opened the door. The room was large, the same size as her living room and dining room, had the same bay window in the west-facing front wall of the house. Long tall windows on the straight-ahead north wall. She could see their outline in the glare cast by the outside lights. The floor was bare hardwood, so the room was as chilly as she'd expected.

Mia felt for the wall switch on her right, found it and flipped on the lights. Four round halogen fixtures were spaced around the high, twelve-foot ceiling; six banks of long fluorescent tubes suspended by chains lit her worktables.

None of the lights were instant-on. The halogens hummed and flickered. The neon tubes fluttered, then lit with a zip of bright white glare that illuminated the wreck of her sewing room.

Her pattern and cutting tables were overturned; most of her supplies swept off the shelves that lined the walls. Yards and yards of fabric had been ripped off their bolts; spools of trim and ribbon tangled in piles. Books were tossed on their crumpled pages and torn jackets. The plastic bins that held notions—pins, thread, seam tape, chalk for marking patterns and material, a zillion things—were emptied and thrown, their contents scattered all over the floor.

Alicia's design. The thought shot like a laser through her head.

Mia left the lights on, the door open, went back into her apartment and shut and locked the door. Her hands shook as she opened her purse, but the design was still there in the pocket. Mia almost fainted. She found Joe's card and called him from the French telephone on the living room desk. He answered.

"Someone broke into my sewing room. Should I call the police?"

"Yes. Are you all right? How about your apartment?"

"I'm fine. My apartment is fine. My sewing room is a wreck."

"Call 911. I'm on my way."

12

JOE THOUGHT HE'D TIMED his arrival at Mia's place just right.

Allowing for slick, snowpacked streets, fifteen minutes for the patrol guys to show up, another twenty for the crime lab techs to unload and set up their gear. But as Joe turned onto Mia's cul-de-sac, he passed one patrol car on its way out. Another sat at the curb in front of her pink stucco house, its emergency flashers blinking patches of yellow light on the snow. The crime lab guys were packing up their van.

Joe parked behind the squad car and swung out of his truck. A frigid wind had whipped out of the north behind the snow, plummeting the temperature into the teens. A nasty night to be a cop on the streets.

The tire treads he followed up the drive were already iced over. Same for the footprints marking the walk. Joe crunched through them to the first-floor front door.

This wasn't his first visit to the vestibule. He'd taken her keys and checked it out last night while Mia slept. The pneumatic glass door on the inside stood open on its rubber-tipped kickstand. Joe stepped past it, his ID ready, and held it up to the patrolman coming down the steps.

"Evening." He read the brass nameplate affixed to the officer's jacket: SGT. M. SMITH. "Joe Kerr. I'm a PI."

Sergeant Smith stopped at the foot of the stairs, read Joe's ID and nodded. "You related to Sam Kerr?"

"Yeah. I'm his baby brother."

"Heard of you. Do you have an interest here?"

"I'm working for Lucien Savard. Savard Creations. Mia Savard's father." Joe nodded up the stairs, then at Sergeant Smith. "You fellas on the night crew work fast."

"The perp is upstairs with the vic." Sgt. M. Smith smiled. "You can pick up a copy of our report on Monday." He handed Joe a card. "Case number is on the back."

"Thanks." Joe tipped the card toward him. "Stay safe."

"Will do." The sergeant nodded and left, kicking the door off its stand and letting it shut with a sigh behind him.

The perp was upstairs with the vic? This Joe had to see. He took the stairs two at a time to the third floor and knocked on Mia's door.

"Come in," she called. "It's open."

Mia sat on her pink-flowered sofa, her hands on her knees. On the cushion beside her stood a Siamese cat. The cat turned its head toward Joe and meowed, its blue eyes so crossed they were painful to look at.

"Who's your friend?" Joe asked.

"This is Becca's cat, Cocoa."

"How did she get up here?" Joe shrugged out of his overcoat.

"A better question is how she got into my sewing room."

"The cops think the cat wrecked the place?"

"I can't blame them, I guess." Mia rested her elbows on her knees and rubbed her hands over her face. "I told them what happened, I showed them the room. The crime lab was just starting to test for fingerprints, when out popped Cocoa from under a pile of velvet."

"Did they dust for prints?" Joe asked, and Mia shook her head no. "Do you want to show me or do you want me to look for myself?"

"I'll go with you." Mia rose from the sofa and led the way.

The cat followed her. It was pigeon-toed as well as cross-eyed and moved like it had arthritis. Joe followed the cat.

The sewing room door was open, the lights on. Joe surveyed the wreck of the perfectly ordered space he'd scoped out last night after the vestibule, then eyed the cat sitting in the doorway. Cocoa meowed. A grating fingernails-on-a-blackboard meow.

"Is that cat as old as she looks?"

"Almost thirteen. She was Becca's sixteenth birthday present."

"My mother had a Siamese that could go on some pretty impressive rampages when it got wound up." Joe looked at the room, then at Mia, standing beside him staring at the mess. "Do you think Cocoa did this?"

"I think she could have done some of it. Knocked the books and the other things off the shelves. I can't imagine how she overturned the tables and opened the plastic bins. They snap shut. Or how she managed to strew the contents all over the floor."

Neither could Joe. "When the cops decided Cocoa

was the culprit, did you disagree with them? Register an objection?"

"No. I didn't know what to say. But I can tell you this. No way in hell did Cocoa unwind twenty yards of velvet from a bolt."

Mia was getting pissed. Joe didn't blame her.

"I'll tell you why the cops nailed Cocoa for this. A burglar wouldn't have bothered with this room. He would've gone for your apartment. Your TV. DVD player. Jewelry. Small valuables he could snatch quickly and sell even quicker, but your apartment wasn't touched. Did they check Becca's place and Robin's?"

"Yes." Mia sighed. "I have keys. I went with them. It didn't look to me like anything was missing."

"I'm guessing there were no signs of forced entry, or the cops would still be here." Joe nodded at the sewing room. "That's why this looked like mischief to them and nothing more."

Mia turned toward him. "Do you think this is mischief?"

Joe studied her face. He had to draw a breath first, so he wouldn't get distracted, so he could focus on what he needed to see, not what he wanted to see—her lashes sweeping down, her lips parting as he bent his head to kiss her.

Her eyes were a little on the glittery side. She was pissed, probably shook up, too, but her voice was steady and her shoulders were loose, her arms and hands relaxed at her sides.

"Yes, I think it's mischief, but not feline mischief. Where's the design for Alicia Whitcomb's new dress?"

"It's been in my purse since last night. I called 911 and

then I locked it in the wall safe in my study. Do you think the thief did this?"

"Besides me, who knew the design was in your purse?"

"No one. I didn't tell anyone where I'd put it, not even Dad."

"Has anyone asked you about the new design?"

Mia thought about it, catching the tip of her tongue in the corner of her mouth. Joe wished she wouldn't do that.

"At Blanko's Jordan asked me if I'd come up with a design for Alicia. I told her I couldn't talk about it. Lucien's orders."

"She knew that Alicia had chosen you over DeMello?"

"Damien couldn't get back to design to tell everyone fast enough."

"At the close of business yesterday, how many people knew that Alicia had chosen you to design her new wedding dress?" Joe held up his left hand, fingers spread. "So far as you know, count them off for me."

"My parents. Luke and Jenna. The governor, Mrs. Whitcomb and Alicia. Damien, Arlene, Kiley, Jordan and Evan."

"What about Becca?" Joe asked.

"She knew when I got to Blanko's last night. No, wait. I'm not sure about that. I may be assuming. If she didn't know before I got there, she did when Jordan asked me about it."

"Your father didn't give you any special instructions? Like guard the new design with your life? He just told you not to discuss it?"

"That's all. I took the design with me because I didn't think it was smart to leave it in the building with a thief running around."

"You made the right call," Joe said.

It irritated him that Lucien Savard had made the wrong call. After the heavy emphasis Joe had put on security with Savard's CEO, Lucien *should* have taken precautions. He was not a stupid man. Set in his ways and arrogant as hell, but not stupid.

"What do you normally do with the stuff on your drawing board at the end of the day?"

"We each have a portfolio. About this size." Mia held her arms out a foot or so, then from her shoulder to mid-thigh in a square shape. "It's basically a big accordion file. Our supply room has a fireproof cabinet that locks. We put our portfolios with our sketches and designs inside in the cabinet."

"Is the lock on the cabinet combination or a key?"

"It's a key, and yes, I have one. So do Damien and my father. Jenna and Luke, probably. My mother might. I'd bet Pete does."

"The other designers?" Joe asked, and Mia shook her head no.

At her feet, Cocoa yawned. Then she stretched, gave one of her rusty-gate meows and started into the sewing room.

"No, Cocoa." Mia scooped up the cat. "I think I'll take her home."

"Does she get out of Becca's place much and wander around?"

"Not often." Mia rubbed Cocoa's ears. "She doesn't sit by the door and wait for a chance to escape. She comes up with Becca. She never goes down to Robin's place. He calls her Cuckoo and she doesn't like it. She got shut up in his place once and peed in his bathtub."

"Has she been in here before?" Joe nodded at the sewing room. "Has she ever done anything like this?"

"She's been in here with Becca and me a couple times," Mia said. "She pokes around at stuff. She's a cat, she's curious. It's what they do. I've never heard Becca say she's destructive."

"Okay." Joe nodded. "Take her home. I'll stay here."

He waited till Mia fetched her keys from her apartment and headed downstairs with the cat. Then he took a slow, careful walk around the sewing room, stepping over and around piles of fabrics and sewing stuff. He didn't believe for two seconds that Cocoa had done this.

"Ay-yi-yi," Mia said from the doorway. "What a mess."

Joe stopped on the far side of the room, near the big windows that faced north above the driveway. He turned and looked at Mia.

"When can I start cleaning this up?" she asked.

"That depends on how you want to play this."

"Play this?" She tipped her head at him. "What do you mean?"

"If Cocoa didn't wreck your sewing room, who did?"

Mia laid a hand on her chest. "You're asking me?"

"I'm asking you. Who do you think did this?"

"I think the thief did it. I think he was looking for the new design."

"If it was the thief and he came for the design, then he had to believe he'd find it here. So tell me again. As of last night, who knew Alicia had chosen you over DeMello?"

"What you mean," Mia said sharply, "is if I'm right and it was the thief who did this, then the thief is either Damien or one of the other designers, my parents, my brother, my sister or my cousin Becca."

"That's what I'm saying, yes."

"Uncle Rudy said today that he can't believe anyone who works for Savard's would do this. Neither can I. And I don't believe anyone *named* Savard would steal the design and give it to Heavenly Bridals."

Joe could've said: *One of them did. One of them took it out of your portfolio or filched it off your e-mail,* but he didn't. He would, but not until Mia was ready to go there with him.

Instead he said, "If the thief didn't come here for the design, then he came for the sole purpose of wrecking your sewing room. He did this to distract me, to give me and my people something else to chase, or he did it to point the finger at someone else."

"Robin or Becca," Mia said. "Access and opportunity."

"I'll make a detective out of you yet."

She missed the smile he gave her. She'd looked away, already moved on, her quick mind caught on something else. Access and opportunity, Joe guessed. She was thinking that over. Or she'd remembered something she wasn't sure she wanted to tell him.

"What did you do when you left your parents' house?"

"I went shopping. The neckline of the dress Alicia and I came up with reminded me of a gown I thought I'd seen someplace else. I hit a few of the bridal boutiques to check it out. I got home about six."

"Were Robin and Becca here?" Joe moved around the room, aware that Mia was watching him.

"No. And they still aren't here. I checked while I was downstairs." That was smart of her, Joe thought. "When I got home, I took a spin in the Jacuzzi, put my pj's on and sacked out for a while. I woke up a little after ten and decided to work on the design. I got dressed, because it's chilly in here, unlocked the door, and you know the rest."

"Did you see anyone? Talk to anyone while you were out?"

"I called Becca on my cell just as I left Mom and Dad's. I asked her if she wanted to go shopping. She didn't."

"Where was she when you talked to her?" Joe stopped prowling and turned toward Mia. "What was she doing?"

"She was home." Mia shrugged. "I don't know what she was doing."

Yes, she did. She didn't pull her gaze away, but something flickered in her eyes. She didn't trust him, and she was still in denial that a family member or someone she worked with every day was a traitor and a thief.

"What do you mean by how I want to play this?" Mia asked.

"You have two choices. One, clean up the mess and pretend this never happened. Unless one of the neighbors asks Becca or Robin what the cops were doing here Saturday night, you might get away with it. Two, make a joke out of it. Tell the world that Cocoa the cat broke into your sewing room and had a field day."

"Okay," Mia said. "Which one do you recommend?"

"Make a joke out of it. The closer you can stay to the facts as they appear, the better. Blame it on the cat, laugh it up and take steps to make sure this never happens again. Change the locks on this door and your apartment and don't give copies to anyone. How many people have keys to your place now?"

"Becca and Robin and my parents have keys to my apartment. I have the only keys to the sewing room."

"No you don't," Joe said as kindly as possible. "No signs of forced entry. Whoever did this has the keys. How about Terence the Bum?"

"No. I offered, but he declined. I don't make a habit of that," Mia added, a slight but becoming flush pinking her cheeks. "Passing out keys to my apartment to men, I mean."

"Do you lock up your purse at work?"

"Um, no. My desk drawer locks, but it's a pain in the neck."

"Then get used to having your neck hurt."

"Wait a minute. You're going too fast." Mia held up one hand. "Do you think the thief did this or not?"

"If not the thief, then he has an accomplice."

Mia's eyes widened. "You mean you're looking for two people?"

"Could be. Do I think the thief came for the new design? Possible, but I doubt it. I think he came to do this and throw me off his trail."

"I hope you're right." Mia chafed her arms, like a chill had run through her. "The design was next door and I was asleep."

"You didn't sleep through this." Joe smiled to reassure her. "As the saying goes, it would've wakened the dead. This was done between the time you left to have lunch with your family and the time you got home."

"I hope you're right about that, too." Mia rubbed her arms again.

"Whoever did this wore gloves, I'll bet, but if it'll help you sleep, I have a print crew of my own. I'm not talking *CSI*, but I can have them dust this room, see if they can find anything."

"Would you?" Mia gave a gusty sigh. "Can they come tonight?"

Joe unclipped his cell phone from his belt. "Let me make a call."

"I'll make coffee," Mia said, and went back to her apartment.

Joe dialed Brian and told him what had happened.

"I'm bettin' Larry will be up for it," Brian said. "I'll call him."

"Jimbo had the tail on Mia Savard today. I want to know where she was and what she did from three till six."

"You got it, Obi-Wan. See you in thirty."

In spite of the lousy roads, Brian made it in twenty with Lawrence Carson, a retiree from the KCMOPD crime lab, another JKI part-timer. Joe met them in the vestibule and, because Larry would be seventy in March, took him and Brian, who lugged his heavy cases, up in the elevator.

Mia was in the foyer. When tall, white-haired and bird-thin Larry stepped out of the elevator, her big dark eyes gave an oh-my jump.

"Mia Savard," Joe said. "Lawrence Carson. The best lab technician the KCMOPD crime lab ever had."

"Mr. Carson." Mia gave Joe a why-didn't-you-tell-me frown, Larry a moment to take off his gloves, then clasped his hand. "Thank you so much for coming out on such a miserable night."

"Larry, please. It's my pleasure. I haven't had a wild ride on icy streets since I retired." He glanced at Brian, struggling with his heavy cases toward the sewing room. "Thanks to young Skywalker, we made it."

Brian put the cases down with a grunt. "No prob, Larry. My X-wing fighter is always at your disposal."

Mia cocked her head at Brian. "You're the new guy in security."

"I am." Brian grinned. "But if you tell anyone I'll have to kill you."

Mia laughed. Joe smiled. She needed to laugh, to shake this off.

"I made coffee," she said. "Who'd like some?"

"My old bones would love a cup." Larry crossed the foyer to the sewing room and glanced through the open doorway. "Did you touch anything, Miss Savard?"

"The doorknob and the light switch. Then I called Joe."

Larry slid Joe a *smart girl* glance. "Have you been fingerprinted?"

"No." Her eyes lit up. "Are you going to fingerprint me?"

"I should, yes. Do you have a small table?"

"A card table. I'll get it." She dashed into her apartment.

Joe had never seen anyone so thrilled at the thought of being fingerprinted. By the time Larry finished, Mia's eyes were shining and she'd lost the pinched look around her mouth.

"Coffee coming up," she said, and skipped into her apartment.

She made good coffee. Joe drank two cups while Brian helped Larry in the sewing room and he watched through the foyer window for Becca and/or Robin Savard. Thanks to Moira he knew that Robin Savard drove a new Thunderbird and Becca Savard a Mazda Miata.

Larry spent an hour and a half in the sewing room. It was nearly two A.M. when he packed up his cases and sat down with Joe and Brian and Mia at her dining room table for a cup of cocoa.

"So you can sleep when you get home," she said to Larry, dazzling him with a smile as she set a super-size mug in front of him.

Hell, Joe thought. He wished *he'd* thought of finger-printing her.

"I found your prints and two other sets," Larry told Mia. "Another woman's, and by their size, a man's. Only your prints are on the shelves, the bins and the big items like the books that are dumped on the floor. So you're right, Joseph. Whoever did this wore gloves." He glanced at Joe, then winked at Mia. "Or you did this yourself."

"Not likely." She winked back at him. "Since I have to clean it up."

"What d'you think?" Joe asked him. "Was somebody looking for something or was this random?"

"Oh, it wasn't random. It was staged," Larry said emphatically. "A person looking for a specific thing would've been methodical. Dumping everything on the floor is no way to find something. It's looking for a needle in a haystack. Whoever did this might like you to think they were looking for something, Joseph, but I think it was done to throw you off."

Mia had her arms folded on the table and her eyes on Larry. She turned her head and looked at Joe.

"That's exactly what you said."

"I get one right now and then."

Mia raised a *hmmm* eyebrow.

When she brought their coats, Brian's beat-up brown

bomber with the moth-eaten fake fur collar and Larry's navy overcoat, she stretched up on her toes and wrapped a long red, white and blue muffler around Larry's turkey-thin neck.

"My mother made this. She spun the yarn, too." Mia made a loose loop under Larry's chin. "It should keep you warm on the way home."

"Thank you, Mia. How very sweet." Larry smiled and pressed one hand to the scarf. "I will cherish this."

Mia gave him a quick hug and turned into her kitchen.

"Be right back," Joe said to her, and she nodded from the sink.

He rode down in the elevator and waited with Larry while Brian slid out to his Chevy Blazer and started the engine. Joe and Brian both walked Larry outside into the frigid night and tucked him into the truck. Brian shut the passenger door and turned toward Joe.

"Jimbo says Mia Savard went shopping this afternoon. She hit six stores on the Plaza, all bridal boutiques."

Joe nodded. "That's what she told me."

"Looks like we got ourselves a smart amateur." Brian's breath puffed white on the cold air. "I'm thinking you'd like me to take Larry home, and then come back and sit on this place."

"Before I tackle Becca and Robin Savard, I want to know what time they come home. I'd do it myself, but my car was here last night and one of them might recognize it."

"Are we going to have to tail the designers and the family?"

"I hope not." Joe shivered and rubbed his hands together.

He was already thinking which of his employees he could pull from other jobs or switch in case he had to put a tail on each of the Savards. Exactly the kind of thing that whoever had wrecked Mia's sewing room wanted him thinking about instead of who had stolen the design.

"Moira will have the background and financial checks on the Savards ready for tomorrow at my place. We'll see where we are then."

"I'll be in touch." Brian swung behind the wheel of his truck.

Joe watched the Blazer slide and spin away up the cul-de-sac, its taillights illuminating the vanity plate that said X-WING. Joe smiled and turned back inside. He'd left the inside vestibule door open, closed it behind him and took the stairs to the third floor.

Mia was in her sewing room, lifting a dress form off the floor. She stood it on its base and smoothed the wrinkles from a dress made of blue velvet, the fabric Cocoa couldn't possibly have unwound from the bolt.

"Pretty dress." Joe leaned in the doorway. "Did you make it?"

"I'm making it." Mia glanced at him. "It's not finished."

"Who's it for?"

"Me." Mia brushed bits of thread off the skirt. "I decided I wanted something new to wear in case someone asks me out for New Year's Eve."

"Where would you like to go?"

She stopped brushing and looked at him. Joe smiled. Mia blinked.

"Did you just ask me out for New Year's Eve?"

"Yes. Providing I find the thief who stole Alicia's dress and wrap this up by then. So I guess I should say 'Maybe.'"

"Why are you just standing there? Go find him."

Joe laughed. Mia smiled, her big, dark eyes shimmering in the glow cast by the floor lamp she'd righted. The shade was crooked. Joe crossed the room and straightened it, standing close enough to Mia to sweep his arms around her and feel her against him.

"Are you going to kiss me?" she asked.

"I'd like to, very much, but I shouldn't."

"It's only a kiss."

"No. It's crossing the line from objective to personal."

"Didn't you cross that line when you asked me out for New Year's?"

"That's not crossing the line. That's balancing right on it." Joe cupped her face in his hands. He shouldn't, but he did, felt how soft her skin was beneath his fingers. "This is crossing."

Mia's eyes widened as he bent his head, then her lips parted to meet his. Joe's mouth still felt cold from being outside, but she didn't seem to mind. She shivered a little, but so did he when her lips parted a bit more. He was still in charge, still in control, till her tongue touched his and a bolt of heat shot through him. Her mouth was soft, warm and tasted so sweet, so good. Good enough to make him forget the reason he was here, till Mia swayed against him and breathed a chocolate-flavored sigh into his mouth. Cocoa. Larry. Fingerprints. *Thief.*

Joe broke the kiss and lifted his head.

Mia blinked and smiled. "Wow," she breathed, her eyes glazed.

"I can do better," Joe said. "But not tonight. Not till I catch the guy who stole the design and wrecked your sewing room."

"Go get him." Mia drew a deep breath. "And be quick about it."

13

MIA WENT TO BED AT THREE. She fell asleep imagining she could still feel Joe's mouth against hers and dreamed about where she wanted him to take her on New Year's Eve. Paris, maybe? Rome, perhaps?

Mia didn't care, so long as she could ring out the old year and bring in the new gazing into Joe Kerr's gorgeous dark blue eyes.

Over flaming Chateaubriand in a five-star restaurant on the Rue de Whatever. (Mia had never been to Paris; she'd have to fill in that blank later.) Or some divine pasta in a bistro with frescoed walls in Rome. Her plate swimming with sauce, the sauce swimming with meatballs . . . one that looked like Robin, another that looked like Cocoa the cat.

Mia's eyes sprang wide open in the dark. *Well, hell.*

If Jordan hadn't blabbed to Robin two seconds after she saw him in Blanko's poolroom, then certainly she'd told him while they were out partying that Alicia had chosen her design over Damien's.

Cocoa didn't have thumbs; she couldn't turn a key. That meant that the thief or his accomplice had locked Cocoa in so Mia would think the cat had vandalized her sewing room.

And that meant the thief not only had keys to her sewing room, but keys to Becca's apartment. Or it meant Becca was the thief and Robin her accomplice, or vice versa.

Mia turned her head toward the clock radio—6:17 A.M.

It was too early to call Joe. He'd left her apartment at 2:45. The man needed his sleep. So did she, but she was wide-awake now, dammit.

Should she add Robin to the list of people who knew Alicia had chosen her design? Should she tell Joe that Becca was out of breath on the phone and that she'd heard something go thump in the background?

This was Mia's worst fear. It had been gnawing at her since Lucien announced the theft. That she'd end up suspecting everyone at Savard's. That she wouldn't be able to look at anyone without wondering, *Are you the one? Did you do this?*

At lunchtime on Thursday she'd caught Robin leaning over her drawing board. He'd grinned when she asked what he was doing and said, "Snooping." Typical Robin? Or a clever thief messing with her head?

Becca had been out of breath and "in the middle of something" yesterday during the hours Joe had outlined as the time frame for the sack of her sewing room. And Cocoa was her cat.

On the other hand . . . she never locked her purse in her desk. Anyone could've taken her key ring while she was out of her office and copied her sewing room keys. Or all her keys and tried every one of them till he found the sewing room keys and Becca's door keys so he could frame Cocoa.

Was that possible? Yes. Was it probable? No.

Becca and Robin had been with her dozens of times

when she'd opened the sewing room. They both knew which keys were the right ones.

"I'm going to stop watching *Law & Order*," Mia muttered.

She got out of bed and made coffee. The carafe was still warm when she took it out of the dishwasher. Which figured, since she'd started the cycle at three A.M. While her Vanilla Bean brewed, Mia made her bed and got dressed, jeans and a sweatshirt, socks and her Reeboks, then looked out the living room window.

The streetlights lit the snowpacked cul-de-sac. Becca's bottle green Miata was parked at the curb, along with a few other cars that belonged to neighbors who couldn't make it up their icy driveways, but she didn't see Robin's red Thunderbird. If the Miata couldn't make it up the drive, neither could the T-bird, so Robin probably wasn't home.

With her first cup of coffee, Mia ate toast, then poured a second and took it to her study. She opened the safe, made sure the design was there, then opened the window blind and looked at the carport.

No Thunderbird. If Robin had made it up the drive he could've parked in the garage. But Mia wasn't about to go out in what looked, in the house lights, like a bitter-cold dawn breaking in pink streaks above the roofs of the houses on the next block. It was barely seven. Too early to go knocking on doors. And maybe too late, anyway.

Access was one thing, opportunity another, but what was the motive? Why would Robin or Becca, or Robin *and* Becca, steal Alicia's design? Because Uncle Rudy was on Prozac and Robin blamed Lucien? That seemed thin. They didn't need money. Uncle Rudy was way better at investing their trust funds than Lucien's broker was at investing hers.

Mia couldn't think of one good reason. She had suspicions and circumstances that seemed to match, but did they?

Before she talked to Joe, maybe she should investigate.

Nine o'clock, Mia decided. At nine o'clock she'd knock on Becca's door. Till then she'd work on restoring order to chaos.

At 8:45 Becca appeared in the sewing room doorway in red flannel sleep pants and a white sweatshirt, mascara smudged beneath her eyes and her dark hair tangled around her shoulders.

"My God, Mia!" Becca gaped at the mess. "What happened?"

Make a joke out of it, Joe said, so Mia put a grin on her face and said, "Ask Cocoa."

Becca blinked. "Ask Cocoa what?"

"How she did this," Mia said happily, sitting on the floor fitting spools of thread over plastic pins on a tray that fit inside one of the umpteen bins emptied on the floor. "I found her in here last night."

"My cat?" Becca gaped at her again. "You think my cat did this?"

"Well, yeah." Mia grinned wider. "That's what the police said."

"The police!" Becca shrilled. "You called the police?"

Wait a minute, Mia thought. *I'm grinning. Why isn't Becca?*

"Well, sure," she said with a breezy shrug. "What would you have done if you'd opened the door and found this?"

Becca balled her fists. "You called the police on my cat?"

"Oh, lighten up, Beck." Mia put the bin aside and got to her feet. "I called the police because I thought someone had broken in. Cocoa didn't come out of hiding till after they got here."

"Who would break into your sewing room?"

"No one broke in. Listen to me, will you? Cocoa did this."

"Cocoa did *not* do this!" Becca huffed indignantly.

"Then who did? And how did Cocoa get in here?"

"Are you accusing me of letting Cocoa in here?"

"I'm not accusing you of anything. I simply asked how she got in."

"I'm telling you I don't know. I don't have keys to this room, which you know, so I can't understand why—" Becca's eyes widened. "You *are* accusing me! You're accusing me of breaking into your sewing room!"

"It wasn't a break-in. The police found no signs of forced entry."

"Did they look all over the house?" Becca demanded. "Did they look in Robin's apartment? Did you let them into *my* apartment?"

"Uh," Mia said. "Yes, I did."

"You had no right to let *anyone,* even the police, into my home!"

"Then why do I have keys to your place? Why do you have keys to mine? Because we decided it could be necessary in an emergency."

"This wasn't an emergency! It wasn't even a break-in!" Becca's face was nearly as red as her sleep pants. Mia was stunned. She'd never seen her cousin go from zero to furious. "You just said so!"

"It *looked* like a break-in. I didn't realize it wasn't and neither did the police till Cocoa crawled out from under a pile of blue velvet. By then I'd already let them into your place and Robin's."

"I'm going to call a locksmith and change my locks!" Becca wheeled away and then spun back. "And *you* will *not* get keys!"

She stalked toward the stairs. Mia followed her as far as the half wall that enclosed the staircase. She spread her hands on the wood-capped top, hung over it and hollered at Becca's retreating back, "I'm changing my locks, too!"

"You do that!" Becca shouted, and slammed her door.

Mia closed up the sewing room and went back to her apartment.

"Well." She huffed out a breath. "That joke didn't go over."

She'd thought she was making light of it. Grin on her face, ha-ha-look-what-Cocoa-did tone in her voice, but *yow*. Becca had gone ballistic. Mia realized she'd hit a nerve. How dare you accuse my cat, how dare you invade my privacy. Was that all, or was there more?

She glanced at the desk, at Joe's card, one corner stuck under the rubber foot of her French telephone. She could give Becca a chance to cool off, and try to talk to her again. Clean up her sewing room, wait for Robin to come home and take a shot at him. Mr. Tight-lipped, I-Don't-Stick-My-Nose-in-Your-Life Savard.

Or she could just call Joe. He was the detective.

She was a designer. Fabric, she knew. Color and cut and line. She had no idea what constituted evidence. She had suspicions that matched circumstances. Maybe nothing more than a string of coincidences, but what if they were more than that? She didn't know a clue from a false lead, wouldn't recognize a red herring if somebody smacked her upside the head with one. And obviously she had no interview skills.

She could wonder and worry, speculate till the cows came home, drive herself crazy trying to figure out if Becca and Robin were traitors, or she could just call Joe. Tell him what she knew, what she'd heard and what she'd seen, and let him do his job. He was the detective.

She needed to do her job. She had six weeks to craft a wedding gown for the governor's daughter. In the best circumstances it could take eight or nine weeks, and that was just Mia's initial guesstimate. She should focus on Alicia Whitcomb's wedding dress, one last gown for Lucien, and get herself free of bridal.

Mia sat down at the desk, lifted the French phone and dialed Joe.

"I've thought of some things I should probably tell you," she said when he answered. "Do you have time to hear them now?"

"Are these things you should probably tell me urgent?"

She thought about it. "I don't think so, but I'm not a detective."

"I'd like to see you, too." Joe lowered his voice and a little thrill shot through Mia, remembering the feel of his mouth against hers. "But we're testing the new security system. Your father and your brother and sister are coming this afternoon to see it. Why don't you tag along and we'll talk then? About two?"

"My office is still mostly in boxes. Meet me there?"

"I'll be there," Joe said, and hung up.

Mia broke the connection and dialed her mother.

"Morning, Mom," she said. "It's Mia. I—"

"No!" Petra barked. "I haven't told him yet!"

Then she slammed the phone in Mia's ear.

Jenna lost interest in the new security system in ten minutes flat.

"I've seen all I care to see." She breezed into Mia's office, swept off one of Petra's shawls, a soft green Irish knit, and tossed it over the blue and white damask wing chair from her mother's Americana period that Mia had rescued. When her back got tired at her drawing board, she sat in it to sketch. "How can I help?"

This was unusual. If Jenna were standing in the kitchen, she'd hire someone to make you a cup of tea.

"I'm not sure." Mia stood over a box of knickknacks, staring up at her like they had no more idea where they belonged than she did. "You'd think I'd remember where I had all this stuff, wouldn't you?"

Jenna picked up a small box and rifled through it.

"Paper clips, erasers, pencils—desk." She sat down on Mia's swivel chair and started filling drawers. "Your eyes are red. Why?"

"I had another late night." Mia carried two of the bride rag dolls she made out of fabric scraps and leftover bits of Petra's yarn to the bookcase and arranged them like shelf sitters. "And not much sleep."

"Were you out with the awfully good-looking Mr. Kerr?"

"No." Mia glanced at Jenna. "Why would you think that?"

"His car was parked in front of your house last night. Very late."

"Why were you out driving around in a blizzard?"

"Enjoying it. We don't get snow in LA. You weren't out with Mr. Kerr. Were you entertaining him?"

"I called Joe and the police. I thought someone had broken into my sewing room, but it wasn't a burglar. It was Becca's cat. Cocoa got shut up in there and knocked everything on the floor."

"Is Mr. Kerr certain the cat was responsible?"

"There were no signs of forced entry and nothing was taken from my apartment, Becca's or Robin's. When are you going back to LA?"

"I'm not sure." Jenna shut Mia's bottom desk drawer, collapsed the box and stood up. "I may be jumping at shadows. This theft is such a shock, but I have a feeling there's more to come. Maybe it's Mother. She seems on edge about something but she won't talk to me."

"I know," Mia said. "She almost bit my head off on the phone."

Jenna leaned on the front of the desk and folded her arms. "I get the feeling she isn't very happy with you. What did you do?"

"I don't recall doing anything," Mia said. *Other than being dragged against my will to Heavenly Bridals,* she wanted to say, but couldn't.

"Luke told me you and mother had a tiff."

"No," Mia said slowly, like she was trying to remember. *God will get you, Luke, if I don't,* she thought. "I don't recall arguing with Mother."

"Any idea why she's so jumpy? What's bothering her?"

"How about Dad yelling and throwing things every five minutes?"

"That's nothing new." Jenna pursed her lips. "Maybe it's Tilde."

"There you go." Mia snapped her fingers. "I'll bet you're right."

Through the glass wall of her office, Mia saw Joe strolling around the corner from the elevator. She was so glad to see him—she would've been glad to see Damien if he'd save her from Jenna—that she smiled.

"Afternoon, ladies." Joe leaned his right shoulder on the jamb, a green tie splashed with blue and yellow and lighter shades of green loosened from the collar of his cream-colored shirt. "Can I dazzle you with the new security system?"

"You've already wowed me with it, Mr. Kerr." Jenna plucked her shawl off the chair and slid Mia a smile. "I'll leave you two alone."

When Jenna disappeared around the corner, Joe raised an eyebrow at Mia. "She'll leave us alone?"

"She thinks we're dating."

"Not yet, but soon." Joe smiled and Mia's pulse fluttered.

With the cream shirt and abstract tie, he wore dark trousers and a deep green tweed jacket. There was a glint in his eyes, sharp as a sword point, and a flush above his unbuttoned collar that said to Mia, *Lucien.*

"Methinks," she said, "that you and Dad had words."

He shrugged and nodded at the boxes in the middle of the floor. "The pile is getting smaller. Do you have time to take a break?"

"Sure." Mia placed the display box that held part of her collection of antique thimbles on a bookshelf. "I'm the queen of break time."

"There's a coffee shop on Broadway, at about Thirty-seventh Street. Do you know it?"

She'd been trying to forget her drunken, butchered

rendition of the Nescafé coffee commercial, "Let's have another cup of coffee, then let's have another cup of joe!" but clearly he remembered it.

"You mean the Cup o' Joe?" she asked, and he grinned.

"That's the one. I'll meet you there in twenty minutes."

Joe strolled away toward the elevator. Mia eyed the dwindling pyramid on the floor. She could do her Martha Stewart thing later. In five minutes she had the boxes empty, their contents shoved in the bookcases, on tables, the boxes collapsed and stuffed in her closet.

She'd changed her jeans and sweatshirt for wheat-colored wool-blend trousers, an off-white turtleneck and a mini-poncho Petra had knitted in teal, pumpkin and burgundy yarns. Mia brushed her hair and her teeth in her bathroom, dabbed Neosporin, lip balm and lipstick on her healing ice hockey injury, tossed a red wool cape over her poncho and headed out.

The sun was bright and brilliant, sparkling on the fresh snow and Mia's new lease on life and love. He liked her, Joe Kerr really *liked* her.

Cup o' Joe sat in the middle of the block, a seen-better-days storefront on the outside, inside a retro-modern mix of black and white and red titles on the floor and halfway up the walls. Red and black armchairs draped with patrons, mostly college kids, and tables scattered with newspapers by the front windows, long-leg tables and stools nearly as tall as Mia. The dark wood coffee bar with a pastry case along the back, the side walls filled with booths, one red, one black, one white.

Joe sat in a red booth. He stood up when he saw Mia come in. He smiled and her stomach flipped. He helped her out of her cape and hung it on a hook next to the booth.

"What's your pleasure?" he asked.

"Another kiss?" Joe raised an eyebrow, and Mia sighed. "Okay. Then I'll settle for a double mocha latte."

"Comin' up," he said, and turned toward the coffee bar.

Three minutes later, the double mocha latte that just yesterday had seemed as unattainable as the moon sat in front of Mia in an oversize white mug, and Joe Kerr's dark blue eyes were smiling at her across the red Formica tabletop.

"So," she said. "Are we officially sneaking around?"

His well-shaped eyebrows drew closer together. "Do you want to?"

"No," Mia said, though the thought of it put a little zip in her pulse.

"Then we aren't doing anything *official*," he said, "but drinking coffee while you tell me some things you think I should probably know."

So Mia told him about Robin "snooping" at her drawing board on Thursday, and about Becca being out of breath on the phone, "in the middle of something," and the thump she'd heard in the background.

"I'm probably just paranoid," Mia finished. "This stuff is probably just coincidence, isn't it?"

"I don't believe in coincidence," Joe said. "Anything else?"

"Well . . ." Mia scooped a spoonful of whipped cream into her mouth. "Becca lost it this morning when I told her Cocoa wrecked my sewing room. I really tried to make a joke out of it. 'Ha-ha, isn't it funny that your cat did this,' but Becca went nuts. How could I call the cops on her cat, I had no right to let anyone, even the police, into her apartment. It was like she stopped listening at the word *cop*."

"Lots of people freeze up like deer in headlights at the word *cop*."

"But why? Why would you if you have nothing to hide?"

"It's not that simple. Cops are authority figures. Big brother is watching you, and all that."

"She thought I was accusing her of breaking into my sewing room."

Joe sprinkled cinnamon into his cappuccino. "Were you?"

"I don't think so, but I guess I can see how Becca might think that. It was just weird. When I told Jenna that Cocoa had wrecked my sewing room, she didn't bat an eye."

"There you are." Joe shrugged. "The difference in people."

He sipped his cappuccino. Mia watched him, wondering what his shrug signified. What he meant by "the difference in people." That Becca had a guilty conscience, but Jenna didn't?

Joe put his cup on its saucer, looked at Mia and said, "Stop it."

"I'm sorry?" She blinked. "Stop what?"

"Trying to divine the hidden meaning in everything I say. Yes, I'm a detective, but I'm also a human being. Sometimes I say things that don't have a point." He smiled at her with the dimple. "And I've been known to shrug my shoulders just for the exercise."

"I didn't realize I was doing that." Mia wrinkled her nose. "Sorry."

"Hopefully I won't be around long enough for you to

get used to it." He sprinkled more cinnamon. "Officially, anyway."

What did that mean? That unofficially he was sticking around?

"Help." Mia bent her elbows on the table, spread her fingers on her temples. "I'm doing it again. Reading things into what you say."

"You'll get used to it. Unofficially, I hope. Is that better?" He smiled at her and Mia sighed. "Yes. Much better."

"Have you decided where you want to go New Year's Eve?"

"How about Paris?" Mia grinned. "I've never been there."

Joe grinned back at her. "You aren't cheap to keep, are you?"

"Oh, no." Mia said gaily. "I'm very high maintenance."

"Why haven't you been to Paris? Isn't that the Mecca of fashion?"

"Luke goes to Paris, Jenna goes, but I'm the baby." Mia rolled her eyes and stirred the melting whipped cream into her latte. "I'm lucky Lucien lets me go to New York or LA by myself."

"He has some major issues with control, your father." Joe raised his cup, the pink on his throat brightening above his collar.

"You tangled with him, didn't you? Over the new security system?"

"It wasn't a major tangle. I've had plenty of difficult clients." Joe put his cup down and looked at Mia. "Thing is, he reminds me of me."

"You're the last person I'd mistake for a control freak."

"I'm in recovery." He smiled. "Hi. My name is Joe."

Mia laughed. Oh, how she liked this man.

"Listen, I know all about Lucien. He's my dad and I love him, but he's a royal pain in the butt at work. I had to turn in my resignation to get him to let me out of bridal, to design for the trousseau line."

"I'm sure you could tell me tales, but I shouldn't make comments about him to you. It's unprofessional. So is this. Being here with you."

"Why are you here with me?"

"I like you, Mia." Joe sat back against the booth and smiled. "More than I should. I've never done anything like this in the middle of a case."

"Like what?" She bent her elbow and leaned her chin on her hand. "Kissed your number-one suspect and asked her out?"

"You fell out of first place last night. Like you said, you had to clean up the mess in your sewing room. How's that going?"

"Slo-o-o-owly," Mia said, and Joe grinned. "I thought of something else. If it wasn't Becca or Robin who did it, then whoever did had to have keys to Becca's place, too, so he could plant Cocoa in the room."

Joe nodded. "I know. When are you changing the locks?"

"I'll call a locksmith tomorrow. Any recommendations?"

"Ask Brian. He'll be on the security desk all day. Do you own the house?" Joe asked, and Mia nodded. "Then you should seriously consider a security system. A neighborhood as nice as yours draws burglars like garbage draws flies."

"The house had one when I bought it," Mia said,

"but Robin kept passing out the code to all his friends. I gave up and had it removed."

"Threaten him with eviction." Joe sipped his cappuccino. "Threaten him with death, but get that system reinstalled."

Mia's stomach clenched. "If you think it's important, I will."

"One of my guys is a genius. He can do it. Want me to arrange it?"

"Yes, thanks. That would be great. I don't know diddly."

"I'll handle it." Joe nodded. "When you say you want to go to Paris for New Year's, I guess you mean Paris, France, not Paris, Texas?"

Mia laughed. He smiled, and nodded at the pastry case.

"They have apple dumplings. Would you like one?"

"Oh, yes, please. Warmed with cream and extra cinnamon."

"Mmmm." He flashed his dimple. "Make that two."

When Joe slid out of the booth, Mia pressed her hands to her face. Her palms felt cool, her cheeks hot. She hoped she wasn't red as a beet. She took her compact out of her purse and opened it. A little pink.

Joe had the bench facing the door. Detective thing, Mia knew from *Law & Order*. She tipped her face up, raised the mirror, and saw over her shoulder and the low back of the booth a man with thinning brown hair and glasses, sitting in one of the chairs by the windows, reading.

"Two apple dumplings, warmed with cream and extra cinnamon."

The smell of hot, buttery apples filled Mia's nose. A second later Joe's taut, flat abdomen filled the bottom half of her mirror as she angled it for a better look at the brown-haired man. A round white soup bowl clinked onto the table in front of her. Joe stepped out of the mirror and sat down across from her, the vinyl bench creaking.

"What's so interesting?" he asked.

"That man with the brown hair and the glasses. I saw him on the Plaza yesterday while I was shopping."

Mia lowered her mirror. Joe craned his neck to look around her.

"Lots of men in Kansas City with brown hair and glasses."

"But not lots of men who wear an Henri Villeauv herringbone peacoat. It's a classic from one of Villeauv's eighties collections. He probably bought it for cheap in a vintage clothing store." Mia shut her compact with a snap, looked at Joe and asked, "Is that man following me?"

14

LIE, JOE TOLD HIMSELF, JUST LIE. Don't risk the investigation. He should've thought of that before he kissed Mia, but it was too late now—she had him cold. And he couldn't lie to her. Reproach and a glint of *I should've known* flickered in her dark eyes.

"Yes. That man is following you," Joe said. "His name is Jim Fields. He works part-time for me and part-time for Barnes and Noble."

"Don't tell me. In the mystery section?"

"Pretty corny, but Jimbo gets a laugh out of it."

Joe smiled. Mia didn't. She just stared at him.

"You said you weren't having me followed."

"At lunchtime Friday, I wasn't. After I interviewed your coworkers Friday afternoon, I was."

"So you *did* follow me to Blanko's."

"No, I didn't. Moira followed you. You aren't a suspect anymore, but you work in design. So does the thief."

Her dark eyes narrowed. "How do you know that?"

"Access and opportunity. Two out of three. I'm playing the odds."

"Then I guess what I don't understand is how you

could kiss me and ask me out while you're having me followed."

"I shouldn't have. I told you, I've never done anything like this."

"I think what you mean," she said, a frigid undercurrent in her voice, "is that you didn't expect me to find out."

"That, too." Joe tried another smile. An apologetic one that Mia didn't return. "So Jimbo's coat is famous?"

"Notorious. Herringbone in a peacoat is just *wrong*."

"You aren't a suspect," Joe repeated. "But you spend all day every day with five other suspects and you socialize with one of them."

"You're following everyone who works in design?"

"I'm trying to find a thief, Mia. The sooner, the better, so we can make plans for New Year's Eve."

Joe hoped that would get a smile out of her. It didn't. She spread her palms on the table and looked at him over her apple dumpling.

"I can't do this. I won't tell Jordan she's being followed. I won't tell Arlene or Kylie or anyone else. I want you to find the thief, Joe. I want my life back and I'd like to have you in it, but not like this." Mia reached for her purse. "I'm sorry. I shouldn't have come."

"It's my fault." Joe started to rise. "I shouldn't have asked you."

He shouldn't have kissed her, either, but he didn't regret it.

"Don't get up." She pushed out of the booth, lifted her cape off the hook and flung it around her shoulders. "I realize this is everyday stuff to you. Having people followed, I mean, but it isn't for me. How you could invite me here, and then sit there flirting with me about

New Year's Eve, knowing that man is sitting there watching me, watching us—"

"Jimbo isn't a voyeur, Mia, and I'm not a pervert. I'm a detective."

"Well." At last she smiled. "I'm a Savard."

She picked up her apple dumpling, upended the bowl and let it fall in his lap with a *plop*.

"Bon appetite." She slammed the empty bowl on the table, spun on her heel and stalked out of the Cup o' Joe.

Jimbo folded his paper, stood up and glanced at Joe, who scooped the dumpling out of his lap with a napkin— thank God it had cooled—and crooked a finger at Jim. He came to the booth and asked, "Would you like a couple wet paper towels from the men's room?"

"That'd be great, Jimbo, thanks."

Jim headed for the men's room. Joe dialed Brian on his cell phone.

"Mia Savard is loose. She made Jim. Doubt she'll head back to the Savard Building, but I thought I'd give you a heads-up."

"No worries. This place is locked up tighter than Area Fifty-one."

He meant the secret UFO base in Nevada that the government denied existed but Brian believed in with all his heart.

"I'm on my way back there," Joe told him. "I want to see how Stink's doing and I want another look at the sewing room."

After the security system orientation, Luke Savard had given Joe a tour of the Savard Creations sewing room, where the custom-made, mostly hand-sewn wedding gowns were assembled. Lucien Savard had trailed along, only half listening, his cell phone pressed to his ear while he and Walter Vance plotted Oren Angel's downfall.

Jim appeared with wet paper towels and sat down in the booth.

"Thanks," Joe said. "I'd better not hear about this at the office."

"My lips are sealed," Jim said. "Why'd you call me off?"

"She recognized your coat from yesterday's shopping foray."

Jim blinked. "My coat?"

"Did you know that a peacoat in herringbone is just wrong?"

Now that Joe saw it up close, he was inclined to agree with Mia. The longer he looked at the pattern, the more his eyes wanted to cross.

"I never heard that one." Jim held out his left sleeve. "I thought it was kind of sharp-looking."

"To be on the safe side, don't wear it on the job anymore. Call Moira tomorrow. I've got a feeling I'll have something else for you."

"Thanks, Joe." Jim headed for the door, turning up the collar on his god-awful coat. Walking away, it was just as busy as it was up close.

Joe eyed his gooey crotch and wondered how he was going to walk away from this booth. Losing his date for New Year's Eve didn't bother him; his years as a cop taught him that New Year's was a good night to stay home and leave the carousing to the professionals. But he felt bad that he'd hurt Mia's feelings, confused her and definitely pissed her off.

Joe scooted clear of the sticky puddle oozing across the bench and wiped the front of his pants.

Inviting Mia for coffee was the second dumbest thing he'd ever done. The first was kissing her, 'cause now that's all he wanted to do; feel the press of her hot little mouth against his.

He of all people knew that you don't play where you work. When things get personal, you lose your objectivity—he was on Brian about it constantly—and still he'd kissed her, had no idea why he'd kissed her.

Oh, that was bullshit. He knew exactly why. Mia's smile, the gleam of intelligence in her eyes—oh man, those eyes—and the laughter that always seemed on the verge of bubbling into her voice.

She didn't appear to take herself seriously and everything seemed to interest her. She'd asked Larry a million questions while he'd fingerprinted her. She'd kept eyeing Brian like she was trying to figure out if he was a Martian or from Venus, and she'd held her own with old Bri, the king of the one-liners.

She was kind. The muffler she'd given Larry had made the old guy tear up. Joe, too, damn near. She didn't panic. No hysterics when she'd called him about her sewing room, just a calm "What do I do?"

She couldn't lie, she couldn't hold her liquor and, apparently, she had her father's temper. Well. If she ever decided to speak to him again, that could keep things lively. He wasn't Irish for nothing.

Joe wasn't lonely, but God he was tired of being alone. He had Moira, his mother and Sam and his wife and two boys, Brian and Stink and Carlos, but it wasn't the same. It wasn't a pink toothbrush next to his, the smell of a woman on his sheets, her clothes in his closet, a TV screen he could actually see 'cause she remembered to wipe off the dust.

There really hadn't been anyone for him since Janine. He'd tried. She'd made him promise. "Find someone, Joe. Give my baby a mother, some brothers and sisters, maybe. Don't be alone. Make yourself happy."

Joe had given it his best shot. He'd had lots of dates, a couple almost serious relationships, all with lovely, intelligent women, but no matter how bright and engaging they were, none of them could fill the empty space beside him.

It wasn't a void, because Joe was aware of it. He couldn't describe it, but he knew it was there. Sometimes he could almost touch it, put his hand out and just barely feel his fingertips brush . . . something.

For a while after she died he thought it was Janine. He'd lie in bed half-asleep and feel it hanging just above him, an awareness of someone hovering, waiting. It was the weirdest damn thing. So weird he'd gone to see a psychic, a woman Brian knew.

She'd told him it wasn't Janine. She'd gone like a rocket, her soul leaving a trail of stars, straight back to the Light. Or God, or the Source, whatever Joe wanted to call it that gave him comfort. Janine hadn't lingered, she had no reason. She'd left her child, her daughter, with Joe, knowing she'd be safe and loved.

The space beside him that looked empty but wasn't, the psychic couldn't see or feel, but she believed Joe that it was there. When he told her that it almost felt like he had an imaginary friend, she'd smiled and said, "That's a good thing to call it. Why don't you give it a name?"

Uh, no. Joe wasn't that far gone into Brianland, but he'd felt better after he talked to the psychic, and after a while, he got used to the feeling. When it seeped into his bed at night or brushed against him in the office or on the street, he'd smile and think, *My shadow's back.*

That's how he felt around Mia, like he'd found his shadow. Or his shadow had finally found him.

Joe gave up on his pants and used the paper towels to wipe the bench. Then he slid his elbows on the table and scrubbed his hands over his face. Two late nights and Lucien Savard were catching up with him. The man could suck the life force out of a mannequin.

The padded bench on the other side of the table sighed. Joe spread his fingers and saw Moira sliding onto it.

"As dates go, Jo-Jo, I'd say this one was a bust."

"Where did you come from, Smooch?"

"The bus stop." Moira tipped her head toward the window, at the Kansas City Area Transit Authority shelter on the curb outside, a tinted Plexiglas shell capped with snow. "When you left the Savard Building and ten minutes later Miss Mia left with stars in her eyes, I followed her."

"We had coffee. Mia had some things to tell me."

"Uh-huh," Moira said. "What happened? She couldn't say it with flowers, so she said it with an apple dumpling?"

Joe bent his left elbow, closed his eyes and rubbed his fingertips up and down his forehead. "What was I thinking? I know better."

"I, for one, am delighted that you didn't think, that you acted on impulse for a change," Moira said happily. "You think way too much."

Joe spread his fingers and looked at her across the table.

"I think," he said. "Therefore, you eat and pay your rent."

"Not that you've asked me," Moira said pointedly, "but I like her. And I would *kill* for her clothes. Where does she shop?"

"She makes most of what she wears." While Mia slept off the Bloody Marys, Joe had gone through her closet. Most of the garments hung on padded silk hangers had satin labels stitched in burgundy ink that said *Design by Mia*. "Her closet is the size of Montana."

"I'm gonna be sick." Moira made a face and tugged her wallet out of her purse. "Want something?"

"Cappuccino. Make it to go. I'm heading back to Savard's."

Moira went with him, his cappuccino and her ice coffee—she drank those ice-cold things all year long—in thick plastic-coated cups. On their way out of the Cup o' Joe, Moira asked, "Do you want me to put someone else on Mia?"

Joe thought about it. "No. Leave her be for today."

He turned his truck into the Savard parking garage ahead of Moira's silver BMW. The security gate accepted the new code and lifted.

Moira being Moira, she had to try to beat the electric eye Stink installed by scooting through behind him. No dice. In his rearview, Joe watched the gate slam down an inch shy of the silver Roadster's front bumper. Moira had to enter the code to raise it again. The eye triggered five seconds behind the BMW and down came the gate.

"Stink," Moira announced with a grin as she swung out of the Roadster, "is a screaming genius."

"That's why we pay him the big bucks," Joe replied. The elevator didn't respond to the call button until the new camera mounted close by swiveled and gave whoever was watching the monitor in the Savard security office a look at them. Took a couple seconds, then the indicator light above the doors lit and the car descended. Joe smiled. No more unauthorized entry on weekends.

Come morning, there were going to be lots of irritated Savard employees when their garage codes no longer worked and they had to be buzzed through manually. He'd told Pete to make a list of everyone who struck him as being pissed off beyond reason.

Uncle Pete had come in for the system orientation, stayed to get comfortable with all the bells and whistles. He turned away from the new bank of monitors on his desk when Joe and Moira entered his office.

"You *can* teach an old dog new tricks," he said. "I saw you two pull in on my screen, pushed the buttons Stink told me to push to turn the camera toward the elevator, pushed the other button Stink said to push and voilà—the elevator went right down to pick you up. This is great, Joe. Gonna make our jobs here in security a lot easier."

Pete grinned and cocked his head at Joe. "What happened to you?"

"Had a run-in with an apple dumpling. Be right back."

Joe took the duffel he kept packed in his truck into the john and stripped, put on jeans, the KCMOPD sweatshirt he'd last worn Friday night when Mia threw up on him and switched the dress shoes Moira had bought for his initial interview with Lucien Savard for his Nikes.

The security office was a suite of three rooms. The front office where Pete sat, the combination kitchen and

break room where he'd met with his JKI people yesterday afternoon and a smaller second office where Stink
had installed the monitors linked to the new security
cameras throughout the Savard Building.

On his way out of the bathroom, Joe stuck his head
into this office, where Carlos sat at a long curved modular table, watching the cameras watch the empty corri-
dors and offices.

"Can you show me the sewing room on four?" Joe
asked.

"You got it," Carlos said.

He worked a toggle on the control board that Brian
said looked like the science station on the bridge of the
starship *Enterprise*. The camera that fed into the second
monitor on the top row of screens blinked, and Joe was
looking at the sewing room Luke Savard had shown him
earlier.

"Can you gimme the split screen?" Joe asked.

"Sure." Carlos toggled, the screen blinked, then split
into eight smaller views that showed every angle the
camera saw.

"Thanks," Joe said, and headed for the elevator.

On his way, he made sure he still had Pete's keys and
text messaged Brian and Stink to meet him. On the ride
up, he walked through the sewing room in his head.

As good as the designers had it—department bathrooms, a kitchenette for coffee breaks and large, well-
appointed cubicles, in each a state-of-the-art PC, cushy
stool and hydraulic drawing table that adjusted with a
touch of a finger—the seamstresses had it better.

"Doesn't look like a room where women sew all day,"
Joe had said to Luke Savard. "It looks like the best suite
in a five-star hotel."

"We pamper our seamstresses. A brilliant design will still look like crap on a rack if it isn't properly and meticulously constructed."

Like the design department, the sewing room was divided into individual areas, eight of them. Each seamstress had her own worktable with wall racks to hold all her tools and threads, high-intensity lamps, some that magnified, and comfortable chairs with footstools—for handwork, Luke said. Each seamstress had her own PC, telephone and sewing machine, plus there were a half dozen more against one wall.

"Why so many sewing machines?" Joe asked.

"Basically, they're set up to do different things," Luke explained. "Buttonholes and loops, specialty stitches, things like that."

The seamstresses had their own bathroom and kitchen for breaks and lunches. Luke showed Joe three other rooms. The cutting room, with long rows of big, flat tables like Mia had in her sewing room, where the gowns were cut, and two other climate-controlled rooms. One where delicate trims and materials were kept in cabinets, the second where the gowns under construction were stored in locked closets.

Joe had looked at the four walls full of closets and stifled a groan. *More effing locks,* he thought, *and more people with keys.*

"Is this where Alicia's dress was made and kept?" he'd asked.

"Yes. It's still here," Luke said. "Alicia hadn't picked it up yet."

Lucien hadn't followed them into what Luke called the back rooms. He'd paced around the main sewing room, still on the phone with Walter Vance. The open doorway and about twenty feet separated them. Luke had stepped closer to Joe and lowered his voice.

"Dad wants the gown moved to the bank. We deal with Lambert Bank and Trust, always have. Dad wants Alicia's dress put in one of their vaults for safekeeping until the trial."

Joe grimaced. "So the battle lines are drawn?"

"Oh, yeah." Luke nodded. "Dad is counterfiling against Oren Angel tomorrow. You and Walter, Jenna and I and Mother all told him a court trial was not a good idea, but he's determined to own Heavenly Bridals so he can take it apart with his own hands brick by brick."

"In that case, stashing the dress in a vault is probably a good idea," Joe replied. "Who keeps the keys to these closets?"

"Our head seamstress, Viola, has keys. So do Damien and my father. Mia might." Luke shrugged. "I'm not sure."

If Mia did, she might have to go back on the suspect list. If that happened, he could forget kissing her.

Brian and Stink waited for Joe outside the sewing room. Brian unlocked the door. Joe led them through the main sewing room, opened the doors to the back rooms and let them look around.

"Here's how things work around here," Joe said, and explained to Brian and Stink how a wedding gown made it from a designer's imagination to finished product.

Joe told them exactly as Luke Savard had told him:

"Once a design is approved, we take the bride's measurements and make the pattern. Four of our seamstresses are also pattern-makers. Mia makes her own—she's Dad all over when it comes to being a control freak about her gowns—Damien can make patterns, but he usually doesn't bother. The pattern is fitted to the bride, then we construct what we call a muslin, which is what it sounds like, the gown sewn in plain muslin. We fit the muslin to the bride, then the gown is cut and constructed. Depending on the complexity of the design and the amount of detail, construction can take anywhere from a month to ninety days."

While Joe talked, Stink walked around the tables in the cutting room, and Brian glared at the vast bank of closets. When Joe finished, Stink came back to the doorway where Joe stood.

"I guess you want cameras in these rooms, too," Stink said.

"If I say yes, how long?"

"I can have the hardware by the end of the day tomorrow, call my guys and have them pull an all-nighter."

"If I want it done, I'll let you know as early tomorrow as possible. How're you doing with Mia's PC?"

"I found the e-mail she sent to Alicia with the final design attached as a PDF file. Nothing obvious like a forward or a blind copy to Heavenly Bridals. Course, anyone who knew the design was e-mailed to Alicia could've forwarded it to their own in-box from Mia's machine or just plain printed it. Once I'm in IT, I'll have access to the entire Savard network, which includes LA and New York, and it'll be lots easier to see if anybody hacked in and snatched the design."

"I wouldn't blow any brain cells on that one, Stink," said Brian as he wandered back from the closets. "Holy hairless wookies, Obi-Wan. There's a zillion ways the thief could've gotten his hands on the design without going anywhere near Mia's PC."

"I know," Joe said. "Scary, isn't it?"

Brian blew out a breath. "It's a freakin' nightmare."

That evening at Joe's house, after they'd eaten Evie Kerr's chili over rice or Fritos (Carlos' favorite) or topped big bowls of it with shredded cheese and sour cream—jalapeños optional—Joe and Brian outlined the ways the thief could've obtained the design to Moira, Betty Sanders, Ricky LeHay, Imogene Tyler, Carlos and Stink:

"Overnight, the designers store their work in a locked cabinet in the design department," Joe led off. "But during the day, their work is in plain view on their drawing boards. While they're at lunch, drinking coffee in the break room or in the bathroom."

"I'm here! I'm here!" Ricky piped in a falsetto voice, waving his hands like mad over his head. "Come and get me! Come and get me!"

"Exactly." Joe grinned at Ricky. "The cabinet where the designs are kept overnight has the flimsiest lock I've ever seen. Brian and I checked it this afternoon. A four-year-old could pick it with a Lego. People who hold keys to this cabinet are Damien DeMello, Lucien and Petra Savard and their daughter Mia, who hasn't up till now kept her purse or her keys locked in her desk, but I believe she will starting tomorrow."

"Want me to find out about DeMello's keys?" Imogene asked.

"Leave DeMello and his keys to me," Joe told her. "I want you to knock his socks off. Be your pretty, efficient self and see what you can charm out of him in general. Specifically about September twenty-first. Did he work late? Did anyone else in design? You have the vantage point for the whole department from your desk, includ-

ing the supply room and the locked cabinet. Eyes and
ears, Imogene."

"I plan to eat lunch at my desk." She smiled. "A lot."

"And now, boys and girls, we come to the sewing
room," Brian said.

He told them what he and Stink and Joe had seen that
afternoon, explained how the design department and
the sewing room worked, how the wedding gowns were
constructed, the giant room full of locked closets where
the dresses were stored.

"Yes, children. That means more keys," he finished.
"DeMello has keys to the closets. So does the head
seamstress, a woman named Viola, and Lucien and Mia
Savard."

"This little Mia girl," Carlos said. "Her name keeps
popping up, and she designed the dress that was stolen."

"She was number one on my top ten list of suspects
until last night." Joe told them about Mia's sewing room
at home being vandalized. "I'm not saying she couldn't
have done it herself to throw us off, but Larry and Brian
agree that that's a long shot."

"You mind, boss," Carlos said, "if I pay special attention to the trash that comes out of her office while I'm
cleaning up nights?"

Had Jimbo spilled the beans already? Had Moira? Joe
glanced at her. She sat on the brick hearth, the fire he'd
lit flickering blue highlights in her hair. She smiled at
him with her sweet, innocent face.

"Not at all," Joe replied. "You pick through Mia
Savard's trash, Lucien's, Rudy's, Becca or Robin Savard's
trash with my blessing. I'll come help you. Let's find who
did this as soon as possible."

"Anyone who works for Savard Creations could have

stolen the design, I suppose," Betty said. "But based on all you've told us, Joseph, I think the thief is in the design department."

"Until one of you can provide me with a better scenario for how the theft was accomplished, that's the one we're going with," Joe said. "The thief is in design."

"Access and opportunity." Ricky turned to look at Moira, his favorite thing to do. "How're we doing with motive, my beauty?"

Ricky grinned. Moira raised a calm-yourself-Junior eyebrow.

"I'm still digging," she said, "but so far I can't find a financial motive for anyone in the Savard family. These people are not hurting. DeMello isn't, either—he's extremely well paid. Makes me wish I could draw. The other designers are also paid very well. Lucien Savard may terrorize his employees, but he makes it well worth their while to put up with his tantrums. I'm thinking revenge. Savard screwed somebody big-time and they're getting even."

"Oren Angel," Joe said. "We need to get our foot through Heavenly Bridals' door. You want to take a run at Angel, Moira?"

She smiled, a gleam in her eyes. "I'd be delighted."

"How does the governor play into a revenge theme?" Betty asked.

"High-profile fall guy," Moira said. "Stealing the dress designed for Whitcomb's daughter guarantees public embarrassment and humiliation, scandal and possible financial ruin."

And it probably would, Joe thought, unless Lucien Savard could be dissuaded from countersuing Oren Angel. He hadn't tried to talk Savard out of it today.

Best to let him vent and rage, plot and scheme, get it all out of his system so hopefully he'd be calm enough to listen tomorrow.

"So the profile of our thief," Brian said, "is a Savard employee with a damn good reason to sell Lucien to Heavenly Bridals."

"Or a Savard employee ripe to be recruited by Oren Angel to help him engineer Lucien's downfall," Joe added. "Either way, we're looking for an unhappy camper."

"A *really* unhappy camper," Moira said. "One who's willing to risk discovery to stick around and watch the show."

15

MIA'S HEART WASN'T BROKEN, but it was bruised. Just when she'd thought that this time she'd found the perfect guy.

The sun vanished with the happy sparkle on her day. It was cold and icy. Only November, and already she was sick and tired of slogging through white crap, but life went on. She had dirty clothes at home, a nearly empty fridge and a wrecked sewing room.

Plenty to keep her mind off Joe Kerr.

Mia stopped at Price Chopper and went through the store, making quick turns at the end of the aisles, hoping to catch the guy in the herringbone peacoat, but he wasn't there. Or if he was, he was ducking behind displays of fabric softener and pork 'n' beans.

She took a zigzag route home, but couldn't tell if there was a particular car following her. Mia Savard, girl detective. *Not.*

Becca's bottle green Miata wasn't on the street. The plow service had cleared the drive, so either her car was in the garage or Becca wasn't home. Mia told herself she didn't care, but she did. Two people she'd thought she could trust had disappointed her today.

"Oh, shut up, Mia," she muttered disgustedly as she parked in the carport. "Get a real problem."

She trucked her groceries upstairs in the elevator. Before she put them away, she opened the safe in her study and made sure Alicia's new design was still there. Then she loaded the fridge, started the laundry with the Bloody Mary aftermath—PU—and hit the sewing room.

A good way to work off what was left of her mad at Joe.

If he thought the thief was in design, why had he let her blather on about Becca and Robin? What was the point of that? To prove she knew nothing about being a detective? She'd already figured that out.

She still couldn't believe she'd thrown her apple dumpling in Joe's lap. Jenna would be proud, but Mia wondered how she could ever face him again. Because she was a fool, her pulse fluttered as she wondered when she might see him again. At Savard's tomorrow? Would he be there?

At six-thirty Sunday evening, her sister showed up to lend a hand with the sewing room. Mia was so amazed—twice in the same day Jenna was *helpful!*—that when they stopped for a cranberry-apple juice break (blech) she blurted out that she'd doused Joe in warmed-up apple dumpling with extra cinnamon and cream.

"If you have serious designs on Mr. Kerr," Jenna said, "let's hope you didn't scald a body part that you might have an interest in later."

"Oooh." Mia winced. Poor Joe. She managed to feel bad for him for a whole nanosecond. "I didn't think of that."

"For that particular area of the male anatomy," Jenna

said, "I recommend something cool and soft. Whipped cream, sour cream—"

"*Sour cream?*" Mia gaped at her, horrified.

"Yes. Fewer calories than whipped cream," Jenna said in a tone that implied she knew of what she spoke. "Yogurt also works very well. Plus, you get extra calcium and protein."

"Oh, my God!" Mia howled with laughter. "Only in LA!"

"Don't knock it if you haven't tried it." Jenna grinned, plucked a cushion from the back of the sofa and bonked Mia on the head.

She laughed harder, snatched up a pillow and whacked Jenna. *Bonk. Whack. Bonk. Whack.*

Jenna was laughing, Mia was laughing, and pillows were flying. Bouncing off walls, rolling behind chairs. Mia snatched one out of the fireplace and flung it at Jenna. She caught it and threw it back. Mia shrieked and dove for the floor.

Bang! Bang! Bang! A fist pounded on the door.

"Well. Whattaya know." Mia puffed, winded. "Becca must be home."

She crossed her living room and flung open the door. Her cousin stood in the foyer, her hands behind her back.

"Yes?" Mia said breathlessly. "Come to complain?"

"No." Becca swung the bed pillow she had hidden behind her. "I've come to join in!"

Mia ducked and ran, screaming and laughing, for another pillow.

The fight ended with the three of them sprawled across Mia's bed, out of breath, clothes askew, hair totally wrecked.

"How'd you know we were having a pillow fight?" Mia asked Becca.

"That's what it sounded like," she said. "I took a chance."

Mia had taken one with Joe, and look what happened. Oh, well, one outta two wasn't bad. She grinned and pushed a pillow in Becca's face.

"That's enough for me." Jenna scooted off the bed, straightened her lilac cashmere sweater and raked her fingers through her hair. "You kids have fun. I have work waiting for me in my hotel room."

"Jen," Mia said. "Why don't you stay with me?"

"Will you wait on me hand and foot? Let me order you around?"

"Uh—no."

"That's why. God knows Tilde won't wait on anybody, either, so I'll stay at the Fairmont. I'll see you two tomorrow."

Jenna kissed Mia, hugged Becca, put on her coat and left.

"I bought a French silk pie," Mia said to her cousin. "Want some?"

"Am I breathing?" Becca said.

Mia brewed a pot of Vanilla Bean and took the pie out of the fridge. They ate two slices apiece, then settled cross-legged facing each other, with their coffee between them, on the big window seat in the living room.

"Why are we sitting here?" Becca looked out at the sidewalk glittering with ice in the pools of light thrown by the streetlamps.

"Keeping an eye peeled for Robin," Mia lied. She was watching for someone watching the house. "Where the heck d'you suppose he is?"

"He and a little blonde seemed awfully interested in each other Friday night. Maybe he got lucky." Becca drank her coffee and looked at Mia. "I'm sorry about this morning. I don't know what got into me. Of course you should've called the police. I would have. I apologize."

"It's okay, Beck. I guess it wasn't funny first thing in the morning."

"Not after a night out with Jordan." Becca grimaced. "I called you back yesterday afternoon, but you didn't answer. Then Jordan called and talked me into meeting her for dinner and a movie."

"If you saw the new Richard Gere movie without me, you're dead."

"We never made it to the movie. Jordan said to meet her at Blanko's and we'd go from there, only we never left. All she wanted to talk about was the theft, which makes sense, but then Terence showed up." Becca's nose wrinkled. "He plunked himself down at our table like he's our best friend and he started on me. Everyone *he* knows knows about the theft. It had to be an inside job, and who did I think did it? Like because my name is Savard, I know everything. I came home with such a headache."

Becca's cheeks were pale, her eyes smudged. After the whomper headache she'd had yesterday, Mia sympathized.

"Have you talked to Uncle Rudy?" she asked.

"This afternoon," Becca said. "I invited him out to dinner but he said he was working. He sounded exhausted. This is a tough time of year for Dad. Mother died a week after Thanksgiving three years ago."

"Is he okay? Thursday night Robin said he was on Prozac."

"I could've shot him for saying that in front of Jordan." Becca beat her fist against her knee. "Now it'll be all over Savard's. Dad realized he needed help. That's why he went to the doctor. Uncle Lucien knows, but Dad did not want the entire universe to know that he's taking Prozac."

"Did he tell you he stopped by Mother and Dad's yesterday?" Mia asked, and Becca shook her head. "Then you don't know. Dad received a subpoena. Oren Angel is suing him for slander and harassment."

"Oh, boy," Becca said. "Here we go again."

Since Moira was headed for Prairie Village and Heavenly Bridals, Joe met her for breakfast Monday morning at Wolferman's in Fairway, Kansas, just across the state line and up the hill from Ward Parkway on the far west side of the Plaza.

While Moira ate an English muffin and filled the time slots in his day planner, Joe read *The Scout,* a local weekly newspaper. He wasn't happy about it—there were no football scores—but the *Kansas City Star* box outside was empty and *The Scout* was something to read.

Joe did his best thinking while he read.

He had a plan to make Lucien Savard reconsider getting tangled up in court with Oren Angel. He was putting the finishing touches on it in his head when he turned the page and his eye caught on a photograph.

A black and white of Petra Savard and Mia, staring wide-eyed and openmouthed at the camera that caught them standing on the loading dock of Heavenly Bridals.

Joe recognized the window they stood next to—he'd looked in it himself Friday morning before Oren Angel tossed him off the premises.

"Holy Jesus Christ," he said.

On the other side of the table, Moira looked up. "What?"

"Read this. Then get moving for Heavenly Bridals." Joe tossed her *The Scout* and pushed to his feet.

On the way to his truck, he fed enough quarters to *The Scout* box to buy four more copies. He skidded on ice leaving the parking lot, made a left at the light and read the short piece beneath the photo while he drove to the Savard Building:

For those of you who live under a rock or have just wakened from a coma, allow me to identify Kansas City's First Lady of bridal fashion. Petra Savard, wife of Lucien Savard, owner of Savard Creations of *el posh-o* Country Club Plaza fame, shown here with her youngest daughter, Mia.

Look like a couple of half-wits, don't they? Think how you'd look if *Candid Camera* caught you peeking in the back window of your fiercest business competitor. For those of you who only get to town once a month, that would be Oren Angel, owner of Heavenly Bridals.

What do you suppose Mrs. and Ms. Savard were looking for? A fabulous new design to boost the company's flagging sales?

Do you suppose this caught-red-handed photo could be the basis of the lawsuit claiming slander and harassment filed by Oren Angel in Jackson County Circuit Court on Friday afternoon?

I wonder how the Savard women will look in this fashion season's hottest new color—jailbird orange . . .

Joe tossed *The Scout* into the passenger seat and gritted his teeth.

The byline belonged to Aubrey Welch, who wrote the "About Our Town" gossip column for *The Scout*. Joe had butted heads with him before and knew there was no way Welch had taken the photo. The angle suggested the photographer stood on the slope adjacent to Heavenly Bridals. Welch was built like the Michelin Man. No way was he nimble enough to negotiate that icy snowpack. One of *The Scout* staffers or a freelancer had snapped the photo.

What Joe wanted to know was, who or what had prompted Welch, a cheap, snarky sensationalist, to start sniffing around Savard Creations?

On his way through the lobby of the Savard Building, Joe stopped at the security kiosk and left three copies of *The Scout* with Brian.

"Read Aubrey Welch's column," Joe told him, "then find Jenna Savard and sit on her. Text me when you've got her."

On his way up to four in the elevator, Joe drew deep breaths. All the silly drivel Mia had told him yesterday about her cousins Robin and Becca, why hadn't she told him about the photograph?

She was sitting at her drawing board when Joe walked into her office. Left elbow bent, chin on her hand. She looked half-asleep, like she was dreaming, the pencil in the fingers of her right hand barely moving.

She wore a pink cardigan sweater with a brown fur collar and rhinestone buttons. The studs in her lobes were probably real, the wedge of dark hair that usually swung toward her chin tucked behind her ear.

She looked up and saw him, straightened and smiled.

"Joe," she said. "I didn't expect to see you." She didn't say *ever again,* but her eyes did.

Joe slapped *The Scout* on her drawing table, tapped the photo with his middle finger and said curtly, "Explain this to me."

Mia glanced down at the photograph. Her lashes jumped and her face drained. Her fingers let go of her pencil and covered her eyes.

"No, you don't." Joe shook the back of her stool. "Tell me."

She dropped her hands, opened her eyes and looked at him.

"Mother wanted Dad to call Oren Angel. She said so at the meeting Friday morning. You were there. You heard her. Dad refused. I had no idea that she intended to drive out to Heavenly Bridals till she made a right when we left PF Chang's after lunch. She said if Lucien wouldn't talk to Oren Angel, then she would. What could I do?"

"You should've stopped her. You could've called me." Joe tapped the photo. "This is what I meant when I told you not to talk to reporters."

"I *didn't* talk to him," Mia said hotly. "He said, 'This way, ladies,' when Mother and I were at the window. We turned around and *click*."

"Does your father know you went to Heavenly Bridals?"

"I don't think so. Mother kept putting off telling him."

"Why didn't *you* tell him? Why didn't you tell *me*?"

She opened her mouth, blinked and shut it. "I don't know."

"This happened on Friday, didn't it?"

"You know it did. That's how I got my ice hockey injury. I chased the guy with the camera and bit my lip."

"What did he look like?"

"I didn't really see him. The flash went off and blinded me. I think he was on the tall side. He had on tan cords and a green suede—"

"Did you or your mother talk to Oren Angel?"

"No. He wasn't there. No one was there. That's why we were looking in the window."

"And whose bright idea was that, to look in the window?"

Mia's chin shot up. "Mine."

"Liar." Joe snatched *The Scout* off her drawing board, left her office and took the elevator to the seventh floor.

Lucien's secretary, Selma, sat at her desk outside the double doors of his office, her bright coral nails tapping on her PC keyboard. Joe stopped in front of her, *The Scout* folded under his arm.

"Would you ask Mr. Savard if he has a few minutes?"

"For Pete's nephew? Sure." Selma lifted her phone, spoke to Lucien and hung up. "Go on in."

The CEO of Savard Creations sat at a gargantuan dark wood desk in front of a bank of windows. The office walls were lemon yellow, the rug the same ugly paprika red as in the conference room.

Savard's shirtsleeves were rolled to the elbow, the surface of his desk scattered with papers.

"Good morning, Joseph." He took off the silver-framed half-lenses perched on his nose. "Would you like coffee?"

"No, thanks." Joe's cell phone vibrated but he ignored it. "I have something I need to show you, something you need to see."

"All right." Savard moved a stack of papers. "Let me make room."

"Here are the ground rules." Joe leaned his hands on Savard's desk. "You will not yell. You will not throw things. You will sit calmly and look at what I have to show you. We will discuss it. If you so much as twitch in your chair, I will put you on the floor. I was a judo instructor at the police academy. I can do it. Do we understand each other?"

Savard's eyes narrowed. "Are you threatening me?"

"No. I haven't gotten to that part yet. Are you ready?"

Savard drew a breath through his flared nostrils. "Yes."

Joe laid Aubrey Welch's "About Our Town" column on the desk.

Lucien put his glasses on and leaned over the photograph of his wife and daughter. His pale blue eyes scanned the article, then fixed on the photo. His face washed vermilion above the loosened collar of his blue on blue striped shirt.

"Petra." His heart broke in his voice. "She never said a word."

"When did she have a chance? You spent the weekend throwing a tantrum." Savard's eyes flashed up at him. Joe tapped the photograph. "Here's your lawsuit for slander and harassment. Your wife wanted you to call Oren Angel. You refused, so she decided to talk to him herself. She took Mia with her. I doubt Angel would've talked to you, but you could have made an attempt. If you had, this might not have happened."

Savard slapped his hands on his desk. "This is *my* fault?"

"Yes. The photograph, the lawsuit, the theft of Alicia Whitcomb's wedding dress. Everything that has occurred is directed at you. Someone is out to get you, ruin you and Savard Creations. Oren Angel may be the mastermind or he may be a dupe, but you are the target."

"Oren Angel despises me. I despise him. He's behind this. I can feel it." Savard leaned back in his chair and gripped the arms. To keep from twitching, Joe suspected. "I *know* it."

"You don't know it and neither do I. Your wife had the right idea, find out if Angel knew the design came from Savard's. If you'd acted on her suggestion and called him Thursday night, he might have answered the question. The second you sent me to talk to him Friday morning, that window closed."

"The only way we can get at the truth now is in court."

"No, that's not the only way. Drop your countersuit against Angel and let me do my job. Oren Angel, *if* he's involved in this, didn't prance through the front door and steal the design. Someone who works here stole it for him. Give me a chance to find out who."

Savard raised a dark eyebrow. "Am I stopping you?"

"Stopping me? No. Making it damned difficult? Yes. Lawyers ball things up. Suits and motions tie my hands. I uncover a piece of evidence and it gets tossed out of court because there was blah-blah or such-and-such a motion in place."

"That's easily handled." Savard sat forward in his chair. "If you and Walter coordinate your efforts, I'm sure—"

"No. Mr. Vance can litigate or I can investigate. Decide which thing you want to do. Rack Oren Angel's balls in a courtroom or find out who's trying to ruin you and your company. Let me know what you decide. I'll be off the clock until I hear from you."

Joe wheeled away from the desk. He'd nearly made it to the door when Savard said, "That was the threat part, wasn't it?"

"Yes." Joe turned around. "Litigate or investigate. Pick one."

"If I drop my suit against Oren"—Savard stabbed the photograph with a silver pen—"can I sue this dung beetle Welch?"

"No. You can't sue anyone I may need to talk to."

"Dammit." Savard fell back in his chair and stabbed the padded arm with the pen. "All right, Joseph. Investigate."

"You'll drop the countersuit?"

Savard picked up the telephone. "I'm speed dialing Walter."

"And you'll leave Aubrey Welch to me?"

"Yes, but I want him when you're finished."

"Fair enough." Joe nodded and left the office.

On his way to the elevator he checked his cell phone. The message was in text from Brian: GOT HER IN PETE'S OFFICE.

Jenna Savard was laughing and Brian was grinning when Joe came through the door of the security office. She stopped laughing when he showed her Aubrey Welch's column and the photo of her mother and sister on Heavenly Bridals' loading dock.

"When did this happen?" She asked, her mouth drawing into a tight white line. "When did my mother and sister lose their minds?"

"At lunchtime on Friday."

"Does my father know about this?"

"I just left his office. It was news to him. How about you?"

"Did I know about this? No. Did you ask Mia about it?"

"Yes. Your mother decided that if your father wouldn't talk to Oren Angel, she would. She took Mia along for the ride."

"Well, did they? Did they talk to Angel?"

"No. He wasn't there. Mia said no one was there."

"In the middle of the day? That's odd."

Joe thought so, too. If it was true, it was damned odd. Jenna looked at the photo again and shook her head.

"All right, Mr. Kerr. What do you want me to do?"

"I've got someone at Heavenly Bridals this morning. I'm leaving now to talk to Aubrey Welch. Hopefully, your mother, too. If you can keep a lid on your father, that would be helpful."

"I'll do what I can," Jenna said. "Give Welch hell."

Mia sat in a daze at her drawing table. Joe hadn't raised his voice, he'd barely looked at her, yet she was afraid to move for fear she'd fall apart in tiny little cut-up pieces.

Lucien Savard could learn a thing or two about slicing and dicing from Joseph Kerr, Inc.

Of all the sleazeballs who could've taken her photograph with her mother on Heavenly Bridals' loading dock, it had to be Aubrey Welch, the man who made yellow journalism look lily white. Mia had lost count of all the times Lucien had threatened to sue him.

Who had put the bee in Welch's bonnet that if he wanted a juicy story he should follow Petra Savard?

Who could have known, or guessed, that her mother might try to contact Oren Angel?

Mia wished Luke, the king of damage control, was still here, but he'd left for New York yesterday. She'd kissed him good-bye in the lobby on her way out to meet Joe, and Jenna had driven him to the airport.

Joe would tell Lucien about the photograph. He'd found it; he'd *have* to tell him. He was probably in her father's office right now, so what was she doing just *sitting* here? She should call her mother and warn her, while Petra still had time to hop a plane for Brazil.

Mia reached for the phone on the windowsill next to her drawing board. She dialed her mother, who despised call waiting, and got a busy signal. She tried Luke and got his voice mail. In the middle of leaving her brother a message, Mia's intercom line buzzed. It was Damien.

"Mia," he said. "Can you come to my office, please?"

"Yes, sure. I'll be right there."

Mia tried her mother again. Still busy. *Damn.* She hopped off her stool and hurried through design, waggling her fingers at Arlene and Evan and Kiley as she passed. Jordan was nowhere to be seen.

The new assistant, Imogene, a very pretty strawberry blonde with pale blue eyes, sat at the only desk not enclosed by a cubicle. Damien had interviewed her Friday afternoon after Alicia gave him his walking papers. Mia smiled at her as she rapped on Damien's door.

"He buzzed me," she said, and Imogene nodded as Damien said, "Come in."

Because her name was Savard, Mia had the office with the windows, but Damien had made up for the lack of natural light with mirror tiles, light colors and pale woods. His signature black garb against the neutral background made him the focal point of the room.

"Your father tells me that you and Alicia agreed on a design for her new gown," Damien said as Mia sat down in the chair in front of his desk. "I'd like to see it, please."

"I can't show it to you just now. With a thief running around the Savard Building, I didn't feel safe leaving it here."

"I understand, Mia, but we have precious little time to construct this gown. We can't begin until we have the design."

"I realize that." Mia had realized it yesterday when she came home from her coffee date with Joe and the first thing she did was check on Alicia's design. Too bad she'd been so busy feeling sorry for herself that she hadn't bothered to come up with a solution. "Still, we have a security issue. One I think we should discuss with Lucien and Mr. Kerr."

"Dick Tracy?" Was there extra emphasis on *Dick* or was she hearing things? "The genius who pissed off half the company this morning because he changed the access codes to the parking garage?"

Mia pointed her finger at Damien. "That's the guy."

"You aren't being difficult and artistic are you, Mia?"

"No, that's Lucien's job." *And yours, too.* "As soon as I feel secure that the design will be safe, I'll produce it. And you'll be the first to see it."

"All right, Mia," Damien said. "If that's the way you want it."

What's that supposed to mean? Mia wanted to shoot back at him, but she didn't have time to get into a snippy fight with Damien. She had to get back to her office and call her mother. The urgency she felt to talk to Petra was making her insides jump.

"It's not a question of what I want, you want or anyone else wants, Damien," Mia said. "It's the way things are right now. So which one of us is going to set up the meeting with Lucien and Mr. Kerr?"

"I will," Damien said, not quite but almost between his teeth.

"Fine." Mia smiled and stood up. "Let me know."

She hurried back to her office, snatched up the phone, dialed Petra and almost screamed at the busy signal in her ear. Wait. Tilde took the phone off the hook when her parents were gone so she wouldn't have to answer it. Maybe her mother wasn't home.

Mia dialed her mother's cell phone and got her voice mail. "It's Mia," she said. "Our picture is in *The Scout*. Call me, then start packing."

She slammed the phone down and stood at her desk, her heart thudding in her throat. Now what? Grab her coat and go look for Petra? Look where? Call Luke again? No. He was in New York, what could he do? The thought of standing here waiting for Lucien to come and breathe fire on her turned her knees to water, but she had to stay here, she had to be here when her mother called.

Mia sat down to check her e-mail, shook the mouse and cleared the Colin Farrell screen saver from her PC monitor.

An instant message from Becca waited: "You-know-who *did* get lucky. Lunch?"

Mia messaged back: "No lunch. Maybe a Last Supper. More later."

16

The Scout WAS PUBLISHED by Plummer Publications, Inc., one of Kansas City's oldest publishing houses.

Nowhere near as wealthy or as grand as Hallmark Cards, but hardly small potatoes. PPI put three special-interest magazines as well as *The Scout* out the door of their three-story brick building near Our Lady of Perpetual Help Church on the corner of Broadway and Linwood.

The first time Joe came here, within four blocks of the Quik Trip where his life had changed, he'd broken out in a cold sweat.

Old man Plummer, Eugene H., chairman of the board, also sat on a handful of civic boards that supported the arts. Joe knew him to nod to; his contact at PPI was Plummer's son, Drew, editor of *The Scout*.

When Joe stepped off the elevator on the second floor of the PPI building, Drew was swinging around the corner, out of the break room, with a mug of coffee in his hand.

"Aw, crap," he said. Joe wasn't sure if Drew meant him or the end of the Scooby-Doo tie trailing in his coffee. "Who's suing us now?"

"Nobody yet," Joe said. "Want to talk about it?"

"Not really," Drew admitted. "But since you're here, come on."

He led Joe down a long hall that branched on the left into *The Scout*'s newsroom and on the right into another large area divided into cubicles, like the design department at Savard's.

The editor's office lay straight ahead at the end of the hall. Around a jog to the right was Aubrey Welch's dirty, grubby little hole. The door was shut tight and locked with three dead bolts. Joe had jokingly asked Drew once if the door to Welch's office was bulletproof. With a straight face, *The Scout*'s editor replied, "You bet your bippy."

"Have a seat." Drew rounded his desk, put his cup down on a blotter that had more rings than a sequoia and dropped into a green chair with a wooden swivel that squealed at his weight.

The Scout's editor's desk was a beat-up, old blond wood behemoth, big as a boxcar, and a dead ringer for every desk that every nun who had terrorized Joe during his school career had sat behind with a ruler.

The chair in front of the desk was slatted wood with arms that helped contain the stack of back issues piled on the seat. Joe lifted the papers onto the floor, gave the office door a push shut and sat.

"Okay." Drew sighed and quaffed his coffee from his mug, which said, *"Editors Do It in Pencil."* "Who has Aubrey offended now?"

Joe took the folded copy of this week's *The Scout* from his pocket, opened it and laid it in front of Drew, who scanned the "About Our Town" column, smoothed his damp tie and groaned.

"What is that crazy old fart doing? Pissing off somebody who has the money *and* the temperament to sue the pants off us?"

"This is just a suggestion," Joe said. "But why don't you read what Welch writes before you print it?"

"June sixteenth." Drew looked up at him. "That's the day the iron-clad contract Welch extorted from my father, to work here and write here, carte blanche, without edits, expires. That's the day I can fire him. That's the day I'm living for. Are you working for Lucien Savard?"

"Yes." Joe hooked his thumb toward Welch's office. "Is he in?"

"No. This time of day Aubrey is out digging in Dumpsters." Drew's mouth twisted. "I mean that literally as well as figuratively."

"Has Welch changed his haunts recently?"

"Since the last time you were looking to throttle him? No."

"Good." Joe nodded. "Then I know where to find him."

"Do you have a cat? A bird? A hamster? Any creature that requires tons of shredded paper that I would be happy to keep you supplied with in perpetuity if you could talk Lucien Savard out of suing us?"

"No pets. If you see Welch before I do, I'd like to know who took that photo." There was no point repeating Mia's nondescription. "One of your staffers or a freelancer? I'd also like to know who or what put Welch on Savard's trail. I'll put in a good word for you with Savard."

"Thanks, man." Drew rose and gave Joe a hand slap. "I'll work Aubrey over with the rubber hose."

Joe folded *The Scout* into his pocket and headed for

his truck. He'd just slid behind the wheel when his cell phone rang.

"Okay," Moira said, an I-want-to-scream-but-I-won't edge in her voice. "Oren Angel has agreed to meet you on neutral turf. With his attorney present, of course. It's the best I could do."

"It's better than I did. Good job." Joe backed the truck out of its parking space, drove to the exit of the Plummer Publications parking lot and braked. "Where am I going, Smooch?"

"The swanky Chinese joint on Eighty-fifth Street in Prairie Village. The Jade Something. Forty-five minutes. You're buying."

"Naturally." Joe made a left toward I-35 to take him to Kansas.

"Angel lawyered up awfully fast. Think he knew this was coming?"

"If he didn't before, he knew *something* was coming when I showed up at his door Friday morning and spoke the name Lucien Savard."

"You ready for this? Angel's attorney, Howard Edwards, was sitting at his elbow when I walked into Angel's office this morning."

"Doesn't surprise me that Edwards is babysitting," Joe said, but it made his jaw clench. "Angel is every bit as volatile as Savard. These two have been looking for a reason to go after each other for years."

"I tried to find out what Angel knew about the design and when he knew it." Moira snorted. "Fat chance with Edwards in the room."

"We'll double-team them at lunch. Maybe we'll get lucky."

Moira was seated at a back booth with Oren Angel

and his attorney, Howard Edwards, when Joe arrived at the Jade Bowl restaurant.

"I'm here to set the parameters of this meeting and see that they are maintained," Edwards said when Joe slid next to Moira in the booth. "My client will not answer any questions about the suit he filed against Lucien Savard."

"How about the basis for the suit?" Joe asked. "The subpoena is a little vague, and shaky on specifics."

"It was enough for the judge," Edwards replied. "And no, Mr. Angel won't answer any questions about that, either."

"And *that* is . . . ?" Joe let his voice trail off.

Howard Edwards, a pudgy man with black hair slicked against his skull and horn-rimmed glasses, gave him a nice-try smile. Oren Angel grinned. Why not? He was sitting in the catbird seat.

Friday morning, he'd had no trouble tossing Joe to the curb like a Hefty bag despite his size. Angel was a lean five-nine and maybe one seventy-five after a lengthy stint at an all-you-can-eat pasta buffet. His red hair was silver at the temples, springy and thinning on top. He wore a quiet, green plaid jacket that suited his pale, ginger-freckled complexion.

"Okay," Joe said. "Who'd like to talk about the Chiefs' defense?"

Edwards smiled again. Angel guffawed.

The waitress, a tiny flawless Chinese girl, bowed up to the table, took their orders, delivered tea and bowed away.

"I'm told," Joe said to Angel, "that you got your start at Savard's."

"You heard wrong. I gave Lucien Savard *his* start. He

had the money, but I had the talent and the genius. I still do."

"That conflicts with another thing I heard. Which is that you put your company name on the gowns created by the designers you employ."

"Of course I do," Angel snapped. "Brides come to my showroom to purchase a gown styled by Heavenly Bridals, not Mary Jane Nobody."

"Makes sense to me." Joe shrugged. "So why does Lucien Savard give credit to the individual designers?"

"Because he's an idiot. Do you know how many first-rate, fresh young designers Lucien has lost?"

As a matter of fact, Joe did. He and Moira spent last evening after the chili party researching Savard Creations, Heavenly Bridals and wedding fashions in general on the Internet, but he looked Oren Angel in the eye and said, "No."

"Dozens, scores. He finds them, he trains them, *helps* them build a name for themselves and then *pffft*—" Angel made a sweep with one arm toward the window behind the booth—"they're out the door."

"To New York or Los Angeles," Moira said, picking up her part of their tag-team strategy. "A savvy move, according to *Women's Wear Daily*. Designers who've matriculated from Savard's don't forget their mentor. Savard Creations has picked up a lot of referrals and made a lot of lucrative connections in the upper echelons of fashion that way."

"Young lady," Angel swung a blistering glare on Moira. "Lucien Savard's great-grandfather was a corset-maker. *A corset-maker.*"

"The first one west of St. Louis." Moira smiled, unfazed. "He amassed a robber baron–size fortune making ladies' foundations."

"Has anyone," Joe jumped in, "left Savard's to work for you?"

"I wouldn't hire anyone who worked for Lucien." Angel swung his on-fire green eyes on Joe. "He's been trying to plant a spy at Heavenly Bridals since the day I opened my doors."

"That's another conflict." Joe used his I'm-just-a-dumb-gumshoe-trying-to-do-my-job voice. "I've heard that you've made several attempts to lure Damien DeMello away from Savard Creations."

"I wouldn't let DeMello clip loose threads. He's approached me, if you want the truth. Don't blame him. He'll never go anywhere with Lucien's brats ahead of him in the hierarchy."

"DeMello is head designer. How much higher could he go?"

"He'll never know, will he?" Angel smiled. "Head designer is just a title. Lucien calls all the shots. His brats get all the perks."

"You never married, Mr. Angel?" Moira asked.

"No," Angel said simply and coldly.

Lunch arrived. When they finished, the waitress cleared the plates, brought another pot of tea and a small dish of fortune cookies and bowed away.

"Gentlemen." Joe lifted his folded copy of *The Scout* from the pocket of his tan corduroy sport coat. "I'd like to show you a newspaper article and ask if either one of you have seen it. May I?"

"If you're referring to Aubrey Welch's column in *The Scout*," Howard Edwards replied, "yes, we've seen the article and the photograph and we have no comment."

The attorney's bland show-nothing expression didn't change, but Oren Angel's jaw tightened and another spark leaped in his eyes.

Joe tucked *The Scout* back in his pocket.

"Mr. Angel, how long did you work for Savard Creations?"

"Twenty years. I was the first designer Lucien hired. That was 1966. I graduated from the Kansas City Art Institute in sixty-four. So did Lucien and Petra. They got married." A snarl crept into Angel's voice. "I went East and did two years at the Parsons School of Design. I worked for Lucien until 1986. The oldest brat, the boy, was fifteen by then and already working summers at Savard's. I saw the handwriting on the wall and got out."

Moira asked, "Were you close friends with the Savards at school?"

"No." Angel bit out the word and his jaw clenched even tighter.

He was about as gifted a liar as Mia. How close, Joe wondered, had she come to calling Oren Angel Daddy?

"But you did *know* them at the Art Institute," Joe said. "That *is* where you met Lucien and Petra Savard?"

"I just said that," Angel snapped. "Are you paying attention?"

"This is all the time we can give you." Howard Edwards laid his napkin on the table. "I'm due in court. Thank you for lunch, Mr. Kerr."

"Thank Lucien." Angel flung down his napkin and shoved out of the booth behind his attorney. "It's the least he owes me."

Joe watched the two men walk out of the restaurant. When Edwards laid his hand on Angel's shoulder, Oren shrugged him off, stepped ahead and pushed through the glass doors into the parking lot.

"Well, well," Moira said. "I'd say Lucien got the girl."

"Would've been nice," Joe replied, "if the girl had told us."

"If Angel was involved in the theft of Alicia's design, then this whole thing is a giant pissing contest."

"Forty years is a long time to wait to get even over a woman."

"What are *you* talking about?" Moira snorted. "You're not over my mother, and it's been ten years."

"I *am* over your mother, and we're not talking about me." Joe gave her the look he'd used when she was twelve and begged to stay up on a school night to watch Letterman. "We're discussing the case. If Angel is in on this, it's not just about Petra Savard."

"She's at the root of it." Moira leaned toward him and narrowed her eyes. "Oh. There it is. I see it now— the how-could-you-disappoint-me face. You chewed Mia out because of the photograph, didn't you?"

"I asked her three simple questions. One, why didn't she stop her mother. Two, why didn't she call me. And three, whose bright idea was it to look in the window."

"She said it was hers, but you didn't believe her," Moira said, just to prove how well she knew him, Joe figured sourly. "That means it was her mother's idea, so why did Petra Savard start looking in windows? A window *behind* the building, no less? That's what I can't figure."

"I asked Mia that, too, if she or Petra spoke to Oren Angel. She said no, he wasn't there. She said no one was there—at lunchtime on Friday. So Petra decided to play Peeping Tom."

"Hmmm." Moira sipped from her tiny round teacup. "I'd sure like to know why Heavenly Bridals was shut down in the middle of the day."

"So would I. Put Jimbo on Heavenly Bridals. I told him you'd have something else for him. Who would you suggest for Angel?"

"Whoa, Lone Ranger. We're running short on ground troops."

"We are?" This was news to Joe. "How come?"

"Why do I e-mail personnel reports if you don't read them? Some of our guys and gals want to go home next week for Thanksgiving. If they have the days coming, I can't say no. I can only ask."

"Ask nicely. Dangle the usual bonus. Worst case, I'll take Angel."

"And leave Brian in charge at the Savard Building? You're brave."

"Don't underestimate Brian, Smooch."

"I'm not. I'm just picturing Brian calling Lucien Savard Darth Vader, and wondering where that will get us."

Joe grinned. "I think it could be a horizon-broadening experience for both of them."

"We need to know what Angel knew about that design and when he knew it." Moira poured the last of the tea into her cup. "How are we going to get around Howard Edwards?"

"If Jimbo can't shake something loose, I have a plan." Joe kissed Moira's temple. "Charge lunch on the corporate card, Smooch, and bill Savard. I have to go dig through the trash."

* * *

For a dirtbag, Aubrey Welch had some high-class haunts.

Joe found him at Le Fou Frog. One of Kansas City's best-known yet best-hidden French restaurants, so far downtown it was nearly in the Missouri River. The pale green walls were covered with framed watercolors of Paris street scenes. The tables were small, clustered together in places to seat large parties; the tops marble, the legs and the padded chairs off-white curved iron.

Maybe this place would work for New Year's Eve.

Joe tucked that away in the I-can't-afford-to-think-about-that-now file. Along with Mia's smile, her snappy, too-damn-smart-for-her-own-good dark eyes and her stricken look when he'd shown her the photograph. She'd blown it and she'd known it.

He'd blown it, too. Last Friday at the meeting in the conference room with Lucien Savard and his family, Walter Vance and DeMello.

He'd missed Petra Savard's accusatory tone when she'd said to Lucien, "*You* should have called Oren," mistaken her husband's glee in announcing that he and Angel hated each other's guts for a business rivalry rather than a personal one. Petra's defense of Angel, her claim that he didn't know the design was stolen; Lucien's snarled response that Oren Angel had done it to provoke him, to incite a war.

He'd missed those cues. He'd realized it when he replayed the tape in his head on the way here and didn't like what he'd seen. He'd blown it, pure and simple, but he wouldn't blow it again.

Welch sat at a table eating an artful pile of mashed

potatoes and a fillet of beef liver curved and curled to stand like a crown roast.

In French cuisine, presentation was everything. A precept Welch had applied to his own life. In these shabby chic surroundings, you wouldn't take him for a sleaze. He didn't dress like one, either. A blue patterned vest with a blue shirt and gray suit, gold cuff links, a stick pin in a muted stripe tie that winked at Joe as he walked up to the table.

"Organ meats will kill you, Aubrey." Joe pulled out a chair and sat down. "Especially liver. It holds all the impurities. Maybe that's why you like it."

"Do join me, Joseph." Welch put down his knife and fork and dabbed his mouth with his napkin. His lips were very pink, framed by a tawny brown and silver goatee. He smiled, a twinkle in his light brown eyes. "You're always such an amusing luncheon companion."

"I do the best I can, Aubrey. Wish I could say the same for you."

"Let's don't go over that old ground again. Will you have coffee?"

Joe nodded. Welch signaled the waiter. The coffee came, the waiter went. Welch finished his lunch, poured cream in his cup and sipped.

"Shall I astound you with my knowledge of who you are working for and why you are here, or do you want me to pretend to be surprised?"

"If it will incline you to be helpful for a change, astound me."

"Lucien Savard hired you to find out who stole Alicia Whitcomb's wedding dress, which appeared in the new issue of *Today's Bride* in an advertisement placed by Oren Angel of Heavenly Bridals."

"Why wasn't that the lead for your column this morning?"

"Because the photograph of Petra and Mia Savard was better."

"Saving Alicia for next week?"

"Yes. She'll likely be my segue into the rest of the story."

"Who was the man behind the camera?"

"A young associate of mine, eager to follow in my footsteps."

"God help us."

"Joseph." Welch tsked. "As if you've never dealt with the unsavory or the unseemly."

"When I do, Aubrey, I like to think it's for the greater good."

"And the nice fat fee you earn has nothing to do with it?"

"Do you work for free?"

"One must eat. Will you have dessert?"

"No thanks." Joe had a fortune cookie in his pocket for later. "Who tipped you to Savard Creations versus Heavenly Bridals?"

"My sources are sacred, and protected by the First Amendment."

"I don't need to know who. Just where the tip came from."

"Narrowing the field of suspects, eh?" Welch snapped his fingers for a dessert menu. "What do I gain if I help you?"

"You mean what's in it for you? What do you want?"

The waiter brought the menu. Welch ordered crème brûlée and eyed Joe over his clasped fingers.

"I want an invitation to Alicia Whitcomb's wedding."

"I don't have that kind of clout, Aubrey."

"I'm sure Lucien Savard does."

"You're joking. After the photo and the smear job you did on his wife and daughter, you expect Savard to reward you?"

"I don't expect anything. I'm telling you what I want. No invitation, no information."

This was one of those times that Joe wished he was Brian. At this point, his former partner would be pulling every last hair out of Welch's chinny chin chin. A tempting thought, but it wasn't Joe's style and he might, God forbid, have to deal with Welch again before June sixteenth.

"If I can arrange an invitation, I'll want the name."

"If you can arrange an invitation to the wedding of the governor's daughter, I'll give you the moon on a bed of stars, Joseph."

"I'll settle for the name." Joe rose and pushed in his chair. "Enjoy your dessert. I'll be in touch."

Liar. OH, THAT STUNG. The fact that it was true only
made it hurt more. Why had she lied to Joe about something as stupid as whose idea it was to look in the window? Why had she even *tried*? She was the world's
worst liar. The beans were spilled, out of the can, all
over the floor. She couldn't protect her mother now, no
matter what she did.

Mia paced between her desk and her drawing board.
She'd been prowling her office all morning, jumping for
the phone every time it rang, checking her cell phone
every two minutes. It was nearly 12:45 and she still hadn't
heard a peep from Petra.

She hadn't heard from Lucien, either—which hung
over her like a black cloud of dread—and now she was
starving.

An hour ago Jordan had offered to bring her a sandwich back from lunch, but an hour ago she hadn't been
hungry. Now she could eat the telephone that was keeping her here trapped like a rat. A lying rat.

Evan or Kylie would probably run upstairs to the
cafeteria for her, but Mia didn't want to rouse their suspicions. Like they couldn't see her roaming her office
through the glass walls, but she did that now and then

when she was thinking. She'd seen Jordan coming on her way to lunch, hopped on her stool and managed to look busy.

Mia's stomach growled. Surely she had *something* edible around here. She searched her desk and found only pencils, paper clips and Post-its, stuff Jenna had put away. Any munchies she'd had stashed were in the boxes she'd tossed in the closet. Or Jenna, the health queen, had thrown them away. Well, fudge. Preferably with pecans.

Her purse. Maybe she had something in her purse.

She'd locked her shoulder bag in the bottom drawer of her desk, as she'd promised Joe she would, and slipped the key in the pencil tray in the middle drawer. Mia unlocked the drawer and put the key back, pulled her purse onto her lap and unzipped it.

Jeez. When was the last time she'd cleaned this thing out? A two-hundred-dollar Prada trash bag. While she dug through her purse in search of food, Mia tossed all the folded and torn bits of paper, mostly receipts and crumpled notes she'd written herself, onto her desk.

She didn't find any crackers left over from salad-only lunches, and no Milky Ways, her favorite candy bar. Only a role of cherry Life Savers. Mia popped one and started sorting through the trash from her purse.

The Price Chopper register tape from yesterday, showing how much she'd saved with her Chopper Shopper Card—$2.32—ATM receipts and two note cards stapled with swatches of material she wanted to look for on her next trip to the fabric store. On one of them, a green 3 x 5, she found three scrawled letters and three numbers—CMK-039.

A license number. Why had she written down a license numb—

Oh God, no! A wave of horror swept Mia. Gushed from the pit of her gnawing stomach, rang like bats in a belfry in her ears and made her empty, not-a-single-brain-cell-functioning head spin.

It was the license number of the Kia Sportage that the man with the camera, the one she'd chased, had leaped into. Oh, God. Mia clapped a hand over her mouth and sucked air between her fingers. Now she remembered—biting the cap off a pen in her mother's Cadillac Esplanade on the drive back to Savard's, fishing the card out of her purse and writing down the license number so she wouldn't forget it.

She'd meant to give it to Joe. As soon as Petra told Lucien they'd gone to Heavenly Bridals. So his friend at the DMV who'd looked up *her* license plate could tell him who owned the dirty gray mini SUV.

Then came Alicia Whitcomb, getting stuck designing her new wedding gown, Blanko's, Terence and one Bloody Mary too many.

Saturday she'd been hungover with the headache from hell, the subpoena arrived and her sewing room was trashed.

And Sunday—oh, hell, forget it. The entire weekend was a disaster.

She'd meant to help. Now, no matter what she said to Joe, not only would she look like a bigger liar, she'd look like she'd withheld evidence.

Mia dropped her hand in her lap and stared at the windows. Too bad they were sealed shut. Otherwise, she could jump.

"Miss Savard?" A voice she didn't recognize spoke behind her.

Mia slipped the 3 x 5 card into the middle drawer of

her desk and swiveled her chair around. A young man she'd never seen before stood in her office doorway, behind a wire mail cart. He had close-cropped red hair and a nice smile. He held a pale burgundy envelope.

"Hello," Mia said. "You're new, aren't you?"

"Yes, ma'am. Ricky LeHay. This is for you." He held out his hand. "Special delivery from Mr. Savard's office."

Uh-oh. Mia took the envelope and said, "Thank you."

"You're welcome." Ricky lifted a clipboard from the mail cart. "Would you sign for it, please?"

Mia blinked. "I beg your pardon?"

"Mr. Savard told me to have you sign for it."

Oh, did he? Mia thought. "Sure," she said to Ricky. She took the clipboard, signed it and gave it back. "There you go."

"Thanks." He tucked the clipboard in his cart and wheeled away.

Mia looked at the envelope. Her name was typed across the front, not handwritten in her father's bold, flourishing script. Lucien had never sent her anything through the interoffice mail that required a signature. She lifted the envelope to her ear to make sure it wasn't ticking.

As she did, a flicker of movement in the design department caught her eye. She glanced up and locked gazes with Damien, standing in the corridor between the cubicles. He flicked her a hi-there wave. Mia waved back and rolled her chair up to her desk.

She slit the flap with her letter opener, took out a single folded sheet of pale burgundy Savard stationery, opened it and read:

Dearest Mia,
You are fired. Effective immediately.
Love,
Dad
P.S. Please give Alicia's new design to Damien, ASAP.

Mia's chin shot up. Damien was gone, but the pneumatic door at the far end of the design department was falling shut. *Hi-there wave, my foot,* she thought. Bye-bye was more like it. Damien knew what was in the letter—he'd probably added the P.S.

Mia could not believe this. She'd agreed to design another dress for Alicia, thereby saving Lucien's butt, and he fired her? Over the photo in *The Scout?* A week ago, in the midst of her fight to get out of bridal and into trousseau, she would've danced for joy at being fired, but now . . .

"No way." Mia slapped the letter on her desk. *"No way!"*

She jumped out of her chair and out of her office.

The closest target was Damien. Mia stalked through the design department. She didn't knock on his door, just pushed it open—no Damien—and spun around to the open space between the cubicles.

Arlene, Evan and Kiley stared at her. Jordan grinned. The new assistant, Imogene, looked at her nonplussed.

"Where is he?" Mia demanded.

"He went thataway." Evan pointed over the top of his cubicle.

Mia pushed through the pneumatic door and turned left toward the sewing room. Savard's eight seamstresses lifted their heads from their machines and their handwork when she came through the door.

"Is Damien here?" she asked Viola, the head seam-stress.

"No," she said. "We haven't seen him all morning."

"Thanks," Mia said, and turned back into the hallway.

On her left was a stairwell. Straight ahead, the shoulder-high wall topped by a two-bar metal railing that over-looked the lobby. She couldn't hear voices from any of the lower floors, and she'd need a box to stand on to see over the rail.

Damien wouldn't jump, anyway. He was too vain, too arrogant, too behind-the-back sneaky. This was an all-new low for him, whining to Lucien that she wouldn't produce Alicia's design, which was *not* what she'd said. Did he really think he could get away with such a cheap shot?

Well, for now he could. What was she doing chasing Damien? She should be on her way to the seventh floor and Daddy Dearest.

Selma glanced up from her PC when Mia came around the corner from the elevator and said, "He's at lunch."

"Thank you." Mia about-faced and headed back to the elevator.

Good, she thought. She could have it out with her fa-ther and then grab something to eat before she fainted from hunger.

On six, she paused in the cafeteria doorway and scanned the tables for Lucien. An awful lot of wooden folding chairs had replaced the mauve and green padded chairs he'd busted up after last Thursday's meeting, when he'd fired the entire company. Is that what firing her was? A restrained-for-a-change tantrum?

The tables weren't that crowded; it was late-ish to be having lunch. Maybe thirty Savard employees were finishing coffee or dessert.

Lucien sat with Jenna at a small table near the middle of the room. He liked to be the center of attention. *Happy to oblige,* Mia thought, and headed toward him.

Jenna saw her first, touched Lucien's wrist and murmured to him. He put his fork down on his plate. Meat loaf with mashed potatoes and green beans and a side of spiced apples. Mia loved spiced apples. She loved her father, too, but his reign of terror had gone on long enough.

Which is what Jenna and Luke had tried to tell her when they launched their campaign to liberate her from bridal. Mia hadn't seen it then, but she saw it now. From the corner of her eye, she saw forks lowered onto plates and heard cups clink against saucers.

Lucien rose to his feet as she stopped across the table from him.

"Why did you fire me, Dad?"

He didn't glance at the heads turning in their direction, but he was aware of them. So was Mia.

"We'll discuss this," her father said curtly, "in my office."

"We'll discuss it here." Mia tapped the tabletop, caught a glimpse of Jenna and the atta-girl glint in her eyes. "Are you going to fire Mother, too, because you were too stubborn to call Oren Angel?"

"Certainly not," Lucien snapped. "Did you give the new design for Alicia Whitcomb to Damien?"

"No. And I'm not going to. The design is mine."

Lucien curved his knuckles on the table, narrowed his eyes and leaned toward Mia. "That design is the property of Savard Creations."

"No, it isn't." Mia spread *her* hands on the table and leaned toward *him*. "I resigned last Thursday. I was a free agent on Friday when I created that design for Alicia Whitcomb. So you can take your termination letter and set fire to it."

"*Mi-ah*." Lucien made two sharp, warning syllables out of her name and threw on the "h," which meant he'd lost patience. "Don't push me."

"I'm not pushing, Dad. I'm leaving."

"*Lucien Savard!*" a woman shrieked behind her.

Mia wasn't positive it was her mother until she spun around and saw Petra, in her silver fox jacket, stalking toward her father with a sheet of Savard stationery clutched in her hand. Mia had never heard her mother raise her voice. Living with Lucien, when did she have a chance?

Mia glanced at her father, saw the startled, wide-eyed expression on his face and realized he'd never heard Petra raise her voice, either.

"I warned you!" A second before her mother crushed the paper and hurled it at Lucien, Mia saw the bold, black "Dad" and realized it was her termination letter. "I told you what would happen if you *ever* fired another one of my children!"

"You run our home, Petra," Lucien said coolly. "I run Savard's."

"You think you run the world! You think all you have to do is shout and people will do what you say, but I won't! Not anymore!"

Before Lucien could open his mouth, Petra snatched the plate of meat loaf, mashed potatoes, green beans and the side of spiced apples off the table and mashed it against Lucien's chest. Jenna leaped out of her chair, around the table and threw her arms around her mother.

Mia stared, openmouthed and astonished. So did Lucien as the plate slid down his chest, leaving a trail of smeared gravy and green beans on his blue-on-blue-striped shirt, and clattered onto the table.

Chairs scraped, feet thudded and the cafeteria cleared in a flash.

"Call Rudy," Petra said. "Maybe you can stay with him."

"Petra," Lucien said, his eyes brimming. "No."

"You see? It works." She smiled. "I didn't shout, but you heard me."

Then she turned on her heel and swept out of the cafeteria. Jenna followed her without a word or a glance at Lucien.

This couldn't be happening. Her parents didn't fight. Lucien raged; Petra waited till he blew himself out and then talked sense to him.

Mia didn't know what to do. Go with her mother or stay with her father? This wasn't her fault; Lucien had crossed a line drawn by Petra. She hadn't caused this, yet she felt responsible. Her heart felt like it was about to crack.

Her father looked at her and gave her a thin smile.

"Go on, Mia," he said gently. "I'll be all right."

She went, almost running, before she burst into tears.

It was nearly two-thirty when Joe stepped into the elevator in the parking garage of the Savard Building and pushed L for the lobby.

If he'd known Friday afternoon, Friday night or even on Saturday that Mia and Petra had gone to Heavenly

Bridals to talk to Oren Angel and someone had taken their photograph, he would've suspected Welch immediately. It was just his style.

If he'd known Friday afternoon, he might've been able to intercept the photo before it reached Oren Angel. Incitement was Aubrey's style, too. By e-mail or messenger, Joe was sure the photo had gone straight from Welch to Heavenly Bridals' CEO. No photo, maybe no lawsuit—or at least, not as soon. Angel might've held off.

But the suit was filed, and the weekend had given Welch, the photographer and the tipster plenty of time to get their stories straight and close ranks before the photo appeared in *The Scout*.

Which meant Joe was playing catch-up. Not his favorite game.

He'd replayed more tapes on the way here from Le Fou Frog, especially the one from Friday night at Blanko's.

Mia had asked him, "Did you have someone following my mother and me today?" When he'd asked if someone had tailed them, she'd blown him off with the story about footprints in the snow on the sidewalk Thursday night and distracted him with her long, dark eyelashes.

Innocently, he was sure. The fault wasn't hers, it was his. She'd all but told him that someone *had* followed her and her mother. If he'd had his mind on the case instead of the tip of her tongue touching the split in her lip, he would have realized it. He *should* have realized it, should've stayed on it till he got the truth out of her.

He wasn't angry with Mia about the photograph. Most people didn't know how to handle situations like that.

That's why they hired private detectives. He was angry with himself for blowing it.

He wouldn't blow it again.

Joe stepped out of the elevator and turned into the lobby.

Brian, in his blue Savard uniform, was on his knees before the pool at the foot of the waterfall, an aquarium-size fishnet in his right hand, poised above the water. When he saw Joe, he stood up.

"Any fish in there?" Joe asked.

"A couple. And a freakin' little frog that won't shut up." Brian went back to the kiosk, sat down and tucked his net in a drawer. "If I catch him, I'm gonna have frog legs for Thanksgiving dinner."

"Good luck, mighty hunter. Anything interesting here?"

"You missed it, Obi-Wan." Brian folded his arms, leaned back in his chair and looked at Joe. "Old man Savard fired Mia, and Mrs. S. threw Lucien's lunch at him. See Betty for details. She was there."

"I'll talk to her." Joe didn't need to guess why Mia had been fired. He knew—the photo in *The Scout*. Retribution was Lucien Savard's style. "Anybody interesting on the visitors list?"

"Not really." Brian passed Joe the clipboard. "See for yourself."

Three account reps from fashion magazines had checked in to see Celeste Taylor in advertising; four reps from fabric manufacturers to see Lucien Savard; Walter Vance arrived at ten A.M., left at eleven-fifteen; Petra Savard signed in at ten minutes past one.

"I signed out Mrs. S. at one thirty-five," Brian said as Joe read the sign-out line and recognized his handwriting. "That woman had fire in her eyes. No way was I getting in her path with a clipboard. Jenna left with her. Mia left at two on the nose."

Joe handed the check-in sheet back to Brian and looked at his watch: 2:35. He hadn't missed Mia by much.

Walter Vance pushed through the revolving door, briefcase in hand, a dark green muffler tucked inside the collar of his black wool overcoat. Joe wondered if the scarf was another Petra Savard creation.

"Mr. Vance." Brian offered him the clipboard. "Back so soon."

"I can't stay away." Vance signed in and nodded at Joe. "Mr. Kerr. Can I have a word?"

They stepped away from the kiosk toward the pool, where the splash of the waterfall would mask what they said.

"I realize it's early days," Vance said. "But, any progress?"

"I'm ninety-five percent sure the thief is in design. Still in design. It's no fun ruining someone's life if you can't hang around to watch."

"Lucien has backed off on counterfiling against Angel. At your suggestion, I understand." Vance smiled. "Thank you."

"I thought you'd be chomping at the bit to get into court."

"Against Oren Angel? No. The animosity between Lucien and Angel is mostly personal. That's a mudslinging match and tough to win."

"I had lunch with Angel and Howard Edwards," Joe said, and gave Vance the highlights. "I'm clear on what's personal between Savard and Angel and why Mrs. Savard thought Oren Angel would talk to her."

"Lucien showed me the photograph in *The Scout*." Vance shook his head. "Petra meant well, but it was ill-advised and not helpful to the litigation or, I would imagine, your investigation."

"I really need to know what Angel knew about the design and when he knew it. Can you get Howard Edwards out of my way?"

"If Lucien counterfiles, then I can depose Angel. Short of that, no."

"That's what I thought. How about this," Joe said, and ran his idea for getting around Howard Edwards past Vance.

"You'd have to script the whole thing," Vance replied. "I'm not sure it would be admissible in court. It could be considered entrapment."

"If it tells me what Angel knew and when he knew it, and I can get answers to a couple other questions that keep coming up, I can catch this guy and we don't have to sweat what's admissible in court."

"All right. If you need help writing the script, let me know."

Vance offered his hand. Joe shook it and they went their separate ways. Vance to Lucien Savard's office, Joe to human resources.

He spent a few minutes with George "Zippy" Burkholtz, the head of HR, in his glass-walled office. In plain view, where all of Zippy's twenty employees, including JKI's Betty Sanders, could see him.

"Lucien wrote the memo you asked for and I sent it out by e-mail this morning," Zippy said. "He made it clear that you'll be in the building until further notice, investigating the theft of Alicia Whitcomb's design, and that he expects everyone to cooperate with you. Each department has a bulletin board. I posted hard copies on all of them."

"That's great, Mr. Burkholtz. I appreciate your help."

"Anything I can do. The sooner this situation is resolved, the sooner things around here will get back to normal."

It wouldn't be the old normal; it would be a new and different kind of normal. Something like a theft, especially an internal theft, irrevocably changed the status quo, but Joe didn't say so. Zippy was a smart man; he'd figure it out. The best Joe could do before he walked out of the Savard Building for the last time was make sure that nothing like this ever happened here again.

He shook hands with Zippy and wandered out into the hallway. With his hands in his pockets, he stood at the company bulletin board reading the usual HR postings, stuff from the Feds and the State of Missouri, notes put up by employees and Lucien's memo.

The bulletin board was near the restrooms and water fountains. Joe paid no attention to Betty when she passed him on her way to the ladies room. He smiled at her when she stopped beside him on her way back.

"Excuse me. I left my glasses at my desk," she said, loud enough for anyone passing by to hear. "Do you see any car-pool notes?"

"There's a couple here." Joe unpinned them from the board and handed them to her.

"Big blowup in the cafeteria," Betty murmured, holding the notes close to her nose and pretending to read them. "Lucien Savard fired Mia. She marched in and asked him why. She asked if he was going to fire her mother, too, because he was too stubborn to call Oren Angel, and she refused to give Alicia Whitcomb's new design to Damien DeMello. She said the design belonged to her because she'd quit last Thursday." Betty paused and shook her head. "I'm told this kind of thing happens a lot around here. You're fired, you're hired, you're fired. How does anyone get any work done?"

She handed one of the notes to Joe and he pinned it on the board.

"Then Petra Savard came in, shrieking like a banshee. She wadded up a piece of paper and threw it at Lucien. Here it is." Betty dipped her hand in the pocket of her skirt and slipped him a crumpled, folded sheet of pale burgundy stationery. "It's Mia's termination letter. I hung around in the lobby and when all the Savards left, I went back and got it."

"You're the bomb, Betty." Joe smiled at her and her eyes twinkled.

"Mrs. Savard said to her husband, 'I told you what would happen if you ever fired another one of my children.' Lucien said, 'You run our home, I run Savard's.' Petra said, 'You think you run the world. You think all you have to do is shout and people will do what you say.' She said she wasn't going to anymore. That's when she threw his lunch at him and I cleared out of the cafeteria with everyone else."

"How many employees witnessed this?" Joe asked.

"Twenty-six. I counted," Betty replied. "I have their names and their departments. Since I'm new, I went around introducing myself."

"Betty." Joe clutched a hand over his heart. "Will you marry me?"

"If I were forty years younger, in a flash." She handed him another note to pin on the board, stepped closer and lowered her voice another notch. "I ducked behind one of the doors and eavesdropped. Petra kicked Lucien out. She told him to go stay with his brother, Rudy."

"Whoa," Joe said. Had Walter Vance come back for this? "Anybody else hear this?"

"I don't think so. Not yet, anyway. E-mail, instant messaging and the chat in the bathrooms is all about Petra shouting at Lucien and dousing him in meat loaf. I have that from Stink. I put a bug in his ear and he's monitoring from IT. Ricky made a mail drop to HR. I slipped him a note and he's got his ear to the ground, too."

"Betty." Joe leaned one arm on the bulletin board and bent his head near hers. "Where do you want to go on our honeymoon?"

18

IT WAS TILDE WHO TOLD PETRA about the photograph in *The Scout*.

Did it surprise Mia that Tilde not only read, but also subscribed to *The Scout*? No. Did it amaze her to find Tilde gone, as in packed up and left in a huff, when she arrived at her parents' house forty-five minutes after her mother and Jenna? Yes. Yes, yes and *yes*!

"Where'd she go?" Mia asked around a mouth full of the Winstead's double steak burger with cheese she'd stopped to buy on her way here.

"To Rudy's house to be with your father," Petra said. "She'll be in high alt taking care of her two darling boys."

"I wonder how her darling boys," Jenna said, "and Uncle Rudy's housekeeper will feel about having Tilde there?"

"I don't know," Petra declared. "And I don't care."

The three of them sat at the half-moon kitchen island, Jenna and her mother sipping chamomile tea and Mia wolfing her steak burger.

Jenna slid Mia a look that asked *Are you buying this*?

"She'll come back with Dad, won't she?" Mia asked.

"No, she won't. *If* your father comes back," Petra

said. "He may not want to when he sees the list of changes that are going to take place around here. One of them is that Tilde goes to live with her nephew."

"It's past time for that," Jenna said. "What else is on this list?"

"No shouting. No throwing things. At home or at Savard's. No firing my children or anyone else without just cause and due process."

"It would be kinder to have Dad lobotomized," Jenna said. "He'll never agree to those things."

"Then he won't be coming home," Petra said, and sipped her tea.

The phone rang. Petra lifted the cordless handset she'd brought to the island, read the caller ID screen and put it down. Mia picked it up and saw the number of her father's private line in his office.

"How many times has Dad called?" she asked.

Petra shrugged. Jenna said, "Seventeen."

"You can't expect him to turn over a new leaf in an hour," Mia said.

"Why can't I?" Petra put her cup down. "He's expected me to put up with his tantrums for the last forty years."

"That's why. Because you've put up with them," Mia said. "You've got to give him time to change."

"He can have all the time he needs. In the meantime, I will have peace because he won't be here."

"Are you doing this because Dad fired me?" Mia asked her mother.

"Yes. I told him Thursday night if he ever fired any one of you ever again, this was going to happen. Obviously, he didn't believe me."

The question of the day was *why* didn't he believe her?

Lucien roared and raged. When he calmed down he took back everything he'd said or done during the storm. Because she engaged her brain before she engaged her mouth, Petra rarely altered her stance on anything. If she said it, she meant it. And she stuck to it.

Mia slipped what was left of her steak burger in its paper sleeve. Her appetite had suddenly vanished.

"Your father didn't say in the termination letter why he fired you," Petra said. "Did he give you a reason?"

"No. I'm guessing he did it because of the photograph in *The Scout,* and what I said to Damien." Mia gave them a synopsis. "I don't know what he told Dad, but I'll bet you it wasn't anything near what I said."

"Damien has been twisting things of late," Jenna said. "Neither Luke nor I will discuss anything with him on the phone. We put it in an e-mail and copy Dad so Damien knows that Lucien is in the loop."

"Well, thanks for telling *me,*" Mia said, annoyed.

"You're the baby and you're right under Dad's nose," Jenna replied. "I'm amazed Damien tried to pull anything with you."

"I'm amazed Lucien sided with Damien against his own daughter," Petra said, a glint in her eyes that said he'd wish he hadn't.

"We don't know that that's what happened," Mia said. "And not to defend Dad, but he had a rough weekend."

"And you and I didn't?" Petra raised an eyebrow at her.

"Because of the photograph," Jenna jumped in. "What in the world were you thinking, Mother, to go out to Heavenly Bridals?"

"I was *thinking* to get at the truth, Jenna." Petra swung

a glare on her older daughter. "I had no idea that Mia and I were being followed."

The doorbell rang. Petra nodded toward the hallway.

"See who that is, Jenna. If it's your father, don't open the door."

"He lives here, Mother," she said. "He has a key."

Petra looked at her. "Did I stutter?"

"Okay." Jenna held up her hands and headed for the door.

"Mom," Mia said. "What if Dad refuses to change his ways?"

"Then I married the wrong man," Petra said, and sipped her tea.

Jenna came back carrying a humongous arrangement of long-stem red roses. The scent of them, soft as a summer garden, and the sentiment that had moved the sender, obviously Lucien, made Mia tear up. Her mother stared at the blooms, dry-eyed.

"Here we have the totally over-the-top, I'm-sorry-forgive-me three dozen roses." Jenna placed the bouquet on the counter that separated the kitchen from the great room and grinned at her mother. "It's *so* Dad."

"You're right to be concerned about Alicia's design," Petra said to Mia. "Even with the new measures Joseph installed, the Savard Building isn't completely secure. Where is the design?"

"In the safe in my study at home."

Jenna brought the card from the flowers to her mother. Petra laid it aside unopened and sipped her tea. Mia wished she'd open it. She was dying to know what her father had written.

Jenna slid onto her stool and asked, "What are you going to do with the design?"

"Keep it in the safe till Dad gets over his snit and tells me I'm not fired." Mia shrugged. "What else can I do with it?"

"How about this." Petra put her cup on its saucer and folded her arms on the island. "Take the design out of the safe and make the dress."

Mia stared openmouthed at her mother. So did Jenna.

"What did I say that's so astounding?" Petra looked at them. "Alicia Whitcomb chose you to design her wedding gown, Mia. You're a seamstress as well as a designer. Why shouldn't you make the gown?"

"You're suggesting this," Mia said, "to get back at Dad."

"How can he learn to make positive changes if we don't help him?"

"I can't see this helping. I *can* see this giving him a heart attack."

"Pish." Petra sniffed and asked Jenna, "How many times has your father fired you?"

"I've lost count," she said.

"And now you've been fired," Petra said to Mia. "How does it feel?"

"Awful. I was *so* angry. I still am, and it hurts."

"I can't think of one Savard employee who hasn't been fired. Thursday was unique, only because Lucien fired everyone in one fell swoop. Nonetheless, everyone who works for Savard's has been fired. Most of them more than once. Except you, Mia, until today."

"What hurts the most," Mia said, "is that I didn't *do* anything."

"Neither did anyone else," Petra said. "Your father loses his temper and fires people. He doesn't mean it. As soon as he calms down, he rescinds the terminations, but that's not the point. The point is that no one should have to put up with it. Talk about a harassment lawsuit." Petra shook her head. "I've told him he should be on his knees thanking God that his employees haven't filed a class-action suit."

"This sounds familiar." A slow smile spread across Jenna's face. "Luke and I have had this conversation several times."

"Luke and I had it over the weekend," Petra said to Jenna, then to Mia, "Except for Heavenly Bridals, Savard's is the only bridal fashion game in town. Your father behaves like a tyrant because he thinks he can get away with it. He needs to learn that he can't."

"And me making Alicia's wedding gown will convince him?"

"Hopefully it will make him realize that he can't run Savard's by himself," Petra said. "He needs every one of his two hundred forty-three employees, and he needs to get it through his head that if he doesn't stop mistreating them, he'll be lucky if he's left with Damien."

"Oh, baloney." Mia snorted. "Dad has been terrorizing Savard's for the last forty years and he still has a whole building full of people working for him. You're trying to talk me into using Alicia Whitcomb's wedding gown to force Dad to straighten up and fly right."

"No," Petra said. "I want you to make the dress."

"I don't," Jenna said. "We'll never have a better bargaining chip than the governor's daughter."

"I think we should forget Alicia and her dress," Mia said. "I think we should just have a mutiny."

She wasn't serious, she was being flip. But her mother's eyes lit, and Jenna's eyes lit, and they looked at each other.

"That was a joke," Mia said quickly. "I was kidding."

Petra smiled, Jenna smiled. Then they both looked at her.

"Jenna told me what you said to your father, Mia." Petra smiled. "I'm very proud of you for taking a stand."

"Now you're sucking up," Mia said. "Technically, the design doesn't belong to me. I was just bluffing Dad. It belongs to Alicia Whitcomb. She might have something to say about who makes her wedding gown."

"Why should she?" Jenna asked. "She's getting it for free. Dad gave her money back. As long as Alicia has a gown to walk down the aisle in on Christmas Eve, I don't think she'll care if the Brownies make it."

"That's in less than six weeks. I only have two hands," Mia said. "There isn't enough time to make a gown as intricate as this one all by myself."

"Hello." Jenna waved her hand. "I went to design school, too."

"So did I. We'll help you," Petra said. "If you're worried about Alicia, I'll talk to her mother. We had a lovely conversation Friday afternoon."

"And where would we make this gown?" Mia asked.

"Duh," Jenna said. "You have a sewing room."

"It's still a wreck from Saturday night."

"Why are we sitting here? Let's go clean it up."

Jenna started to swing off her stool. So did her mother.

"Wait. Stop." Mia slapped her hands on the island and caught each of them by a wrist. "I haven't agreed to this. I think it's insane. I think it will break Dad's heart."

"I think it could be his salvation," Petra said. "I love your father, Mia, but he can't go on like this. None of us can."

"And you just realized that today?" Mia said. "Dad's

been throwing tantrums and firing people for forty years, but all of a sudden *today* it has to stop? Why does it have to be today? And why do I have to be the one to do it?"

"Because you have the design," Jenna said. "You have the power."

"I don't *want* the power," Mia declared. "I don't want to do this."

"You don't have to do anything." Petra came around the island and put a kiss between her eyebrows. "It was just an idea."

Then she picked up the teapot and carried it to the sink. Jenna picked up the cups and saucers and followed Petra.

"I didn't say I wouldn't do it," Mia said. "I just said I don't want to."

Petra turned on the faucet and rinsed the teapot. Jenna opened the dishwasher and loaded the cups and saucers on the top rack.

Mia picked up her steak burger and left, started the Forester and checked her cell phone. Two missed calls and two messages: one from Jordan, one from Becca.

From Jordan: "Oh, my God! Damien just announced that you're fired! I can't believe this! See you at Blanko's?"

From Becca: "Oh, Mia. I just heard. This is awful. Call me."

The two missed calls were from Lucien. Mia dialed his private line.

"Dad. It's Mia. Can I come and talk to you?"

"I wish you would," he said so fervently that Mia's eyes filled.

On her way to the Savard Building, she finished her steak burger. She didn't park in the garage, she found a spot on the street, and pushed through the revolving door at two minutes past four. Pete Onslow sat at the security kiosk in the lobby. He looked up at her and smiled.

"Hi, Pete." She dropped her elbows on his desk. "Since I'm a former employee, do I need to sign in?"

"Nah." Pete made a face. "I don't imagine you'll be former for long."

"Is your nephew Joe still around?"

"No. He left a while ago. I'm working nights this week."

"I'm on my way to see Lucien, but I have something I need to give Joe. Something I found in my office." That wasn't a lie. Her purse was in her office when she'd found the 3 x 5 card with the license number. "I have Joe's business card. Do you think I could catch him at his office?"

"I'm not sure. Is this something important?"

"Yes." Mia nodded. "I think it is."

"Tell you what." Pete wrote on a scratchpad, tore off the sheet and gave it to her. "Joe's home address. In case you miss him at the office."

"Thanks, but—is it okay for you to give this to me?"

"I think it's okay to give it to *you*." Pete grinned. "I wouldn't flash it around. Lot of the young things around here would like to have that."

"Gee, Pete. I'm unemployed, you know." Mia waved the small square of paper. "I might be able to make a few bucks off of this."

"Start with your friend Jordan. I came on at three and she was down here at three-oh-five, sniffing around about Joe. Is he married, where does he live. I didn't tell her zip."

That was another lie. Well, a sin of omission, keeping it from Jordan and Becca that Joe wasn't married. Some friend she was.

"I'll guard this with my life." Mia slipped Joe's address in the pocket of her purple stadium coat, which she'd picked up from the dry cleaner on her way to her parents' house, and headed for the elevator.

Her heart banged all the way up to the seventh floor. She had no idea what she'd say to Lucien, or what he might say to her. She was still angry that he fired her, but he was her father, and she loved him.

"Go on in." Selma sighed unhappily when Mia came around the corner. "He's waiting for you."

Lucien was staring out the window, his chair turned partway from his desk, elbow on the arm, his index finger pressed to his cheekbone. He heard the door close and swiveled his chair. He'd changed his shirt from the meat loaf–smothered blue-on-blue stripe to a pale mint green with white collar and cuffs.

When he saw her, Lucien smiled. It was the saddest smile Mia had ever seen on her father's face.

"Well," he said, "this is a fine mess we've gotten ourselves into."

"What *we*?" she snapped. "What did I do? Why did you fire me?"

"You have to ask?" Lucien snapped back. "You took your mother to Heavenly Bridals against my express wishes."

"I did *not* take Mother to Heavenly Bridals! She was driving. She took me. I told Joe that this morning. Didn't he tell you?"

Lucien looked absolutely stunned. "I didn't believe him."

"You mean you didn't believe *me*," Mia accused.

"It was your mother's idea." Lucien repeated it like he still couldn't believe it. "Why would she do such a thing?"

"Why would *I*, Dad? You know Oren Angel. Mother knows him. I wouldn't know him if I fell over him on the street. Why would I drive out to Prairie Village, Kansas, to talk to a man I've never met?"

"Tell me." Lucien shoved to his feet, leaned his fisted knuckles on his desk. "Tell me every word that bastard said to your mother."

"Mother didn't talk to him. Angel wasn't there. No one was there. Heavenly Bridals was locked up tight. Didn't Joe tell you that?"

"No. Joseph didn't tell me. Jenna did." Lucien fell back in his chair and swept a hand over his eyes. "I didn't believe her."

"You thought Jenna and I lied to you? We've never lied to you!"

Lucien dragged his hand down his face and looked at her.

"I'm sorry, Mia. Oren Angel pushes every button I have."

"You didn't believe me. You didn't believe Jenna. If Mother'd *had* a chance, between your tantrums, to tell you over the weekend, I don't think you would have believed *her*. No wonder she threw you out."

Mia turned on her heel and headed for the door.

"Just a moment, young lady. I want Alicia Whitcomb's design."

Mia spun around and saw Lucien on his feet behind his desk, a thunderhead glower on his face.

"You can't have it. I'm going to make the gown for Alicia."

Then she wheeled and ran. Out of Lucien's office, past Selma's desk and the elevator, into the stairwell and down three flights to the fourth-floor landing before she stopped to catch her breath and listen.

No echo of footsteps. Her father hadn't followed her. Mia hadn't expected him to, really. She drew a deep breath. Opened the stairwell door, swung around the corner and through the lobby, past the elevator, and made a left into the hallway that led to the design department.

Damien was in her office. She saw him through the glass wall, standing at her drawing board, rifling through her portfolio.

A gush of anger surged straight to Mia's head and pounded in her ears. She rushed through the doorway and swung her purse on her desk with a smack that made Damien start and look up at her.

"What do you think you're doing?" she demanded.

"Such drama. You Savards are all full of it." Damien closed her portfolio and slid it on the shelf beneath the slanted top of her drawing board. "On Lucien's orders, I'm looking for Alicia's design."

"It isn't here. I told you that. Get your hands off my things."

From the corner of her eye, Mia could see Jordan, Arlene, Evan and Kiley almost falling out of their cubicles to watch. Imogene was perched on the corner of her desk.

Damien stepped away from her drawing board and folded his arms.

"Where is the design, Mia? We need to get started on the gown."

"Savard Creations isn't making Alicia's wedding gown. I am."

That wiped the smug expression from his face.

"You are not snatching that feather from my cap. Alicia chose you to design her gown, but I will be in charge of its construction."

"No, you won't." Mia grabbed the phone and punched 3 for the security kiosk. When Pete answered, she said, "I need a new lock on my office door until I can remove my personal effects. Would you send maintenance up? I'll wait."

Then she slammed the phone down. "Get out of my office."

Damien went. As he passed her, Mia could almost feel the fury rolling off him, but he didn't say a word. By the time he crossed the hallway to the design department, Jordan, Kiley, Evan and Arlene had resumed sketching, and Imogene was at her desk.

Damien didn't slam things. Lucien slammed things. When his office door closed behind him, Mia sat down on her desk chair.

Her knees were shaking and her ankles felt numb. She raised an icy hand to her stinging hot forehead. She was probably beet red. How did her father survive this many adrenaline rushes in one day?

Mia shrugged out of her coat. She bumped the mouse, cleared the Colin Farrell screen saver from her monitor and saw the instant message from Jordan: "Sorry"—sad face emoticon—"We tried to stop him."

"It's OK—" Mia IM'd back—"See you at Blanko's."

The maintenance guy was another new face. A tall, broad Hispanic man with a paunch, but muscled forearms and upturned, warm brown eyes that looked like they were smiling. His name was Carlos.

"You like that Irish dude?" He shook his head at Colin Farrell. "My daughter, Leesia? She's fifteen. He's all over the walls in her bedroom. Me? I think somebody should take hedge trimmers to his eyebrows."

Mia laughed and felt her quivering insides start to relax.

Carlos had three children: Leesia, Carlos Junior and Joaquin. Five o'clock came and went while Carlos talked about his kids, put a new knob on her office door and everyone in design, including Damien, left for the day.

"This lock has three keys." Carlos gave them to her when he finished. "I'll let you decide who gets the two spares."

"Savard SOP regarding keys," Mia told him, "is one to security, one to maintenance and one to the office occupant."

"You don't tell, I won't." Carlos winked, closed his toolbox and left.

Mia shut down her PC, put on her coat, picked up her purse and locked her office for the first time since she started at Savard's two weeks after her graduation from design school. Joe had told her that the sooner he found the thief the sooner things would get back to normal. Mia wondered what he'd say to her if she called him a liar.

She wasn't psychic, but she had a hunch things would never be the same at Savard Creations.

She walked to the elevator, glad that she could feel her ankles and that her knees had stopped shaking. On the ride down to the lobby, she leaned against the back wall and closed her eyes. Her head didn't hurt, but her eyes felt funny, like they were too big for their sockets.

Pete was still at the kiosk. Mia gave him the extra keys.

"Could you do me a favor and misplace these for a couple days?"

"Keys, Mr. Savard?" Pete smiled at her. "What keys?"

"Mr. Savard is okay. It's Mr. DeMello I don't want in my office."

Maybe my former office. The possibility chilled Mia.

"Keys, Mr. DeMello?" Pete said. "What keys?"

What if all this—the theft, the estrangement between her parents, the battle over who was going to make Alicia's wedding gown—blew up in her face and everybody else's and she never saw Pete again? She should say something, just in case, but her throat clenched and all she could do was blow him a kiss and scurry through the revolving door.

Mia belted and locked herself in her Subaru, gripped the wheel and stared at the windshield. It was nearly dark, the oncoming headlights stinging her eyes. And it was snowing. Again. Not hard, just flurrying. But still. If she wanted to live at the North Pole, she'd move there.

Which right now sounded like a pretty good idea. But that would be running away. Which also sounded like a pretty good idea.

Now that she was alone and sitting down, Mia felt the ache in her muscles, her shoulders and the back of her neck especially. Adrenaline crash. She had Joe's address in her pocket, the 3 x 5 card with the photographer's license number in her purse, but she just couldn't face him and the shadow of recrimination in his gorgeous blue eyes.

Mia dug her cell phone and Joe's card out of her purse and dialed.

He answered with a crisp "Joe Kerr," the white noise of traffic, or maybe it was static, in the background.

"It's Mia," she said. "Sorry to bother you, but I have something—"

"You've had a hell of a day," he cut in, but not unkindly. "Me, too. I could use a beer. Are you headed to Blanko's?"

"Yes." Mia's heart sank. She should have headed for the North Pole while she had the chance. "I'm at Savard's."

"I'm north of the river." The Missouri River, which meant North Kansas City, Gladstone or any number of other places south of the airport. "I'll meet you in half an hour."

Joe disconnected. So did Mia, wondering how he knew she'd had a hell of a day.

19

MIA DIDN'T BOTHER trying to find a place to park on the street. She drove straight to the parking garage a block from Blanko's. While she cruised looking for a spot, she dialed her mother.

"I'm in. Let's do it," she said when Petra answered. "Let's make Alicia's wedding gown."

"Excellent," Petra said. "Jenna and I will see you in the morning."

Mia found an empty space and parked the Subaru, put on her gloves and pulled up her hood as she got out of the car, made sure she pressed Lock and Alarm on her keypad and shivered down the public-access stairs to the street.

Lousy day to wear a skirt. The wind had kicked up with the snow, and even with tights her legs were cold by the time she reached Blanko's.

Jordan, Becca and her amazing, disappearing brother, Robin, sat at their usual table. With pastel Hawaiian leis around their necks and red felt beanies with yellow propellers on their heads.

"I give," Mia said. "Is this a *Hawaii Five-0* or a *Gilligan's Island* party?"

"You wish." Robin stood up, a red beanie in one

hand and two leis, one pink, one yellow, in the other. "We have come to initiate thee into the Infernal Order of the Sacrificial Lambs."

"The what?" Mia hung her coat and purse on the back of a chair.

"A sacred, secret society," Robin intoned gravely. "Founded and fostered by those of us whose jobs have been sacrificed time after time after time on the altar of our god, Lucifer Savard."

Robin spun his propeller. So did Becca and Jordan.

It wasn't funny, and yet it was. In a daffy blow-off-steam kind of way. Mia laughed.

"Silence, supplicant," Robin said sternly. "This is serious stuff."

"Your pardon, oh great . . . ?"

"Leader of the Pack," Robin said. "Who comes before us seeking entry into the Fold?"

"I do," Mia said, and bowed. "Mia Savard."

"Ahhh." Robin drew out the syllable. "Meekest of the meek."

Becca and Jordan spun their propellers.

"And what proofs do you bring to show your worthiness?"

"None," Mia said. She'd last seen her termination letter as a paper wad aimed at her father's head. "I forgot my you're-fired letter."

"That's okay." Robin shrugged. "There will be others."

He draped the leis around her neck, gave the propeller on the beanie he held a mighty spin and placed it on her head.

"It is done. Welcome Sheep Two Hundred Forty-three. Our number is now complete."

Robin bowed. Mia bowed. Becca and Jordan spun their propellers.

And then they all laughed. It beat the heck out of crying.

Robin held Mia's chair. She sat, he sat and Bev appeared between them with a tray of drinks. Four Shirley Temples speared with swizzle sticks loaded with fruit and jaunty paper umbrellas.

"A toast." Becca raised her glass. "To sacrificial lambs."

They clinked glasses and drank.

"I've always wondered," Mia said, "how those of you who've been fired every time you turn around cope. Now I know. This is great."

"Funny how a goofy hat," Robin said, giving his propeller a flick, "can put a brighter spin on your day."

Mia, Becca and Jordan groaned. Robin grinned.

"I especially like Lucifer Savard," Mia said. "That's inspired."

"We'd like to take credit for it," Robin said. "But the truth is, Evan came up with it on the night of his induction."

An awful thought struck Mia. Damien had been fired three times.

"If DeMello belongs to this club, you can have your beanie back."

"Mia. Please," Jordan said. "Do you honestly think Damien would be caught dead wearing a beanie?"

"Caught dead. Now, there's a picture," Mia said, and then shook herself. "What am I saying? Sorry about that."

"I've never seen you so angry," Jordan said. "Honestly, we tried to stop Damien, but he was determined to find Alicia's new design."

"I told him it wasn't in my office. I told Lucien it wasn't in my office." Mia's heart pounded, she was getting angry again. "I've lost track of how many people called me a liar today."

"Why isn't it in your office?" Robin asked.

"Because we still have a thief running around Savard's."

"Ah. Good point." Robin nodded. "In that case, wherever you have the design stashed, I hope it's safe."

"Oh, believe me," Mia put her hand over her heart, "it's safe."

"Why are you keeping it?" Becca asked.

It was on the tip of Mia's tongue to tell them she intended to make Alicia's wedding gown—What difference did it make? She'd already announced it to Lucien and Damien—but she didn't. Defying her father was one thing. Humiliating him in public was something else.

"I'll give it back," Mia lied. "I'm just making Dad sweat. It's the least he deserves for siding with Damien and firing me."

A snatch of digital music engulfed the table. The Stones' "I Can't Get No Satisfaction"—Jordan's cell phone.

She plucked it out of her purse and her eyes lit.

"Ooh. It's Brad," she said to Becca. "The blond hottie we met at the party Friday night. 'Scuse me while I vamp this guy's pants off."

Jordan swung away from the table, her phone pressed to one ear, her finger over the other.

"Welcome to the fold, mite." Robin spun the propeller on Mia's beanie. "I'm gonna belly up for a beer and a chat with that redhead."

Mia and Becca watched him take off his beanie and his leis and sidle up to the bar beside a svelte young woman with titan hair halfway down her back.

"Two redheads," Becca said. "That would be a scary mix of genes."

"Robin isn't interested in mixing his genes, is he?"

"Not that I know. Dad would like grandchildren, though. It would give him something to look forward to." Becca sipped her Shirley Temple. "I think it will help him to have Uncle Lucien around for a while."

"Oh," Mia said with a wince. "So you know?"

"Dad called me into his office this afternoon. He was excited, making plans. What they'd have for dinner, that kind of thing."

"You do know that with Lucien comes Tilde?"

"So does Dad. He's even excited about Tilde."

"Well, Beck," Mia said. "Maybe Uncle Rudy *is* crazy."

They laughed. Mia glanced at the window. The snow was tapering off. Yippee. It was too damn cold to scrape ice off a windshield.

"Well, girls, I have a dinner date." Jordan bounced back to the table, picked up her purse and her coat and looked at Mia. "When do you think you'll be back in the salt mine?"

"I don't know." Mia squelched the *Maybe never* that ran through her head. "I'll keep you posted."

"You and me, lunch tomorrow," Jordan said to Becca, and left.

"You are beyond brave," Becca said to Mia, "to defy Uncle Lucien."

"I'm not brave," Mia said. Truthfully, she was scared to death. Jenna was brave. Her mother was fearless. Thank God they were on her side. "I'm just pissed off. Don't worry. I'll give the design back."

* * *

That Blanko's was packed on a Monday night didn't surprise Joe. It was one of the most popular hookup spots for single professionals. And warm after the bite in the sharp, snowy wind.

He saw Bev, the waitress who'd helped him pour Mia into his truck. He nodded to her. She smiled and pointed at a table, the same table from Friday night, where Becca Savard sat by herself, with two paper leis around her neck and a red beanie with a yellow propeller on her head. When she saw him coming, she snatched it off.

Two more leis, one pink, one yellow, and another beanie sat on the table in front of a chair draped with Mia's purple coat.

"Mr. Kerr." Becca Savard smiled as he sat down in the vacant chair next to Mia's. "Mia said you were stopping by."

"And here I am." Joe smiled back at her, picked up the red beanie and spun the propeller. "You people have the most interesting parties."

"This isn't a party," she replied. "This is Mia's induction into the Infernal Order of the Sacrificial Lambs."

Just the name made Joe smile. By the time Becca Savard finished explaining the Infernal Order of the Sacrificial Lambs he was grinning—and Mia was on her way back to the table.

Probably from the ladies room. Head down, brushing the front of her above-the-knee skirt, the wedge of dark hair that swung toward her chin catching a gleam of light, which made Joe's pulse leap.

"Hey, Mia!" a voice called, and she turned, lifted a hand to wave and stepped toward a close-by table to talk to a young couple.

Joe watched her, waiting for the right second. When

she leaned away from the table, he spun the propeller on the beanie. When she turned in his direction, he put the beanie on his head. She lifted her gaze, saw him, stutter-stepped and blinked.

The look on her face said that of all the people in the world she could picture in a beanie, he was not one of them. Joe couldn't see himself in one, either, and was glad. Very glad. Then Mia laughed and came toward him, her eyes shining, and he didn't care how ridiculous he looked.

"Unhand my beanie." She plucked it off his head, plunked it on her own and sat down next to him. She looked as cute as a bug's ear. "Only Sacrificial Lambs get to wear these and you can't be one unless or until my father fires you."

"For a hat that cool, it might be worth getting canned."

"Flattery will not earn you a beanie. Will it, Becca?"

"'Fraid not." She smiled, put her beanie in her purse and rose from her chair. "Yoga class starts in half an hour. Nice to see you, Mr. Kerr."

"You, too." Joe nodded at the fruity drink on the table on the other side of Mia. "Your brother wouldn't happen to be here, would he?"

"He was till about ten minutes ago." Becca slipped into her coat.

"He left with a redhead," Mia said, as if that explained it.

"Call me when you can," Becca said to Mia. "Good night."

"'Night, Beck." Mia watched her walk toward the door, then turned toward Joe and clasped her hands in her lap. The happy, joking-around shine was gone from her eyes. "I have several things to tell you and something to give you. Where would you like to start?"

"I'd like to start with dinner." Joe smiled. "How about you?"

"I'd like that very much, but . . ." She reached beneath her coat, withdrew a green 3 x 5 card from her purse and handed it to him. "I think you need to see this first."

"Cee-em-kay-zero-three-nine," Joe read, and looked at her. "This is a plate number."

"Yes. It's the license number of a gray Kia Sportage, driven by the man who took our picture at Heavenly Bridals. I wrote it down so I wouldn't forget it. I didn't intend to withhold it. I meant to give it to you as soon as my mother told my father, but . . ."

She let her voice trail off and looked at her clasped hands.

"Well. You were in on the weekend." She gave a small shrug and rubbed her right thumb over her left. "You know what happened. I'm not excusing myself. I'm just saying."

"How did you get his plate number?"

"I chased him—and I talked to him. He said, 'This way, ladies,' and we turned around and he took our picture. He asked me 'Which kid are you?' and I said, 'Mia.' *Stupidly.*" She smacked the heel of her hand on her forehead. "I ran down the steps and chased him to his truck."

"Did you catch him?"

"No. He was taller and faster. I only got close enough to hit the back window with a snowball and get the license number before he drove off."

"Nice work. Can I keep this card?"

She glanced up, tucked her hair behind her ear and nodded.

"I had a fabric swatch stapled to it." She touched the two tiny holes near the top. "I took it off."

"Okay." Joe slipped the card inside his navy wool sport coat. "Where would you like to have dinner?"

She raised an eyebrow. "You don't mind eating with a liar?"

"I'm guessing that you said looking in the window was your idea to protect your mother from your father's temper. Did it work?"

"I didn't get a chance to find out." She dipped her head and her hair swung out from behind her ear. "Unbeknownst to Jenna or me—I'm not sure about Luke—Mother told Lucien if he ever fired any of us ever again, she was going to kick him out. So. She kicked him out."

"You did have a hell of a day."

"You said you did, too." She looked up, tucked her hair again.

"I'll tell you about it over dinner. Are you ready?"

"Yes." Mia took off her beanie and stood up.

Joe lifted her coat from the chair and held it for her.

As they stepped outside into the frosty dark, the wind gusted and nearly snatched Mia off her feet. Joe caught her and tucked her under his arm. Small as she was, she filled the Grand Canyon–size empty space beside him perfectly. He felt it in a warm brush up the back of his neck and smiled, thinking Brian would have a field day with this.

"Where's your car?" Joe asked her.

"Parking garage." She nodded up the hill behind Blanko's, her eyes tearing in the cold wind.

"Mine, too." He pulled her closer, his arm around her

shoulders, and drew her up the sidewalk. "Do you like Italian?"

"I do." Mia shivered and burrowed closer to him.

"We'll take my truck, then I'll bring you back to your car."

When they reached the parking garage, she went ahead of him up the steps. On the street, the wind only buffeted pedestrians. In the stairwell, it howled like a banshee, pushed Mia's purple hood off her head and swallowed sound. Joe could barely hear her footsteps ahead of him, and he had ears like a bat.

The guy waiting in the shadows at the top, in dark clothes and a dark ski mask, must've had sonar to hear her coming.

He leaped on Mia and grabbed her shoulders, flung her around and reached for her throat. He didn't have a knife, because she yelled—she didn't scream, she yelled furiously and kicked at his ankles.

"Hey!" Joe shouted, and barreled up the last three steps.

Dark Man swung his masked face toward Joe—eye and mouth slits stitched in red—and let go of Mia. She stumbled away from him, still on her feet. He whirled at a run for the far end of the parking garage.

"Stay there! Do *not* move!" Joe shouted at Mia, and ran after him.

He wasn't a professional. A pro would've snatched Mia's purse, pushed her down and been long gone before Joe cleared the top stair. He wasn't very tall, either. Joe had a head—maybe a head and a half—on him, but the guy was slim, wore black track shoes, and he could run like a gazelle.

Joe was no slouch, but he'd dressed for a day at

Savard's. The fancy wingtips Moira had made him buy had slick leather soles. He wished he had a nightstick he could throw under Dark Man's feet to trip him and bring him down. He'd been an ace with a nightstick, but those days were gone, and Dark Man was pulling away, veering toward the stairwell in the far back corner that led down to the street.

Not a pro, but smart enough to stay out of the parked cars where a side mirror could smack him and slow him down or he could get hung up on a bumper. Joe filled his lungs with air and poured on the speed, snaked out his arm and just touched Dark Man's shoulder. He twisted sideways, wrenched away and leaped like a rabbit for the stairwell.

Joe jumped with him, clutched a fistful of thick, scratchy fabric—then lost his grip and went down like a ton of bricks when he hit a patch of ice at the top of the stairs and his feet shot out from under him.

He still had good reflexes from all those years of falling on his ass as a cop, managed to roll partway and take the brunt of the slam on his right shoulder rather than the back of his head. Still he saw stars, all the breath whooshed out of him—and Dark Man got away.

Over the blood thudding in his ears, Joe heard the *tappy-tap-tap* of Dark Man's rubber-soled feet flying down the steps. And a laugh, throaty and muffled by the ski mask, echoing up the stairwell.

"Joe!" Mia cried. He heard her running toward him, her footfalls ringing on the concrete. "Are you hurt?"

He rolled on his back and sucked air, blinked and saw Mia bending over him, her worried face upside down.

"I'm not hurt." Joe gripped the cold metal handrail of

the stairwell with his left hand, pulled himself up and sat on the top step. "But my dignity is in tatters."

"To hell with your dignity." Mia dropped to her knees on his right side and sat back on her heels. "Did you hit your head?"

"Wouldn't have mattered." Joe smiled to keep from gritting his teeth at the throb in his shoulder. "It's harder than concrete."

"Look at this." Mia opened her coat. Dark Man had ripped half a dozen rhinestone buttons off her pink cardigan, torn the fur collar loose from the neckline and shredded her paper leis. Joe could see her left collarbone and a thin white bra strap. "Why didn't he take my purse?"

"He didn't want your purse. He wasn't a rapist, either," he added quickly at Mia's wide-eyed look of horror. "He didn't have a weapon."

He might've had one, and he might've used it if Joe hadn't surprised him, but he didn't tell Mia that. He grabbed the handrail and pulled himself to his feet. Mia stood up beside him. When he turned away from the stairwell, she threw her arms around him.

"I'm glad you're okay." She pressed her cheek against his chest.

Joe closed his arms around her. She was trembling. Not shaking like a leaf, just shivery. Partly from cold, the rest reaction to being grabbed. Mia Savard did not cave. She'd yelled at Dark Man and she'd kicked him. Joe hoped the SOB would at least have a couple bruises.

He bent his head and rubbed his lips in her hair. It felt soft against his mouth and smelled like citrus and something softer, maybe vanilla.

Mia sighed and raised her head. The shimmer in her

eyes, thank-God-you're-okay, thank-God-you-were-here look caught at Joe's heart. He bent his head a bit more and their mouths meshed. Hers felt cold for maybe a second, then heat flared and her lips softened. Opened for him, enticing him. He touched her tongue with his, just barely, then broke the kiss. A small disappointed sigh escaped her.

"We survived our first mugging. Think we have a chance?"

"I don't know." Mia said, her eyes dazed. "You'll have to kiss me like that about a billion more times before I can be sure."

"This isn't the best place in the world to lose track of what I'm doing." Joe put a tiny kiss on her nose. "Are you still up for Italian?"

"You bet," she said. "But I should probably change first."

"I'll follow you to your place." Joe spotted her gold Subaru Forester and led her toward it. Once she was behind the wheel and he'd locked her into her seat belt, he smiled. "Drive safely. I'll be right behind you."

20

FOR DINNER, JOE TOOK MIA to Sophia's in Brookside. He loved their lasagna and he wanted to see how Mia handled herself outside of her high-dollar swank and to-the-manor-born element.

She did just fine. Their corner booth was upholstered in gold velvet. It had a few shiny wear spots, but Mia didn't turn a hair. She slid her small, shapely fanny onto the banquette, spread her napkin in her lap and smiled. Composed, relaxed, a first-date sparkle in her eyes.

To look at her, you'd never guess that less than an hour ago she'd been jumped and manhandled in a parking garage. She was something else.

Someone special. The right someone for him—and he the right someone for her—remained to be seen, but he had hopes. And dreams. Joe was sure Mia did, too, and he itched to hear them.

But first, he had a thief to catch.

When they'd stopped at her apartment so she could change, Mia went straight to the safe in her study to check Alicia's design.

"All right and tight," she'd told him, a flicker of relief in her eyes.

Joe wondered if she was trying to connect Dark Man

to the design as she'd tried to connect it to her sewing room. He was, too, but at the moment he had no proof that Dark Man was anything but a mugger.

He'd washed up while Mia changed, then he'd called Stink and told him she needed a security system.

"ASAP, Stink. When can you do it?"

"Lunch tomorrow I can look the place over if you can get me in."

"I'll get you in," Joe said. In the truck on the way to Sophia's he'd talked to Mia about Stink and the security system.

"No problem," she'd said. "I'll be home all day."

He ordered lasagna, Mia shrimp fettuccine. They shared a toasted artichoke. Watching Mia peel the petals, suck them and lick her fingers sent Joe's imagination into overdrive picturing the things she could do to him with her long, slim fingers. She had lovely hands, artist's hands, he supposed, and oval nails painted a pale, flesh-toned pink.

"Why exactly," he asked, "did your father fire you?"

"Because I took Mother to Heavenly Bridals. You told him Mother took *me,* but he didn't believe you. He didn't believe Jenna, either, when she told him that Oren Angel wasn't there and that Mother and I didn't talk to him. Mother told me she'd dated Oren Angel for almost a year when the three of them were in art school."

"That's pretty much the story I got from Angel," Joe said, and Mia's eyes widened. "Moira and I had lunch with him and his attorney today."

Joe gave her a recap of the conversation, which held her attention and kept her fingers off the artichoke. Thank Jesus.

"Dammit." She ripped off a petal when he finished,

tore at it with her fingers and looked at him. "If you could find out how Angel came by the design, that might give you a clue about who gave it to him. Or, as Jordan thinks, sold it to him for a boatload of money."

"I'm sure money changed hands, but I doubt that was the primary motive. I think somebody has it in for your father. Big-time."

"Dear, darling, adorable Lucien?" Mia's eyes held a glint, her voice a knife edge. "How can you say such a thing?"

"A beanie with a propeller doesn't do much for the sting, does it?"

"Not much." She lost interest in the artichoke petal and tossed it on her plate, bent her elbow on the table and put her chin on her hand. "Can Walter Vance get you past Angel's attorney?"

"No. I asked him. Angel enjoyed the hell out of stonewalling on the design. He especially enjoyed that your father paid for lunch."

"What a charmer." Mia smirked. "What did Mother see in him?"

The centerpiece candle glowed in her eyes. Joe thought he could see his future there. Premature, maybe, but he'd known Janine was the woman for him the second he'd laid eyes on her.

Joe wondered what Mia saw when she looked at him.

"Do you think your mother and father will patch things up?"

"I can't see them flushing forty years down the toilet, but it won't be easy on Lucien. My mother is up to here"—Mia took her hand out from under her chin and held it up to her eyebrows—"with his temper and his tantrums. She wants changes, and if Lucien wants to go home, he'll have to make them."

"Will your father *un*fire you?"

"He will if he wants to sleep in his own bed." Mia put her chin back on her hand. "I hate being a bone of contention between them."

"You didn't make yourself a bargaining chip. Your parents did."

Mia sighed. "That's what Jenna said."

"Pretty sharp cookie, your sister. When's she going back to LA?"

"Wednesday, I think. She'll be back next week for Thanksgiving. After that, she's staying for a while." Mia straightened and put her hands in her lap. "That's another thing I need to tell you. My mother's plan to convince Lucien to stop behaving like a tyrant."

"Let me guess," Joe said. "Anger management therapy?"

"Good idea, but no. Mother and Jenna and I are going to make Alicia's new gown. Mother thinks that will force Lucien to realize he needs all of his employees to run Savard Creations and that if he wants to keep them he'd better knock off the tantrums and yelling at people."

The waitress appeared with their entrées, served them and left.

"Where are you going to make the dress?" Joe asked.

"In my sewing room at home. Tomorrow, we'll finish cleaning up the mess and get started."

"Does your father know you intend to do this?"

"Yes." Mia nibbled on a shrimp and told him about her termination letter and storming up to the cafeteria to confront her father. "I was just pissed when I said the design was mine, but that's what gave Mother the idea. That freaked me out and sent me back to Savard's to talk to Dad. When he said he didn't believe me or Jenna, I was so mad and so hurt, I told him I was going to make the dress for Alicia."

"Did he have a stroke on the spot?"

"I didn't hang around," Mia said guiltily. "I ran downstairs to my office and into Damien going through my stuff. On Lucien's orders, he said, to find Alicia's design. I threw him out, called maintenance and changed the lock. I have one key, Pete has the other two."

"DeMello is on my list for tomorrow. How often does he work late?"

"Rarely. If there's a crunch in the sewing room, if Viola and her girls need to stay late and my father doesn't stay with them, Damien will, but that's it so far as I know."

"Was there a crunch to finish Alicia's dress on schedule?"

"The first one? No. This one? Oh, yes. It will be a crunch. We can do it, but it's going to be a killer."

"Will Alicia care who makes her dress?"

"Jenna thinks not and Mother agrees. She's going to talk to Mrs. Whitcomb. They hit it off and Mother thinks it won't be a problem."

"What do you think?" Joe asked.

"I think it's going to be a disaster, but I'm committed. Or maybe I should be. I don't know." Mia sighed and shrugged. "I won't bail on Mother and Jenna, but I think this will rip Lucien's heart out."

"Are you sure he has one?" Joe winked, signaling that it was a joke, an attempt to make her smile, but Mia's eyes filled with tears.

"You should've seen his face when Mother said maybe he could stay with Uncle Rudy. Dad sent her three dozen red roses and she looked at them like they were a vase full of weeds. Oh, boy." She gave a watery laugh and dabbed her eyes with her napkin. "Aren't I a fun date?"

"You had a rough day, ladybug. Give yourself a break."

She paused in mid-dab and blinked at him. "Ladybug?"

"The first time I saw you I thought you were cute as a bug's ear." Joe tugged a breadstick out of the napkin-lined basket, broke it and offered Mia half. "I thought you'd like *ladybug* better than *cockroach*."

"Oh, I do." Mia laughed and her tears changed to little stars of light in her eyes. "I'll draw black spots on my beanie and I'll be all set."

Joe grinned. So did Mia, and took the half breadstick from him.

"Making the replacement gown for Alicia off-site takes a load off of me," he said. "I don't have to keep this design out of the thief's grubby little paws. I just have to catch him. I wish I'd thought of it."

"I wish *I'd* thought of it when I was telling Dad," Mia said. "I would have looked like a responsible grown-up rather than Lucien Junior."

"If you'd like, I'll be glad to point out the advantages to him."

"Would you? Maybe it'll smooth things between him and Mother."

"I'll talk to him in the morning," Joe said. "First thing."

Mia ate maybe half her fettuccine, every scrap of her

tiramisu, and nearly licked the dish. They both had coffee.

"This stuff with my parents." Mia poured cream in her cup. "I got the feeling from Mother that it's been festering for a while. The theft brought it to the surface. Well, maybe not the theft. Maybe Oren Angel."

"I'd put my money on Angel," Joe said.

He put money on the table for the bill, stopped their waitress on their way to the door and told her to keep the change.

"Hey, look." Mia cocked an eye at the dark, starry sky as she shivered to the SUV next to Joe. "For once, it's not snowing."

The roads weren't bad, but they weren't great. The Explorer slid a bit as Joe braked at a red light, and he glanced at Mia. She sat sideways in the seat looking at him, her left foot hooked under her right knee.

"When you were a little boy," she said, "what did you want to be when you grew up?"

"A cop, like my father. That's all I ever wanted to be."

"How did you end up being a detective?"

"A lot of guys make the switch when they leave the force."

Mia's eyebrows went up. "You were a cop?"

"Runs in my family, like making wedding gowns runs in yours. My brother, Sam, is a cop. You probably know my uncle Pete retired from the force." Joe glanced at Mia and she nodded. "That's how my parents met. My mother, Evie, is Pete's sister. My dad was Pete's partner. I was a cop for ten years. Went to school, got the degree, the whole nine yards."

"Why did you quit the police force?"

The light changed. Joe accelerated through the intersection.

"I don't like guns. They scare the crap out of me."

"I can't envision you being afraid of anything."

Joe gave a short laugh. "I've got you fooled."

"Come on. The way you chased that guy in the parking garage?"

"He didn't have a gun." Joe grinned at her. "If he'd had a Glock in his pocket, I would've let him have you."

Mia laughed, then asked, "You don't carry a gun?"

"In this job, I've never needed one." *Thank God,* Joe thought, and made a right off Ward Parkway. "What did you want to be?"

"What I am, a designer. Only I wanted to design for Barbie."

She told him about the bride rag dolls she made out of scraps and her mother's yarn. She gave one to every bride she designed for, from the fabric and trims left over from the gown.

"Will Alicia Whitcomb get two dolls, then?" Joe asked.

"If I have time to make another one, she— Oh, my God!" Mia shot upright in the passenger seat. "Turn around, Joe. Take me to Savard's."

He whipped the SUV into a driveway and glanced at Mia. She looked like she'd been struck by lightning.

"What is it?" he asked, and backed the SUV into the street.

"Alicia's doll is wearing an exact mini-replica of her dress. It was in my office. I think. I don't remember seeing it on Thursday when I quit and packed my stuff. I *know* I didn't see it when I unpacked."

Joe stepped on the gas and headed for the Savard Building.

Mia jumped out of the SUV in the parking garage and raced for the elevator. No need to rush, he could've told her. If the doll was gone, it was gone, but he let her dash off the elevator in the lobby and punch the call button on the opposite bank of elevators, which serviced the upper floors.

"Hey, Pete." Joe raised a hand to his uncle, who was turning his chair away from the security kiosk. "We're on a mission."

The middle car opened and Joe followed Mia into it. On the fourth floor he stood aside as she fumbled, because her hands were shaking, with the new key. She got the door open and shoved it out of her way, flipped on the lights and raced toward the tall wooden shelves lined against the walls, where at least a dozen bride rag dolls sat in front of books, on top of books and next to books.

"No. No. No." Mia grabbed three dolls and flung them out of her way. "Alicia's doll isn't here. Hell! Where *is* it?"

It wasn't in the boxes in the closet that still had stuff in them. It wasn't on the closet shelves, in Mia's desk drawers, in the oak lowboy storage cabinet against the windows behind her drawing board.

Mia searched, rifled, rooted through every nook and cranny. She had Joe move the furniture, in case Alicia's doll had fallen behind something.

"The last time you saw it," he said, "was it here in your office?"

"I don't remember." She stood in the middle of the room, her gaze darting frantically, her eyes overbright. "Last Thursday I was so upset with Lucien because he wouldn't move me out of bridal, I wasn't paying attention, I was just throwing stuff in boxes to get out of here."

"What do you do with the dolls when you finish them?"

"I sit them on the shelves in here, where I can see them from my drawing board, so I can look at them and make sure I don't want to change anything. The hair maybe, or the face. When I'm happy with the doll, I wrap it up in a cellophane bag, do a nice bow, write a note to the bride, and give it to Viola to put in the bag with the gown. *The bag!*"

Mia whirled and ran, snatching her keys off her desk as she raced out the door toward the storage rooms adjacent to the sewing room. Joe followed, hoping Lucien Savard hadn't already moved Alicia's gown to the vault at Lambert Bank and Trust. He thought Mia might have hysterics.

The gown was there, sealed in a heavy opaque plastic bag—to protect it from dirt and sun damage, Joe recalled Luke Savard telling him. He didn't see exactly how the bag closed, because Mia ripped it open and nearly jumped inside in search of Alicia Whitcomb's bride rag doll.

"It isn't here. It should be, but it isn't. It's gone." Mia had dropped to her knees on the floor, sat back on her heels and looked up at Joe, her eyes huge and stricken in her face. "The thief took Alicia's doll. That's how he got the design."

"Maybe." He dropped to his haunches beside her. "Could Angel have copied the design from the doll's dress? Is it that close a match?"

"I told you, it's *identical*. Otherwise, what's the point?"

Mia pushed to her feet. So did Joe. She shut and locked the closet.

"Thursday, September twenty-first," he said. "Did you work late that night?"

"I never work late. I'm the empress of outta here at five on the nose. What's special about September twenty-first?"

"There was a false alarm at 11:38 P.M. on the third floor. Somebody went through the fire door there onto the garage roof. Was Alicia's doll finished by then?"

"That depends on when her gown was cut. Let's find out."

Joe followed Mia into the design department storage room, where she flipped through the multitude of keys on her ring, found the right one and unlocked the file cabinet drawer Jordan Branch had opened on Friday. Mia removed Alicia Whitcomb's envelope and opened it on the table next to the file cabinet.

"Here it is." She held up the spreadsheet/production schedule that Jordan had copied for him. "Alicia's gown was cut on September first. That's when I got the scraps. Once the gown is cut, Viola brings me the leftover fabric. I gather up the trims and anything else I need myself, so sometime that week I started Alicia's doll."

"How long does it take you to make a bride rag doll?" Joe asked.

"A couple weeks, tops. I sew them at home. I keep a supply of blanks—the bodies sewn and stuffed—so all I have to do is make the gown, dress the doll and do her hair and her face. I work from a Xerox of the design and a photo of the bride—we photograph all our brides—so I can get the hair color and the eyes right."

"If Viola gave you the scraps on or around September first, would you have had the doll finished and sitting on a shelf in your office on Thursday, the twenty-first, the night of the false alarm?"

"I can't swear to it, but I'd say yes, more than likely. I make the doll as soon as I get the fabric, while the design is still fresh in my head and I'm excited about the gown. Oh, my God." Mia clutched her temples. "This is all my fault."

"No it isn't." Joe tugged her hands away from her head and held them gently, felt the tremble in her fingers. "You didn't steal the design."

"The thief didn't, either," she shot back. "He stole Alicia's doll!"

"He could have, but that doesn't make you responsible. How long have you been making the bride rag dolls?"

"Since day one. I came up with the idea in design school. I thought the dolls would make a nice keepsake for the brides. Oh, God."

She tried to take her hands back, but Joe held on.

"Are you going to pull your hair out by the roots?"

She tried to smile, but couldn't. "No. I'm going to put this stuff back."

"No hair pulling." Joe held up finger. "I like your hair."

"Me, too." Now she managed a smile. "I'd look goofy bald."

She slid the production schedule into Alicia's envelope, filed it under W, locked the drawer and turned to face him. She almost but didn't quite look at him, her gaze slanted slightly away from his face. She did that, Joe had noticed, when she was thinking.

He was thinking, too. He thought while he helped Mia straighten the mess she'd made in her office, while he helped her into her purple coat and locked the door. While they walked to the elevator, rode down to the lobby, called good night to Pete, rode down to the parking garage. While he tucked Mia into the Explorer, got in behind the wheel, fastened his seat belt, started the engine and drove her home.

When they reached her house, he parked in the carport, opened her door and offered Mia a hand. She took it, hopped down from the high seat and said, "Thanks." She still wasn't quite looking at him.

"Do you have any dolls here at home that are finished?"

"A couple, yes. They're in my sewing room." Mia took her keys out of her coat pocket as they walked toward the back door, the ice that had formed when the sun went down crunching under their feet. "Jenna and I found them yesterday when we were cleaning up."

"Would you go back to work if your father apologized?" Joe followed her up the steps to the small concrete back porch.

"I'd like to." Mia glanced at him as she unlocked the door. "But I can't abandon my mother and Jenna. It's going to take all three of us to make Alicia's gown in time for her wedding."

"Stairs or elevator?" Joe asked once they were inside.

"Elevator." Mia sighed. "I'm wiped out."

He was sure the day was catching up with her. It was catching up with him. His shoulder wasn't throbbing anymore, but it ached and felt stiff. Time to go home and ice it and do a little reading.

Mia unlocked her door and turned to face him. Her

eyes looked red and overworked, like they'd seen too much today.

"Would you like a cup of coffee?"

"Thanks, no. I'm maxed out for today." It made his teeth grit, but Joe spread his arms across the doorway. "I suppose you'd like a kiss."

"If it's not too much trouble." She smiled tiredly. "Yes, please."

"Me, too. I'd like a kiss and a whole lot more. I'm yours if you want me, but not yet. Not till I catch this guy. Can you wait?"

"I don't know." Mia circled one of his shirt buttons with a fingertip and looked up at him through her lashes. Those long, lush lashes that had made him catch his breath in Blanko's on Friday night. "Can you?"

"A kiss might make it easier."

Mia caught his lapels, drew his head down and kissed him. Warm, soft mouth, a little tongue, a universe of promise.

"Don't make me wait too long," she whispered.

Then she stepped inside and closed the door.

Joe hung on the frame, smiling. And wondering. What Mia was hatching in that quick, sharp little brain of hers.

21

"I'M YOURS IF YOU WANT ME, but not yet. Not till I catch this guy."

Joe Kerr. Tall, dark and delicious. Smart, funny, brave, no matter what he said. He'd stood in her doorway smiling at her with those eyes. Those dark blue, almost navy eyes, half-lidded with desire. For her.

Talk about motivation.

Mia rolled out of bed at six on the dot. While her Vanilla Bean brewed, she made the bed. While her egg poached and her bread toasted, she heated two strips of Oscar Mayer Ready to Serve Bacon in the microwave and washed it all down with a big glass of orange juice.

She'd need a tiger in her tank today, for sure.

Mia brushed her teeth and pulled on old jeans and a sweatshirt to tackle the sewing room. Before the vestibule buzzer went off at seven-thirty, she'd selected the perfect power ensemble to wear later.

She'd even thought of a foolproof way to get rid of her mother and Jenna without raising red flags or their suspicions—she'd work them to death.

It didn't take long. By eleven their butts were dragging. Poor babies were used to household help. Tilde was worthless, but Petra had a biweekly service and Jenna a live-in housekeeper at her Malibu condo.

Mia had a spotless sewing room.

"This is great!" she gushed. "Thanks a lot!"

She had dirt under her fingernails, dust up her nose, but she was high on Joe. Petra was filthy and pale with fatigue. Jenna collapsed on the chair at Mia's sewing machine, elbows on her knees, her head hanging.

"Oh, my God," she moaned. "I can see my reflection on the floor."

"Four coats of old wax. Whoddathunkit? But you know," Mia said, "we're going to be working with very delicate fabrics in here."

"We're going to be *making a dress* in here, for Christ's sake," Jenna snapped. "Not performing open-heart surgery."

She lurched to her feet and staggered out the door.

"I'd better take her home," Petra said. The drained look on her face said *Before we both collapse.* "Tomorrow we'll hit the fabric store."

"Great!" Mia enthused. "I'll start on the pattern this afternoon."

She helped her mother and Jenna into their coats and the elevator, blew them a kiss and dashed for the shower.

She completely forgot about Joe's friend Stink until she turned off the water and heard the buzzer going nonstop. Mia let him in, told him where the basement door was and agreed to meet him in the first-floor hallway once she dried her hair and threw on some clothes.

Andrew Stinkensky was the epitome of a geek. Not much taller than she was, and she was pretty sure she outweighed him. He was cute in an aw-what-an-ugly-puppy-he's-*adorable* kind of way, but he dressed well—

Tommy Hilfiger from the skin out, she guessed—he was well spoken and he had great hair, a thick, rich chestnut. Mia instantly wanted to find him a girlfriend.

"Joe is a god," Stink announced to her, and proceeded to tell Mia, while she showed him around the triplex, why.

"With all my heart I wanted to be in law enforcement, but I'm the kid who got shaken down in the hall for his lunch money. I couldn't pass the physical. I thought my life was over. But Joe hired me. The cops can't do it all, he said, that's when we, Joseph Kerr, Inc., come in. I'm not Arnold Schwarzenegger, but I have a brain." Stink tapped his temple. "Gray matter solves more crimes than big muscles and big guns."

Stink was JKI's technology wizard, responsible for the new security system in the Savard Building.

"Very impressive," Mia said, although what she knew about high-tech electronics would fit in the eye of a needle.

"Joe said you used to have a system in here," Stink said.

They were in the back hallway on the first floor and he was feeling around the back door frame.

"Yes," Mia said. "But I don't think it was much of one."

"Here's the existing wires. I can use some of what's already here, so this won't be a big deal. I can grab what I need tonight. If my boss will let me off, I can do the installation tomorrow afternoon."

"Since your boss said this was ASAP, that shouldn't be a problem."

"I don't mean Joe. I'm JKI's mole in IT at Savard's." Stink grinned. "Joe lets me do this every once the while, work undercover."

"Oh." Mia nodded. How many moles did Joe have at Savard's, she wondered. "If I reveal your true identity, will you have to kill me?"

"No. That's Brian's line. My line is electronics and computers. I spent all day yesterday peeking into your Outlook files, looking to see if the design you e-mailed Alicia went someplace it shouldn't have."

"Did it?" Mia was almost afraid to hear the answer.

"Not that I can find, and I'm damned good at this. When we figure out how the design was stolen, it should point us toward the who."

Mia hadn't a clue about who, but she thought she knew how. Now all she had to do was prove it.

"Tomorrow afternoon would be good for me," she told Stink.

If she was right about how the design was stolen, hopefully no one would kill her for the who she had to go see to find out.

"Cool." Stink turned toward the door. "Call you in the morning."

Half an hour later Mia was ready. Hair perfect, makeup perfect, her cardinal red power suit kick-ass, even if she said so herself.

The jacket had a single button closure, a pearl-studded circle she'd paid fifty bucks for in an antiques store. No lapels, so underneath she wore a white silk wrap blouse. She had decent legs for a pygmy, so she wore the skirt she'd designed with a flirty vented pleat at her knees. Her three-inch platform heels were cardinal red, her envelope clutch cardinal red, her soft-sided alligator tote bag cardinal red.

Mia gave her reflection a critical once-over in the trifold mirror on the back wall of her walk-in closet. A mini Joan Crawford. Not her usual look, but it *should* telegraph to Oren Angel that he'd better think twice before he messed with her.

The baby of the Savard family no more. A woman on a mission.

On her way out the door, Mia wrapped one of her mother's ice white shawls around her shoulders. In her Subaru, she switched off her cell phone and shut it in the console between the seats.

She was incommunicado, rigged for silent running.

Forty minutes later, Mia pushed through the double glass doors she and her mother had pressed their noses against last Friday and stepped into the front lobby of Heavenly Bridals.

The cloud-spun angel in the logo on the wall was still the dopiest thing she'd ever seen, but now that she saw it up close, it struck Mia that the angel's face bore a resemblance to her mother.

The young woman at the reception desk wore a headset and about an inch of dark roots with her platinum hair. *Honey,* Mia wanted to tell her, *Madonna moved on a looong time ago.*

"Mia Savard," she said firmly. "Would you please tell Oren Angel that I'm here?"

"Like I'm gonna lose my job for you." Madonna snorted. "Yours is a name we don't speak around here."

"Then don't speak it." Mia reached into her tote for one of the bride rag dolls she and Jenna rescued from her sewing room. She'd pinned a hundred-dollar bill to the white satin bodice. "Just give him this."

The blonde unpinned Ben Franklin, stood up and slipped him in her pocket, took off her headset and said, "Wait here."

When she turned down a hallway, Mia sucked a deep breath and retreated to the farthest corner of the lobby. A long and narrow gold-veined mirror hung between two chairs. She stepped in front of it and checked her knees. They weren't knocking; they just felt like it.

She heard running footsteps and turned on one foot.

"Brace yourself," Madonna said, and dove into her chair.

Oren Angel barreled out of the hallway and around the desk. One hand was clenched on the doll, the other in a fist. Friday morning he'd thrown Joe into the snow. Mia thought she was about to follow him, until Angel slammed to a stop halfway across the lobby and cocked his head.

It wasn't a particularly attractive head. His wiry, gray-threaded red hair looked like a rusty Brillo pad. He wasn't as tall as her father, but he was broader through the chest and shoulders. His eyes were green.

"It's you," he said. "You're the one in the photograph with Petra. Which one of Lucien's brats are you?"

"My name is Mia. I'm the youngest."

Angel stalked up to her and thrust out his chin. In her Joan Crawford heels, Mia could look him in the nose.

He held up the doll. "Where did you get this?"

"I made it," she said. *I knew it!* she exulted. "I make one for every bride who chooses one of my designs."

"You'd better come back to my office."

"Don't you want to blindfold me first?"

The corners of Oren Angel's mouth lifted, not much, but enough to make her heart sigh and slide with relief out of her throat.

"Nothing to see along the way," he said, and spun on his heel.

Mia followed. Angel swung his arms as he walked, like a soldier on the march. The jacket of his tan plaid suit was well cut to disguise the fact that his torso was longer than his legs.

His office wasn't as palatial as Lucien's, but it was large and very contemporary. Lots of stainless steel, smoked glass and clutter. Heaps of sample books, magazines and computer printouts bound in blue covers. The carpet was cream, the steel-framed chairs pale leather. Masculine but not very inspired. And it felt lonely.

"Sit down." Angel dropped into a beige executive chair behind a glass-topped teak desk and waved Mia into a smaller chair.

She sat, put her tote on the floor, leaned her cardinal red envelope clutch against the leg of the chair and folded her hands in her lap.

"Why should I take your word for it that you made that doll?"

"Would I be here if I didn't think you already had one?"

"What makes you think I do?"

"If you don't, why did you come charging out to the lobby?"

Angel didn't reply. He bent his elbow on the arm of his chair, slid his thumb under his chin and stared at her.

"I don't believe you had anything to do with the theft of Alicia Whitcomb's design. My mother doesn't, either. That's why we were here on Friday. She came to talk to you, but the doors were locked. It was midday. We thought that was odd. That's why we looked in the window."

"Lucien sent her, didn't he?"

"No, he did not. Mother wanted him to call you

Thursday night when we found the Heavenly Bridals ad in *Today's Bride,* but Lucien—"

"Is that what you call him?" Angel interrupted. "Lucien?"

"At Savard's I do. At home I call him Dad."

"Are you aware, young lady, that if I hadn't been a stupid young fool who couldn't keep his pants zipped, you might be calling me Dad?"

"Yes. Mother told me. Lucien told her that his tongue would rot out of his mouth before he spoke to you. So we drove out here. Mother brought me along because she didn't want to come by herself."

"But you came alone."

"I'm not my mother. You didn't two-time me."

"You're a lot like Petra. But you look like Lucien." Angel scowled and made a fist. "That almost got you tossed out on your fanny."

He was trying to scare her. At least Mia hoped he was only trying.

"I would've gotten up and come right back in."

"Are you Daddy's girl or Mommy's girl?"

"I'm my own girl. Lucien thinks you advertised Alicia's gown to incite him. My mother thinks you were duped. I think you got greedy. But I also think you're too smart to advertise a design you knew was stolen from Savard's in a publication that we're guaranteed to see."

Oren Angel didn't say anything. For a moment, he didn't move. Then he opened a drawer and tossed the bride rag doll she'd made for Alicia Whitcomb on his desk.

"Now what?" he asked her.

"How determined are you to sue my father?"

Angel grinned. "How determined are you to stop me?"

"Very. Extremely. Totally." Mia drew a breath. "Pick an adverb."

"How about I pick a restaurant and you buy me lunch?"

Joe spent the morning chasing Damien DeMello from one floor to another, one department to another, all over the Savard Building.

The flip little wave DeMello tossed him as he vanished ten steps ahead of Joe into Celeste Taylor's office suggested that he was not being deliberately evasive. He was just being an ass.

Annoying, but Joe had been jerked around by more accomplished egomaniacs than Damien DeMello.

He checked his watch. Three minutes past one. Savard should be in his office by now. Joe headed for the elevator.

If Otis Elevator awarded frequent-flier miles, he would've earned two trips to Hong Kong since nine o'clock, when he'd taken his first ride up to the design department with Imogene. It was just the two of them.

"DeMello occasionally stays late if the seamstresses need to and Lucien Savard can't stay with them," Imogene said, which Mia had already told him. "DeMello doesn't punch a clock, but the seamstresses do. He can't remember if he stayed late September twenty-first. Viola, she's in charge of the sewing room, says he did because Savard had a dinner or something. Viola also keeps an overtime log. The log says she and her girls left at eight-thirty. Viola says DeMello didn't leave with them."

"Good work, Im," Joe said. "Keep those eyes and ears open."

Imogene got off on four. Joe rode up to seven, where Selma, Lucien Savard's secretary, told him that the boss would be out all morning.

"Big doings someplace?" Joe asked.

"You could say." Selma crooked a finger and he leaned closer over her desk. "He went to see Rudy's therapist this morning."

"No way," Joe said, and Selma nodded gravely. "Way."

Now there's a man singing "Show Me the Way to Go Home," Joe thought. To Selma he said, "Did you feel the earth shift on its axis?"

She grinned and winked. "He'll be back by one."

As he got off the elevator on seven at five minutes past one, Joe's cell phone rang. It was Jimbo, who had the watch on Heavenly Bridals.

"You aren't gonna believe this," Jimbo said. "Five minutes ago Mia Savard got out of her car with a red tote bag and walked through the front door of Heavenly Bridals. I wandered up to the building, doing my lost-guy-trying-to-find-an-address routine. Nice big windows in the lobby. Oren Angel came charging out. He stuck his face in hers, then took her back someplace in the building. She's still in there."

The elevator slid shut behind him. Joe glanced around. No one in sight; still, he moved to a far corner of the hall and lowered his voice.

"Did anybody see you, run you off?" he asked Jimbo.

"Nope. Made it back to my car just fine."

"You aren't wearing the herringbone peacoat, are you?"

"No, I retired it. I've got sunglasses and a hat."

"I'll call Moira. If Mia Savard surfaces before you

hear from one of us, use the shades and the hat and stick to her like a fly on garbage."

"Will do," Jimbo said, and disconnected.

Joe called Moira and gave her the lowdown.

"Oh, Jo-Jo, I'm sorry," she said. Then quickly, "I'm sure Mia thinks that whatever she's doing will help."

"I shouldn't have dropped the tail on her. Who've we got that we can send out to Heavenly Bridals and give Jimbo a hand?"

"I'll find somebody ASAP. Don't sweat it. Jo-Jo—"

"Leave it alone, Moira. I pulled a Brian and now we've got a loose cannon on our hands. I'll put a stop to it."

Joe slapped his phone shut and shoved it on his belt.

Last night he'd known Mia was up to something. He should've put someone on her then, but no. He'd driven home with a goofy smile on his face and the taste of her mouth, coffee and tiramisu on his tongue.

He seriously doubted that Mia was at Heavenly Bridals confabing with her cohort in crime, Oren Angel. He was sure, as Moira said, that whatever she was doing she thought would help. Maybe it would.

He hoped to God that it wouldn't destroy the small inroads he and Moira had made with Angel at lunch yesterday. He'd intended to follow up with Angel in a day or two. Maybe if he'd told Mia she would've held off, but probably not. Her name was Savard.

And his name was Bonehead. There would be no more kisses, no more dinners till this was over and done.

"He's ready and waiting for you," Selma said when Joe came around the corner from the elevator. "Go on in."

Lucien Savard sat at his desk. Hands laced together,

not a single sheet of paper in sight. On his right in a snazzy crystal holder flickered a blue and white marble candle.

"It's a serenity candle," Savard said before Joe could ask. "It's supposed to keep me calm."

"Shall we put it to the test?" he asked.

Savard nodded. Joe sat down in the chair in front of his desk.

"Mia told me about the bride rag dolls she makes," he began.

By the time he got to Alicia Whitcomb's missing doll, Savard had stared at the candle flame three times.

"Mia is convinced that this is how the thief stole the design," Joe said. "I'd like to test her theory."

"How do you propose to do that?"

"By having Mia submit Alicia's new design for production. Not the real one, a decoy. In a week or so I'd like to see her prop a bride rag doll that matches the dummy design on the bookshelves in her office."

"While you're baiting a hook for the thief, what's going on with Alicia's *real* gown? Her wedding is barely five weeks away."

"Construction on the real dress will continue off-site."

"You mean in Mia's sewing room."

"Yes. I'll go through the motions here at Savard's, make it look like I'm standing watch on the decoy, but it won't be a close watch. Meanwhile, Mrs. Savard and Jenna will make the real gown in Mia's sewing room, but Mia won't be there. She's the designer. She needs to be here to shepherd the decoy through construction, which is her normal m.o. If she doesn't keep to her usual routine, the ruse won't fool anybody."

"How many people are we trying to fool with this decoy?"

"Everyone who works for Savard's, with the exception of yourself and Mrs. Savard, your children, me and my people."

"My brother and his children? They can't be included?"

"No. The smaller and tighter the loop, the better."

Lucien Savard's eyes lit. Joe had just lifted the lantern to light Lucien's path from the doghouse to the big house. Rehiring Mia for the sake of the investigation would save him from losing face or looking like he was caving in to his wife. A man with an ego his size needed an out.

Savard glanced at the candle, then back at Joe, pursing his lips to make it look like he had to think about it.

"So you want me to rehire Mia."

"Yes. So we can catch this guy."

"What makes you think the thief will strike again?"

"The first theft failed to achieve the desired result, which is the public relations disaster and ruin of Savard Creations."

"It's only been five days," Savard pointed out. "Why would the thief think he's failed so soon?"

"Because you and Oren Angel aren't at each other's throats. Things aren't playing out the way he planned. I can't guarantee that dangling a decoy dress and doll will draw the thief out. He's not happy because events aren't unfolding as he expected, but at the moment he feels safe. He hasn't been found out yet, we're nowhere near discovering his identity. He's hanging on the sidelines, right here in the Savard Building, watching the show. A decoy might tempt him."

"Are there any risks? Any potential for harm to anyone?"

"Negligible. This guy isn't a violent felon. Indiscretion is the only risk. If this escapes the inner circle, it'll spread like a flu bug through the whole company, and then it won't work."

"I can assure you that my family will be discreet." Savard sighed. "It bothers me that I can't include my brother Rudy in the loop."

"You can't," Joe said firmly. "Your wife and Jenna have to know because they'll be constructing the real gown. Mia has to know because she's part of the ruse. Luke has to know so that he can pick up Jenna's workload and back her up on whatever reason she gives for staying in Kansas City. But that's it. That's as far as it can go."

"You'll make it look like you're guarding the decoy, but what about the real dress? Have you no security concerns there?"

"I've got a boatload," Joe said frankly. "Mia lives with Robin and Becca. They won't be in the loop so they can't catch so much as a whiff of what's going on upstairs. I'll provide a driver for your wife and Jenna. Their cars cannot be seen. I'll have someone on the outside and someone on the inside to head off any buttinskis. My tech guy is putting a security system in the house tomorrow."

"All right, Joseph. You seem to have this well thought out, all known contingencies covered." Savard unlaced his fingers and spread his palms on his desk. "Let's proceed."

Joe said, "Let's hope it works."

"I'll call Mia now and ask her to come in and talk to me."

"I'd give it the rest of the day," Joe said. "She was still pretty pissed last night."

Surely she'd had brains enough to turn off her cell phone, but if she hadn't and she was camped in Angel's office, the last thing she needed to do was take a call from his arch enemy.

"If she's at her drawing board by Thursday, that'll be fine."

"She'll be there," her father said. "Count on it."

"One more thing," Joe said. "No tantrums while we're running this ruse. You can't fire anyone. You might fire the thief."

"All right, all right," Lucien grumbled. "You sound like my wife."

When Joe closed Savard's office door behind him, Selma shook her head at him. "A candle. Two hundred and fifty bucks an hour for a candle. I'm in the wrong line of work."

"Selma, honey," Joe said to her, "some days we all are."

He wasn't especially hungry, but he could use a cup of coffee. Joe took the stairs down to six. As he swung out of the stairwell, his cell phone vibrated with a text message from his contact at the DMV:

CMK-039 REGISTERED TO ALAN RYDELL, followed by Rydell's address.

Joe saved the message, strolled into the cafeteria with his hands in his pockets and took a look around from the doorway.

Ricky sat in the back with two girls about his age. He didn't so much as glance at Joe. Neither did Damien

DeMello, engrossed in a conversation at a table with Celeste Taylor. Well. This was convenient.

DeMello didn't see him till Joe had nearly reached the table. When he did glance up, he clamped on a glare. DeMello was caught and he knew it, but he didn't like it. Aw. Too bad.

"Mr. Kerr. Hello," said Celeste Taylor, a fiftyish blonde with elegant features. "We're just finishing lunch. Will you join us for coffee?"

"I'd love to join you." He'd love a cup of coffee, too, but he didn't dare head for the line to grab one and give DeMello a chance to slip away. "You're a busy beaver today, Mr. DeMello."

"I'm still a busy beaver. I have a meeting in fifteen minutes."

"That's plenty of time." Joe gave DeMello a glare of his own, one that said, *I dare you to try and get up from this table.*

"I'll see you in Lucien's office, Damien." Celeste Taylor picked up her purse and rose. Joe rose with her and held her chair. She smiled. "If I can be of any more help to you, Mr. Kerr, please don't hesitate."

She'd been a big help Friday morning, told him everything she knew about Alicia Whitcomb's design and magazine advertising.

"Thank you, Mrs. Taylor." She turned away and Joe sat down, folded his arms on the table and looked DeMello in the eye. "You've been avoiding me. Why? I'm trying to find the viper in your bosom."

"I don't believe we have a viper. I believe we had a break-in."

"And Alicia Whitcomb's design was the only thing taken?"

DeMello shrugged. "It's possible."

"It's ridiculous." Joe wanted to snort but didn't. "Did you work late on Thursday, September twenty-first?"

"I don't recall." DeMello looked at his watch. "I rarely stay late."

"Viola says that she and two of her seamstresses worked late that evening and that you stayed because Mr. Savard had a social engagement."

"All right," DeMello said. "If Viola says I was here, then I was here."

"She says they left at eight-thirty. What time did you leave?"

"If I don't remember being here," DeMello snapped, "how can I tell you what time I left?"

"Let's try an easier question. Did you leave with the seamstresses?"

"Are you deaf or stupid? I don't remember being here. How can I—"

"Viola says you were still here when she and the other two left."

DeMello's glare clamped even tighter. "You're trying to trap me."

"I'm trying to account for who was in the building late on September twenty-first. There was a false alarm that evening. That's likely when the design was stolen."

"Are you referring to the break-in that didn't happen?"

"There was no break-in. This theft was an inside job. If you didn't take Alicia Whitcomb's design, then one of your designers did."

A nasty glint narrowed DeMello's brown eyes.

"You have absolutely no proof of that. It's a complete fabrication. You're making things up as you go along.

Lucien Savard is not stupid. Eventually he'll realize that there is no thief, that there never was. This is nothing more than a tempest in a teapot, created and fostered by you, to suck as much money out of him as you possibly can."

"I didn't fabricate the ad in *Today's Bride*. The employment offers you received from Oren Angel? I had lunch with him yesterday. He never made them. He said he wouldn't let you clip loose threads from a hem." Joe shook his head and tsked. "You made them up."

DeMello pushed to his feet. So did Joe. A few heads turned in their direction. Not many; still, Joe leaned toward him and kept his voice low.

"How long did it take you to realize that all you had to do was mention the name Oren Angel and Savard would up your salary or toss you a few perks? Anything to keep you from going over to the enemy, no matter how crappy a manager you are or how mediocre your designs."

Joe never saw the sugar dispenser coming. One of the heavy, old-fashioned round glass jars with a screw-on metal cap and a flap. One second it was on the table; the next, it was in DeMello's hand.

The next thing Joe knew, he was on his back. His head hurt. His eyes were closed. A fierce white light throbbed against his lids.

"Jo-Jo?" It was Moira, her voice hushed. "Are you awake?"

"I'm not asleep." His throat felt singed and raw. "I'm drugged."

"Yes. The ER doctor gave you a hypo before he stitched your head."

"Where am I?"

"Private room, fourth floor, Saint Luke's Hospital."

"How many stitches?"

"Six."

"Six?"

"The sugar dispenser broke. That's how hard he hit you."

Joe swallowed. His stomach felt like a box of gravel. The light was about to pierce his skull.

"Smooch. Turn that damn light off."

Her footsteps reverberated, magnified in his head. Aw, crap. He had a concussion. He'd been here before. Two years before he'd quit the force, he'd been clocked with a flashlight.

The flick of the wall switch made him jump, but the vicious white stab against his lids faded and he could crack one eye at Moira as she settled into the chair next to his railed hospital bed.

It was still daylight. Slats of opaque winter sky showed between the half-closed blinds on the window behind her head.

"I'm never gonna live this down. Coldcocked with a sugar bowl."

"If DeMello had hit you an inch lower and half an inch to the right, I'd be having this conversation with your spirit in the morgue."

"Smooch. C'mon. I've got a head like a brick. What happened after I went down? I assume I went down."

"Like a felled tree, Ricky said. Lucky he was in the cafeteria. He used his JKI beeper to summon the cavalry and called 911. He made sure you weren't dead first, which gave DeMello time to get away."

Joe cracked his eye a bit wider. "Got away to where?"

"Out of the building. Probably slipped into a stairwell, waited till the stampede to the cafeteria passed, then ran like hell for the parking garage. Brian is out hunting him. Sam is hunting Brian."

"DeMello better hope Sam finds Brian before Brian finds him."

"Uncle Sam wants to know if you want to press charges."

Joe started to shake his head, thought better of it and didn't, but he moved just enough to make his stomach roll with nausea.

He drew a breath and said, "No."

"I told him you wouldn't. Once DeMello is charged with the theft of Alicia Whitcomb's design, assault would be a little redundant."

"Whoa, Smooch. When did I say DeMello stole the design?"

"He didn't? Then why did he try to fracture your skull?"

"He wasn't trying to fracture my skull. He was trying to keep me from telling Lucien Savard that he's been scamming him for years with those bogus job offers from Oren Angel."

"Oh," Moira said, and nodded. "No wonder he clubbed you."

"Yeah. No wonder." Joe closed his eye. "A sugar bowl."

"When Savard found out, he fired DeMello in absentia."

"He can't. I need DeMello there." Joe swallowed, his stomach still kicking, and told Moira about the decoy dress.

"What if DeMello won't come back?" she asked.

"He will. Where else has he got to go? Anything from Jimbo?"

"Mia left Heavenly Bridals with Angel at one-thirty.

Jimbo tailed them to Denny's. When he checked in last, about twenty minutes ago, Mia and Angel were still there, hunkered in a booth, drinking coffee."

"What time is it?" Joe cracked his eye, saw Moira push up her right sleeve and look at her watch. "Quarter till four."

Joe sighed. "Time sure flies when you're having fun."

"You took a really hard shot. The doctor wants you to stay overnight for observation."

"Fine," Joe said. He'd been down this road and knew what would happen if he didn't stay flat on his back at least until morning.

"Just tell me one thing, Smooch."

"What is it, Jo-Jo?"

"Tell me you didn't call Ma."

22

OREN ANGEL DIDN'T DRINK ALCOHOL, but he drank enough coffee, black with two sugars, to float an aircraft carrier.

"Booze was the lubricant for my zipper," he told Mia. "I haven't touched a drop in forty years, since the day your mother walked out on me and went straight to Lucien."

He was brusque and prickly, but he knew a ton about fashion, particularly bridal fashion. He'd been at Savard's for its first twenty years and told Mia stories she'd never heard from her parents. Some of them were hilarious. He didn't laugh at them, but Mia did.

"Those were great years," he said. "And good times."

"If my mother broke your heart, why did you work for Savard's?"

"I broke my own heart." Angel scowled. "I would've dumped me, too, if I'd been sober. Petra made the right choice. She did me a favor. Got me off the sauce. I was bent out of shape for a while, but I'm not a complete fool. Lucien's offer was too good pass up. We shook hands, buried the hatchet, and I became Savard Creations' first head designer."

"Why did you leave?" Mia asked.

Angel took a giant swig of coffee. "Petra didn't tell you?"

"No." Mia shook her head. "No one has ever told me."

"You should hear it from her, not me."

Oren Angel set his jaw and glared. Subject closed.

"Tell me again about the doll," she said.

"Why?" Angel barked. "You weren't listening the first time?"

"I have to repeat it. I want to make sure I've got it right."

"I told you I'd think about talking to that detective." Angel pointed a finger at her. "I told you not to push me."

"I'm not pushing. I want to hear the details again, that's all."

He shoved a napkin at her, took a pen out of his inside suit pocket and gave it to her. "Detectives write things down."

"I'm not a detective. I'm a designer."

"A damn fine one. Truly gifted. That's all I saw when the hippie girl came in with the doll. The dress. It's brilliant. I told her I wasn't interested in hiring her to make keepsake dolls, but I'd give her five hundred bucks for that one if she'd sign over the rights on the dress. She said okay, signed the paper, I paid her in cash and she left."

Mia wrote "Greedy," underlined it and then scribbled through it in case Oren Angel could read upside down.

"Write this down." Angel tapped his blunt index finger against the table. "Hippie Girl was on the tall side, but she had on platform sandals with two- or three-inch heels. Blond, Lady Godiva hair down to her ass. Low-rider jeans, pierced nose, tie-dyed peasant shirt, smocked at the neck and the elbow. Huge sunglasses, rainbow lenses. Now that I think about it, she didn't look dressed. She looked like she was costumed."

"And she came to see you when?" Mia asked.

"Early October. Yes, for the second time, I have the agreement she signed, with the date and her name on it, but no, I won't give a copy to you, the real detective or anybody else until Lucien calls off his dogs."

"My father didn't sic anyone on you," Mia said. Jenna would in a heartbeat, but she didn't tell Angel that.

"Who else would call my two major fabric suppliers and tell them I'm a thief? Who but Lucien would know that the design I purchased in all innocence and good faith was one of yours? Who else has clout enough to hint to my suppliers that if they continue doing business with Heavenly Bridals they can kiss Savard Creations good-bye?"

"You know my father," Mia replied. "You know that's not his style."

"All I know is that someone is out to ruin my business, and me personally. The only person who hates me enough to do that is Lucien."

"You received these calls on Friday morning?" Mia asked.

"Yes. The first one not five minutes after I threw the detective out. I was supposed to believe that was a coincidence? A private cop working for Lucien shows up at my door, then I get a call from Ribbons and Bows, yanking the rug out from under me?"

Mia knew the name. Ribbons and Bows supplied most of Savard's laces and fancy trims. She wrote it down.

"An hour later Everything Bridal calls. Looked like the handwriting on the wall to me. I sent everybody home, shut the doors and called my lawyer. He said it sounded like slander and harassment. Fine, I said. Call it that and slap a suit on Lucien Savard to shut him up. Then I got on a plane and flew to Chicago, where Ribbons and Bows and Everything Bridal have regional offices."

"You sued Lucien because of the phone calls, not because my mother and I got caught on camera looking in the window?"

"First I knew of the photograph was Friday night. I flew back to Kansas City around nine, landed about ten."

Very doable, Mia thought, since Chicago was less than an hour's flight from Kansas City. She jotted the time on her napkin.

"I went to the office to check messages and e-mail. On the floor inside the front door I found a manila envelope somebody had pushed through the mail slot. Plummer Publications return address, inside the photograph, Aubrey Welch's business card and an invitation to lunch from that cockroach. I tore it up."

"Here's what happened to me on Friday . . ." Mia told Oren Angel about Terence the Bum showing up at Blanko's and what he'd told her he'd heard from his fellow model Terri Baxter at the gym.

"Bad news travels fast," Angel said. "But that's awful damn fast."

"The same with the phone calls. Unless the thief was ready and waiting for Lucien to discover the ad in *Today's Bride* so he could drip poison to Everything Bridal and Ribbons and Bows. Or maybe not."

Mia stopped and thought for second. She was trying to think like Joe, which was tough, because all she wanted to do was think *about* Joe.

"No. He couldn't have waited till last Thursday. That's less than twenty-four hours. That's still too fast." Mia shook her head, frustrated. "He must have started his smear campaign on you before that. But how could he unless he knew your ad was going to be in that issue?"

"You're right." Angel lifted the coffee carafe and refilled his cup for at least the twentieth time. "You're not a detective."

"The real detective," Mia said, "thinks that someone is out to get Lucien. The thief didn't steal just any design. He stole the design for the governor's daughter. I think the thief used you to make it public, to humiliate and embarrass Savard's and wreck our reputation."

Angel glowered. "What about my reputation and my business?"

"Maybe the thief is out to get the both of you," Mia suggested.

"That's not what I mean. Image, name, reputation. That's our stock in trade, that's what brings customers through the door. I want mine restored. How are you going to do that?"

"Me?" Mia blinked, startled. "You expect *me* to do that?"

"Why do you think I'm here?" Angel said bluntly. "For my health?"

"If you were concerned about your health," Mia snapped, "you wouldn't drink so much coffee."

"Ah. There it is." Angel pointed his finger at her. "I knew you had some Lucien in you someplace. He's your father. He started this."

"No, he did *not*. You fired the first shot." Mia pointed her finger at Angel. "Lucien should've listened to my mother and called you Thursday night. He didn't. That was a mistake, not a lawsuit. Instead of calling your lawyer Friday morning, why didn't you call Lucien?"

"I swore twenty years ago when I left Savard's that I would never speak to Lucien again, and so help me God, I won't."

"So says Lucien about you. Are you two businessmen or little boys slugging it out on the playground? I'm not helping either one of you."

Mia folded the napkin in her purse and slapped two twenties on the table, slid out of the booth where she'd been sitting so long her fanny was numb and flung the ice white shawl around her shoulders.

"You can't leave." Oren Angel slammed his cup on its saucer and glared at her. "We're not finished."

"Yes, we are." Mia picked up her clutch and her tote bag. "Thank you for telling me about the doll. Good luck to you, Mr. Angel."

Mia pushed through Denny's front door into a face full of dry snowflakes swirling on a sharp wind. She was really starting to hate snow. She pressed the keypad to unlock her Subaru as she crossed the parking lot, opened the door, tossed her clutch and her tote in the passenger seat, swung in behind the wheel and started the engine.

Her shoulders hurt, her neck hurt. Her heart hurt. What had gone so wrong between Lucien and Angel, filled them with such hate that they'd risk losing their life work rather than speak to each other?

Mia didn't realize she was staring off into space with her hands wrapped on the wheel till Oren Angel punched the heel of his fist against her window. She jumped and glanced at him.

He was still glaring, but she lowered the window anyway.

"All right," he growled. "I'll talk to the real detective."

Mia took Joe's card out of her wallet. She didn't need it anymore, she'd memorized his number. Angel tucked the card in his pocket.

"It took guts for you to come out here," he said.

"The theft, the lawsuit. Those things aren't good for business. Heavenly Bridals or Savard Creations. Nobody wins. Everybody loses."

"You're a smart girl. You remind me of Petra," Angel said brusquely, and turned away toward his tan Lincoln Town Car.

What a greedy, grasping, unhappy man. Mia was exhausted from simply being with him and being on her guard every second. That's why she felt tears in her eyes.

She waited till Angel drove away, then turned the Subaru out of the lot toward I-35, which would take her back to the Missouri side of the metro area. While she sat at a red light she glanced at the dashboard clock—4:45—and took her cell phone out of the console.

Holy smoke. Seventeen messages in four hours.

Three from her father, two from her mother, two from Becca, eight from Jordan, one from Stink, the last and latest from Jenna.

The light changed. Mia selected her sister's message, stuck the bud in her ear, adjusted the tiny microphone on a wire near the corner of her mouth and listened while she drove through the intersection.

"Call me as soon as you get this."

Short, curt, calm. So not like Jenna. Mia speed dialed her sister.

"Where are you?" Jenna asked.

"Just turning onto I-35, heading home."

"Call me back when you get off the freeway."

Jenna disconnected. Mia frowned, wondering what was up. Jenna was never calm. Well, maybe when she slept.

She was heading east, away from the sea of headlights winding toward Kansas in the westbound lanes. Quicker than she expected, she was off I-35 and on Ward Parkway. She redialed Jenna.

"I'm back," she said. "I'm about six blocks from home."

"Mother would like you to come to Saint Luke's. Dad is here." Mia felt every drop of blood in her body drain to her feet. "He's all right, at least the cardiologist thinks he is. He had chest pains this afternoon. By the time he got here his EKG was normal. He's in room 438."

"I'm on my way." Mia disconnected, pulled the bud out of her ear, shut off her phone and drove.

On the fourth floor the elevator opened into a small waiting area, tranquil colors, subdued lighting. Jenna sat on the edge of a chair, elbows on her knees, hands clasped. She sprang to her feet when Mia stepped out of the car, and threw her arms around her.

"The doctors don't think it was a heart attack. They suspect it was an anxiety attack. He'll have a stress test and an echocardiogram tomorrow. Mother is with him. At least they're talking."

Mia pulled away from Jenna. "What happened to bring this on?"

"What didn't?" Another car opened and Jenna pulled her into it. "I need a cup of coffee to tell you."

Coffee was the last thing Mia needed, but she tagged along to the hospital cafeteria. Jenna ordered two cups of coffee, one to take upstairs to Petra; Mia a Sprite, which she nearly spilled when they settled at a table and Jenna told her that Damien had whacked Joe with a sugar dispenser and that he, too, was a patient at St. Luke's.

"Just down the hall from Dad. Room 457," she said. "He has a concussion and six stitches in his head. Pete called an ambulance for Mr. Kerr, then went upstairs to Dad's office to tell him. Pete said he went ballistic. There was a candle on Dad's desk. I've never seen him burn candles, but—Pete said he threw it across the room, bellowed that Damien was fired, grabbed his chest and fell back in his chair. Pete called 911 and Mother and here we are."

Mia couldn't speak. Her brain and her tongue were stuck. So were her hands around her plastic glass of Sprite.

Jenna raised an eyebrow, nudged the glass and said, "Drink."

Mia gulped the whole thing and gasped. Her eyes watered and she belched, but the carbonation and the sugar kick-started her brain.

"Sorry." She pressed her fingertips to her lips. "I've never seen Damien slam a door. What provoked him?"

"No one knows." Jenna shook her head and sipped her coffee. "One second they were sitting in the cafeteria talking. The next—*bam.*"

No wonder Jordan had called her eight times.

"You don't suppose that Damien is the thief?" Mia said. "That he stole Alicia's design?"

Jenna smirked. "That's almost too much to hope for."

"Damien hit Joe over the head, Dad had chest pains. Then what?"

"Mother came here, I went to Savard's. It was chaos. Pete was at the kiosk in the lobby. Brian Hicks—I assume you know he works for Mr. Kerr—the rest of Pete's men and I swear almost everyone who works for Savard's were turning the building upside down looking for Damien They didn't find him. He got away."

"Just what the world needs. Another lunatic," Mia said to make her laugh. "Thank God he's only armed with a sugar dispenser."

Jenna smiled. "C'mon. Let's go see Dad." In the elevator, she cocked her head at Mia. "Why are you dressed like Joan Crawford?"

"Long, long story." Mia sighed. "I'll tell you later."

The side rail on Lucien's bed was down. Petra sat on one hip beside him, her right hand tucked in his left. She glanced over her shoulder when Jenna and Mia came through the door.

Lucien smiled. A lump rose in Mia's throat at the wires sticking out from under his hospital gown, wires attached to the monitor beside the bed that was tracking his heart rate in digital green blips and waves.

"There you are, mite. Where did you go off to today?"

"Here and there. Driving mostly." Mia leaned over the rail and kissed her father's forehead. Did he feel warm? Did he look pale?

"I apologize for firing you," Lucien said. "You're re-hired."

Mia glanced at her mother. Petra nodded.

"All right, Dad. I'd love to come back."

"First thing tomorrow. Savard Creations needs a head designer."

The gears in Mia's brain jammed again. Her father smiled broadly.

"You choose what you want to design. Bridal or trousseau. Your call. You're the boss. Well, no. You're not *the* boss. That's me."

And this is where everything started. Last Thursday morning in Lucien's office. Bridal versus trousseau. It seemed so far away now, so unimportant. And it was, truly. Nonetheless. Mia's fingers itched to rip a couple of the sticky diodes off her father's hairy chest, stamp her little foot and shriek, "Would you *please* make up your mind?"

But she didn't. She wasn't the baby anymore. She was head designer for Savard Creations. She bent over and kissed her father.

"Thank you, Dad. I love you."

The door pushed open with a creak. Uncle Rudy, Robin and Becca stepped into the room. Mia moved aside, Becca with her.

"You heard about Damien?" she whispered, and Mia nodded. "We'll talk later at home. Break out the French silk pie."

Becca turned toward Lucien's bed with Uncle Rudy and Robin. Mia slipped out of the room and hurried down the hall to room 457.

Joe's door was half-closed. Mia paused, didn't hear anything—no murmur of voices—and knocked. No answer. Maybe he was asleep. She wrapped her fingers on the edge of the door and pushed gently.

The bed was empty, the sheet and light blanket thrown

back. The room was dim, lit only by a floor lamp in the corner nearest the door.

The bathroom was on the left, the sink in an alcove straight ahead. Joe stood there, his right hand spread on the laminated vanity, his head turned to the right, his left hand raised to the gauze bandage above his ear. Like Lucien, he wore a hospital gown tied at the neck and the waist.

And nothing else. His feet were bare. So was the rest of him under the thin blue cotton gown that barely came to mid-thigh.

Mia knew she should shut the door, but she didn't. She tried to keep her gaze fixed on his legs, long, muscled, lightly covered with dark hair, but her eyes refused to obey. They lifted and locked on the most stunning male tush she'd seen since last Wednesday, when Jordan had flashed the latest issue of *Playgirl* at lunch.

Round, firm buttocks—flexing like well-oiled steel pistons as Joe shifted his weight onto his right foot and leaned closer to the mirror.

Mia moaned, gasped—something. Joe grabbed the back of his gown, wheeled on his right foot and stumbled.

Mia gave the door a shove and rushed toward him, reached him and slid her left shoulder under his right arm just as Joe caught himself on the vanity. His arm looped around her and he blinked.

"Mia." He sounded surprised, like he hadn't seen her at the door. Maybe he hadn't, but if he had . . .

"I'm sorry I startled you. I was"—there was no way to say it, but to say it—"ogling you."

"Really?" He smiled, half-asleep or groggy. "Like what you see?"

"Oh, yes," Mia said on a half-sighed breath.

"Good." He swept her closer, bent his head and kissed her.

Openmouthed, warm and lengthy. Mia laid her hand on his chest, felt the heat in his skin and the strong solid thump of his heart. He smelled faintly of antiseptic and sighed when he lifted his head.

"I swore I wasn't going to kiss you again till we catch the thief."

"Oh." Mia sighed, too, disappointed. "You mean it's not Damien?"

"Could be, but I don't think so. He doesn't feel right for it."

"Why did he hit you with a sugar dispenser?"

Joe winced, like remembering made his head hurt, which Mia realized it must. He had a concussion and six stitches.

"Are you supposed to be out of bed?" she asked.

"Shhh." Joe pressed a finger to his lips. "Potty break."

Mia laughed. Joe leaned off the vanity. She slid her arm around his waist and walked him back to bed. Once he was tucked under the covers, she pulled up a yellow vinyl side chair.

"Unh-uh." Joe patted the bed beside him. "Up here."

Mia sat beside him, her right foot tucked under her left knee.

The head of the bed was up in a half-sitting position. Joe leaned back against the pillow and looked her over. The track of his dark blue eyes left a shiver and a trail of heat.

"Nice suit. I like this." He gave the pleated vent in the front of her skirt a flip. "Did you make it?"

"Yes." Mia quivered at the brush of his fingertips against her knee. "Tell me why Damien hit you."

He did, and Mia's mouth fell open with shock.

"That sonofabitch. Did you tell Lucien? Does he know that Damien fabricated all those job offers from Angel?"

"Not yet. Jenna was in here a while ago and told me about your father. Have you seen him? How's he doing?"

"He's wearing a heart monitor, but he looks fine. No, he looks great. He looks happy. Mother is sitting on his bed holding his hand."

Joe laid his left hand, palm up, on his thigh. Mia laid her hand over his, tucked her thumb under his. His hands were large, twice the size of hers, firm and strong, not callused but tough. Joe smiled.

"Kind of like this?" he asked.

"Close enough." So was she. Close enough to lean over and rest her cheek against his chest, so she did. His hospital gown was thin enough that she could feel the warmth of his skin.

"C'mere, ladybug." Joe let go of her hand, looped his arm around her shoulders and pulled her down to him.

Mia kicked off her heels and stretched out beside him, laid her head on his shoulder, her hand on his chest. Joe rubbed his palm up and down her arm, buried his nose in her hair. The stroke of his hand and the warmth of his body eased all the tension out of her.

"This is nice." She sighed. "I could get used to this."

"Me, too." Joe nuzzled her temple. "My bed is way more comfy."

Mia tilted her head back to look up at him. Joe was smiling; his eyes half-lidded. She hoped with desire rather than drugs.

"Think we'll ever get there?" she asked.

"Oh, yeah." He bent his head. "We'll get there."

Soon, said the long, deep kiss he gave. He let go of her mouth slowly, lingering at the corner to nibble. Mia moaned and he chuckled, touched his lips to her nose and leaned back on the pillow, drawing her closer. Mia cuddled into his shoulder and sighed.

"I went to Heavenly Bridals today," she said.

Joe kissed the top of her head. "I know."

"Am I being followed again?"

"No. Your friend Jimbo in the herringbone peacoat? He's keeping an eye on Heavenly Bridals. He followed you and Oren Angel to Denny's."

"Did he call you and tell you?"

"No. He called Moira. She told me. Why did you go to Heavenly Bridals, Mia?"

"I told you I had a couple of bride rag dolls at home. I took one with me, gave it to the receptionist with a hundred bucks and asked her to give it to Oren Angel. She did, and guess what? He talked to me. He spent three hours talking to me. At Denny's, but you already know that."

"What did Angel say to you?"

Mia told him about the calls from Everything Bridal and Ribbons and Bows, Angel's trip to Chicago, finding the envelope from Aubrey Welch with the photograph inside on Friday night. About the hippie girl who sold him Alicia Whitcomb's rag doll.

"I was right," Mia summed up. "That's how Angel got the design."

"Excellent work, ladybug. I'll make a detective out of you yet."

"He agreed to talk to you again. I gave him your card."

"Good. Now we'll see how much of what he told you holds up."

"Holds up?" Mia repeated. Joe was rubbing his hand up and down her arm again, melting her bones. "What do you mean?"

"He says he has the document Hippie Girl signed. If he can produce it, then we'll know he's telling the truth about how he got the design."

"You mean he could've been lying to me about the doll?"

"He could've been lying about everything. The phone calls from his suppliers." Joe pressed another kiss into her hair. "Who handles purchasing at Savard's?"

"Robin. He places the orders. He works with and talks to the reps from our suppliers all the time. He's on the phone most of the day."

"I didn't get to him today. He'll be first up in the morning."

"You're going to be at Savard's tomorrow?"

"I may be walking around with a barf bag, but yes. I'll be there."

"So will I." Mia sat up while she still could, before she oozed off the bed in a puddle of desire. "I am the new head of design for Savard Creations."

She expected Joe to say, "Congratulations." He said, "Oh crap."

"Crap?" Mia raised an eyebrow. "That's not very supportive."

"It's great. Congratulations. But there's a problem."

Joe explained the decoy dress, the decoy doll and the part he wanted her to play. He told her, too, that Lucien had agreed to the plan.

"This was before DeMello cracked me with the sugar bowl." He just touched his fingertips to the bandage on his head and flinched. "Your father has every right to terminate DeMello once this is over. Until it is, I need him at Savard's. I need everyone who was in the design department when the doll was stolen to be in their places."

"Well," Mia said flatly, "you don't want much, do you?"

"Do you want to take over a department with a thief in it?"

"This is isn't about my promotion." Mia's heart was pounding, her neck and shoulders stiff and tight with temper. "Damien is a nut job, which comes as no surprise to those of us who've worked with him, let me tell you. I can't believe you expect me and Jordan and Arlene and Kiley and Evan to keep working with him."

"If it's any help or any comfort, I don't think it will be for long."

"It's no help and it's *zero* comfort." Mia slid off the bed and into her shoes. "Damien has been lying and manipulating my father for years. He cracked you over the head. When Pete told Lucien, he had chest pains. Even if that was only an anxiety attack, my father shouldn't be within five hundred miles of Damien DeMello."

"You're doing it again." Joe frowned. "Taking this personally."

"It *is* personal. My father had chest pains. I'm amazed he hasn't long before now, but that's not the point. The point is, you want to throw the man who caused this attack, or whatever it was, in his face."

"It's not your decision," Joe said. "It's your father's company, your father's reputation and his call to make."

"If Damien shows up tomorrow. What if he doesn't?"

"He'll show. Where else has he got to go? Angel won't hire him."

"You say," Mia shot back. "What if Angel was lying to *you*? What if Damien has been working for him on the sly this whole time?"

"If DeMello is Angel's man, this gives him another chance to show his true colors."

Mia had tears in her eyes. Hot, angry, overwhelmed and frightened tears. She was running out of things to throw at him and he had an answer for everything. So did her father. She hadn't believed Joe when he'd told her on Sunday that he used to be Lucien—now she did.

"My mother might have something to say about this."

"I'm sure she will. I'm sure your father will listen to her," Joe replied, unfazed. "And I'll say it one more time, it's his decision."

Mia gave up with a gusty, frazzled sigh.

"That was my last, best shot. If you and Dad decide to do this, I won't be part of it. I hope it works, but count me out. That's not pick one, me or catch the thief. I know he has to be caught. I know it's important to you and to Savard's. It's just that . . ." She flicked at the one tear that refused not to fall. "I can't. That's all. I just can't."

"If you can't show up with your game face on, you'll be a liability. So if you can't, it's best that you don't show up at all." Joe gave her a curt nod and this time he didn't wince. "And that's your decision."

"Then consider it made." Mia turned on her heel, catching the door to pull it shut behind her. "Good luck to you and your fellow lunatic."

* * *

Joe was half-asleep when his fellow lunatic crept into his room.

He heard the door whoosh, opened his eyes and in the dim glow of the floor lamp saw Lucien Savard, a crimson silk robe tied over his hospital gown, holding a finger to his lips as he eased the door shut.

Joe found the bed controls and raised his head. Savard crossed the room, leather mules on his feet, and sat on the yellow vinyl chair.

"I thought you were hooked up to a heart monitor," Joe said.

"It malfunctioned, so they unplugged me. They're bringing another one, so I don't have long. How are you, Joseph?"

"I'll live. And I'll be at Savard's tomorrow."

"Good. So will I. I'll stay the night and let them hook me up again until morning, but my blood pressure is fine. The echocardiogram and the treadmill I can do as an outpatient. Petra isn't happy, but she wasn't happy with me, anyway. By the way, I'll cover all of your expenses here."

"You scared the hell out of Mia," Joe said.

"So did you. She refuses to participate in the ruse."

"You still want to go through with it?"

"Absolutely. Unless you think it won't work without Mia."

"Mia's not the problem. It's DeMello. I need him at Savard's."

"Yes. Mia told me. She's refusing to return to work because of Damien. She thinks I'll fall over dead at the sight of him." Savard gave him a shark smile. "I'll survive for the pleasure of firing him in person."

"Mia's heart is in the right place. She's worried about you."

"She needn't be," Savard replied. "I'm tougher than I look."

"So is Mia," Joe said, "in case you haven't noticed."

"She gets it from her mother. A very determined woman, my Petra. I worship her. She's furious with me. She was before, now she's siding with Mia and taking a stand about Damien." Savard shook his head and sighed. "I'm not sure they realize what's at stake here."

"Sure they do," Joe said. "You mean more to them, that's all."

Lucien smiled. "Do you think so?" he asked, almost shyly.

Insecurity. The chink in every egomaniac's armor.

"I know so. Every other word Mia says is *Lucien* or *Dad*."

"I'm flattered. However"—Savard capped his hands over his silk-draped knees—"if I'm the only topic of conversation between you and my daughter, Joseph, then I've misjudged you woefully."

"We've touched on a couple of other things. I'm taking her out on New Year's Eve. She wants to go to Paris."

Her father laughed. "That sounds like Mia. Will you take her?"

"Not on New Year's Eve. Maybe on our honeymoon."

Lucien Savard blinked. "That's—awfully fast."

"When you know, you know." Joe smiled. "I know."

"A better question is, does Mia know?"

"At the moment we're not speaking, so no."

"If it matters to you, I approve."

It didn't matter to Joe, but it would to Mia, so he said,

"Thank you. Are you up for DeMello? Can you handle him?"

"I abhor violence, Joseph. I'm appalled that this happened to you. But for the short term, knowing I can see his face when I speak the words *You're fired,* yes. Do you honestly believe he'll come back?"

You bet, his ego is as big as yours, Joe wanted to say, but didn't.

"I'm positive," he said. "Where else has he got to go?"

23

Joe was so confident that Damien DeMello would return to Savard's on Wednesday morning that he ordered Brian to call in sick.

It was almost ten-thirty Tuesday night, long past visiting hours. Joe was almost asleep, almost beyond the reach of the razor-slice pain in his head, when something told him he wasn't alone. He opened his eyes and saw Brian sitting in the yellow vinyl chair beside his bed.

"I have failed you, Obi-Wan." Brian prostrated himself on the foot of Joe's bed. "Take my light saber."

"Couldn't find DeMello, huh?" Joe asked around a stifled yawn.

"No, man, and it is seriously pissing me off." Brian dropped into the yellow chair. "I know every haunt, every hidey-hole in KC, but it's like this Johnny Cash wannabe freak got sucked into a black hole."

"I hope not. I need him at Savard's tomorrow."

"Goody, goody. I'll be waiting for him in the lobby."

"No, Bri. You won't. You're going to call in sick in the morning."

"No can do, Obi-Wan." The only light in the room came from the hall through the door Brian had left ajar.

Even in the near dark Joe could see the glint in his eyes. "This guy is mine."

"No, Brian. He's mine. Drop out of warp drive and listen up."

Joe outlined his plan for the decoy dress and doll.

"You don't have a part for me in this play?" Brian asked.

"Can you remember that you are not my personal protector? Can you keep your hands off DeMello?"

"Tell me my part," Brian said. Joe told him and Brian grinned. "Cool. I can dangle him off the roof of the parking garage when this is over."

"Swell. But you're still skipping tomorrow morning. Come in after lunch. The big show will be over by then."

At eight-thirty the next morning, Mia sat in her pajamas at her dining room table with a pink mug of Vanilla Bean and a big-time case of the blues.

She should be at Savard's. It was killing her that she wasn't.

The phone rang. It was Becca and she was laughing.

"Somebody has a wicked sense of humor," she said. "Check your e-mail. I just sent you a memo supposedly written by Uncle Lucien."

She had nothing else to do, so Mia took her coffee into her study, logged on to Outlook Express, found the forward from Becca and read:

Date: November 16, 2006
Memorandum to: All Employees
From: Lucien Savard, CEO

Dear Valued Staff Members of Savard Creations:
  Please accept this formal written apology for my

*outburst of Thursday last. I am honored and moved
by your show of support in returning to your positions with Savard Creations.*

   This has been a trying week for us all.

   *However, there is good news. I invite you to share in
it at 1 P.M. this afternoon in the employee cafeteria—
promptly, please—so that we might all rejoice together.*

   My sincere good wishes to you all,
   Lucien Savard

Mia was laughing like a loon when Becca called back.

"If Robin didn't write the memo," Mia said, "I'll eat
the design for Alicia's dress."

"Brace yourself," Becca said. "Uncle Lucien wrote it.
He dictated it to Selma last night from Saint Luke's.
Selma e-mailed it to herself at Savard's and shot it out
first thing. What do you make of that?"

"I don't know what to make of it," Mia said, and bit
her tongue. She couldn't tell Becca that she thought it
was part of the decoy plan.

"I wish you were going to be here for this meeting at
one o'clock."

"Me, too. Keep me posted, Beck."

Mia printed the memo in case her mother showed up
and knew nothing about it. Petra could be at the hospital with Lucien. More likely, she was taking Jenna to the
airport for her flight to LA. Wherever she was, she was
doing something. Time for her to be doing something,
too.

She'd talked to Stink last night. He'd be here at two to
install the security system. That gave her all morning to
work on Alicia's gown.

Mia was half dressed when Stink called.

"Big to-do here at Savard's at one o'clock, so I can't cut out till past two, probably," Stink said to her. "Will you be here for this?"

She wanted to be there. It was *killing* her that she wouldn't be there, but Mia said, "No. I'll be here, so whenever."

Mia hung up and sighed. She wanted to be with Joe. She wanted to be at Savard's. She wanted, she wanted. And here she sat on the side of her bed in her underwear, frustrated and sulking. With nothing and doing nothing.

Last night she'd started the pattern for Alicia's dress. If she got off her duff she could finish it this morning. She still didn't know if her mother was coming. She'd tried to talk to her as they left the hospital last night, but Petra had flung up a hand.

"*Not now,* Mia. I don't want to hear about Alicia or her gown."

"All right," she'd said. "Then let's talk about—"

They were in the elevator, just stepping out of it on the first floor.

"*Mi-ah,*" Petra snapped, spinning at her on one foot. "What part of *not now* don't you understand?"

And off she'd stalked to her Cadillac Escalade.

Mia supposed it was her fault that her mother was upset again. She should've kept her mouth shut about Lucien rehiring Damien in order to make Joe's plan for the decoy dress and doll work. If she had it to do over she wouldn't have said a word, but there were no do-overs.

Mia pulled on jeans and a sweater and headed for her sewing room with her coffee and the cordless phone. It rang in her hand as she let herself out of her apartment. It was Jordan.

"Damien is *here*," she said in a low voice. "Strolled in on the stroke of eight like he owns the place. Like it was somebody else who went berserk yesterday and bonked Joe Cool upside the head."

"Unbelievable," Mia said, her throat tightening with anger. "How is Kylie? Is she a basket case?"

"She's in the bathroom throwing up. Arlene claims to have a recipe for poisoned matzo, and I don't think she's kidding. Evan says it *is* possible to strangle someone with a feather boa. The new girl, Imogene, just looks confused. What happened? I thought Lucifer fired Damien."

"You know Lucien. Fired one minute, hired the next."

"Yeah, well, this time we'd all hoped he *meant* it." Jordan sighed. "It would be easier if you were here. You take the edge off Damien."

"You mean I draw his fire away from you guys."

"Well, *yeah*." Mia heard the grin in Jordan's voice. "Your name is Savard. That's your job, isn't it?"

"Ha-ha. If he comes back from lunch with a sugar bowl, duck."

"Ha-ha," Jordan shot back. "Blanko's later?"

"No. I'll be with my parents." One of them, at least. "Dad's okay. It was just an anxiety attack, but I feel like I should be with him."

Mia's heart kicked a little as she unlocked and opened the sewing room door, but the room looked exactly as she and her mother and Jenna had left it yesterday. Spotlessly clean and perfectly ordered.

She turned on the lights, put the phone and her coffee on a tabaret near the pattern table. She'd left her apartment door open so she could hear the buzzer. When it sounded at ten-thirty, she hurried across the foyer and pushed the intercom key.

"I love you, Mia," Petra said. "I'm sorry I snapped at you."

"It's all right, Mother. As days go, yesterday was a bust."

"A complete bust." Petra sighed. "Pour me a cup of coffee."

Mia buzzed her in and retrieved her mug from the sewing room, filled one for her mother and put it on the dining room table with Splenda packets and nondairy liquid creamer. Petra swept in, out of her silver fox jacket and wrapped her arms around Mia.

"We have to help them," Petra said, hugging her fiercely.

"No, Mother." Mia held her just as tightly. "We don't."

"Yes. We do." Petra held Mia's arms. "I don't think the decoy dress will work, but that's my opinion. Pete called me. Damien had the *gall* to show up this morning, so objecting to his return is moot."

"No, it isn't. Would you like to know why?" Petra nodded and Mia told her that Damien had been scamming Lucien for years with bogus job offers from Oren Angel. "Joe had lunch with Angel on Monday. Angel told Joe. Joe confronted Damien and that's why Damien hit him."

"That sonofabitch," Petra said, her voice a hiss of fury. "Twenty years ago I knew Damien was a snake. When he cost Oren his job as Savard's head designer, I *knew* it."

"Whoa," Mia said. "I never heard that story."

"Sit down and I'll tell you."

They sat, Petra doctored her coffee, took a swallow and told Mia:

"You know I went back to Savard's when you were

ten. I was bored at home. I'd always worked in design, so that's where Lucien put me. In design, working for Oren. There was no reason for your father *not* to put me in design. The past was the past. Oren and I, your father and Oren, were friends. Damien was new at Savard's. I despised him on sight and I couldn't hide it. He fawned all over me, trying to impress me, the boss's wife. I rebuffed him."

"Knowing Damien," Mia said, "that's when he turned nasty."

"Every time I turned around, there he was. Sliding around corners, hanging outside my office listening to my phone conversations. I caught him snooping in my desk, also my drawing board. I never told Oren or your father. I wrote him off as a toad-eating pest. My mistake." Petra sipped her coffee and her mouth tightened. "Your father and I had a huge fight at work, in his office. Another mistake. I was too upset to go back to design, so I went down to the warehouse. I loved to go out there and look at the fabrics. Very soothing for me.

"It was late in the day. Oren wandered in for something. He could tell I was upset. We talked a while. I felt better and thanked him. He gave me a hug, a there-there-everything-will-be-all-right hug. Out jumped your father with a big, "Aha!" just like you see in B movies. He accused us of having an affair.

"I denied it, Oren denied it, your father took a swing at him. I had to call Pete to break them up. It was awful. Of course, your father fired Oren. I left in a huff. Your father came home and gave me a notebook, given to *him* by Damien, with so-called documentation of our affair. He'd taken little things, coffee here, lunch there, twisted them and blown them out of proportion. I told your father that Damien DeMello was a liar, that he shouldn't take any one person's word for anything.

"Lucien proceeded to check Damien's so-called facts with the other designers, everyone else at Savard's with whom Oren and I interacted, and realized he'd been hoodwinked. He tried to apologize, but Oren wouldn't speak to him. Your father called Damien to his office to fire him. Damien gave him empty client files that should have contained designs and *had* contained designs, which I knew because I'd seen the designs in those files myself that very morning. Damien intimated, your father assumed, and before I could tell Lucien what I knew, he'd hunted Oren down and accused him of theft. The police had to break up that fistfight."

"He's your father. He started this," Angel had said to her. *Oh, my God,* Mia thought. Was this what he'd meant?

"What did Dad say," she asked, "when you told him you'd seen the designs in those files?"

"I didn't tell him." The flush had drained from her mother's face. She looked white, almost ill. "I've never told him."

"Mother!" Mia cried, shocked. "How could you *not* tell him?"

"I couldn't face another battle. I was sick all the way to my soul. Your father had to hear it from other people before he believed that I hadn't had an affair with Oren. I can't tell you how that crushed me. I resigned and went home. I bought my spinning wheels and I spun, I bought my looms and I wove. Lucien and Damien deserved each other. I told myself that one day Damien would go too far. And he finally has."

"Holy smoke." A thousand thoughts spun through

Mia's head. Her brain didn't know which one to chase first. "If you want to help the decoy plan, you can't tell Dad, but I think you should tell Joe."

"Yes. I'll tell him." Petra sighed and drank her coffee. "I did try later once or twice to tell your father, but it was impossible. You know how he reacts when he hears the name Oren Angel."

And now Mia knew why. Why her father went off the deep end and why Petra had changed her mind about helping with the decoy plan.

"Mother." Mia reached across the table and caught her hand. "This isn't your fault because you didn't tell Dad that Damien emptied the files. Lucien believes what it suits his mood or his purpose to believe."

"Believe, me, Mia, I know that." Petra laced their fingers. "Still. I can't help but wonder."

"You know, don't you," Mia said, "that if we do a one-eighty on this decoy thing, we're going to look as schizo as Lucien."

"So what?" Petra smiled. "We'll just say it runs in the family."

The pills they gave Joe at Saint Luke's so he could stand up without puking were also helping his right shoulder. By one o'clock the lingering ache and stiffness from his collision with the icy concrete in the parking garage was pretty much gone. He didn't miss it.

It was standing room only in the employee cafeteria. Literally. Lucien Savard had busted up a lot of chairs last Thursday.

Brian had shown up at twelve-thirty, which was close enough to after lunch. He was helping Pete set up more folding metal chairs with padded seats, which kept him a safe distance from Damien DeMello, who sat on a dais at the far end of the room with Rudy and Lucien Savard.

He did not look enigmatic in his black duds today. He looked pale, almost waxen. Like he was coming down with something.

A bad case of your ass is outta here.

The pallor lingered from the jolt DeMello took when he'd sailed into the boss's office an hour ago and came face-to-face with Joe.

"What is this, Lucien?" he'd demanded.

"Sorry about yesterday." Joe offered his hand. "I was out of line."

DeMello eyed him warily, shook his hand and wisely kept his mouth shut. It would drive him nuts trying to figure out if Joe had told Lucien about the fabricated job offers, keep him awake nights staring at the ceiling, wondering when the ax might fall.

"Now that we're all friends again," Savard said brusquely, "let's discuss the announcement I'm going to make."

He laid it out crisply for DeMello, almost word for word the way Joe had given it to him. By the time Savard finished, the nervous glitter had left DeMello's eyes and he was smiling. Preening. Cock of the walk.

He didn't think DeMello was the thief. Accomplice or dupe maybe. Lying, scheming manipulator for sure. If he could take him down for that along with the thief, his work here would be done.

Joe lurked in the back of the room, letting the wall hold him up. When he heard the doors brush open against the carpet, he turned his head and saw Mia and Petra Savard slip into a row of metal chairs. Were they here because they were curious, Joe wondered, or contrite?

The last of the chairs were unfolded, all the employees seated.

Lucien Savard rose from his chair and stepped to the front of the dais, his hands folded behind him. Joe had suggested the stance to give his audience the impression of an open, humble man.

"Why not light a serenity candle, too?" Savard had growled.

Now he swept the room with a smile.

"Thank you all for coming," he said. In the crowd Joe saw a couple of like-we-had-a-choice glances exchanged. "Last Thursday was a black day for Savard Creations. Today, however, I have good news.

"Alicia Whitcomb, the daughter of our governor, has graciously agreed to allow us to craft for her another wedding gown." Lucien paused for a round of applause. "Thank you. Thank you all. Without you, each and every one of you, this would not be possible."

Savard paused again. Joe looked at Mia and saw the eyebrow Petra raised at her and the where-have-I-heard-that-before smile on her face.

"The weeks between now and Alicia's wedding on Christmas Eve will be very hectic. In light of last Thursday's events, and to insure the safe delivery of Alicia's gown, Mr. Joseph Kerr, of Joseph Kerr Private Investigations, will be supervising the construction process."

Perfect. Savard delivered the line exactly as Joe had told him. The thief was sitting somewhere in this room, listening avidly. The carrot was dangling. Joe held the string and the stick.

Now it was a game of catch me if you can.

"Our head of design, Damien DeMello," Savard went on, "will be in charge of this most prestigious project."

No applause for DeMello, which made him stiffen in his chair and frown. A few heads turned toward Joe. One of them Mia's. He glanced at her. She flicked him a small, hi-there smile and turned away.

"Last," Lucien Savard said. "I want to remind you all and invite you personally to our annual Thanksgiving buffet, where we come together to give thanks for another successful year and watch the Country Club Plaza Lighting Ceremony. The festivities begin at four P.M., which should give us all plenty of time to make our way here ahead of the crowds that flock every year to watch the ceremony on the streets. From the Savard Building, of course, we have an elevated and very warm view."

A few chuckles rippled through the audience. Savard smiled.

"Thank you all again," he said. "Now get back to work."

That drew a laugh, and a few sighs of relief from those in the crowd who were wondering if they'd fallen down the rabbit hole with Alice or if Lucien Savard had had a lobotomy. All part of the plan to keep the thief and his accomplice, if he had one, off balance.

DeMello and Rudy Savard rose from their chairs and stepped down from the dais. Joe caught Pete's eye and nodded. Pete moved closer to Brian in case he had to be restrained, but Brian stood aside and let DeMello sweep past him ahead of the crowd.

In his wake, Brian pantomimed pulling the pin out of a grenade with his teeth and tossing it after DeMello.

Joe chuckled. A little zip of pain shot beneath the bandage above his left ear, but it wasn't bad. Great pills, whatever they were.

Mia appeared in front of him, her eyes squeezed nearly shut, her nose and her mouth scrunched together.

"This is my game face," she said. "Whattaya think?"

"Needs a little work," Joe said. "Are you here for the show or are you here to stay?"

"I'm here to stay," she said, relaxing her features. "Are you?"

"I told you I was." Joe lowered his voice. "If you want me."

"Do I want coffee first thing in the morning?" Mia smiled, a shine in her big dark eyes. "You betcha."

Joe crooked his finger. Mia stepped closer. He bent his head and murmured in her ear, "How about Joe in the morning?"

"Sounds like a great way to start the day," she whispered, her soft breath brushing his jaw and raising the hair on the back of his neck.

"Mia." He managed not to groan. "You're driving me crazy."

"I know. That's *my* plan," she murmured. Then she stepped back and said, "My mother would like to talk to you about yours."

Joe raised his head. Petra Savard stood near the chairs across the room, where she and Mia had sat during the meeting, her silver fox jacket folded over her arms, her head tipped, a what's-this smile on her face.

"Is this going to be a lengthy conversation?" Joe asked. "If so, I'll take her to lunch."

"She'll like that," Mia said. "I'm going to have lunch with Dad."

It was a late lunch, a delivered anchovy pizza, which Mia and Lucien loved and everyone else in the family despised.

They ate it at the conference table in Lucien's office, a mini version of the cherry monster in the formal conference room next door.

When Lucien finished, he crumpled his napkin, lifted Mia's hand to his mouth and kissed it.

"I can't tell you how much it means to me that you're here. How long will it take you to create a decoy design?"

"I have one. A design I've been playing with at home." Mia lifted the small portfolio she'd leaned against the leg of her chair, withdrew a sketch and laid it on the table. "What do you think? Will it work?"

Lucien moved his half-lenses from the top of his head to the tip of his nose and studied the design.

"I think this style would look spectacular on you." He lifted just his eyes to her face and smiled. "Could this be the wedding gown you never intend to wear because you're finished with men? Because you don't want to be a bride, not ever?"

"Is that what I said?" Mia grinned. "When did I say that?"

"Last Thursday morning, right here."

"Will it work for Alicia, or is it too obvious a decoy?"

"I doubt that even Damien DeMello will question the choice of the governor's daughter." Lucien handed her the sketch. "Yes. It will be fine."

"I'll take it downstairs and give it to Damien." Mia slid the design in her portfolio. "Then I'm off to buy the fabric for Alicia's real gown, rather than risk the wrong person seeing me take it out of our warehouse."

"And the decoy doll? When will you have that ready?"

"I can't start it till the gown is cut. Joe said we can't

veer from our usual way of doing things or it will look suspicious."

"I told the cutting room to expect Alicia's gown on Friday."

"If I don't sleep this weekend I'll have it finished by Monday."

Lucien smiled, a twinkle in his eyes. "Then don't sleep."

"How d'you feel?" Mia laid her hand on his chest. "Calm? Relaxed?"

"I'm fine, Mia." Lucien laid his hand over hers. "Get to work."

She laughed and kissed him, picked up her portfolio and headed for the design department.

The new assistant, Imogene, glanced up from a stack of filing on her desk when Mia came through the department, and said: "He's in."

Mia didn't knock. She turned the knob and pushed the door open, stepped into Damien's office and shut the door behind her.

He was on the phone, a cell phone, and he sounded angry.

"I don't frighten easily. Don't think for one second that I—" Damien glanced up, saw her and slapped the phone shut. "Do I have to lock *my* office, too?"

"Here's Alicia's design." Mia took the sketch out of her portfolio and laid it in front of Damien. "I'm back, by the way."

He laid the cell phone aside and smiled. "We'll see for how long."

"I'll tell you what you'll see," Mia said, then froze and blinked.

When she'd laid her hand on Lucien's chest, she felt it.

A flicker of memory, a hey-remember-this nudge from her subconscious. Monday night in Blanko's. Robin saying that wherever she had Alicia's design stashed, he hoped it was safe, the pat over the heart she'd given herself when she'd replied, "Oh, believe me. It's safe."

"Yes?" Damien prodded with a raised eyebrow. "What will I see?"

Mia blinked again, shaking off the memory and a chill.

"You'll see me," she said. "First thing in the morning."

On her way out she caught the knob and pulled the door shut.

Arlene, Kiley, Jordan and Evan—with a feather boa stretched between his hands—stood in a semicircle in front of Imogene's desk.

"If you'd been in there another twenty seconds," Jordan said, "we were coming in for you."

"You guys are the best." Mia dropped her portfolio, stepped into their midst and opened her arms for a group hug. "I'll be here in the morning and then we'll take back the fort."

24

THE MUGGER IN THE PARKING GARAGE hadn't grabbed her purse. He'd grabbed the front of her sweater and ripped off the buttons.

Had he been looking for something other than to cop a feel? Perhaps the new design for Alicia Whitcomb's wedding gown?

If so, then the thief had been sitting in Blanko's, close enough to hear what she'd said to Robin and see her pat her heart.

He'd left Blanko's ahead of her and waited for her in the parking garage. Mia couldn't think how he'd known where she'd left her car.

Joe had almost caught him, which gave her hope that he could catch him again, for good this time, with the decoy dress and rag doll.

She was sitting in her Subaru, engine idling, her seat warming, in the parking lot of the best fabric store in town, wondering *how* the thief had known where her car was, when her cell phone rang.

Mia's heart leaped. She hoped it was Joe. It was Jenna.

"How's Dad?" she asked. "How did he do at work today?"

"He did great." Mia told Jenna about the memo, the meeting, and Lucien's announcement to the whole company that Savard's was making another wedding gown for Alicia Whitcomb. "I'll bet it was Joe's idea. He's letting the thief know there'll be another dress in the building."

"How goes the dress in your sewing room?"

"I'll finish the pattern tonight, start the muslin tomorrow night."

"What's Mother doing? This was her idea. Isn't she helping?"

"I'm sure she will, Jenna. Dad ending up in Saint Luke's yesterday knocked the pins out from under her. She'll regroup."

"I'll have everything here in LA lined out by closing time Friday. I'll be back Friday night, so Mother had better regroup by then."

Here we go, Mia thought. General Jenna in charge.

"We'll be ready." She hung up, put the Subaru in gear and headed for Blanko's to give Becca and Robin the code for the security system.

Mia hadn't seen Joe since the meeting. She had no idea if he'd taken her mother to lunch, where he was—or where Petra was, for that matter. She'd asked Stink when he'd shown up at three o'clock to install the system, but he'd known less than she did. Mia felt like she was floating around in a bubble all by herself. A weird feeling.

It was ten minutes past five, the pale winter light fading rapidly from the sky. It would be dark by the time she reached the Plaza. If she hurried, she might be able to find a spot on the street and stay out of the parking garage, which sounded like a Jim Dandy idea.

The parking gods smiled and opened a spot for her just a few paces uphill from Blanko's. Mia had lowered the car's cargo cover over the fabric for Alicia's dress to keep it out of sight.

Singles and a few couples were swinging off the sidewalk through Blanko's heavy wooden front doors. Mia joined them, squirming through the crush in the foyer to see if Becca and Robin were there.

They weren't, but Jordan was, at a table near the bar, with Terence.

Leaning up on her elbows, leading with her mouth to meet his in a deep kiss over the candle flickering in a glass cup between them.

It was Jordan who'd told her that Terence was meeting someone at Blanko's. *Their* place then, clearly Terence and Jordan's place now.

The kiss went on. It was still going on when Mia reached the table and said in a chirpy voice, "Hi, love-birds. When's the wedding?"

They broke apart, fell back in their chairs and stared at her.

"Don't stop on my account." Mia pulled out a chair and sat. "So. How long have you two kids known each other?"

"Mia," Jordan said, stricken. "I didn't know how to tell you."

"How about this?" Mia suggested. "I'm dating Terence."

"Mia," Terence said in his oh-you-poor-thing voice. "There's no need to be mean."

Mia turned her head and looked at him. What had she ever seen in him? What on earth did he see in Jordan? She couldn't think of two people who were such complete opposites in every way.

"This is my last night here, Terence. Starting tomorrow Blanko's belongs to you, but for now it's still *my* night, not yours. Please leave."

He glanced at Jordan. She bit her lip and nodded. Terence rose and pushed in his chair.

"There's no reason for you to stop coming here."

"Yes, there is," Mia told him. "I've moved on."

So did Terence, with a backward wave at Jordan, toward the door.

"I don't know why," Mia said to her, "you didn't just tell me."

"I was afraid it would ruin our friendship."

"It helps our friendship to find you in a lip lock with Terence?"

Jordan's chin lifted. "You said you weren't coming tonight."

"You're the someone Terence was seen with, aren't you? What a backhanded way to tell me."

"It wasn't backhanded," Jordan said, but she couldn't quite look Mia in the eye. "I didn't start seeing Terence till the two of you were over."

"Oh, Jordan," Mia said sadly. "Don't make it worse." She got up, walked to their usual table and sat down. Bev slid a Shirley Temple with three swizzle sticks loaded with fruit and a smiley face paper umbrella in front of her. Mia laughed. Bev sat down.

"I wondered when you'd walk in here at the wrong time." Bev patted Mia's wrist. "Here come Robin and Becca."

Mia glanced up, saw them and waved.

"That detective you were with the other night? Joe?" Bev said. "He looks like a keeper to me."

"He does to me, too," Mia said, and smiled. "Thanks, Bev."

"Sure, kiddo." She winked and walked away from the table.

"Mighty mite! Quick!" Robin dashed up to Mia, turned his back to her and looked at her over his shoulder. "You can see them, can't you? Tell Beck you can see them."

Mia swallowed half a swizzle stick of fruit. "See what?"

"The lash marks." Robin faced her. "From the rubber hose Mr. Kerr worked me over with this afternoon."

"For ten whole minutes." Becca came up to the table on Mia's other side, shaking her head. "The agony of it all."

Robin dropped into a chair opposite Mia and Becca, folded his arms on the table and looked at them. "You're a tough crowd tonight."

"It was a tough day." Becca shrugged out of her coat and sighed. "Took forever to balance the payroll. That's why I'm late."

"I'm late because I was being grilled," Robin said. "Can't imagine why Mr. Kerr wants to know about Savard's wholesalers, but I gave him the short course. I directed him to Dad for the advance class."

Joe was checking out what Oren Angel had told her, seeing how much of his story held up. How much was truth, how much wasn't, but she couldn't tell Robin or Becca.

Bev came to the table. Becca ordered a margarita, Robin a beer. When their drinks came, Becca licked salt and sipped.

"We saw Jordan on her way out," she said. "Brad again?"

"Yes," Mia said. If it wasn't Terence who'd called Jordan Monday night, she'd eat her paper smiley face umbrella. "Okay, roomies. Here we have the code for the new security system at home."

Mia took two of the three business cards printed with the code out of her purse, gave one to Becca and one to Robin. As he reached to take it, she held on to one corner.

"If you give this code to anyone, I'll hand you over to Tilde and tell her that you're the Thanksgiving turkey."

Robin grinned. "Can I tattoo it on my forehead?"

Mia threw her paper umbrella at him. Robin stuck it behind his ear. They laughed and talked and by the time Mia finished her Shirley Temple, the sting of Jordan's duplicity had faded.

She'd been coming to Blanko's almost every night after work since she'd started at Savard's. She'd had a lot of fun, a lot of laughs, but the atmosphere, Mia realized, had been wearing thin since Terence.

She wasn't the baby anymore. She really had moved on.

To the top design job at Savard's when the thief was caught. She'd thought about the position but never imagined it would be hers this soon, if it all. How many colors would Jordan turn when she found out the friend whose boyfriend she'd stolen was going to be her boss?

That would be fun, and Jordan deserved it. Not for snatching Terence, but for fibbing about it. Five minutes of squirming ought to do it, then she'd put an end to it. As Mia was sure Terence would put an end to Jordan when boredom set in. For the likes of Terence the Bum,

Mia wasn't about to lose an excellent designer. Or a friend.

She was tired and she was hungry. Mia said good night to Becca and Robin, gave Bev a hug on her way out and drove home yawning.

When she turned the Subaru into her cul-de-sac, the headlights swept ahead, illuminating the snowpacked curbs, the patches of ice on the street—and her mother's Cadillac Escalade parked in front of her house, with Petra and Lucien in the front seats, locked in an embrace.

Mia put the Subaru in the garage, walked around the house and met her parents on the front walk.

"We come under the cover of Chinese carryout," Lucien said, holding up four white paper bags, "to help you with Alicia's gown."

"Wonderful." Mia inhaled a nose full of cashew chicken and sighed, her breath puffing on the cold night air. "I'm starving."

She reset the alarm once they were through the vestibule and led the way upstairs. Her parents followed, splitting the food bags between them so they could hold hands.

They were so cute sitting at her dining room table feeding dim sum to each other. Watching them made Mia smile and wonder what Oren Angel was doing tonight. She could almost see him hunched over a microwave meal with a cup of coffee in a kitchen as lonely as his office.

After dinner her parents carried the yards and yards of delicately wrapped and carefully bagged fabrics from the Subaru up to her sewing room and set to work on Alicia Whitcomb's wedding gown.

The pattern that Mia thought would take at least another hour, Lucien finished in twenty minutes. The master at work. The next step was to cut the pattern out of muslin and fit the cotton garment to Alicia.

"My love," Lucien said to Petra as they wound muslin off the bolt Mia had purchased. "Did you make arrangements for Alicia's fitting?"

"Yes. She and her mother are coming at two o'clock Friday."

"*Here?*" Mia squeaked. "How fast can I clean my apartment?"

"Mrs. Whitcomb and Alicia are coming to our house for tea," Petra said. "We'll fit the muslin there."

"What about the muslin for the decoy gown?"

"There won't be one." Lucien gave Mia a sly smile. "If Alicia doesn't have time to fit a muslin, what can we do?"

"Oh, man. Damien must be having a cow about that."

"He was peeved at missing an opportunity to brown-nose," Lucien said. "But one does not argue with the governor's daughter."

Mia sat on a stool near the pattern table, watching her parents. Measure, pin, chalk and cut. A word here, a word there, but mostly they didn't need to speak. They knew each other so well.

This was how it must've been in the early days of Savard's. Lucien, Petra and Oren Angel. Working together, laughing together, panicking when they discovered skirt panels cut against the grain of the fabric, not with it, scrambling to correct the error, celebrating with a pizza.

Then Damien DeMello came along and wrecked everything.

Mia hoped Petra had told Joe what she knew about Damien. When she brought her mother her silver fox jacket, she quietly asked, and Petra whispered, "Yes," as she kissed Mia good night on the cheek.

The pattern was finished, the muslin cut. It was just nine o'clock.

It wouldn't take long to run the seams in the muslin. Mia could do it easily before she went to bed. All she had to do was sit down at the sewing machine, but she was having trouble breathing. There wasn't much air left inside her bubble.

Her mother had told Joe about Damien. Should she tell him about the mugger, what she'd said to Robin that she thought had prompted the attack? Was it stretching coincidence to the breaking point? Was she looking for a reason to talk to Joe? A reason to see Joe? Yes.

Mia turned off the lights and locked the sewing room.

Her parents had brought a vat of egg drop soup. Most of it was still in a Zip-Lock container in her fridge. She put it in a white paper bag from the Chinese restaurant, put on her purple coat, and pulled out of the pocket the slip of paper with Joe's address that Pete had given her.

Before she could change her mind, Mia picked up her purse, the egg drop soup, locked her apartment and headed for her Subaru.

He might not be home. He might be asleep. He might not be alone. He had a brother, his mother and the divine Moira.

Mia had an ache in her heart, a bubble that was collapsing around her. The bubble was her life, her old life as Mia the baby. Little mite, mighty mite, Robin called her. She wanted to hear Joe call her ladybug.

He lived in Brookside, a nice neighborhood of older,

mostly brick homes with wide porches and neat lawns. Covered in snow that glistened in the Subaru's headlights as Mia drove slowly down Joe's block looking for his address. She found it at the end of the street.

A brick house wider than it was tall, kind of a bungalow, although Mia could see that it had a second story. Unlike most of the lawns, Joe's was level, with a slatted wood fence along the sidewalk and gates that stood open. One on the walk leading up to the porch, the other across the driveway, where he'd parked his Ford Explorer.

His truck was here. The lights were on. He was home.

She parked in the drive behind the truck. It was filthy, streaked with slush and road salt. On the back window someone had written "Wash Me" and drawn a frowning face. Kids probably.

When Mia shut off the engine, the headlights went out. She drew a deep breath, picked up her purse, the white paper bag, locked the car and picked her way across the snowy front yard, up the concrete steps, onto the porch and rang the bell.

The light came on, a brass fixture on the right side of the door. Mia blinked in the glare. Her heart jumped into her throat as the inside door scraped open and there stood Joe, in jeans, a navy sweatshirt and white socks. The screen was still in the storm door. No glass between them for his breath to fog. She could see his smile and relaxed.

"Mia Savard, girl detective," he said. "You found me."

"Pete gave me your address." Mia held up the white paper bag. "It's egg drop soup, not chicken. Think it will help your head?"

"My head is fine." He pushed the storm door open. "Come in."

"Are you sure?" She caught the metal handle. "Should I be here?"

"Mia." Joe smiled wider. "Come inside."

The front door opened into a living room with a brown brick fireplace, separated from the dining room by side walls solid halfway, then with spindles to the high ceiling. Hardwood floors, a little dusty. A big over-stuffed couch and chair in cranberry plaid, a closet behind the front door where Joe hung her coat.

There was another room beyond the closet wall, closed off with glass doors and mini-blinds on the inside. No lights on. A bedroom?

An upright piano stood against the paneled staircase wall in the dining room, which really wasn't a dining room. There were desks, computers, a couple long tables and filing cabinets. Joe's home office.

"Can I be nosey?" Mia asked, nodding at the framed photographs on top of the piano.

"Sure." Joe followed her into the dining room and stood behind her, putting names to the faces.

His mother, Evie, pretty with permed gray hair and snappy blue eyes. His brother, Sam, Joe's twin almost, Sam's wife and two sons. But most of the pictures were of Moira. High school and college graduation, prom dresses and dates. A couple framed snapshots of Moira with Evie and her grandsons, one of Joe with his arm around Moira in front of a blond brick building.

"That's our office," he said. "Joseph Kerr, Inc., Private Investigations."

"Is that you?" She pointed at a man in a dark blue Kansas City Missouri Police Department uniform.

"My dad. He's gone. Line of duty when I was seventeen."

Mia turned and faced Joe. "And you still became a cop?"

"I did. My mother was not happy. Want some coffee?"

Mia followed him into the kitchen. The cabinets were painted red, the countertops butcher block, the appliances white. There were more photos in magnetic frames on the fridge, on a shelf above a round table in a breakfast nook tucked into a bay window curtained in red gingham.

While Joe filled the carafe with water, Mia drifted toward the photos on the wall shelf. Moira, Brian, Evie and Sam. In a group shot taken outside Joseph Kerr, Inc., Private Investigations, Mia recognized Stink and the new assistant in the design department.

"Well. What do you know." She glanced at Joe. "Imogene."

"She's one of my best." Joe poured the water in the coffeemaker, slid the carafe under the drip spout, leaned against the cabinets and folded his arms. "The pictures of Moira's mother are upstairs."

"I wasn't really looking for pictures of her," Mia said.

"I'm thirty-eight. I'm not married. I adopted another woman's child and you aren't curious about her?" Joe tsked. "Not much of a detective."

"I'm not a detective. I'm a designer."

"Go look, Mia." Joe nodded at the doorway. "Top of the stairs, first door on the right. Moira's old bedroom."

Mia smiled. "I'll be right back."

Joe flashed his dimple again. "I'll wait."

She found the wall switch, turned on the lights and climbed the creaky steps covered with carpeted treads. Moira's bedroom was pink, her girlhood furniture white

French provincial. Her bed had a canopy. On the dresser Mia found pictures of her mother. Moira looked just like her.

The woman Joe had loved and lost was beautiful, just like her daughter. In some photos she had long dark hair, short in others, and in two that made Mia's heart wrench, no hair at all, a yellow bandanna tied around her head, a preteen Moira with braces on her teeth standing in front of her in the circle of her arms.

Her name was Janine. Moira had pressed her memorial card under the glass top of her desk. Mia read her date of birth, the date she died and did the math. Only twenty-eight. With a beautiful young daughter and Joe Kerr to love her. Oh, God. What a heartbreak.

Moira had clipped her obituary from the newspaper and pressed that under the glass, too. Mia sat down on Moira's white desk chair and read it, elbows bent, tears running down her face.

"Ovarian cancer," Joe said from the doorway. "She fought like hell."

"For Moira." Mia bent her elbows and pressed her index fingers to her lower eyelids to stop the tears. "I don't know why I'm crying."

"It was tragic, Mia, and you're a good person. If you weren't crying, I'd be showing you the door right about now."

She gave a watery laugh, wiped away tears with her fingertips and looked at Joe, leaning on his left shoulder in the doorway.

"Do all your girlfriends have to pass this test?"

"You're only the third woman I've ever let come up here."

"What happened to the other two?"

Joe smiled. "They weren't you."

Mia's heart flipped. She turned sideways on the chair to face Joe and pressed her clasped hands between her knees.

"When I saw you kiss Moira in the parking garage and I thought you were married, I was so relieved. The second I saw you, when you helped me up outside Savard's, I thought, 'Oh God, help me. I could really make a fool of myself over this man.' "

"Here's your chance." Joe pushed off the door frame and held out his hand. Mia rose and took it. He pulled her close, wrapped his arms around her shoulders. She slid hers around his waist and laid her cheek against his chest. "Do you want to see my bedroom?"

"That's not why I came. At least I don't think it's why." Mia sighed, closed her eyes, felt his body warming hers. She hadn't realized she was cold. "I wanted to see you, talk to you. Be in the same room with you."

Joe kissed the top of her head and rubbed his nose in her hair. "Last time I checked, my bedroom is a room."

Mia heard his voice in her ear and felt the thrum of it in his chest. She raised her head and looked at his face. His chin was stubbled, his eyes red and bloodshot, half-lidded, a darker blue than usual.

"You have a concussion," she reminded him. "Six stitches in your head. And you haven't caught the thief."

"I will, but not tonight. Tonight I want you in my arms, in my bed, making love." He put a kiss between her eyebrows, his whiskers raising a shiver. "You might as well be. You're already in my heart."

"I am?" Mia caught the breath that was trying to escape in an oh-God-thank-you sigh. "Wow. And I thought I was a fool for love."

"Come with me." Joe took her hand. "I'll show you a fool for love."

He led her down the stairs, through the dining room, the living room and pushed open the glass doors. Enough light spilled through the doorway from the living room to show Mia the black and white and gray plaid coverlet on a king-size bed. Joe switched on a lamp with a low-watt bulb on a table and nodded at a doorway on the far side of the bed.

"The bathroom, if you need it." He kissed her forehead. "I'm going to lock up, turn off all the phones and kill the lights."

Mia scooted into the bathroom, closed the door and leaned against it. Her heart was thumping in her throat. Was this smart? Probably not. Were they rushing things? Probably yes. Would they regret it?

"Oh, I hope not," she sighed fervently.

Mia used the toilet and washed, found Scope in the medicine chest and gargled away her cashew chicken. She undressed, wrapped herself in a big gray towel that hung past her knees and opened the door.

Joe was sitting on the side of the bed. The plaid coverlet and the sheet were turned back, but he was still dressed, the lamp lit on the other side of the bed making his hair shine blue. He'd closed the doors and the mini-blinds that covered their glass panels.

"This is the only condom I could find." He showed her the single foil packet between his fingers. "I have no idea how long I've had it. I can't remember the last time I needed one. Could be iffy."

"Are you iffy about me? About us?"

"No and no. Are you?"

"A little," Mia admitted, her voice shaky. "I could

love you for a long time, Joe. The rest of my life. I've never said that to a man. I've thought it, but I've never said it, which is good, because I was wrong."

He smiled. "Are you trying to scare me?"

"No. I'm trying to warn you. You might not get out alive."

"Are you afraid I'll hurt you?"

"Hurt me as in break my heart? Yes. Aren't you afraid?"

"No," Joe said gently. "As scary as it is to love someone, the only thing that's scarier is not to love anybody."

"You're very wise. Must be because you're so much older," Mia said, and he laughed. "Maybe older than that condom."

"It's not that old." Joe rose from the bed, peeled off his sweatshirt and popped the snap on his jeans. "Come over here and unzip me."

"Oh," Mia gasped. "*Joe.*"

His chest was gorgeous. Broad, sculpted, clockwise swirls of dark hair on his pecs, washboard abs, a big black bruise on his right shoulder that made her catch her breath, scoot across the floor, stand on her toes to kiss it and look up at his face, his head bent, his lashes lowered.

"The parking garage?" Mia asked, and he nodded. "Poor baby."

She kissed the bruise again. He tipped up her chin, opened her mouth with his tongue, wrapped his arms around her and lifted her. Mia clutched his shoulders and hooked her legs around his waist. His tongue thrusted, his hands slid under her towel and cupped her bare bottom. Her legs spread and Joe groaned. Mia felt it in her throat. He pulled his mouth away from hers, sucked a breath and put her on her feet.

"Unzip me," he repeated, his heart beating in his voice.

The steel shaft of Joe's erection behind the zipper made Mia's fingers tremble as she caught the brass tab and eased it past the teeth. He wore boxers, not briefs, a Black Watch Plaid. Mia touched the head of his penis through the cloth and felt him quiver.

"Look at me," Joe said, and Mia raised her face to his. His irises had almost disappeared, his pupils were so large. "Take off the towel."

She tugged the end she'd tucked between her breasts, kept her eyes on Joe's face and let the towel fall. His nostrils flared and her breath quickened. He cupped her breasts, his thumbs almost touching.

"Not much there," Mia said, her voice shaking, the strength in his hands and the warmth of his fingers pooling heat between her legs.

"Plenty for me," Joe whispered, and bent to kiss her.

Thrusting his tongue in her mouth, gently kneeding her breasts, touching her nipples with his thumbs till she whimpered. He caught her before her knees buckled, let go of her mouth, scooped her up against his chest and let her feel his heart thundering against hers.

"Are you still scared?" Joe asked, his voice ragged.

"No." Mia kissed him, kept kissing him as he bent one knee on the mattress and laid her on the gray and black and white plaid sheets.

She opened her eyes when he backed off the bed, hooked his thumbs in his jeans and his boxers, tugged, shucked, kicked and stood in front of her, gloriously naked, *incredibly* erect.

"Wow," Mia breathed, her voice part moan, part gasp of wonder.

Joe blushed. It was so adorable, so endearing. Mia held up her arms to him and murmured, "Come and love me."

He slid down beside her, nuzzled her ear and murmured, his voice deep and suggestive, "Don't you mean love me and come?"

"Well." Mia twined her arms around his neck. "If you insist."

"I do," Joe said, and swept his mouth over hers.

He insisted till Mia could barely breathe, with kisses and nibbles, caresses and long strokes, featherlight brushes with his fingertips and lips. On her breasts, her belly and her hip bones, the insides of her thighs, brushing her curls with his nose, just touching, barely tasting her with the tip of his tongue. She moaned and almost exploded.

Joe went up on his knees, tore the packet with his teeth and gave Mia the condom. He quivered while she covered him, sighed when she finished, took her mouth and made a slow, easy thrust inside her.

He was big and thick, beyond hard, but very gentle, very tender, stretching her as he moved, caressing her as he stroked, resting and withdrawing partway, pushing again till she could take all of him and her hips lifted, her back arched and she moaned.

"Oh, Joe." Mia nipped his bottom lip. "Love me."

"I do, ladybug, I do," Joe rasped, and drove into her.

Once, twice, and the heat he'd built inside her with such patience blew in a fountain of stars, lifting her like a rocket through spirals of comets and great wheeling galaxies. Or not. Maybe it was all in her head, or all inside of Joe, the best, the most giving man she'd ever known.

He made the trip with her, only a stroke or two behind. Mia caught the tail end of it in a kiss, held his face in her hands and his lips against hers while he plowed and pulsed inside her and collapsed in a sprawl on top of her, shuddering and gasping for breath.

"Did you see the stars?" Mia whispered.

"Little white specks streaking by really fast?"

"Some were pink. A couple were purple."

"I thought they were blue, but yeah, I saw them."

"Oh, good." Mia sighed. "I wasn't out there all alone."

Joe chuckled and rubbed his lips on the side of her neck.

"I'm not sure I can move. You may have to push me off."

"You can stay forever, as far as I'm concerned."

"Not tonight, ladybug." Joe kissed her temple and rolled out of the bed, drew the sheet and coverlet over her and went into the bathroom.

Mia tucked the covers under her chin and closed her eyes. She could still feel Joe inside her and smiled. The toilet flushed and the water ran. When the door opened, she scooched over to make room for him. He slid in next to her and lay on his back, put her head on his left shoulder and put his arm around her.

"I think our friend Mr. Condom did his job." He kissed her hair. "Just in case, better start thinking of some names."

"How about Joseph Junior or Mia Junior?"

"Very inspired," he chuckled, and stifled a yawn. "I'm not tired. It's this headache. It's a doozey."

Mia pushed up on her elbow. "You said your head was fine."

Joe looked at her and smiled. "I lied."

"Speaking of liars." Mia slid her bent elbow between the pillows and leaned her head on her hand. "Did what Angel told me hold up?"

"Your cousin Robin gave me the names of the reps he deals with at Ribbons and Bows and Everything Bridal. Moira talked to them. She's very persuasive. These same reps handle Heavenly Bridals. They both received anonymous phone calls warning them about Angel, intimating that he was involved in the theft of a design from Savard Creations."

"How anonymous? Where did the calls come from?"

"No name, no number on caller ID. The reps assumed the calls came from someone at Savard's."

"Oh, no," Mia groaned. "Do you think it was Robin?"

"No, I don't. Your cousin told me that the Savard family invented nepotism. I say good for him, otherwise he'd be unemployable."

Mia stuck out her tongue. Joe took a nip at it that missed, dropped his head back on the pillow and winced.

"Based on what your mother told me today, I'd say it was DeMello."

"He's dripped poison before. Would you like a couple Tylenol?"

"I've got some pills." Joe pushed up on an elbow and squinted, like the light, low as it was, hurt his eyes. "My jacket pocket."

"I'll get them." Mia laid a hand on his chest. "Where's your jacket?"

"Back of my chair in the office," he said, and lay down. Mia retrieved the gray towel from the floor and wrapped it around her. She found a small amber prescription vial in Joe's pocket, in the kitchen filled a glass with water and went back to the bedroom.

He'd closed his eyes, opened them when he heard her footsteps, smiled as she sat down on the edge of the bed beside him. He took two pills, drank all the water, then lifted the covers for her.

"Shouldn't I go?" Mia kissed him and gently brushed his hair back from his forehead. His eyes looked puffy, and that bruise on his right shoulder. It made her wince to look at it. "Don't you need to rest?"

"No, don't go. I'll rest better if you're here." Joe patted the sheet beside him. "Right here, where you belong."

"Oh-*kay*," Mia said happily, and dropped her towel, switched off the lamp and slid into bed.

Joe tucked her against him and laid her head on his shoulder, wrapped her in his arms and the covers and fell asleep. He snored like a steam engine. *Oh, how adorable*. Mia rubbed her nose in his chest hair, sighed and closed her eyes.

She was almost asleep when it dawned on her that she'd forgotten to tell Joe about the mugger.

25

It surprised Joe that Mia didn't ask when the calls were made.

Must've been the mind-wiping kiss they'd shared over their first cup of coffee. God knew he'd blanked out for a couple seconds.

Both reps received phone calls sometime last Thursday, the day the December issue of *Today's Bride* hit the newsstands. Both shrugged them off till word of the Heavenly Bridals ad spread like wildfire. Which it did within hours of Celeste Taylor making the discovery and telling Rudy Savard, who told his brother Lucien.

Neither rep could remember the exact time of the call. Moira took a different tack and contacted *Today's Bride* at their corporate offices in Chicago. No one returned her calls, so bright and early this A.M., she'd hopped a plane to see what she could wheedle out of them in person.

Joe sent Mia home to shower and change for work, their good-bye kiss carefully contolled, then he headed for Plummer Publications.

Drew Plummer had a zillion more coffee rings on his desk blotter and another goofy tie. The Incredible Hulk versus Spider-Man. *Who the hell dreams these things up*, Joe wondered.

Alan Rydell, freelance photographer and driver of the Kia Sportage that followed Mia and Petra to Heavenly Bridals, had dodged two of Joe's people plus Moira—not an easy thing to do—half the day Tuesday and all day yesterday. Last night before Mia rang his bell, literally and figuratively, Joe called Drew and asked him to take a shot at Rydell.

"Zero, zip, zilcho," he told Joe. "That's what I got out of Rydell. I can drag my feet on paying his invoice when it comes in, but that's all the leverage I have and it could take a while. Wonder what Aubrey bribed him with to keep his mouth shut?"

"An invitation to Alicia Whitcomb's wedding would be my guess," Joe said. "Welch tried to shake me down for one."

"I despise his tactics," Drew said, "but I admire his balls."

Strike one with the reps, strike two with the photographer.

He could sure use a slow floater over the plate about now.

As Joe pushed outside into the bright November morning, he put on a pair of sunglasses he'd found in the glove compartment. Driving to the office this morning, he'd nearly gone blind and his headache had soared from the glare of the sun bouncing off the snow.

His cell phone rang. It was Oren Angel.

"I have something for you," Angel said. "Get out here."

"I'll be there in forty minutes," Joe said.

"Don't be late. I'm a busy man."

What Angel had was a Xerox copy of his agreement with the hippie girl, who signed and printed beneath her signature the name Molly Chandler. The document was dated October 3.

"You do realize," Joe said to Angel, "that this is likely a phony name?"

"I didn't then. Can't you consult a handwriting expert?"

"I can," Joe said. "And I will."

But it could take weeks to compare Molly Chandler aka Hippie Girl's signature against everyone who worked for Savard's.

"Here." Angel scrawled a couple of lines on a sheet of Heavenly Bridals stationery and handed it to him. "Start with me."

"Does your attorney know you're talking to me?"

"To hell with Howard. I make my own decisions. I told him to drop the suit against Lucien Savard."

"That's a big change of heart."

"I don't have a heart," Angel growled. "Get out. I'm a busy man."

"Can I tell my client that you've dropped the suit?"

"Tell who you want. Rent a billboard. Go away."

Joe went, folding the copy into his pocket, climbed into his truck and sat behind the wheel. Strike two and a half. Time to do some thinking.

He drove to the Plaza, parked and walked into Tivol Jewelers, the Tiffany's of Kansas City. Reading price tags in this place ought to shock something loose in his head.

He cruised the cases—just browsing, he told the elegantly dressed sales clerk. The diamonds inside the glass flashed and dazzled his light-sensitive eyes. He reached

for his shades so he could actually see what he was looking at and felt something brush his cheek. A sigh, maybe
a breath, but there was no one standing beside him.

*The one in the middle. The one with three stones. That's
the one.*

A whisper in his head, a voice he knew but hadn't
heard in over five years. The hair on the back of Joe's
neck stood.

He bought the ring, the one in the middle with three
stones, put the red velvet case in his pocket and pushed
through the door. The sigh, the breath, touched his jaw
like a kiss. Then it was gone in the sharp, cold wind buf-
feting the sidewalk and Joe as he went back to the truck,
got in behind the wheel and opened the red velvet box.

Three stones, square cut, the largest in the middle, gold
band.

His cell phone rang. It was Moira.

"This was a waste of time," she said. "No one will say
boo about the Heavenly Bridals ad, when the space was
reserved or when the final copy was submitted. Last
Thursday Lucien Savard called the editor-in-chief. She
could've heard him without the phone, she said. Savard
threatened her with death, dismemberment and a lawsuit. Their lawyers advised her not to discuss anything
with anyone until the dust settles."

Joe snapped the ring box shut. "That's lawyers for
you."

"Do you think Savard called the wholesalers, too,
while he was still in his chair-busting rage?"

"Don't know. Don't know that it matters, either, but
I'll ask."

"Are you okay, Jo-Jo? You sound . . . funny."

He opened the red velvet box with his thumb. The big diamond winked at him. Or was it Janine?

"I bought Mia a ring this morning."

"*Yes,* Jo-Jo!" she screamed happily. "Woo-hoo!"

"Your mother picked it out."

The happy hooting Moira was doing in Chicago snapped off.

"Dad," she said. She never called him Dad. "You do remember that you have a concussion?"

"Sorry, Smooch." Joe snapped the box shut and dropped it in the console between the seats. "I shouldn't have told you."

"I strongly suggest that you *don't* tell Mia."

Joe chuckled, put his key in the ignition, started the engine. "I won't, but I'll ask Savard about the suppliers. I'm on my way there."

First he stopped on the fourth floor to see Mia.

She was at her drawing board, totally involved in what she was drawing; the pencil in her right hand moving in arcs and sweeps and slashing lines. So involved, she didn't hear his footsteps.

Perched on the edge of her stool, wearing a skirt, a teeny tiny little plaid scrap hardly bigger than a towel, that showed her legs. The sleek, smooth legs he'd lain between last night and couldn't wait to lie between again. A white V-neck sweater slipped toward her left shoulder as she drew, exposing her collarbone and a thin white bra strap.

She didn't realize he was there until he stopped on the opposite side of her drawing board and spread his hands on the top edge. Then she looked up, tucked her wedge of glossy dark hair behind her ear and smiled, a spark lighting in her big dark eyes.

"Joe. I meant to tell you this last night, but I forgot."

She told him about the mugger, that's what she called Dark Man, and Robin Savard's comment about keeping Alicia's design safe.

"I told Robin it's safe, believe me. And then I did this." Mia laid a hand over her heart and gave herself a pat. "The mugger didn't grab my purse. He grabbed my sweater and pulled off the buttons."

"You think he was sitting in Blanko's listening?"

"I don't know," she said, but her eyes said that's exactly what she thought. "I'm not a detective. What do you think?"

"I don't know, but I'm glad you told me." He was also damn glad he'd insisted on a security system in her house. "You never know. The oddest little thing can sometimes break a case."

Mia sighed. "I wish this one would break."

"I'm working on it, ladybug."

If his plan held together, this would all be over with next Thursday, Thanksgiving. The thief caught, Damien DeMello booted to the curb before the mayor of Kansas City threw the switch to light the Country Club Plaza for the Christmas season.

"Really?" Mia put her chin on her hand. "Do tell."

"I'll tell you tonight. Make me dinner and I'll bring a can of whipped cream and make you dessert."

The tops of her breasts just showed above the V of her sweater. The flush that pinked her cheeks started there and spread.

"Make it chocolate whipped cream and you've got a deal. I'll be home straight after work." She smiled. "Like a rocket."

"I'll see you at six. Preferably naked."

Lucien Savard was on the phone, Selma told Joe.

"He was on the phone most of last Thursday, wasn't he?"

"Oh, you bet. Screaming at everybody on the planet he could think of to call and scream at." She glanced at her phone. "He's off. Hang on."

Selma announced him and Joe went into Savard's office.

Lucien sat at his desk in an orchid shirt and a blue and purple and yellow tie. How many shirts, Joe wondered, did Lucien Savard own?

"Last Thursday you called the editor of *Today's Bride*. Did you call the sales reps at Ribbons and Bows and Everything Bridal?"

"Dammit. If I'd thought of them, I probably would have, but no."

"Someone did and intimated that if they didn't drop Heavenly Bridals, they could kiss Savard Creations' business good-bye."

"I don't make threats. I keep promises. How do you know this?"

"The sales reps. Oren Angel is dropping his suit for slander and harassment. Walter Vance should receive notification from the court in a couple days. You might want to call and give him a heads-up."

If Savard was astonished, his face didn't show it.

"Do I have you to thank for this, Joseph?"

"No," Joe said. "Thank Mia."

From Savard's office, he went around the building, touching base with Celeste Taylor and Zippy Buckholtz. He ate lunch in the cafeteria with Rudy Savard, physically a ringer for his brother, temperamentally the polar opposite of Lucien.

In a quiet voice, he told Joe more than he needed to know about Savard Creations' financial holdings and accounting practices. Sharp mind, nobody's fool, but he seemed weary. Lucien had told him that Rudy had lost his wife Rose three years ago. God knew for how long after Janine died Joe had dragged himself through days that never seemed to end.

He thanked Rudy Savard for his time and crossed him off the list.

After lunch he cruised by the sewing room, grinned and shook his head at the OFF-LIMITS, NO ENTRY sign lettered in red Magic Marker and signed with a flourish by Damien DeMello.

"Protect your turf while it's yours, pal," Joe murmured, "'cause it ain't gonna be much longer."

Then he checked in with DeMello's merry band. Made a ten-dollar bet on the Chiefs game on Sunday with Evan Larsen, tried not to scare Kylie Northcote and looked at the latest snaps of Arlene Bitterman's grandkids. Jordan Branch looked wan and subdued, only smiled, no flirting. Even the high priestess of fun had an off day now and then.

Joe had no idea whipped cream came in chocolate, but he found a can in a Hy-Vee store. He opened it in the truck and took a hit. Swirled his tongue through it and imagined licking it off Mia's nipples. Not a smart thing to do. He was hard and ready just thinking about her.

He parked in back of her house and entered through the front. Mia buzzed him through the vestibule and he took the stairs two at a time. Every ounce of blood in his body was pulsing in his cock when he reached the top and Mia opened the door, a short, white silk robe loosely knotted at her waist.

"I was naked," she said, "but I got cold."

"You won't be in a second." Joe shut the door, threw the dead bolt. Yanked off his jacket and Mia's robe, lifted her and wrapped her legs around him and slid his tongue in her mouth. He could feel her nipples, already hard, against his chest. He pulled his mouth away and looked at her eyes, nearly black with desire. "I want to be inside you right now."

"Take off your pants," she said, and slid her tongue in his mouth.

Joe carried her into the bedroom. She'd turned the bed down, lit candles. He kicked the door shut and laid her on the bed, on deep pink silk sheets that whispered when she stretched her legs out and opened them. The candle flames flickered on her breasts.

"Hey, Joe," she murmured. "Love me and then come."

He was out of his clothes in a flash, snatching one of the condoms he'd bought out of his pocket, ripping it open, rolling it on. He slid onto the bed, between Mia's legs and pushed inside her. All the way, smooth as the silk sheets, that's how wet she was and ready for him.

"Oh, God." Joe slid his arms under her pillow and lowered himself on top of her, keeping most of his weight on his knees so he wouldn't crush her. "Oh, God, Mia. You feel so good."

"I've been like this all day. On the verge, just thinking about you."

She was moaning, almost whimpering with want for him. It made his heart swell and killed the urge he felt to plunge and empty and be done. He stayed still, slid an arm out to catch the sheet, gave it a pull, let it flutter over them and gathered her close.

"Shhh, ladybug." Joe kissed her temple, nuzzled her ear. "There's plenty of time. I'm here. I'm inside you. We've got all night."

She let go of the noose she'd made with her arms around his neck. Joe kissed her and soothed her till she sighed and relaxed and stroked the back of his neck with her fingertips.

"Joe? Don't be mad, but—is there anybody else in this bed?"

"Just you and me and Mr. Condom." She laughed and tightened around him. "Janine didn't take any part of me with her. She left me whole. She wanted me to find someone. I wasn't sure I would, but then, whoops, there you were. Falling out of a revolving door at my feet."

"Oh, Joe." He heard tears in her voice, felt them catch in her throat. "If the theft hadn't happened, do think we would've found each other?"

"Are you trying to scare me again?" She laughed again, tightened again. Joe groaned and said, "Philosophical conversation over."

He started to move, made two thrusts, and Mia climaxed, clutching him and arching her head back with a cry. She clamped around him, pulsing, and he went right with her, hard and fast and blinding.

"Oh, Joe." She sighed and went limp. "Oh, oh, ohhhhh."

He kissed her and withdrew, covered her with the sheet and the quilt and went into the bathroom. He came back with a towel that he tucked between her legs as he slid into bed, cupped her and massaged her till she curled like a cat in his arms and started to purr.

He didn't remember falling asleep, but it was dark when he woke up, the bed empty beside him. The candles were out, the door partially shut. He heard rattling, slid out of bed and into his pants, put on his socks and buttoned his shirt as he walked into the kitchen.

What he'd heard was the potato masher in Mia's hand knocking around inside a stainless steel pot. She had on socks and a set of pink velour sweats, glanced at him when she heard the door open and smiled.

"Ready for dinner?" Mia whacked the masher on the pan and put it down on a spoon rest. "Dinner is ready for you. Meat loaf and green beans and spiced apples."

Joe loved spiced apples. So did Mia. She told him while they ate.

"So does Lucien," she said, and pointed her fork at her plate. "This is the meal Mother tossed at his chest."

"I can't imagine your mother doing that."

"I can't imagine her dating Oren Angel, but there you are."

"I'm sure he was a different person forty years ago."

"I hope so. I'd hate to think he's always been so miserable."

"I saw Angel this morning. He's dropped the lawsuit. He gave me a copy of the agreement with Hippie Girl. She signed it 'Molly Chandler.' No one by that name has ever worked for Savard's. Zippy did a search. I keep a handwriting analyst on retainer. Zippy is gathering samples from all Savard employees. I don't hold out much hope, but I'll follow through."

"You have an *amazing* follow-through." Mia slipped him a kiss, picked up their plates and carried them into the kitchen.

While she poured coffee, Joe told her about Moira's trip to Chicago, that her father had called *Today's Bride* but hadn't called the sales reps from Ribbons and Bows and Everything Bridal.

"So your day was a total bust," she summed up for him.

"Not entirely." Joe smiled as Mia settled into the chair catty-corner from his at her glass dining room table. "I'd like you to meet my family."

Mia bent her elbow on the table and rested her chin on her hand. "What do you think they'll think of me?"

"I think they'll love you. Not as much as I do, but that'd be tough."

Mia unbent her arm and slipped her hand into his. "Okay. When?"

"How about Thanksgiving, or will you be too busy?"

"You mean the buffet at Savard's? No. That's catered. I know." She squeezed his fingers. "Invite your family. The food is fabulous and the view of the Plaza lighting ceremony from the seventh floor is spectacular."

Joe thought about it. Not long enough to raise Mia's suspicions, just long enough to review the plan in his head, decide that it could and would proceed without Mia, her family or his knowing anything about it.

"Great idea. Ma won't have to cook and I won't have to eat mincemeat pie."

"Oh, but you can." Mia grinned. "It will be on the buffet."

"Will there be chocolate whipped cream on the buffet?"

"No," Mia said, her voice dropping to a husky purr.

"Then come with me." Joe pulled her out of her chair and into his arms. "Tonight's dessert awaits in the bedroom."

26

Mia woke up Friday morning with a bright, shiny new bubble. Plenty of air, plenty of room to grow. Plenty of room for Joe Kerr.

Formerly Joseph Kerr, Inc. Now Joe Kerr the Love of Her Life.

This time she had it right. This time she had the perfect man.

Perfect for her. Strong, steady, solid. Sexy and funny. Fall-on-your-face-and-drool gorgeous. And his eyes. Oh, those dark blue eyes.

Not even Damien could take the shine off her day when he cut her off at the pass in the doorway of the pattern room.

"Need I remind you," he said, "that your father put me in charge of constructing Alicia Whitcomb's new gown?"

Mia had no problem controlling the urge to snip back at him. She simply thought of Joe and chocolate whipped cream.

"That's right." She snapped her fingers. "Have a *great* day."

Damien scowled. Mia batted her lashes and went

back to her office. The umpteenth instant message in the last two days from Jordan blinked on her monitor.

Are we OK yet? Lunch?

No lunch, Mia tapped out on her keyboard. *OK will get here quicker if you just let it happen.*

OK, Jordan typed and tagged on a frowning emoticon.

Mia clicked off IM and went back to her drawing board. She had a couple bridal designs to finish. But on the QT, being careful not to let Damien see, she was piddling with some stuff for trousseau. Conferring with Arlene in whispers and e-mails, having a ball.

She was drawing away, happy and oblivious, when a typed white sheet of paper dropped over her sketch. A résumé. Mia blinked at the name: Petra Savard. Her gaze lifted and swung and locked on her mother standing beside her.

"A little bird told me that you're going to be hiring soon," she said with a smile. "I'm applying for the job."

"You're hired." Mia spun away from her board and threw her arms around her mother. "At last I get to boss you around."

"Only in the design department. I'd like to begin my third career at Savard's by sucking up to the boss and taking her to lunch."

"I'd love to, Mother, but I'm having lunch with Joe."

At his house, in his bed. Last night, looking at her schedule for the weekend and his for next week, they determined it was their only chance to be alone.

"Ah," Petra said in her mother voice. "How's that going?"

"Joe's bringing his mother, his brother, his brother's wife, their two sons and his own daughter to the Thanksgiving buffet on Thursday."

When she came back, Damien was pacing outside her office.

"Are you *ever* going to leave?" he demanded.

"Yes," Mia said coolly. "Right now."

Damien hovered while she slipped her bridal designs into her portfolio and locked it in the metal cabinet in the design department supply room. Her trousseau sketches she tucked in a tote bag.

"What's that? What are you doing? What are you taking?"

The phone in Damien's office rang as he started toward her. A cell phone rang—in his pocket, Mia thought—as he stepped into her office. He paused, unsure what to do. His office phone rang a third time, the cell phone a second. Damien snatched it out of his pocket, flipped it open and wheeled away toward his office, nearly at a run.

Saved by the bells, Mia thought. She tugged her purple coat out of the closet and shrugged into it, opened her middle desk drawer and took out the key to open the bottom drawer, retrieved her purse and her keys and locked her office door behind her.

It was almost two o'clock. She hadn't meant to stay this late. She'd hoped Joe would stop by her office to help her torment Damien, but since she hadn't seen him—and it didn't look like she was going to—she drove to her parents' house.

Her father was in the garage, of all places. The door was up, the spot where her mother usually parked her Cadillac filled with broken chairs from the employee cafeteria. Lucien was sorting through them, in a jacket, gloves and a red KC Chiefs baseball cap. His white Nikes looked out-of-the-box, his Levi's sharply creased.

The words *dress down* were not in Lucien Savard's vocabulary.

Mia parked near the back door and walked into the garage.

"Hi, Dad," she said. "What are you doing?"

"Penance," he said cheerfully. "Repairing the chairs I broke."

"Need some help?" Mia asked, not at all sure it was a good idea to leave her father alone with a hammer in his hand.

"No, no, I'm fine. Quite enjoying this, actually. I'll be in shortly."

"Okay," Mia said, and turned toward the house.

Her mother was in the kitchen making cocoa the old-fashioned way, from Hershey's powder, in a big saucepan over a low burner.

"Mia." Petra smiled, stirring the cocoa with a wooden spoon.

"I've never seen Dad fix anything in his life," she said.

"Neither have I," Petra said. "Perhaps he'll surprise us both."

"I need to tell you something, Mother." Mia swung up onto a stool at the half-moon island. "I went to see Oren Angel."

"Last Tuesday? The day your father had chest pains? The day you were dressed like Joan Crawford?" Petra asked, and Mia nodded. "I wondered if that's where you'd been."

"Does Oren Angel know that it was Damien who emptied the files and cost him his job?"

"No, but your father does," Petra said. "Since he's still trying to get back in my good graces, I decided I'd never have a better opportunity. I told him when he came home this afternoon."

"You did? And he's out in the garage playing Bob Villa?"

"We had a small rant about Damien, which I didn't mind." Her mother smiled. "On the whole, he took it well. He was very thoughtful. I think he might actually call Oren, now that Oren's dropped his lawsuit."

That's what gave Mia the idea.

She thought about it while she drank cocoa with her parents when Lucien came in from the garage, and when Jenna, who had driven her mother's Escalade to the airport to pick up Luke, came in with him.

She thought about it as she drove home, while she took a bath and shaved her legs. She decided to wash her hair in the morning, climbed into bed at ten o'clock and turned on the news to catch the weather.

That's when Joe called.

"Hey, ladybug. Sorry. Long day. We're taking a break."

"We?" Mia pushed Mute on the TV remote. "Where are you?"

"The Savard Building. There'll be two hundred forty-three plus people here tomorrow. One of them is a thief, perhaps a thief with an accomplice. We're making sure everything is protected."

"Everything but Alicia's bride rag doll, I hope you mean."

Joe chuckled. "I really will make a detective out of you yet."

"No, you won't," she said firmly. "But feel free to keep trying."

"I love you," Joe said softly. "See you tomorrow."

Mia hung up, thought about her idea some more and got up.

In her study, she fired up her PC, checked the Internet White Pages, consulted MapQuest, smiled and went back to bed.

She slept late Thanksgiving morning, got up at ten, put on her robe and slippers and went downstairs to Becca's apartment to pig out on cinnamon rolls with her cousins. Becca had her mother's recipe, and her cinnamon rolls were melt-in-your-mouth scrumptious.

Mia ate two and fed bits to Cocoa the cat under the table when Becca wasn't looking. She did it every year and had yet to get caught.

Robin and Becca were headed to Uncle Rudy's for turkey and all the trimmings before the buffet later at Savard's.

"Dad is doing this just to humor Tilde," Robin said. "God only knows what she'll stuff in the turkey."

"I say thank God Tilde wants to stay with Uncle Rudy," Mia said, and headed upstairs to wash her hair and dress to meet Joe's mother.

She decided to wear a cranberry corduroy jumper over a rose pink turtleneck. Conservative, preppy, middle of the road. Jenna would call it a Martha Stewart outfit.

She waited till the last possible minute to leave, then climbed into her Subaru and headed for Prairie Village, Kansas.

At one-thirty, she rang Oren Angel's doorbell. She had to push the button three times before he flung the door open and scowled at her.

"What are you doing here?" he demanded.

"Happy Thanksgiving. I'm here to take you to a party."

"The buffet at Savard's." Angel snorted. "You're out of your mind."

"You told me about the doll. You dropped the lawsuit. The least I can do is give you a turkey sandwich on Thanksgiving."

"Not interested. Go away." Angel slammed the door.

Mia brushed her purple coat under her skirt, sat on Oren Angel's cold concrete front steps and looked at her watch. She could afford to stay there until three o'clock. It took Angel ten minutes to open the door again. She stood up and turned to face him.

"Will DeMello be there?" he asked.

"With bells on."

"Wait for me in your car."

It took Oren Angel twenty minutes to turn himself out in a sharp blue suit, camel topcoat and a snappy fedora with a small red feather.

On Thanksgiving, the Plaza was cordoned off except for pedestrian traffic. Lucien hired a private bus company to ferry his employees from Loose Park, on the hill above the Fairmont Hotel, down to Savard's. Mia timed their arrival just right to catch the last bus at twenty past four.

The streets were already filling with the thousands of people who came every year, no matter the weather, to watch the ceremony that would light up the Plaza and transform it into a city where elves lived and made toys.

Almost everyone had already arrived at Savard's.

Pete was in the lobby, unlocking the doors to let people in, taking coats, which he passed to one of his guards, and handing out claim checks. He smiled at Mia, glanced curiously at Angel. She saw recognition click in his eyes and the quick, startled handshake he offered.

"Oren. Long time. Good to see you."

"Pete," Angel said gruffly, but shook his hand.

The party was in full swing on six. A quintet played Christmas music in a corner, Savard's employees and their families clustered in groups and milled in couples. The scents drifting out of the cafeteria—turkey, stuffing and fragrant vegetables—made Mia's stomach growl.

It had been a long time since Becca's cinnamon rolls.

And an even longer time, twenty years, since Lucien Savard and Oren Angel had laid eyes on each other.

Her father saw them first. Lucien was working the room, a glass of wine in one hand, when he turned his head and saw Mia and Oren Angel coming toward him from the elevators.

Mia saw the startled leap in her father's eyes, felt Angel's hand tighten on her elbow and his step falter, but that was it. After that first flinch, neither of them moved. They just stared at each other.

She'd gotten them this far. Now Mia didn't know what to do. She looked around frantically for Petra.

Where was her mother when she needed her? Nowhere.

But there—oh hell—there was Jenna the Knee Breaker, coming toward her and Oren Angel, wearing a purple Donna Karan pantsuit and her General Savard Supreme Commander face.

"Oren Angel." Jenna snapped to a halt in front of them and stuck out her hand. "Jenna Savard. Thank you for coming."

"It was her idea." Angel took Jenna's hand and nodded at Mia.

"Yes, we know." Jenna slid her a sideways look that

said *We all know and we are reserving the right to kill you later.*

How did they know? Mia wondered, till she felt two large, warm hands settle on her shoulders.

"Mr. Angel," Joe said behind her. "Happy Thanksgiving."

"You're here, too?" Angel turned and glowered at Joe. "Don't you people have anywhere else to be?"

There was a growl in his voice, a flicker of I-shouldn't-be-here panic in his green eyes as he glanced around the lobby. So did Mia, still on the lookout for her mother.

There she was—stepping out of the crowd a short distance away, splendidly dressed in a shell pink wool pantsuit draped with one of her shawls, one side of her blush blond hair swept up in a diamond comb.

She saw Mia first, then Angel. She glanced them a smile, turned and walked to Lucien's side, tucked her fingers in the curve of his arm and pressed a kiss to his cheek. She whispered something in his ear that made him smile and sweep her against him in a one-armed hug.

Lucien stopped a passing waiter. Petra lifted a glass of wine from his tray, her father took another and they started toward Oren Angel.

"Nice to meet you," Angel said to Jenna. "*You . . .*" He pointed at Mia, started to scowl, then smiled. "Don't forget my turkey sandwich."

"I won't," Mia promised. "It'll be ready when you are."

Angel nodded and moved forward to meet Lucien and Petra.

She was a little worried about the glasses of wine her father held, but he passed one to her mother and offered his hand to Oren Angel. Since he was the one who'd started this, with a boatload of interference from Damien DeMello, Mia thought it was a nice touch.

Petra passed Angel a glass of wine and lifted hers. So did her father and Oren Angel, and all three smiled. Then they drank.

"I never thought," Luke said behind them, "that I'd see this day."

"That makes two of us," Jenna said, and turned toward Mia. "How did you do this? *Why* did you do this?"

"Not now, Jen. It's Thanksgiving. Let's dance." Luke took Jenna's hand, paused to lean toward Mia and put a kiss on her forehead. "Good work. Should I worry about you and the CEO's chair when Dad retires?"

"Nope," Mia said. "I'm going to be a detective when I grow up."

Joe gave a hoot of laughter. When Luke towed Jenna away to cut a rug in front of the band, he turned her into his arms and hugged her.

"You were having me followed again." Mia raised her face from his chest. "That's how Jenna knew I was showing up with Oren Angel."

"After what you told me about the mugger," Joe said, planting a kiss on her nose, "it seemed like a good idea."

"I can see that, I suppose, but I wanted this to be a surprise."

"Oh, it was, believe me, when Jimbo called and said you were sitting on Oren Angel's front steps. It gave your mother time to talk a little turkey to your father and for Lucien to prepare himself."

"Speaking of turkeys," Mia said. "Is Damien here?"

Joe nodded. "He's here. Keeping a low profile."

"How about your mother and Moira? Your brother and his family?"

"They're not going to make it. Sam's boys started throwing up this morning, so Ma, Sam and his wife, Carol, are hip deep in puking kids."

"Oh, darn," Mia said, hoping she sounded disappointed rather than relieved out of her mind. "That's too bad."

"Not to worry, ladybug." Joe looped his arms behind her and tucked her against him. "There's always Christmas."

His cell phone vibrated against Mia's ribs. She stepped out of his arms; he unclipped the phone from his belt and glanced at the screen.

"Uncle Pete," he said. "He needs a hand in the lobby. I'll be back."

Joe turned toward the elevators, leaving Mia to circulate, threading her way through Savard's employees, stopping to say hello, exchange a few words. The whole time keeping watch for Damien.

His presence had convinced Angel to come. Her mother said Angel didn't know that Damien was the one who had emptied the files, but what if he did? What if he'd somehow found out over the years or put two and two together?

Too late now, but maybe she should've given that more thought.

All she could do now was find Damien and keep an eye on him.

It took her half an hour to find him, skirting the perimeter of the crowd in the cafeteria lobby like the shadow he resembled in a black suit and shirt. Mia stayed on his tail at a discreet distance, still circulating, still mingling, always keeping Damien's dark profile in sight.

She hadn't seen her parents and Angel since they'd toasted one another. By the shocked, frozen halt Savard's soon-to-be-ex–head designer came to when the three of them emerged from the crowd, laughing, Damien DeMello had no idea that Oren Angel was in the building.

He stared at them for a moment, pale and unblinking. Mia imagined that Damien could see his world and his career crumbling before his eyes. Then he spun on one foot and raced for the stairwell.

So did Mia. He had a good jump on her, but she was smaller and quicker and could dart through the crowd easier than he could. The stairwell door was slowly shutting when she reached it and pushed past it, paused and listened. She heard footsteps, running and echoing.

Down, of course, to the design department. Where else?

Mia ran after him, counting on the ring of his footsteps to mask hers. On four, she caught the stairwell door before it clicked shut, slipped past it and soundlessly eased it shut behind her.

Upstairs, all the lights were on. Here, only every third ceiling spot was lit. The elevator lobby was dim and shadowed, but not dark. Mia listened, heard nothing and crept around the corner.

The design department was dark, the door shut.

The door to her office was open, the lights on.

Damien stood by her bookshelves and beside him— Mia recognized his dark navy peacoat, the ski mask with red-stitched mouth and eye slits, and her heart nearly stopped—the mugger from the parking garage.

Damien and the mugger were playing tug-of-war with Alicia Whitcomb's decoy bride rag doll.

"Give it to me," Damien hissed. Mia was close enough to hear the fury and the panic in his voice. "This won't work!"

"Sure it will!" The mugger gave Damien a shove that sent him stumbling. "It worked once! It'll work again!"

A chill crept up Mia's back. Did she know that voice?

"It won't! Angel is *here*!" Damien regained his feet. "He's upstairs at the party!"

He leaped for the doll, but the mugger snatched it away and held it out of reach.

"I told you that stealing the first doll was a mistake, that it would be smarter to steal the design!" Damien railed, his fists clenched. "But no, you said. She'll never miss it. She'll think she tucked it away in the bag with Alicia's gown! Well, she didn't!"

"The design was too obvious!" The mugger shot back. "It would've pointed the finger right back at us!"

"And stealing the doll didn't?" Damien made another grab for the doll, stumbled and nearly fell.

"I trusted you!" The mugger shoved him again. "You said Savard wouldn't look any further than Oren Angel! There'd be no police! No damned detective! Just lawyers, accusations, enough mud stirred up and thrown that no one would see us! You said it would all blow up, rip the family apart, finally get rid of them so the rest of us have a chance! Well, it *didn't*! That little bitch Mia is still here and I'm still second chair!"

There was a shrill in the mugger's voice now and a sob that shot Mia with gooseflesh. It wasn't a man behind the mask. It was woman, and she knew her voice. It was Jordan. Oh God. It was Jordan.

"We can still make it work," Damien said, a desperate edge in his voice. "If you put the doll back."

"*No!*" Jordan shrieked, her voice muffled inside the mask but unmistakable now to Mia. She shook the doll in Damien's face, pushed him back with it. "This is my ticket! This little doll is taking me to New York! And you can go to hell!"

Jordan gave Damien one last shove and whirled toward the door.

Mia whirled, too, across the elevator lobby into the far back corner, where she prayed the light was dim enough, the shadows deep enough, that Jordan wouldn't see her when she came around the corner. Mia pressed herself against the wall and held her breath, wanted to close her eyes but forced herself to keep them open.

Jordan bolted around the corner and through the stairwell door.

Mia dashed after her, praying Damien wouldn't be hot on Jordan's heels, or hers. He wasn't. She made it through the door and raced down the steps. This was good. This was perfect. Joe had gone down to the lobby. He'd catch Jordan when she came out of the first-floor stairwell.

Only, Jordan didn't head for the lobby.

Mia reached the landing between the fourth floor and the third in time to see Jordan shove the fire door on three out of her way, the door that led outside onto the roof of the parking garage. The alarm should've sounded the second Jordan pushed the bar, but it didn't. Oh no!

"Jordan!" Mia shouted, and dashed down the half flight of stairs.

Jordan spun around in the open doorway, her dark figure and the darker roof behind her lit only by the backwash of the lights from the surrounding buildings. Jordan pulled off her mask and Mia felt her heart wrench at the tears in her eyes, her ragged, gasping breath.

"Let me go, Mia. Let me have the doll and let me go." She was nearly sobbing. "You'll never see me again. I swear."

Mia sucked back her own tears. She might've said yes, might've let her go, if Jordan hadn't raised the doll and cried, "You owe me this!"

Then she spun away and out the door onto the roof.

Mia shot through it like a rocket behind her, outside into the cold evening air. A second before she smacked into what felt like a brick wall, a very warm brick wall, she heard Jordan shriek. Mia blinked in the near darkness, looked up and realized she'd run into Joe. She swung her head past him and saw Jordan caught from behind, trapped in the circle of Brian Hicks' arms, struggling and kicking and sobbing to be free.

Mia grabbed Joe's lapels and buried her face in his chest. She sucked a deep breath, swallowed her tears and looked up at him.

"Did you know it was Jordan?"

"Not till she went for the doll. We've got her and DeMello on tape. Stink put a camera in your office over the weekend." Joe kissed her hair, raised her face and gave her a gentle chuck under the chin. "Game face, Mia. Go back inside. I'll be in as soon as I can."

"What about Damien? Do you suppose he got away?"

"From Imogene? Not likely. She's a champion kickboxer. Go on, ladybug." Joe gave her a push toward the door. "I've got stuff to do."

In other words, she wasn't a real detective, get out of the way. But that was okay. Mia went back inside. She climbed the stairs to the fourth floor and turned the corner toward her office.

The lights were on but there was no sign of Damien. Imogene had nabbed him. Mia hoped she'd slapped him around some.

There was a camera hidden in her office, but she didn't care. Mia climbed onto her stool, bent her elbows on her drawing board, buried her face in her hands and cried.

It was over. The thief caught, Damien unmasked. The damage he'd done and the breach he'd caused between her parents and Oren Angel repaired. Her family wasn't ripped apart as Damien had intended, and Savard Creations had survived. Mia'd gained Joe, but she'd lost Jordan.

Stealing Terence was one thing, but stealing her design for Alicia's dress . . . Had Jordon hoped that Lucien would blame her, fire her, that she'd be arrested, sent to jail? Mia felt cold all over. That would've cleared her from Jordan's path. Could it have happened?

She took her hands away from her face, laid her arms on her drawing board and her forehead on its laminated surface. Mia kept her head down till the tears stopped. By then her back was in such a cramp, she wasn't sure she could sit up without falling off her stool.

"I thought you might be here," Joe said gently.

From the sound of his voice, he was standing behind her table. Mia's eyes filled again. She swallowed a sob and kept her head down.

"Are they gone? Jordan and Damien? Were they arrested?"

"Taken into custody," Joe said. "If your father presses charges, they'll be arraigned. More than likely, they'll get bail."

"Does Lucien know what happened?"

"Yes. He's with Walter Vance in the conference room. You okay?"

"I'm crying," Mia said, her voice quavering. "I have no idea why."

"You were backstabbed by someone you thought was your friend."

"I had no idea that Jordan hated me."

"She doesn't hate you. She wants to be you. First Terence, then Alicia's design. She was stealing your life in little pieces."

"Does my mother know?"

"She's with your father and Vance. So is Oren Angel."

"No way!" Mia pushed up on her hands, so quickly that her back spasmed. Joe stood behind her drawing board, smiling at her, just his head and shoulders visible above the top edge. "You lied."

"It got you off your face." He stepped around the table and handed Mia the decoy doll she'd sewn her fingers bloody to make over the weekend. "Jordan dropped this. I thought you'd like to have it back."

"Thanks." Mia took the doll, licked her finger and rubbed a smudge of dirt off the painted cloth cheek. "This is so ironic."

"What is?" Joe asked.

"Jordan stole Terence, the design for Alicia's dress, and then she tried to steal mine." She held the doll up to Joe. "That's what this is. The wedding gown I designed for myself."

"No kidding." He took the doll from her, looked it over, raised just his eyes and smiled. "You'd look absolutely beautiful in this dress."

Mia's heart leaped. "Do you think so?"

"Well," Joe flashed his dimple, "I'd have to see you in it."

"Would you like to?" Mia asked, and held her breath.

Joe smiled and leaned in to kiss her. "Very much."

His cell phone rang. Mia nearly jumped off her stool. Joe frowned, snatched the phone off his belt and flipped it open.

"Joe Kerr," he said, and listened. Mia watched his face, saw his jaw tighten and a muscle jump. "Okay. I'll be right there."

"What's wrong?" Mia asked. "What happened?"

"I don't believe this." Joe slapped the phone shut. "DeMello got away from the cops."

27

A ROOKIE WORKING CROWD CONTROL for the Plaza Lighting Ceremony, commandeered to keep an eye on Damien till the paddy wagon could make its way through the pedestrian-clogged streets, turned his back for just a second and DeMello vanished. Handcuffs and all.

Dispatch issued an APB, and the manhunt began.

"A dragnet for Damien?" Mia said to Joe, when he called to tell her at eight-twenty Friday morning. "He isn't number one on the Ten Most Wanted list. He's a designer. This is crazy."

"This is Kansas City's finest trying to save face." Joe yawned in her ear. He'd been up all night and was still searching for Damien. "And trying to find DeMello before the media gets hold of the story."

That's exactly who got hold of the story—Aubrey Welch.

It was Damien who'd tipped Welch about Alicia Whitcomb's stolen design. When he had nowhere to go and no one else to turn to, Damien threw himself on Welch's mercy. He turned up at Plummer Publications a little after ten A.M., his cuffed-together hands hidden by a filthy Army jacket a homeless man had thrown over his shoulders in an alley.

Welch called Joe. Joe called his brother, Sam, first, then Brian, and sent him to pick up DeMello.

"I'm glad," Damien blathered, on the verge of tears, to the local TV crew that caught him on tape on the way to his three o'clock arraignment. "So *grateful* to be in custody."

Mia sat with Joe on the flowered sofa in her living room, his arm around her shoulders, watching the spectacle on the six o'clock news.

"Brian, Brian," he tsked, but he was grinning.

The ten o'clock broadcast carried the highlights of Aubrey Welch's press conference. He stood behind a bank of microphones, in a tailored Italian suit, his beard immaculately trimmed, a stickpin glistening in the folds of his perfectly coordinated tie. Lavishing praise on the KCMOPD while modestly pooh-poohing his role in Damien's capture and listing every rotten, lying, cheating, stinking thing DeMello did.

". . . to destroy the happiness of the lovely Alicia, daughter of our great Governor Whitcomb and our beautiful first lady."

"Hey!" Mia shouted at Welch, loud enough to wake Joe. "You left out the part where you did as much as Damien to create a scandal and ruin Savard Creations!"

"Whoa, ladybug," Joe said groggily. "Calm down."

Mia bounced around on her bed to look at him, half asleep against her pillows, the pink silk coverlet drawn up to his bare, dark-haired chest. He looked fabulous and not a bit girly in pink.

"And not one *word* about you," she complained. "Or Joseph Kerr, Inc., Private Investigations."

"I'm a detective, honey," Joe said. "Having my face plastered all over a newscast is not good for business."

"Oh. I guess not." Mia turned back to the TV. "No one has said a word about Jordan, either."

"No one will," Joe told her. "I made a deal with Welch."

Mia didn't have to ask why; she knew. For her. She twisted around and looked at Joe, his eyelids at half-mast and closing fast.

"What did that cost you?"

"Don't ask," he said, and fell back asleep.

His kissing-up press conference earned Aubrey Welch an invitation to Alicia Whitcomb's wedding reception, held at the Governor's Mansion in Jefferson City, following the ceremony at the Presbyterian church the Whitcomb family had attended since Alicia was in Sunday school.

Mia was at the wedding with Joe, Lucien, Petra, Luke and Jenna, squeezed into a pew in the middle of the crammed-to-the-gills church. When Alicia passed them on her way up the aisle on her father's arm, Joe leaned close and whispered in Mia's ear, "Nice dress."

Alicia wore the first gown Mia had designed for her; the lace and pink chintz with the bow-tied tiered skirt, the dress that brought Joe into her life. It was Alicia's first choice, the gown she loved best.

"Why shouldn't I wear it?" she'd said to Lucien when he personally delivered the replacement gown Viola and her seamstresses and everyone else at Savard's had killed themselves to finish on time. "Hardly anyone saw it in that magazine."

Because *Today's Bride,* to avoid being named in a lawsuit, had yanked every copy of their December issue off newsstands.

Lucien didn't bat an eye. He murmured and bowed

over Alicia's hand, drove home, kissed Petra and went out to the garage.

The cafeteria chairs he'd broken were beyond repair, but they made great therapy. Lucien emerged twenty minutes later, ready to face the next crisis with a serene and smiling face.

"What happens when he's busted all those chairs down to a pile of kindling?" Mia asked her mother.

"Not to worry." Petra smiled. "I'm shopping thrift stores and garage sales to keep your father supplied."

At Alicia's reception, against the backdrop of the Governor's Mansion, a grand old Victorian set high on a bluff above the Missouri River, with its red plaster walls and gilt chandeliers, the lace and gingham gown looked spectacular. An inspired design, one of Mia's best.

"That really is a nice dress," Joe said, giving Alicia the once-over as she stood in the receiving line in the first-floor Great Hall.

"The price was certainly right. Free," Mia said. "I see a bright future in politics for the new Mrs. Bowen."

"Two for the price of one." Joe shook his head. "I'm still amazed that your father gave her the replacement gown, too."

"What else could Lucien do? He gave his word."

"It's a tax write-off." Joe shrugged. "What about the other dress?"

"That gown is *mine*. Remember? We were in a crunch for a decoy dress, so I used the design I came up with for *my* wedding dress."

"Oh yeah." Joe nodded. "I remember now."

"The gown is finished. Hanging in a bag at Savard's," Mia said, biting off the "just waiting" she wanted to add.

"Too bad it's not your size. Want some champagne?"

No! I want to get married! Mia wanted to scream, but said, "Half a glass."

"Be right back." Joe kissed her forehead and turned away.

"Five words, Mia." Jenna tapped her from behind and turned her around. "*The gown can be altered.* Why didn't you say them?"

"I'm *trying* to be subtle," Mia said. "And it is *very* trying."

Since Thanksgiving night when he'd returned the rag doll wearing *her* wedding dress and told her how beautiful she'd look in it, Joe hadn't said another word about the dress. Like when—meaning, how soon—he'd like to see her in it.

"Don't hint," Moira had advised Mia the last time they'd had lunch. "Hit him over the head. A concussion usually gets his attention."

In lieu of whacking Joe with a sugar bowl, Mia had started carrying her bride rag doll with her everywhere she went. She'd lost count of all the times she'd asked Joe to hold it while she dug through her purse to look for something and he handed it back to her without a word.

She'd propped it on the dashboard of her Subaru, smack in the middle so he'd have to look at it during the drive from Kansas City to Jefferson City. She'd unpacked the doll first in their motel room and put it on the bed—where the obtuse jerk probably expected her to make love with him tonight—only to have him stare at it, nonplussed.

Mia was giving Joe till New Year's Eve to propose. If he didn't ask her to marry him then, she was going to ask him on New Year's Day.

Oh, but she loved him. So much that when she caught sight of Joe weaving his way toward her through the throng of wedding guests with two flutes of champagne, one with only a thimbleful of Dom Perignon, her mad and her frustration melted into a pool of kiss-me-you-fool lust.

She and Moira had double-teamed Joe into a midnight blue tuxedo from the Lucien line. He was so well put together, had such a great body for good clothes. "Too bad he's such a slob," Moira had said, but Mia had designs—about a dozen of them—to rehab Joe's wardrobe.

Mrs. Whitcomb gave them a tour of the mansion. On the gallery above the Great Hall, she thanked Mia for the gorgeous wedding gown she'd designed for Alicia and left them to make their way down the grand main staircase— which they did, just as Aubrey Welch started up.

"Steady, ladybug," Joe said, tucking Mia's hand firmly in the curve of his elbow and holding it there so she couldn't smack Welch.

"Ah, Joseph." Welch stepped to one side out of the flow of traffic on the stairs, beamed at Joe and ignored Mia, which suited her just fine. "So good to see you here."

"I'm amazed to see you here, Aubrey. It was deftly done."

"Yes, it was, wasn't it?" Welch swept the Grand Hall, and then Joe, with a benevolent, I-love-the-world smile. "I have you to thank."

"Oh no." Joe threw up a hand. "Leave me out of it, Aubrey."

"You're too modest, Joseph. This experience has inspired me. My resolution for the new year is to be a kinder, gentler muckraker."

Welch winked, clapped Joe on the shoulder and moved on.

So had Savard Creations in the wake of Jordan and Damien.

"I knew you were lying," Mia told Joe while they danced. "When you said things would get back to normal as soon as the thief was caught. Things will never be the same, will they?"

"Look on the bright side," Joe replied. "You're head designer now and your father has given up tantrums for your mother."

"It is *so* freaky," Mia said. "To see Lucien skipping around, almost singing and smiling at people."

"A kinder, gentler tyrant," Joe said. "Who would've expected it?"

"Jordan sure didn't."

Becca had told Mia the week before, after she talked to Jordan's sister, "She's astonished that she got probation, that Uncle Lucien didn't throw the book at her. She's finished in fashion and she knows it. Her sister says she's going to go to beauty school."

"I wish her well," Mia had said, and thought, *Well away from me.*

"Oh yeah," Becca'd added with a grin, "Terence dumped her."

Lucien had not been so forgiving when it came to Damien DeMello. Not only did he throw the book at him, he offered to dig Damien a cell under the jail. When Oren Angel punched DeMello in the nose while he was out on bail, Lucien laughed all the way downtown to bail Angel out of jail and then took him home for dinner.

On Christmas morning after Alicia's wedding, Joe drove Mia home to Kansas City in her Subaru. It felt weird to be in the passenger seat, but Joe looked mighty damned fine behind the wheel. She'd given up on the doll, stuffed it in her suitcase and pinned her hopes on finding a ring box under the Christmas tree in her living room.

Joe didn't give her a ring. He gave her a necklace, a diamond circle. *Maybe he's getting there,* Mia thought. *At least it's round.*

She wore it to his mother's house for Christmas dinner, met Joe's brother, Sam; his wife, Carol and their two boys, Sam the Third and Joseph.

"And you sneered," Mia muttered in Joe's ear. "When I suggested Mia Junior and Joe Junior."

While she helped Evie Kerr rinse the dishes after dinner, Evie turned from the sink to admire Mia's necklace.

"You know," she said, "you're the only girl Joe has brought home since Moira's mother, Janine."

Mia didn't know if she wanted to cry or rip her hair out.

After the winter they'd had so far, Mia expected a blizzard on New Year's Eve and whatever secret Joe had planned for their big night out to be canceled, but the day was sunny and warm, almost fifty degrees. Half of the huge pile of snow in Mia's front yard had melted by the time he picked her up at seven-thirty.

"Wow," he said when she opened her apartment door wearing the diamond circle with the blue velvet dress he'd last seen on the form in her sewing room. "You look gorgeous. Are you ready?"

"Ready as I'll ever be," Mia said nervously. Once they

were in Joe's truck, she asked, "Are you going to tell me now where we're going?"

"Nope." He plucked a black velvet scrap of something from the sun visor and handed it to her. "Put this on."

It had a string, it was oval shaped—it was a mask. Mia laughed.

"It's Moira's." Joe grinned. "She sleeps in it sometimes."

"Are you going to put me up against a wall and shoot me?"

Joe laughed. "No. I don't like guns, remember? Just wear it, please. And no peeking. This is a surprise."

"Okay," Mia said, and put on the mask.

He drove for twenty minutes. When the truck stopped and Joe shut off the engine, Mia reached for the mask, but he caught her hand.

"Not yet. Be patient."

"You aren't going to shoot me. Are you going to push me off a cliff?"

"No. I'm going to walk beside you and steer you."

"Might work this time. I'm not drunk."

Joe laughed, and came around the truck for her. He guided her across an expanse of pavement, opened a door and steered her onto a floor that clicked under her heels.

"Okay. Here we are." He caught the string of her mask and slipped if off her eyes.

Mia blinked. They were in a restaurant. A French restaurant, judging by the Parisian street scenes framed on the pale green walls.

"Welcome to Paris. It's all yours for the night. You can sit anywhere you want." Joe swept his arm across the red-tiled floor dotted with empty white iron tables. "As busy as I am right now, this is the best I could do."

"Oh, Joe!" Mia laughed and hugged him. "It's wonderful!"

So, too, was the food and the service provided by the owner and his wife. Mia couldn't imagine what it cost Joe to reserve the entire place for the night, but she figured she could kiss a ring good-bye.

"For mademoiselle," said Andre as he served her coffee. "Your favorite, Vanilla Bean."

"Thank you," Mia said to him. To Joe she said, "You went all out."

"There's more." Joe reached inside the blue jacket Moira had bought him at Jack Henry's. "Close your eyes."

Mia's heart nearly stopped. *Oh boy! Here it comes! My ring!*

"Eyes closed," she said as she shut them. She heard something rustle, then Joe said, "Okay. You can look."

Mia did, her heart leaping, then crashing when she saw two paper envelopes from United Airlines on the table.

"Tickets to the real Paris," Joe said. "The one in France."

"Oh," Mia said, so disappointed she couldn't look at him.

"I thought we'd get married first," Joe said. "You know, make a honeymoon out of it."

Before she could raise her eyes, Joe put a red velvet box in front of her and opened it. A gold band with three diamonds caught Mia's breath.

"I," Joe said, touching a fingertip to the first stone. "Love," he said, moving to the second. "You," he finished, his fingertip on the third stone. "Will you marry me, Mia?"

Her heart jumped for joy. So did she, out of her chair. So did Joe, catching her in his arms and lifting her off her feet as she came around the table. He kissed her till her head spun.

"Yes." Breathless and so happy she could scream, Mia caught his face in her hands and gazed into his gorgeous dark blue eyes. "I will marry you, Joseph Kerr. And I will love you beyond forever."

"Great." He kissed her again, hard and quick. "Let's go to my place and get started on Mia Junior."

"No." She laid a finger on his lips. "Joe Junior."

"Whatever," he said, and carried her out the door, laughing.

In the truck Mia unzipped him. Joe slid one hand up her skirt.

They were both breathing hard and half-undressed, their mouths locked together, when they tumbled onto Joe's bed and made quick, hot, stunning love to each other. Mia didn't scream, but Joe did.

He rolled on his back and took her with him, his heart thundering in her ear, his lips trembling against her temple.

"We gotta do this again," Joe said raggedly. "Tomorrow night."

"Speaking of tomorrow," Mia murmured. "By proposing to me tonight, you saved yourself from a horrible fate."

"I did?" Joe kissed her nose and Mia sighed. "What horrible fate?"

"A sugar bowl in the head."